HUSH

HUSH

SARA MARSHALL-BALL

First published in 2015 by

Myriad Editions
59 Lansdowne Place
Brighton BN3 1FL

www.myriadeditions.com

1 3 5 7 9 10 8 6 4 2

A CIP catalogue record for this book
is available from the British Library

ISBN (pbk): 978-1-908434-58-6
ISBN (ebk): 978-1-908434-59-3

Designed and typeset in Sabon LT
by Linda McQueen, London

Printed by CPI Group (UK) Ltd
Croydon CR0 4YY

For my parents

prologue

Lily built her memories around nothingness, like so much false smoke around an absence of fire. Tiny glimpses of the earth beneath; a faded photograph, the odd fingerprint here and there. A hairbrush, its few buttercup strands still clinging to the redundant bristles. A mirror, so dusty that she couldn't really see the face that was reflected. No great loss there; it wouldn't be the face she was expecting to see anyway.

It had been twenty years since she'd set foot in that house.

Floorboards, thick with dust, audibly protested her presence. There were dark patches where the rugs had once been. An empty bed-frame, curtainless windows. And yet, clothes still hung in the wardrobe. A shirt. Two dresses, too large ever to have been hers.

She heard Richard moving around downstairs, filling the place with noise, as he tended to do. Connie would be here soon. There would be things to do, conversations to be had. It would be better left to Richard, really. He was good at that sort of thing. But that wasn't fair. Not his family; not his responsibility.

She picked up the hairbrush and lifted one of the strands away. Others followed, tangled together, and then split apart, brittle with age. Dust clung to the broken threads and followed them to the floor.

She replaced the brush on the dresser, taking care to put it back exactly, so no dustless space was exposed.

Flickering faces. Daylight. And voices, which seemed to fade in and out of her hearing, some words unaccountably louder than others.

*– Well if you **will let** her **do** this to you but I **didn't I'm telling** you I didn't I just **said** I **know what** you said I heard **you** –*

Connie, eleven, wearing a pink vest, white shorts, ankle socks but no shoes. Laughing, hair flying in her face, or around her face. Movement. Maybe she was running.

No, she'd been shaking her head.

Or she'd spun around, too quickly, to share the joke.

But it couldn't be sharing. Not when Lily wasn't laughing.

*– But **Mama** I **only** asked her if she wanted to **and then** she and now it's all gone –*

Scent of lavender through open windows. Blood. Hers?

*– gone **wrong** well you know **how she** gets but I –*

Connie, taller than she should be. And her mother, crouching. On the floor. Shoelaces undone. Or tied together?

And her mother's voice.

We only get what we deserve.

'The wanderer returns.' Richard was smiling, holding out a cup of tea, and Lily was momentarily confused. Where did he get tea bags? Was there even water, or electricity? Then she remembered the camping stove, the provisions. All lined up on the counter now. Orderly, though they weren't staying.

'Hmm.' She took the tea, walked hesitantly towards the patio doors. The kitchen felt smaller, even with the absence of clutter. The stools, red plastic diner stools, had disappeared. So had the blinds. Maybe Connie had taken them. It would be the kind of thing she would do: assuming ownership of something that was shared.

'You okay?'

'Yeah.'

Richard walked around her to open the doors, and stepped outside. The expanse of the garden – the lawn, gently sloping into flowerbeds, then woodland, all overgrown now, impenetrable. Lily followed him, her steps tentative. It was improbably bright, and still there was that feeling of abandonment. Except not quite.

Whispers of ghosts, gone as soon as they arrived.

It was she who had done the abandoning.

'Not like the city, huh?' Richard placed his mug on the wooden table, which was scarred, weatherbeaten, carpeted with moss. It wobbled when he put weight on it, but held.

'I'd forgotten how quiet it is here.' She stepped further down the patio, until her toes peeked over the edge, hovering above the lawn. She could remember leaping off, from land into the sea, full of crocodiles.

'It's nice. I could get used to it.' His voice was reassuring, optimistic. Unfazed by her silence, or her hesitation. 'Do you want to give me the tour, then?'

No.

'Okay.'

The crunch of tyres on gravel, distant, but there nonetheless. Saving her from her insincerities.

Darkness, or sun obscured by trees. Spots of sunlight, or stars, or maybe lights from the house. Watch missing? Or intentionally left behind. Connie, always laughing, always ahead. Lily trails behind. Unnoticed. Or ignored.

*– but Mama **she always ignores** me it's not fair you've just got to learn to live with it –*

No, the watch is there. Pink plastic reflects the time, but it's gone. Numerals blurred, hands vanished. Digital or analogue? Flashing zeros, no time at all.

*– you see Lils there's **this secret** place but you can't tell Mama or I'll never **speak** to you again but **Mama said** we shouldn't come down here I know that's **why it's a** secret silly now shut up because I **don't want** Billy to know you're here –*

Definitely dark. The house had been asleep, floorboards creaking all the way down the stairs.

But then hadn't she been up there, watching? Twigs snapping underfoot. Carpet between bare toes. Which?

'You wouldn't believe how long it took us to get here!' Connie, letting herself in through the front door, weighed down with bags, which she left in a pile on the kitchen counter. She grabbed them both in awkward hugs. 'Oh, I'm glad you remembered to bring tea, I completely forgot.'

'Where are the kids?'

'Just getting out of the car. Luke! Tommy! Where have you got to?'

Within seconds they were underfoot. Lily crouched down to hug them, and stayed there, perched awkwardly, when they moved away. Richard made tea, while Connie bustled around him, unpacking her own provisions. 'Cake, anyone?'

'Cake! Cake!' the boys chorused. Eight and five. Same difference in age as her and Connie. Tom was the protective older brother, making sure Luke got his share, that he didn't drop it on the floor. They took after their father.

'Where's Nathan?'

'Oh, working, you know. He apologised. What are you doing still on the floor, Lils? Get up and give me another hug.'

The second hug was as awkward as the first. As soon as Connie backed away, Lily followed the boys, who had already retreated to the garden. They circled her eagerly, begging for stories, games, treats. She gave them her crocodiles, and watched as they jumped in and out of the water, screaming with pleasurable fear.

'How's she been?'

'Oh, not great. You know. I think... Well, you know how she gets.'

They didn't realise the window was open. Or didn't care. Their words floated out into the air, caught on a breeze, and dissipated into the sunlight.

She could hear them but not see them. Dark, very big. Black. Obscuring faces, hands, feet, fur.

Teeth. All manner of things.

Which came first, blood or screams?

No, not yet.

*– I'm not **sure** I like it out here I want to **go home** stop being such a baby we're going to the **secret place** but I can't see you I don't **like it** where's Mama **oh go** on then run home to Mama see if I care –*

She was there, warm hands, kind face, shhhhh, all okay now.

Not yet.

No carpet now. Twigs, moonlight on skin. Eyes wide. Mouth open. Gape. Footsteps, two sets, tap, crunch, tap. Branches like fingers in hair. Cobwebs on face.

*– are you sure **this is the right** way of course I'm sure I've been here **a thousand** times but not in the dark it's different in the dark will you **just stop** whining –*

Monsters in the dark. But no, of course not monsters.

This is no fairytale.

'Lils. Hey. Lily.'

She spun around. Richard and Connie were standing behind her, twin expressions of concern on their faces.

'Hi. Sorry. Drifted off for a minute.'

'Yeah.' Connie's voice. 'This place does that to you.'

Does it do it to you?

'Mmm.'

The boys had gone further down the lawn, to the edge of the flowerbeds. She hadn't noticed them go. Tried not to think of what lurked beyond.

'We were thinking: we should probably start going through stuff now. Before it gets dark. I don't think this place has electricity any more, you know.'

'No. I don't suppose anyone's been paying the bills.'

'Well, Mama did for a while...' Connie trailed off, awkward. 'Yeah, you're right, I suppose.'

'There's not much here.'

'Well, no. No one's lived here for ages. She was in care for over two years, at the end.'

'I thought there might have been stuff. That was left behind.' Lily found herself groping for words, and giving up. It was exhausting. Why did no one else seem to be having any trouble?

'I got rid of some of it,' Connie said, carefully. Watching her for a reaction, but Lily had already turned away, looking back towards the bottom of the garden. 'There's still a lot around, though. Maybe we should make a start?'

Lily's voice was small, petulant. 'Richard can do it.'

'No.' Gentle, but firm. 'It's got to be you.'

Lily looked at her face. Unrelenting.

'Right. Me, then.'

Blood. All obscured by. And dark, of course. But blood blacker than the dark.

– *I thought you **knew the** way that's not the **point just help me** –*

No screams now, all quiet. Except that she wouldn't stop crying.

Which one? Did she feel tears? Hadn't ever cried as a baby. Mother told everyone. *The quietest child...*

– he's too heavy not moving I –

And then Mother, crashing, fighting undergrowth. Twigs snap snap snap all over the place.

– What are you girls doing out here –

And silence.

Shhhhh, okay.

We only get what we deserve.

It didn't take long, in the end. They found the important paperwork in one of the kitchen drawers. Made a half-hearted attempt at clearing away some of the residue of their mother's life, but Lily's mind was on other things and Connie didn't want to force her.

Lily didn't go back upstairs. Didn't need to feel the absence of carpet on bare toes. Knew what she'd see if she looked out of the window.

They locked the door behind them, and Connie pocketed the key.

part one

then

The funeral service for William Edward Thompson was held in the church at the centre of the village. Connie had walked past it every day for as long as she could remember, but had never attended a funeral before.

Her grandad – her mother's father – had died two years beforehand, but she'd been deemed too young to attend the service, despite the fact that she'd been old enough to watch him die. She'd tried to sneak out to the church, she remembered; the neighbours' teenage daughter was watching her, but not really watching, and she'd managed to get out of the back door and halfway round the house before she'd been seen. She'd screamed when she was caught, a roaring embodiment of a week and a half's worth of pent-up rage and sorrow that they'd heard, distantly, in the dusty muteness of the church.

They wouldn't make the same mistake twice. Anna Emmett held her eldest daughter firmly by the hand and all but dragged her to Billy's. Connie wore a dress that restricted her breathing and shoes that pinched her feet, and she was miserable, not for Billy, but for the sorry state she found herself in. She cried endlessly, bitterly, while the entire church stared and whispered.

When she got home they didn't speak of it, as if by prior agreement. Her father hadn't come to the service – he'd been visiting Lily, who was at their grandparents' house – and Connie and Anna resumed their normal lives as if nothing had ever happened. Connie understood that they would not talk about it, would not talk about why Lily had gone, would not even talk about the fact that she had gone. These were not topics for discussion.

She didn't ask when Lily would be back.

Instead she went upstairs to her room and she fought her way out of the dress that didn't fit and she lay down in the middle of her floor, wearing only her pants, lying deliberately half-across the rug so that its edge would dig into her shoulders and so that her head was resting on cold unpolished hardwood floor. It made her neck ache, but she stayed that way, her head tilted so that she could see, not the ceiling directly above her, but the open window behind her, the curtains that fluttered in the breeze.

Lily's room was next door. They were almost identical in size and shape, and Lily and Connie had arranged the furniture so that the rooms were mirror images. Their beds were against the shared wall, so that they slept inches apart. Their desks, in the far corners, were where they retreated when they fought, so that they could be as far away from each other as possible.

Connie lay in the same position, staring at the open window, until the sun set, trawling its shadow laboriously across her body before slinking off behind the woods. She stared at the string that was tied to the outside of the window; the string that was attached similarly to Lily's window, which could easily be untied, which the two girls used to pass things from room to room, when they were supposed to be asleep. In the shadow of the setting sun she watched it tremble in the wind, until darkness took hold and she closed her eyes to stave it off.

Lily had been at her grandparents' house for two weeks. Her father had turned up twice, both times at Saturday lunchtime, his car horn honking cheerfully as he pulled up outside. The first time, he had stayed a long while after lunch, and spent the whole afternoon asking Lily questions while she stared at him blankly. This time, on the day of the funeral, he seemed to have got a hold of himself: he spent the afternoon talking quietly to his parents in the kitchen, leaving Lily to sit alone. She sat in the living room, perched on the windowsill, and watched the traffic pass by, separated from her by the expanse of grass in front of the house and a low, neatly trimmed hedge.

The living room was dim, and decorated mainly in shades of brown. Framed photos showed her father at all ages: from grinning blond child to humble teenage graduate to proud father of two, arm slung casually around his wife's shoulders. Lily found it odd to see photos of her father as a child next to photos of her at the same age. It was as if she were in a photographic race to catch him up.

Marcus Emmett came into the sitting room to find her, placing a cup of tea and a glass of juice on the table before sinking into the sofa. 'Come and sit with me,' he said, patting the cushion next to him, and she obliged, curling herself into him and letting him put his arm around her shoulders. 'You know it's Billy's funeral today?'

Lily nodded. She didn't sit up or look at him, but she knew he would feel the movement.

'Do you wish you'd been able to go?'

She shook her head. Her father squeezed her shoulder, and fell silent for a while. Shaping his mind around phrases that wouldn't require her to respond in words.

'I didn't want you to go,' he said finally. 'Your mother thought it would do you good. But I think you've seen enough.'

Lily sat up and reached for her juice. The glass was cold, slippery with condensation, and she had to concentrate to make sure she didn't drop it.

'I've been talking to Grandma,' he said, 'and we've come up with a plan, for the time being. We think it would be better for you to stay here, away from everything that's gone on at home. Grandma could teach you, because she used to be a teacher. And it would take some of the pressure off your mama.' There was a slight strain in his voice as he said the last sentence, but he hid it well. 'What do you think? Does that sound okay to you?'

Lily looked into her glass. There was a single black hair floating in the opaque orange juice, swirling round in circles in the centre of the glass. Nothing here was quite right. The juice wasn't right. The bedroom that she usually stayed in with Connie wasn't right, now that Connie wasn't here to share it with her. The food that Grandma cooked didn't taste right and the bath wasn't the right shape and the toothpaste wasn't the right colour.

But then she thought of the house, and the woods behind the house, and Billy, and Billy's funeral, and thought that maybe things not being right wasn't such a big deal after all.

She nodded, and took a long swig of her juice. She drained half the glass in one go, and, when she looked at it again, the hair had disappeared.

The day after Billy's funeral, his story reappeared in all the newspapers. Connie, walking past the village newsagent's, caught sight of his face in the newspaper stand outside and flinched as if someone had hit her.

She took a paper without paying for it – the old man behind the counter watched her take it without comment – and made her way through the village, down to the river, tiptoeing along the pebble-dashed shore until she found a spot where no one would come to look for her.

She climbed up the bank and sat down in the grass

with her legs straight out in front of her. She smoothed the newspaper over her legs so that Billy's face came to rest, childish and grinning, over her knees. They had used a different photo last week: a school one, with a less genuine smile. This one was more casual; it had caught him off-guard. He was wearing a ThunderCats T-shirt that Connie had been coveting for the past year.

She found she was crying, without quite knowing how it had happened.

She read the words beneath his face, picking them apart as she knew others would. Her name was there, and Lily's. *It is alleged that two of Billy's schoolmates were with him at the time of death – Connie Emmett, 11, and her sister Lily, 8. It is not known why the three children were out of the house in the middle of the night. Their parents have refused to comment.*

There wasn't much more detail than there had been last week – *rumours of brutal injuries, coroner refuses to comment* – but they picked apart his funeral in detail. Took all the beauty from it and left dry, empty words where before there had been something more. They spelled his father's name wrong and confused the names of the songs.

She got to the end and read it again, just to be sure. No new information, but there was still the hint of accusation when they spoke about her and Lily. Not so much that the paper could be accused of outright speculation; just enough to plant the seed in people's heads.

She folded the newspaper over and tossed it to one side. The police hadn't wanted to speak to her again since last week; she supposed they, at least, thought the possibility of her and Lily murdering someone was out of the question. Or maybe they didn't. Maybe they hadn't believed her version of the story, and were just waiting until they could talk to Lily, to see if her story would tally.

Lily was showing no inclination towards speaking, though, from what Connie had heard. Connie lay back on the grass, staring up at the sky, her vision still half-blurred with old tears. She was exhausted and confused, and she wanted so much to talk to Lily, to find out what she saw, what she remembered; to confirm that they hadn't done anything wrong.

That this wasn't their fault.

Because the longer Connie went without talking to her about it, the more possible it seemed that the past would be lost altogether.

The village in which they lived didn't have a secondary school, so Connie had to get a bus into the nearest town with the thirty or so other children who lived nearby. Her first day was just over two weeks after Billy's funeral – two weeks which she had spent sitting in the garden, or the nearby park, or walking in the fields on the outskirts of the village. She had avoided the woods that connected her back garden with Billy's, but otherwise she didn't worry about being by herself. In fact, she preferred it.

Her father, when he was there, tried to engage her in conversation, but she deflected his interest. Truth be told, he had other things to worry about, another daughter who was in a far worse state than Connie. Connie was a trooper. She'd be fine.

Her mother didn't talk to her, and she didn't talk to her mother.

In the fields on the other side of the village, ten minutes' walk from her house, there was a barn that had probably once been used for storing tools. There was no purpose to it now: there was nothing inside it; no one owned it. One of the windows had been smashed, long before Connie had ever been there, and the remnants of glass still littered the wooden floor inside. There were shelves on the inside, with empty jars, or old boxes full of nails and screws that had no purpose to serve.

She had been here before, with Billy, sheltering from the rainstorms at the beginning of the summer. They had been soaked through, and huddled together for warmth, watching the rain driving against the one remaining windowpane, and forming window-shaped puddles on the floor in the places where there was no glass.

They'd talked about starting secondary school. They'd agreed to sit together on the bus, at least on the first day. They hadn't thought beyond that. It was the first day that had loomed ahead, unknown, unknowable. The first day that they'd created contingency plans for, in an attempt to unravel the knots of terror they'd constructed around it.

When it came to it, Connie sat alone, halfway down the bus, and huddled against the window for comfort. It was raining now, too, and she watched the water as it clung momentarily to the glass, attempted to worm its way across, and then was flung off into the road by the movement of the bus. She spoke to no one, and no one spoke to her, and she bit the inside of her cheek for the whole twenty-minute journey. Her mouth was filled with blood by the time they arrived.

now

Throughout the four years that Richard and Lily had been together, Richard had met Connie for dinner around once a month. Originally it had just been an exercise in getting to know each other; it was hard to speak freely when Lily was around, almost as if her awkwardness with words spread outwards into everyone in the room, making them all curiously muted. Over the years it had developed into a strange kind of companionship, almost a parental relationship: Richard sometimes felt that they were united by their shared interest in Lily.

There were unspoken rules to their conversation, subjects that were permissible and things that were left noticeably unbroached. Richard never asked questions about Lily that she would not have answered herself; it would have felt like a betrayal, delving into her past without her explicit permission, and, besides, he had no interest in hearing details of her personal life from anyone except her. But Connie could be useful in the sense that she seemed almost to be able to read her sister's mind at times, and could advise Richard on changes in Lily's mood that he sometimes missed.

Now, though – a month after her mother had died, less than a week after they'd visited her house – Richard needed no help to translate Lily's silences.

'She's okay, I think,' he said, spearing a piece of steak on his fork and lifting it halfway to his mouth before changing his mind and replacing it on the plate. 'I mean, she's certainly not showing any signs of being actually upset. But she's even quieter than she was before, and I'm not sure whether I should be doing something about it or not.'

Connie watched him from across the table. They were in the same restaurant they always came to – a small place halfway between both of their houses, which was cosy without being overly intimate, and was one of the few local places capable of cooking steak to both of their tastes. 'She hadn't seen Mama for years,' she said, the tone of her voice carefully even.

'Yeah, I know. But it's got to have an effect, hasn't it? She was still your mother.' Richard stopped abruptly, realising how insensitive he was being. 'I'm sorry. Are *you* okay about it? I haven't even asked.'

Connie laughed. 'It's fine. I, at least, am capable of telling you when I'm not okay. And, besides, I'm not your responsibility.'

'That doesn't mean I don't care.'

'I know.' She smiled, kindly. 'I'm not so bad. I don't miss her or anything – I hadn't seen her for months either. I'm just – I don't know. Sad that she had such a miserable existence, I suppose.'

He nodded. They ate in silence for a while, letting the murmur of the other diners wash over them.

'Have you decided what you're going to do about the house yet?'

'No. I need to talk to Lily about it.' Connie laughed dryly. 'That'll be a fun conversation.'

'It might be a bit one-sided,' Richard said, with a smile.

'I suppose we should probably sell it, really. I can't imagine either of us wanting to live there. It's not like we have many happy memories of the place.'

'There must have been some good times, though?'

Connie took a sip of her wine, and shrugged.

'None that springs to mind. Oh, it wasn't all completely awful,' she added, seeing the look on his face. 'But we were both glad to move on.'

'Hmm. Well, it's a nice place. Shouldn't be too hard to find a buyer.'

'That's what I'm hoping. The thought of actually selling it, though… It just seems like so much effort.'

'If you find a decent estate agent it shouldn't be too hard.'

'True.' She nodded, chewing slowly. 'I suppose I should talk to Lily about it sooner rather than later.'

'Might be an idea. Maybe we could all have dinner at some point. It's been a while, hasn't it?'

'Yeah. That would be nice.'

Richard poured them both some more wine. 'Would you not think of moving back to the house? Bringing the kids up somewhere quieter?'

Connie made a face. 'No. Drayfield is too weird, too insular. I want them to grow up somewhere with a bit more life to it.'

'And Nathan? Does he feel the same?'

'I don't know. He's got this idealised view of living in the countryside, I think. Knowing everyone by name and keeping horses and so on. But he's never said anything about moving.'

They ate and drank slowly, their conversation skimming over subjects that held no controversy: Richard's job, what the boys had been up to, Connie's latest forays into the world of socialising with the mothers at school. They lingered over the wine, and Connie described the relief of having her mother buried at last, after long years of worrying about her as she went in and out of hospital, and trying to arrange her care.

'I can't miss her, because there was nothing left to miss,' she said, her voice blunt and uncharacteristically harsh. 'All the goodness, the personality that she might have once had disappeared years ago. All that was left was bitterness and self-pity.'

'But you didn't see her much, did you? Do you think she was different when you weren't there?'

Connie shrugged. 'I doubt it. She'd been that way for years. Since we were kids, really.'

'Do you think there was a reason for it?'

Connie looked away. 'Probably lots of reasons. But she'd had plenty of time to get over them.'

Richard looked at her curiously, but she didn't say anything else, and he didn't press her. Connie might find conversation easier than her sister, but there were still some subjects on which silence was resolutely upheld.

There was a documentary on the TV. Something about the Great Depression, though Lily had stopped watching it fifteen minutes ago, flicking the sound off so it wouldn't interfere with her thoughts. She was in the kitchen, a good six feet from the battered old fourteen-inch TV that had seen her through her days at university, and she could only just see the shapes as they flickered across the screen. Richard kept suggesting they buy something bigger, more modern, but neither of them could bring themselves to spend money on upgrading something they only ever used as background noise.

The whole flat was a mishmash of things that they should probably have updated or thrown out long before now. It was something Connie commented on every time she came over, though Lily had never asked for her opinion.

Lily was trying to remember how it felt to sit on the red plastic bar stools in her mother's house. She'd been walking backwards and forwards between the living room and the kitchen, trying to work out when she'd last sat on one. She couldn't possibly have been older than twelve, and therefore the seat would have been huge in comparison to her legs; the whole length of her thighs would have been pressed against the plastic, with just her shins dangling over the edge. And yet. She could so clearly remember the feeling of being perched on the edge of a stool, with the tips of her toes brushing the coolness of the kitchen floor, as they would be now. As if she'd been sitting on one just last week.

She knew she was just superimposing memories of later times. False memories were a fact of life. But it was picking, gnawing at the edge of her brain. Making her restless, so that she walked to the kettle, got stuck at the sink, left the tap running for minutes before she shut it off, went back to the sofa, back to the kitchen, back. Paused at the kitchen window, which looked down over a glimpse of street, always empty, lit with its own, personal, grimy-England-orange glow. If she pressed her nose against the glass she could make tiny, clear holes in the fog on the pane. She could feel the conversation between the heat of her skin and the coolness of the condensation.

She loved this flat. Loved everything about it. When Richard was out she spent hours wandering from room to room, picking up objects, looking at bookshelves and picture frames and ornaments from different viewpoints. She tried to imagine how other people saw it. Spread out on the bed, or the sofa, or the floor, she would focus on individual freeze-frames of her flat and imagine what they said about her. About her-and-Richard.

When Richard was around everything was bustling, busy. The radio was on, or the TV, whichever, it didn't matter as long as there was inane chatter going on somewhere in the background. When he was there the phone rang all the time and people came to the door and Lily's contact with the outside world was real, tangible, there for everyone to see. She was a genuine, real-life person.

When he went out, which he did often, and left her alone, she retreated back into herself. She became just Lily.

She didn't mind. In some ways she liked it best when she had breathing space. Thinking space. Imagining space.

But she was always glad when Richard came back.

The flat was dark when he got home. He let himself in quietly, placing his keys on the table by the door, slipping off his shoes and nudging them with his toes, into line with Lily's battered once-white trainers. The front door opened directly on to the living room, the familiar furniture and debris of their life together lit only by the silvery-orange glow of the moonlight and the street-lamps outside.

He padded through to the kitchen to get a glass of water, automatically registering the objects that had moved since he was in here last, subconsciously taking note of the clues which were his daily insight into Lily's state of mind. It was tidier than when he'd left, indicating restlessness, dissatisfaction. His unopened mail, neglected that morning owing to an early meeting, was piled neatly in the middle of the table. She'd been thinking of him, then. It wasn't all bad news.

He took the water through to the bedroom, opening the door as quietly as possible. The hinges always creaked slightly, but if he opened it slowly enough then the creaking didn't reach the pitch required to wake Lily up; rather, it was a low groan, unobtrusive. She slept sprawled across the bed, wearing a T-shirt and knickers. Her dark blonde hair was loose, tangled around her face. Her mouth was set in a stubborn line, and she breathed out tiny huffs of air, as if exhaling her discontent with the world.

He placed his glass of water on the bedside table and stood for a moment, watching her sleep. It wasn't the only time she was peaceful. But it was the only time he ever had a chance of being able to guess what she was thinking.

then

Lily had been at her grandparents' for two months before Connie's parents broached the subject of taking her to visit. Connie had begun to get used to being an only child: the silence Lily had left behind her now seemed almost normal. She was okay with her parents arguing, with being the sole focus of attention. She didn't like it, but she no longer hated it.

She wasn't sure how she would feel about going to her grandparents' house, a place they had always visited together, and finding Lily there by herself. Her grandparents would presumably now be much closer to Lily than they were to her. Perhaps she and Lily would no longer feel like sisters, but like friends, or strangers even: people who were separated by the differences in their daily lives.

In the end, though, they didn't go to the house. They met halfway between the two houses, a two-hour drive for each, in a pub with a playground in the garden. The weather was cold but sunny, and Connie took Lily outside while the adults chatted and waited for food to arrive.

'You want to play on the swings?' Connie offered. Lily nodded, and climbed on to a swing, clutching the chain tightly on each side with her hands. Connie pushed her, making sure she didn't go too high. She remembered the last time they'd done this: maybe six months ago? Connie had been less cautious then. Pushing her sister carelessly, wanting her to fly, without sparing a thought for what would happen if she did. Now Connie realised she thought of her as fragile; something to be protected.

She wasn't sure she liked it much.

After the swings they played on the slide, Connie going down first, Lily following with a wordless swish and a smile. They landed side by side in the dirt.

'How about we go down together?' Connie suggested. Lily nodded, so they climbed up together, fitting their feet into the ridges in the wood. The slide wasn't wide enough for them to sit alongside each other, so Lily sat between Connie's legs, Connie holding on to her waist. When they landed at the bottom they heard a cheer; Marcus had been watching them from the doorway.

'Do it again,' he urged, so they did. By the end of the third time Connie found the back of her jeans was covered in mud.

'No more, Dad, please,' she said, when he seemed about to ask.

He laughed. 'Okay, then. I was only supposed to be coming to tell you the food has arrived, anyway.'

They trooped back inside, their mother clucking disapprovingly over the state of their hands as soon as they sat down, ordering them to go and wash them. They obeyed, Connie muttering under her breath about selective parenting.

Over dinner the main topic of conversation was the inquest, which had taken place the day before. Lily stared at her plate and gave no indication that she heard anything that was said around her. Connie glared at her mother, who spoke in hushed tones, as if that would somehow soften the blow of her words.

'We thought we'd better go,' she said. 'I mean, the police had already told us what they were going to say, and they didn't need us as witnesses, but I really think it's better to know what's being said. I wanted to be on hand, in case they mentioned the girls.'

'And did they?' Her grandmother's question, but it was Connie who held her breath, awaiting the answer.

'They mentioned that they were there, obviously. Quoted Connie's statement, explained that Lily couldn't talk about it. They recorded a verdict of accidental death.'

'So they're not holding anyone responsible?'

'Officially, no. Basically they don't really have any idea how it happened, but there were no definite signs of foul play, so they just have to assume that it was an accident.'

There was no response to this. Connie tried to chew the food in her mouth, but it was suddenly tasteless, with the texture of damp paper. Lily was completely motionless, staring silently at her plate.

'Anyway,' Marcus said, his voice full of false cheer, 'the main thing is, it's over now, isn't it? So we can all go back to normal.'

The conversation moved back to less painful subjects, and, if anyone noticed that Connie and Lily didn't eat another bite, they chose not to mention it.

'As I said yesterday, there are lots of different types of energy. We've looked at electrical energy, chemical energy and thermal energy. Does anyone know of any more?'

Connie didn't look up, in case the teacher caught her eye. The lack of response wasn't quite a silence; there were low mutterings, the odd giggle. The students weren't not communicating, just steadfastly refusing to communicate with the teacher.

'Anyone?'

In among the quiet murmurs she could pick out individual voices. The odd sentence here and there.

I heard she killed someone.

'Okay, well, today we're going to be looking at *kinetic* energy.'

Connie looked up, following the squeaking strokes of the whiteboard marker as it traced words across the board: 'kinetic energy'. Except that the 'r' and the 'g' weren't clear, had melded together to form an uncertain squiggle. If Connie squinted slightly, she could see the word **'enemy'**, emblazoned on the board for all to see.

I heard it was her sister that killed him and that she got sent away so they couldn't put her in jail.

Connie closed her eyes. Tried to tune in to the teacher's voice, while the whispers behind her seemed to scratch at the back of her mind.

'Kinetic energy is motion energy. All moving things have kinetic energy, even tiny ones, like atoms, and huge ones, like planets. Today we're going to do an exercise to look at the way kinetic energy is transferred, and why it might be of importance to us.'

There was a general shuffling as the teacher started writing instructions on the board. People turned to their partners, started talking more loudly. Connie leaned forward on her desk and switched on the gas tap for the Bunsen burners. Released a tiny cloud of gas into the air, with a minute hiss that only she could hear. She flipped it off again.

I thought her sister went crazy and they sent her to a mental institution.

She had a Walkman at home. Maybe she could bring it in. The teacher probably wouldn't notice, so long as she looked as if she was paying attention. It would use a lot of batteries, though. Her parents would notice if she kept taking all their batteries.

'Okay, so if you want to divide into pairs...'

Connie didn't bother to look around for a partner. It had been nearly three months since she'd started secondary school, and every lesson had been the same. She would sit here until the teacher assigned her to a pair. A different one every time; it wouldn't be fair for anyone to have to put up with her for more than one lesson.

Look at her. I think the whole family's crazy.

'Connie, could you make a three with Natalie and Emma, please?'

She gathered up her books, awkwardly levered herself down from the wooden stool. Taller than the plastic bar stools at home. And the noise the metal legs made, screeching across the linoleum. Grating her eardrums.

Natalie and Emma were two tables away. Far enough that she couldn't hear the whispers of the girls behind. They didn't talk to her, but there were no snide comments as there were with some of the others. This was fine.

She could get used to this.

Connie came in through the patio doors, hoping to avoid her parents. No such luck. They were sitting at the breakfast bar, a pot of coffee untouched in the space between their hands. They both looked up as she walked in.

'Good day?'

'Mmm.'

'That's hardly an answer, is it?'

Connie took a deep breath. Allowed the traces of bitterness left in the air by Anna's tone to dissipate before she responded. 'It was okay.'

'What lessons did you have?'

Her father had evidently been training himself in asking questions that required direct responses. Can't have two silent daughters. Keep this one talking.

'English. Maths.' She paused. Tried to pluck something out of the day that would be worth mentioning. 'We're learning about energy in science.'

'What kind of energy?'

'All kinds. I've got lots of homework.'

'Okay. You'd best get on with it, then.'

Connie went upstairs, closed her bedroom door behind her, dropped her bag on the floor next to her bed. Went to the mirror that hung above her dresser. She looked the same as she had that morning. More tired, perhaps. She leaned close, examined the dark circles beneath her eyes. Some of the other girls wore make-up that gave their faces a powdery orange tint. Maybe she would get some.

She could sense her parents downstairs, talking about her. Talking about Lily. Or maybe they weren't talking at all. Communicating via silent thought-transmissions.

It seemed that silence was its own mode of communication, these days.

She went to her bed, knelt down, and reached a hand underneath, fingers tracing the dust on the floorboards until she found what she was looking for. Her hand closed around hard plastic casing. The radio that her parents had given her for Christmas two years ago. That she had barely used since her father had finally relented and bought a television a year later.

She switched it on. A muted buzz whispered its way through the air. She twisted the dial, and found a voice. A man's voice, joined a moment later by a woman's. They laughed. *Oh, Jim, you know me so well.*

She turned the volume down low enough that she could hear the voices without being able to make out the words, and placed the radio on her windowsill.

She hadn't been lying about the homework, but she couldn't be bothered to do anything about it. Her parents wouldn't check. The teachers wouldn't comment. She was in limbo, outside the normal rules of society, temporarily. Temporally.

Lily had never been able to say *temporarily*.

Connie lay down on her bed and stretched out as much as she could without touching the wall. Not much leeway with a single bed. Sometimes, when her parents were out, she spread out on their bed like a starfish, trying to touch every corner. It was supposed to be a secret, but she could never make the bed as neatly as they could and they always knew. Her father didn't mind. It was only Anna who complained.

She liked their room. It didn't have the sense of emptiness that hers did, regardless of whether or not they were in it. Perhaps it was the fact that it was shared space, the lives of two people combined in one area. It gave a sense of conversation in the room, even when there was no communication between its living occupants.

Downstairs she could hear their voices begin to rise. She pulled a pillow around her ears to muffle the sound. Not that she could ever hear the words. But she could make out the vibrations in her mother's tone that would indicate when she was near tears.

Through the open window she could hear the birds as they bade farewell to the fading day. The sound mingled with the murmurings from the radio, the low growl of voices from the kitchen. And Lily's voice in her mind, stumbling over syllables she could not pronounce. *Tempery. Temporally. Tempo-rarity.*

Connie closed her eyes and wished: for silence or for graspable sound, she could not quite decide.

The following day she decided to go into town after school. Set off on the same route she took every day. The buses from Farnworth back to Drayfield went every hour, with one leaving straight after school. She usually took a later bus. Avoiding people she knew. And it was better to be out of the house.

She headed down the alley next to the school. Kept to the left, clear of the garages where older kids went to smoke. Concentrated on stepping around the cat shit which was liberally scattered among the gravel.

Didn't notice the people emerging from the garages, walking behind her.

The first blow caught her on the ear and knocked her sideways, into the wall. She stumbled, dizzy, and someone grabbed her hair, pulling her to the floor. Face-first, so that the gravel bit into her cheeks and split her lip. She closed her eyes and tried to curl into a ball.

'Coward. Weren't so cowardly when you were killing that guy, were you?'

She didn't know how many there were. At least three, she guessed. They kicked her repeatedly, until she lost count of how many blows landed on her body, and she could no longer feel the individual impact. Just the juddering of her whole body as shoe collided with skin.

'We thought we'd give you a lesson in the transference of kinetic energy,' said one voice. A hiss, venomous, but also amused. It was the amusement that made Connie feel genuinely afraid.

It didn't last long. Maybe a minute before they spat in her hair and left her on the ground. She heard laughter as they retreated, and the lighting of cigarettes.

She lay there for just a few moments too long; when she got to the bus station the early bus was leaving, its brake lights waving cheerfully as they disappeared around the corner. She could think of nowhere else to go, and so she sat at the bus station for an hour, until the next bus arrived. The bus driver looked at her when he pulled up – dirt-smudged, gravel-grazed – but he made no comment, and she sat down without a word.

now

Lily was the first person in the department most mornings. She shared an office with two other members of the faculty: a lecturer in algebraic topology, Eric, who insisted on drinking out of a mug bearing the slogan 'To a Topologist This Is a Doughnut', and Marianna, a German who specialised in archaeostatistics and being quiet. They tended to work in near-total silence, which was only ever interrupted by Eric, whose opinions fluttered out of his mouth and settled ineffectually on the indifference in the room.

Lily treasured the early mornings, when she could work without interruption. She hated sharing an office; had several times considered moving to a new institution just for the privilege of having her own space in which to work. But Richard didn't want to move. And when it came right down to it, nor did Lily. So she came in early, worked hard, taught for the required number of hours, and went back home to capture a few uninterrupted hours of productivity before Richard arrived home.

She set up the coffee machine, switched on her computer, and raised the blinds to let in the first struggling signs of daylight. The sky was blue-grey, without any genuine promise of becoming brighter later in the day. It was the claustrophobic darkness of mid-October, the kind that in the evenings carried with it promises of trick-or-treating, bonfires, hot chestnuts and tinsel, but in the early mornings merely pledged drizzle and murky, rain-bleached sunlight.

Checking her emails took considerably longer than usual. It was her first day back in the office. They'd offered her compassionate leave, but she didn't see the point. The longer she was out of touch with the academic world, the harder it would be to fight her way back to the centre. Besides, excessive thinking without an object on which to focus thought was the quickest route to insanity, in her limited experience.

When she was most of the way through her inbox, Marianna came in, and they exchanged awkward conversation for a previously unheard-of length of three minutes. How are, where have, did you, and, here we are. Three minutes to establish that nothing in their working relationship had changed, or needed to change. Then back to the silence in which they were both most comfortable.

The phone rang ten minutes later.

'Lily Emmett.'

'Lils! Richard said you were going back to work today.'

Lily didn't respond, but shifted the receiver to rest between her ear and her shoulder, so that she could continue typing while Connie spoke.

'How are you feeling?'

'Yes, fine, thank you. And you?'

'Fine. Well, you know, not *fine*, obviously not. I know you're not either. We should meet up soon. The kids would like to see more of you, and of course Nathan...'

'I'm at work.'

'I didn't mean *now*.' Deliberately missing the point. 'Look, Lils, there's stuff we need to talk about. I was wondering if we could do dinner.'

'Mmm.'

'Don't just make noises at me. What does that mean? Does it mean yes?'

'Yes. Of course. When?'

'When are you free?'

35

Lily was momentarily confused. 'Um. Always?'

'Oh, Lily, don't make it sound like that.' A pause, for Lily to speak, but she couldn't think of a single thing to say. 'How about tomorrow, then?'

'Yes. Fine. At your house?'

'Yes. Bring Richard.'

'Of course.'

'Good. See you tomorrow, then. Take care.'

'Yes.' A pause, before Lily remembered, and started to say 'you too', but Connie was already gone; a tiny click followed by an endless and impenetrable buzz.

then

'I still don't understand why we couldn't all spend Christmas together.'

Connie was slouched in the back seat of the car, feet resting high on the seat in front of her, roughly in line with her mother's shoulder-blades. Her mother stared out of the window and did a very good impression of not being able to hear anything. Every now and then she lifted a hand, to rub a clear patch in the condensation on the window; otherwise she was motionless.

'Your grandfather was ill,' Marcus said, his voice stubbornly calm. He was staring straight ahead, watching where he was going, and all Connie could see were his eyes in the mirror, dark and strangely expressionless. 'It wouldn't have been nice, to barge in on them when he wasn't feeling well.'

'They could have come to us,' Connie said. She was aware she was being petulant. They'd been having the same argument all morning.

'Yes, they could have done, but they didn't want to and it would have made things difficult – '

'You mean Lily didn't want to.'

'Lily hasn't said a word on the subject,' Marcus said. Connie glared at him in the mirror. 'Sorry. Bad time to try to be funny, I suppose.'

'It would help if you were actually funny.'

'Yes, I suppose it would.' Marcus sighed, tapping his thumbs on the steering wheel as he slowed the car to a stop at the end of a queue. 'Anyway, it's nothing to do with Lily. It was me and your grandmother who made the decision, really.'

'And no one else,' her mother said pointedly.

'I *asked* you whether you wanted to go for Christmas, Anna – '

'And I said I didn't want to go *at all*. And yet, here I am.' Anna was still staring out of the window, her voice utterly expressionless. Connie shifted further down in her seat, trying to make herself inconspicuous.

'What, you'd rather not see Lily at all?'

'That's not what I meant.'

'Well, that's basically what you said, isn't it?'

Anna shrugged. The car juddered slightly as it waited to resume its movement. Outside, ahead of them in the queue, someone was honking their horn. Connie tilted her head to peer through the gap between the seats, trying to see what was causing the hold-up, but she was slouched too low to see anything but dashboard and sky.

Christmas had been a strange and dismal affair. Her parents had attempted the customary festivities, but there had been a flatness in the air, a lack of enthusiasm. Connie had failed to get out of bed at the usual time – she was usually woken early by an excited Lily. She'd lain awake for almost an hour, listening to the wind stirring outside the house, before she remembered that it was traditional at Christmas for the children to drag the adults out of bed. When she'd knocked on her parents' bedroom door she'd found them both awake, as puzzled and uncertain as she was.

There had still been presents, of course, and they had still made dinner; but, where once it would have been Anna's job to cook while Marcus entertained the girls, Anna now seemed unable to remember what she was meant to do, and she'd left most of it to Marcus. Connie had stayed in her room until late in the morning, reading a book with the radio on low, only stirring when she heard the sound of the patio doors slamming shut beneath her. She'd climbed off her bed and gone to the window, just in time to see her mother striding through the garden, past the lavender borders – all overgrown now, and nothing but a collection of grey-green weeds at this time of year – straight into the depths of the woodland beyond. Connie had watched her until she was out of sight, even her shadow slipping away beneath the trees, and then she'd pulled herself away from the window and joined her father downstairs.

Her mother had come back in time for dinner, and they'd made a valiant attempt at good cheer, before disintegrating into silence and stupor, and eventually retreating to separate rooms.

Connie couldn't help thinking about what it had been like the year before, when Lily had been given a pair of roller skates and Connie had pushed her up and down the patio for an hour, trying not to let her fall off the edges on to the grass. Her mother had watched them from the kitchen window while cooking dinner, and Marcus had hovered with his camera, shouting encouragement from all sides. After dinner Billy and his father had come round, and the adults had sat around drinking wine, getting louder and more out of control. They'd forgotten to send them to bed, and Connie remembered crouching in the doorway to the kitchen, watching them, with Billy on one side and Lily on the other. Billy had whispered in her ear, 'We could steal some of their wine; they wouldn't even notice,' and for a moment Connie had been excited by the prospect, until she'd realised that Lily was there – Lily who she was supposed to be responsible for – and she'd shaken her head. Instead they'd gone upstairs to Lily's room and Billy and Connie had taken turns reading her stories until she fell asleep, twisted in her duvet, left thumb in mouth, right arm thrown out recklessly above her head. Not long after that, Billy's dad had called him downstairs and they'd gone home.

The car started moving again, and Connie shifted so that she was upright in her seat, her feet on the floor. She could see out of the windscreen from this angle, the long line of brake lights arcing off into the distance. 'How much longer?'

'Depends how long the traffic lasts,' Marcus replied. 'Half an hour, maybe?'

'Hurrah,' Anna muttered under her breath.

It turned out to be almost an hour. When they pulled into the tiny terraced street lined with box hedges and rosebush borders, it was to find Marcus's father out in the front garden, trowel in hand, squinting gloomily at the clouds overhead. 'Looks like rain,' he said by way of greeting, giving his son a hug and kissing his daughter-in-law on the cheek. He put an arm round Connie's shoulders and kept it there, squeezing her gently towards him. 'Was the journey okay?'

'Largely uneventful.' Marcus hoisted a large rucksack on to his shoulders, shifting awkwardly under its weight. 'Mum inside?'

'Yeah, she's making lunch. Lily's in her room, I think.'

'I'll go and say hi.' He disappeared inside, Anna trailing behind like a lost child.

'And how have you been, trouble?' He ruffled Connie's hair and then released her from his grip. 'They been taking care of you?'

'Of course.' She looked at the ground, tracing a circle in the lawn with her toe. 'How's Lily?'

'Oh, she's fine. I expect she'll be back home with you soon enough.'

'Is she talking yet?'

'No, not yet. But no need to rush these things, hmm?' He ruffled her hair again, looked as if he might say something, and then thought better of it. Instead he turned to the nearest rosebush, which was almost as tall as Connie. 'Have you met Fred? He'll be on top form by June.'

She followed him around the front garden for a while, looking at shrubs on command, listening politely to the names and the histories even though she knew she would forget them as soon as she went indoors. It was something they did every time she came to visit, but she never remembered the details.

After a while it did start to rain, so they went inside, to find Anna and Marcus standing in the doorway of the kitchen. The house smelled the same as it always did: slightly dusty, slightly flowery. The scent of roasting ham skated over the top of everything else.

Her grandma stood at the hob, stirring something in a pan, and she beckoned Connie over when she saw her. 'Do you want to try this? It should be about done. Have a taste and tell me what you think.'

She held out a spoonful of soup and Connie sipped it obediently. 'Mmm. It's good.'

'Excellent. That means lunch is ready, then. Do you want to go and tell Lily?'

Connie shuffled upstairs, leaving the adults talking loudly as they pulled plates out of cupboards and set the table. The noise receded as she climbed the stairs, and was barely a whisper by the time she was outside Lily's room. She knocked on the door, waited, and then realised she was being ridiculous: there was not likely to be any answering call of 'come in'.

The room was almost eerily still when she pushed open the door. Lily was sitting on her bed, staring out of the window; she turned her head for just long enough to confirm that it was her sister at the door, and then turned back to the outside world. 'Hey, Lils,' Connie murmured, but there was no answering response.

She crossed the room and crawled on to the bed next to her sister. Lily shifted slightly to the left to let her sit down. Together, they looked down on the outside world.

The room was at the back of the house, and from the window they could see a patchwork quilt of gardens stretching out into the distance: tiny strips of land, bordered by wooden fences and hedges, joined by trees which crept over the borders and spilled into neighbouring gardens. Connie could see her grandparents' garden, with more of Grandpa's beloved roses trailing the pathway on either side; the neighbouring gardens, less well tended but still obviously cared for; the gardens that backed on to the ends of them, wild and unruly, allowing their untamed hedgerows to push through the fences. The rain was still falling, and no one was outside; it was a dismal picture, grey sky as far as the eye could see and droplets of water slipping down the window-pane, blurring the view.

'Grandma said to tell you lunch is ready,' Connie said, her voice soft in the silence of the room. Lily didn't move, and her expression didn't change.

'Mama and Dad fought all the way here. I don't think Mama wanted to come. I think – well, I think she wanted you to come home, though she won't admit it.'

Connie watched out of the corner of her eye, but Lily still didn't move.

'You'd find some way to tell us if you hated it here, wouldn't you?'

There was no response for a minute, and then Lily slid off the bed and left the room. Connie sat and listened to her soft, plodding eight-year-old's footsteps on the carpeted stairs. She waited until they'd reached the bottom and disappeared before she made a move to follow.

Connie was surprised by how animated Lily seemed around their grandparents. She still didn't speak, but she was noticeably more responsive – she made eye contact, she smiled, she looked as if she was paying attention to the world around her. She barely glanced in Connie's direction, despite the fact that they sat opposite each other; but, positioned at the end of the table, with her grandmother to one side and her father to the other, Lily almost looked like a normal child having a normal dinner with her family.

'We've been working on reading and writing,' Grandma was saying, as she pushed the bowls from their soup starter to one side, and reached for the meat in the centre of the table. 'Lily's getting very good at writing. She's been writing us letters, haven't you, Lily?'

Lily nodded, but didn't look up. Connie watched as she pushed a slice of tomato backwards and forwards through a pile of salt. 'You don't need so much, Lils,' Marcus said, but she ignored him and popped the tomato in her mouth, her eyes briefly meeting Connie's before darting back to her plate.

'She's very good at maths, as well. I don't think you've got anything to worry about.'

'I got in touch with the school, actually,' Marcus said. Anna looked up, and Connie could see the surprise in her expression, though she didn't say anything. 'They're happy to send out some guidelines to help you. Just some of the subject areas they'll be working on each term, you know. Do you think that would be helpful?'

'Absolutely. Though it depends how long you want her to stay here, obviously. There's no point putting together a whole curriculum and then having you turn round and say you want to put her back in school in two weeks' time.' Grandma's voice was firm, and Marcus looked slightly guilty.

'Mum, you know if it's too much to ask at any point – '

'That's not what I'm saying at all.' Connie saw Grandma's gaze flick towards Lily, but Lily was still absorbed in her food and didn't look up. 'We love having her here. We love having *all* of you here,' she added, with a pointed look at Anna. 'But being a teacher is a lot of work, and, as much as I enjoy it, I would like to know whether there's a long-term plan.'

'Wouldn't we all,' Anna muttered.

'Don't start,' Marcus said. 'This was as much your idea as it was mine.'

Anna shrugged, and picked sullenly at her ham, saying nothing. Connie, looking around the table, wondered whether anyone would notice if she got down from the table and didn't come back.

'How about we work on a month-by-month basis, for now?' Marcus suggested. 'That way you don't have to plan too far ahead and we can keep an eye on Lily and see how she's getting on.' Marcus looked directly at Lily, as if remembering she was still there. 'Does that sound okay to you, Lils? We don't want to send you back to school before you're ready, do we?'

Lily nodded, too focused on her plate to look up. Connie watched her, willing her to make eye contact, but there was no response.

'Sounds good to me,' Grandma agreed. 'What about you, Connie? Have you been enjoying school lately?'

Oh, so you do know I'm here, she thought, and then felt bad. It wasn't Grandma she was angry with. She thought of the bruises on her ribs that were only just healing, and shrugged. They hadn't caught her after school since that last time, but they'd become bolder in other places – tripping her up as she walked past them in the school halls, pinching her arms and pulling her hair when they sat behind her on the bus.

'Well, secondary school's a big adjustment,' Grandma said, her voice gentle. 'Especially after everything that's happened.'

'Maybe you'd like to look after Connie as well? Since she clearly can't cope either?' Anna's voice was bitter, making Connie flinch.

'Anna, there's no need to be like that.' Marcus sounded stern, parental. Connie's eyes went to her grandparents. Grandpa was focused on eating his food, and looked as though he'd barely registered what was being said, but her Grandma was looking directly at Anna with what looked like pity.

'Maybe we could go and have a drink, Anna?' she suggested. 'I've got some wine I've been meaning to open.'

Anna, looking torn between shame and anger, nodded. She didn't meet Connie's eye as they disappeared into the kitchen.

'I guess that's dinner done with, then,' Connie muttered. 'You could have just left her at home. She'd have been much happier.'

'We're a *family*, Connie.' Marcus's voice was sharp, but there was an undertone of weariness, and he pushed away his plate with a sigh. 'How about we go and sit in the living room? We could play a game.'

The four of them went and sat on the living room floor. Marcus and Grandpa leaned their backs against the sofas and spread their legs out in front, their feet almost meeting in the middle. Lily lay on her stomach in the middle of the floor, while Connie sat cross-legged opposite her. Grandpa found a deck of cards and they played a few rounds of Sevens in ponderous silence. From the kitchen Connie could hear the low murmuring of her mother and grandmother talking, but the words were too faint to catch.

'I hope they're getting things sorted,' Marcus said, to no one in particular.

'They'll be fine,' Grandpa said, his voice firm and reassuring. He leaned forward so he could lay the jack of clubs on the nearest pile. 'You know what your mother's like. She can sort out anything.'

'Hmm.' Marcus looked doubtful. 'Anna's been pretty difficult lately. And she's been so negative about this whole situation; it's like she thinks someone's trying to steal her children away...' He trailed off, looking around the room, as if he'd just noticed that both his daughters were within earshot. 'I just don't want you or Mum to think we're ungrateful,' he said finally.

Lily, focused on laying down a card, didn't give any indication that she'd heard. Connie studied her own cards, so she wouldn't say what she was thinking: that maybe they didn't need to be stolen. Maybe their mother had given her children away.

'We know it's a difficult situation,' Grandpa said, his voice light. 'You just focus on worrying about yourselves. Your mother and I are old enough to let you know if something's upsetting us.'

Marcus nodded, and the conversation moved on. After a while Connie put down her cards, mumbling something about needing the toilet, and slipped into the dining room, pushing the door closed behind her.

The room was empty, and strangely dim with the door closed: the sky was steadily darkening outside, as the rain grew heavier and the day crept towards the night. The dishes from lunch were still scattered across the table, casting strange shadows, and the door to the kitchen was open a crack, a shaft of light throwing itself carelessly across the carpet. Connie could hear the low voices of her mother and her grandmother from the other side of the door.

'I know it sounds petulant,' Anna was saying, 'but I feel as if Marcus is punishing me because I wasn't there to help them. It's as if he's gone, *Well, you weren't around to help then, so I'm not going to let you help now.* What other reason can there be for him sending Lily away, other than that he thinks I'm incompetent?'

'Anna, you need to talk to him about this. He doesn't think you're incompetent. He thinks you're stressed and he's trying to avoid putting any more pressure on you.'

'By taking my daughter away? How is that relieving the pressure?'

'She's hard work, Anna. You know that – you can see what it's like. Looking after someone who won't communicate is a full-time job, and it can be pretty hurtful, knowing that despite your best efforts they still don't want to talk to you. Especially if it's your own child. I think Marcus just wants to protect you.'

Connie waited for the response, barely breathing in her attempt to not make any noise.

'Well, he hasn't protected me,' Anna said, her voice blunt and full of hurt. 'He's just made things worse. He's probably ruined my relationship with my daughters, and he's made me lose all respect for him. I don't know if I'll ever be able to forgive him for that.'

The door swung open so suddenly that Connie didn't have time to move; light filled the room, and Anna appeared in the doorway, her features contorted almost unrecognisably. Connie froze, terrified that she'd be seen, but she needn't have worried – Anna made straight for the stairs, and never once looked in her direction.

now

'I invited Lily and Richard round for dinner tomorrow.'

Connie was stretched out on the sofa, her feet resting in Nathan's lap. He was painting her toenails, his eyes inches away from her left foot, concentration blurring his features. Blood red. Blood Dread. She preferred more quirky shades – blue, green – but Nathan could rarely be diverted from the red.

'Did you speak to Lily? Or Richard?'

'Lily.' She paused, stretched. 'At Richard's suggestion. He thinks I should talk to her.'

'He's right.' Nathan and Richard talked on the phone on a semi-regular basis. Their primary topic of conversation was the insanity of their partners, which they spoke of with admirable fondness.

'Are you done yet?'

'Nearly. Stop wriggling. Did Lily definitely say they would come? I don't want you to go to all that effort and have them not show up again.'

'It's not any effort; I'm only going to cook what I usually would for you and the boys. But yes, she said she would definitely come.'

'Want me to ring Richard and mention it tomorrow morning?'

A beat, and then, 'Yes, okay, then.'

The stereo murmured in the corner, classical music that Connie couldn't place. She preferred the stuff that was on the radio: loud, upbeat, popular. The only CDs she owned were the ones Nathan had bought her when they'd first got together, when he'd still presumed she could develop an interest in music just because he had one. She didn't know band names, or genres. But she knew the lyrics to half the songs on Radio One. The ones that didn't sound like dance music being played on a car stereo two streets away.

'Do you think Richard's spoken to Lily about the house?'

'No.' Connie followed her husband's delicate brushstrokes with her eyes. 'I think he's waiting for me to do it.'

'Well, that's fair enough, I suppose.'

'Is it, though? I don't see why I got landed with all this responsibility.'

Nathan finished, screwed the lid back on the nail varnish, and gently negotiated his way past her feet until he was sitting close enough to kiss her. 'It's because you're responsible.'

'I'm not really, though.'

'More responsible than Lily, then.'

'That doesn't take much.'

'Connie – '

'Yes, I know.' She shifted position until her head was resting on Nathan's shoulder. 'I do love you, you know.'

'I know. I love you, too.'

Connie smiled, closed her eyes. Together, they sat in silence, and the music gently filled the space between them.

'So the job's going well?'

'Yeah, not so bad.' Richard speared a piece of chicken with his fork and pushed it back and forth through the sauce of Connie's home-made cauliflower cheese. 'I think it'll take me a while to get to the point I'm aiming for.'

'And what exactly *are* you aiming for?'

Connie and Nathan sat on one side of the table, alternating questions, as if they were an interview panel. Lily sat next to Richard, her eyes on her plate. It was impossible to tell whether she was following the conversation.

'Well, obviously editor-in-chief would be nice, some day.' They laughed as Richard chewed. 'I don't know. For now I'd just like to get put on some more interesting stories.'

'What was the last story you did?'

'You read it, silly.' Connie nudged Nathan with her elbow. 'I showed it to you.'

'The one about the Hallowe'en celebrations?'

'Hmm. Investigative journalism at its greatest.' Richard took a sip of his wine with his left hand, slipping his right one under the table to find Lily's. One long squeeze. *Okay?* Short squeeze in response. *Yes.* He let the tip of his thumb run the length of hers, then returned his hand to the table. 'What about you, Nate? Any interesting patients lately?'

'Actually, I did have one guy the other day...'

As Nathan recounted the story of a patient who had eaten nothing but doughnuts for a month in an attempt to gain weight, Richard let himself tune out somewhat, turning half of his attention to Lily. She had been eating the food earlier, but now she was pushing it around her plate. She stared downwards with the expression of someone who was seeing straight through the table to the plushly carpeted floor beneath.

'Sometimes I can hardly believe these people exist,' Connie said, laughing loudly.

'Maybe they don't,' Richard said, not really thinking about what he was saying. 'Maybe they're an invention of the world, put there solely for your entertainment.'

Connie hesitated in her laughter, her smile flickering. 'But... they'd still exist, even if they were an invention of the world, wouldn't they?' Her eyes were narrowed, as if she was trying to work out whether or not Richard was laughing at her.

'Of course,' he said quickly. 'Of course they would.'

Out of the corner of his eye, he saw the ghostly presence of a smile on Lily's face, in place for just enough time for him to recognise it for what it was. Then: gone.

She'd had more wine than she usually would, though not enough to feel drunk. Just pleasantly hazy round the edges. Connie was drunk, or getting there, her cheeks flushed as if someone had injected her skin with food colouring. Nathan wasn't. He never drank much. Richard, who was driving, had only had one glass of wine, then on to the water. As a result he was constantly getting up to go to the toilet. Every time he left, Lily could feel his absence, a gap almost as tangible as his presence.

Lily could see Connie building up the courage to talk about it. The house. Exhausted just thinking about it. Would happily give it away. Except...

Always an objection, prickling away at the back of her mind. How would she ever remember, if the focus of her memories was gone?

'Do you ever think about it – I mean, *really* think about it? Do you ever try to internalise what it means?'

'What are you talking about?' Lily was confused, had lost the thread of the conversation. Connie's expression, so intense. Eyes glittering with tears, or malice. Never easy to tell the difference. But no, she wasn't malicious. Just unintentionally mean.

Mean: petty. Or average. Or perhaps – Richard would be proud of her for this one – to mean, to connote. Connie, connote. Connite. Connive.

It was the wine, going to her head.

'Being an orphan. Have you thought about it? The fact that you're an orphan now?'

'No.' Her voice no more than a whisper, but it made no difference.

'They're gone. That's it. No more childhood, no more falling back on Mama and Daddy when something goes wrong. We're adrift.'

At sea. I see.

'Dad's been dead for years. And it's not like Mama was someone you could rely on.'

'Well, yes, of course – '

'Is this about the house?' Richard, intervening on her behalf. There was really no need, though Lily was not unappreciative. Connie was far more intimidated by silence than by words.

'No, it's not about the bloody house. It's about the whole *meaning* of our *lives* – '

'Excuse me.'

Lily stood up so abruptly that her chair wobbled, but it didn't fall over. As she walked up the stairs, marvelling as she always did at the softness of the carpet beneath her socked feet – so plush, so *springy* – she heard Richard lecturing Connie. She couldn't understand the words, but she knew the tone of voice, felt its comforting presence wrap itself around her. Even when his voice faded from her hearing, she carried it with her still, a cocoon that seemed to find its home in her very skin.

He waited half an hour before going looking for her. He found her in Luke's room, in Luke's bed, her adult body curved protectively around his child's frame. They were both sound asleep.

As gently as he could, he lifted her up, managing to do so without waking her nephew. He carried her to the car, and drove her home through the city, the glow of the street-lamps illuminating her face in regular intervals all the way home.

She didn't stir; not once.

then

Marcus awoke on the morning of his second daughter's ninth birthday to blazing sunshine and an otherwise empty bed. It took him a moment to register that Anna wasn't there; it was unusual for her to rise before him, and the sheets were still imprinted with her sleeping shape. Usually when he got up to go to work she was still unconscious, buried under a mound of blankets, only her eyelashes and her tousled blonde hair poking out over the top, and he would think how alike she and her daughters looked, especially Lily, whose hair was exactly the same shade of wheat-gold.

He threw the covers off and rose from the bed in one fluid movement. There were clothes scattered all over the floor – his and Anna's discarded outer layers, mingled together in unidentifiable dark clumps on the carpet – and he dug through them until he found yesterday's jeans. He pulled a clean T-shirt out of the wardrobe, and then fussed for a moment in front of the mirror on the inside of the wardrobe door, trying to get his hair to lie flat. Always a losing battle, but he found he didn't mind so much this morning; in casual clothes, with messy hair and a five o'clock shadow, he looked about five years younger than he did when he was on his way to work.

When he opened the door he was hit by the sound of voices. He checked his watch, surprised; it was even more unusual for Connie to get up early than it was for Anna. He found them standing side by side in the kitchen, packing cupcakes into tins. It was so unlike any family scene that he'd come across in the last ten months that he actually stopped and stared, and it was only when Connie looked up and started laughing at the expression on his face that he realised he was frozen in place.

'You're looking like you've never seen us bake before,' Connie said.

'Well, to be fair, it's been quite a while.' Marcus took a few steps forward and leaned over to inspect the cakes. 'Can I have one?'

'Nope,' Anna said briskly. She looked considerably less good-humoured than Connie, though she did give him a wan smile when he raised an eyebrow at her. 'We've made exactly the right amount. We're going to ice them when we get there, and lay them out so they say *Happy birthday Lily*.'

'Nice.' Marcus nodded approvingly. 'And when did you decide to do this?'

'I woke up at five and couldn't get back to sleep, so I thought I might as well do something useful. Connie joined me about an hour ago.'

Marcus made coffee while they finished packing the cupcakes away. The radio chattered softly in the background, competing with the sound of the birds in the back garden and the distant hammering of one of their neighbours.

'What time were you thinking of leaving?' Anna asked.

'Whenever we're ready. I said we'd be there for lunch, so I guess we should aim to be on the road for about nine? How does that sound to you?'

'Yeah, fine. In that case I think I'll go and have a shower.' She slipped upstairs without looking him in the eye, leaving the coffee he'd made her on the counter. He wondered if he should be worried; she was always odd when they all went to visit Lily, and he supposed it made sense that she might behave more strangely on an occasion like Lily's birthday.

'Has she seemed okay to you this morning?' he asked Connie.

She shrugged. 'Same as usual. She didn't say much when I came downstairs, but I figured that was probably because it was half-six in the morning.'

'Not the most talkative of times.'

'Nope.'

Connie was concentrating on shaking out Frosties into a bowl, pouring at least twice as many as she could reasonably eat and making Marcus wince.

'I don't understand how you can eat that stuff.'

'What's wrong with it? It's just cereal.'

'Underneath about an inch of sugar.'

She grinned. 'The sugar is what makes it taste nice. Plus, it gives me energy.'

'For about half an hour. And then you'll have a massive sugar crash and probably spend the whole car journey whingeing like a five-year-old – '

'Chill out – I eat this every day.' She poured milk right to the brim of the bowl, and then leaned down to slurp some of the excess away so she could carry it without spilling milk everywhere.

'That explains a lot.'

'Ha, ha.' She carried the bowl to the table and started leafing through a magazine, flicking droplets of milk on to it every time she lifted her spoon.

Marcus watched her while he sipped his coffee. She'd changed in the ten months since Lily had gone away. She looked thinner; she had dark circles under her eyes; she looked older. She rarely smiled. She seemed distant, and he sometimes felt as if he was watching her from a long way off.

'Do you have much homework to do?' he asked.

She looked up, surprised. 'Not too much. I'll do it when we get back tomorrow.'

'Okay. But remember we won't be back until late.'

'Yeah, yeah. Stop worrying.' She waved a hand carelessly in the air – dismissing him, he thought with a smile – and turned back to the magazine.

He took his coffee and went upstairs. He could hear the sound of running water from the bathroom. Anna had been in their room before she got into the shower; all Lily's birthday presents were laid out on the bed, neatly wrapped. He picked up the nearest one, trying to guess what it was. He'd wanted to go shopping, but Anna had insisted on going alone, and she had refused to show him what she'd bought. 'Buy your own, if you're that bothered,' she'd said, but he'd worried about getting duplicates and ended up with nothing.

The space between them had expanded in the past few months. Things had seemed as if they were getting better, briefly; when they'd come back from his parents' house after the New Year he'd felt as if Anna had been making an effort. But it had only taken a few weeks for them to slip back into the habits of the previous months, and most days now he found she would barely speak to him.

He often wondered what life would be like if Lily came home. Tried to imagine them all slipping back into the easy family roles they had once played. But when he really thought about it he couldn't see a way back; they were not, after all, the people they'd been before.

He lay down on the bed, curling his legs awkwardly to avoid lying on Lily's presents. Anna came in a few minutes later, wrapped in a towel, tiny rivers of water running down her arms and her neck. She barely glanced at him as she walked to the wardrobe. 'You're going to make us late,' she said.

He considered responding, and decided against it; it seemed unlikely he would be able to find any response that wouldn't provoke an argument. He got up and went to the bathroom, leaving her there alone, dripping on the carpet.

They arrived an hour later than they should have done, and found lunch already laid out, birthday banners hung around the table. Lily was lying on the grass in the back garden, reading a book, and she turned around when she heard the door open. 'What have you got?' Marcus asked, crouching down, and she held out the book for his inspection: a title he didn't know, but the front cover indicated it was sci-fi. 'From Grandpa?' he guessed, thinking back to the presents he'd received from his father as a child.

Lily grinned, and nodded.

'Well, come inside in a minute,' he said, standing up again. 'We've got lots more presents for you.'

Lily opened her presents at the table, the food temporarily forgotten in favour of unwrapping. Anna hovered to one side, taking photos, the flash intruding on the scene at regular intervals. 'Can't you switch that off?' Marcus asked after a few minutes. 'It's daylight; there must be enough light in here.'

'There's never enough light inside,' Anna replied dismissively. Marcus grimaced at her, but said nothing.

Connie, next to her sister, inspected each present in turn, making exclamations of approval where necessary. 'Oh, look, we can play this later,' she said as Lily unwrapped a board game Marcus had never seen before. Lily nodded, placing it carefully to one side and reaching for the next one. 'Oh, *wow*,' Connie said, as Lily ripped off silver foiled paper to reveal a camera.

'It's not a fancy one,' Anna said as Lily examined it. 'Just one to get you started. So you can see if you like it.'

Lily nodded again, and placed the camera on top of the board game.

After they'd eaten lunch Anna disappeared into the kitchen while the rest of them retired to the living room. They played the board game, which seemed to involve solving puzzles, though Marcus wasn't entirely clear on the rules. After a while he gave up and left the rest of them to it, and went to find his wife.

He found her hunched over a cupcake with a bag of icing, tears running down her face as she tried to keep her hands steady. 'What on earth's the matter?' he asked.

She flinched, but didn't turn round. 'It's nothing,' she muttered.

'It can't be nothing. Anna, you're – you're crying.' He wondered for a moment how long it was since he'd seen her cry, and realised he couldn't remember. 'Let me help you.' He reached out a hand to put it on her shoulder, but she shook him off before he'd even really touched her.

'I don't need your help,' she said, her voice low and controlled. 'It's just – the icing didn't turn out the way I wanted. But it's fine. I don't need any help.'

Marcus stood behind her, watching the back of her head as she picked up the icing bag and carried on with the cake she was working on.

'It looks good,' he said, hesitant. *HAPPY BIRTHD* was laid out in the line on the counter. He couldn't see anything about the icing that would have reduced her to tears.

'No, it doesn't,' she said bluntly.

'Honestly, Anna, it's – '

'Can you stop it?' She put down the icing bag and spun around to face him, her blonde ponytail flicking sharply as she moved. 'I don't need babying. I'm a mother, okay, not some kind of invalid.'

'You're my wife.'

'I'm not just your *wife*.' Her voice was venomous, and it surprised him. 'I'm Lily's mother. I'm going to do something

59

nice for her, because it's her birthday, and I'm perfectly capable of doing it, and I don't need your help. Okay? Is that okay with you?'

He took a step back, unsettled by the expression on her face. 'Yes, of course it is. But I don't understand why you think I would be taking something away from you if I helped you.'

She turned back around without answering him, and carried on icing the cake in front of her, a large pink *A* taking shape beneath the piping bag. After a while he realised she was never going to answer him, and he went back to the living room.

His parents had gone elsewhere while he'd been in the kitchen, and he found his daughters sitting with their backs to him, crouched over something he couldn't see. 'You can't just take pictures for the sake of it,' Connie was saying, and Marcus realised it was the camera they were looking at. 'Film is expensive, so you have to only take pictures of things you really want to remember. Okay?'

Lily looked up at her, solemn, and nodded.

'As it's your birthday, though, today is special, and you're allowed to take pictures of anything. Also, it's the first day of owning the camera, so you can practise a bit before the pictures start having to be special. Do you understand?'

Lily nodded again.

'Good. Shall we go outside and find things to take photos of?'

They didn't seem surprised to find him in the doorway when they turned around. 'We're going outside,' Connie said, taking her sister's hand, and Marcus followed them as they made their way into the back garden. He sat on the back steps and watched as they walked down the lawn, Connie pointing out photo opportunities as they went.

A rose.

Snap.

A bird.

Snap.

A garden gnome, peeping out from behind a bush.

Snap.

Every time Connie pointed, Lily lifted the camera, snapping obediently. Capturing Connie's gaze on film rather than her own. Marcus watched them for half an hour, smiling to himself, until a useless clicking indicated that the film had run out, and his mother appeared in the doorway to tell them to come and eat cake.

now

'I'm going to tell you a story.'

'Okay.' Lily was sitting on their bed, cross-legged, back very straight, like a child practising her posture. Richard sat in the chair five feet away, one leg crossed over the other, hands clasped around his knee – the picture of an ageing professor, only slightly ruined by the stubborn prevalence of his youth. His reading glasses had slipped down his nose, and he looked at her over the top of them.

'In the beginning was the word. And the word was...' He paused, expectant. She was grinning widely.

'Dim sum.'

'Aha! Dim sum, indeed. Hungry?'

She only smiled, waiting for her story.

'Well, as you know, dim sum is a Chinese dish. And so our story begins in China, with a little girl called Jia-li. Jia-li lived with her parents in a house on the side of a mountain, which looked out over the village below it, and the ocean beyond. Her parents, who were growing old, rarely went down into the village, but they didn't need to, because Jia-li was there to do everything for them. She looked after their needs, and in return they looked after hers. Her mother taught her how to cook, how to make their house a beautiful home, how to weave mats out of bamboo. Her father taught her how to think, how to add numbers and how to tell stories. She was the happiest girl she knew, and wanted for nothing.

'Sadly, though, those who are happiest have the most to lose. One day, when she was shopping for food in the village, a strange man took her aside and offered her fish, special fish, at a reduced price. Because her parents were too old to work in the way that they once had, and they didn't have a lot of money, Jia-li found that she was tempted. She examined it for a long time, but she could see nothing wrong with it, and so she bought it. The strange man's eyes were glinting in the sunlight as she left, but Jia-li, thinking only of the wonderful meal she would cook her parents for dinner, didn't see a thing.

'That night, they ate the most sumptuous feast; when they went to bed they were all smiling widely. But when Jia-li awoke in the morning it was to find her parents crying uncontrollably. She tried to comfort them, but nothing she did made any difference; they could not stop themselves.

'Terrified, she went to the village to summon help. She found the local *yī shēng* – doctor, to you and me – and dragged him back to the house with her. By the time they arrived there was a puddle of tears on the floor around her parents, and still they could not stop crying.

'The doctor examined them carefully. He looked in their ears, their mouths, their noses; he took their temperatures and listened to their chests. After a while, he took Jia-li to one side, where her parents could not overhear him, and he gave her his diagnosis. "I am sorry to tell you," he said, "that your parents are suffering from broken hearts."

'"But how is that possible?" Jia-li asked, shocked.

'"I don't know for sure," he replied, "but I have seen cases like this before. It is usually because some kind of bad spell has forced its way into their body. Have they eaten anything unusual in the last day?"

'Jia-li said that they had eaten nothing out of the ordinary. And then she remembered about the fish, and she told him about the strange man who had sold it to her. "But it tasted normal," she told him. "And I ate it too, and I am not broken-hearted."

' "Are you quite sure about that?"

'At his words, Jia-li realised that the sight of her parents crying in such a way had indeed left her broken-hearted. The only reason she was not crying herself was because she couldn't stand to cause them further pain. "Whatever will I do?" she cried in despair.

'The *yī shēng* told her that, because it was food that had caused their distress, it would be food that fixed it. But he could not help her further than that, and he left her wondering how she would ever find food so powerful it could mend a broken heart.

'For the next week, she did everything she could for her parents, but they did not stop crying. They spent all day outside, watering the flowerbeds with their tears, because when they were inside they were in danger of flooding the house. They slept with empty bowls next to their beds, and when they awoke the bowls were full to the brim with water. Every day Jia-li cooked them a different meal, the most elaborate and wonderful food she could conceive of, but nothing seemed to help.

'After a week of such meals, Jia-li was running out of money, because in their current condition neither of her parents was able to work. Though she tried not to show it, she was very worried. She could not afford to buy more food, and her parents would never get better if she didn't find the food to cure them.

'It was at this point that a wonderful thing happened. The villagers, hearing of Jia-li's plight, had been eager to help her in some way, but they had not known what they could do. When they saw her shopping in the market, and buying much less than she usually did, they realised that she must not have the money to buy enough food. And so they decided that they would each donate some food to her family, to help them get better.

'Because the villagers were very poor, they could not give much. They got together and decided they would each give a little, and in this way there would be a lot. They each gave a little meat, or fish; and, to keep it safe, they wrapped each food parcel in an edible wrapping. Then they all gave their offerings to a young boy, Ning, who carried them in a basket up the hill to Jia-li's house.

'Jia-li was overcome with emotion when she saw what Ning had brought, and she invited him to join them for dinner. She spread out a selection of the food – keeping some back for later, because she was not of a greedy disposition – and they all sat down to eat. For a while there was silence, as they ate and appreciated their meal. And then, very slowly, Jia-li and her parents came to realise that the flow of tears had stopped. Their hearts had been healed.

'The food that the villagers made came to be known throughout China as *dim sum*, or "speck heart" – the sort of food that can touch one's heart and invigorate it.'

Richard had been watching his hands while he told his story. As he fell silent, he looked up at Lily, searching her face for signs of emotion. She was leaning back against the headrest, and had her eyes closed, though he knew she was still awake. Her bare toes were still clenching and unclenching, rhythmically. 'That was wonderful,' she said, finally, opening her eyes just enough for him to glimpse the flash of blue beneath thick lashes.

'I'm glad you liked it. Does that mean you're ready for bed now?'

She smiled silently, and offered no resistance as he switched off the light, climbed into bed, and pulled the covers gently over the two of them.

then

Connie took a long time getting ready on the first day back at school. Summer had been endless and uneventful, most of her time taken up with visiting Lily or hiding from her parents. She had no friends, and so she saw no one, but she found she didn't mind too much. It was infinitely nicer being on her own than being around people who hated her.

She found her school uniform, clean and ironed and hidden at the back of her wardrobe, and pulled it on without enthusiasm. The skirt felt shorter than it had done six weeks ago, the shirt tighter. She wondered whether she had actually grown, or whether it was just her reluctance to be back in uniform that made the clothes uncomfortable.

Last week, she had snuck out to the shops and purchased foundation, mascara and lipstick. She'd spent most of yesterday evening trying them out, borrowing some of Anna's eyeshadow, copying looks out of the magazines that she'd started stashing under her bed when Anna had deemed them 'inappropriate' for girls of her age. She did the same now, hoping to achieve something that looked at least vaguely similar to what the rest of the girls in her class did. It took longer than it had the night before, and she ended up skipping breakfast in order to get to the bus stop on time. As she left the house she found herself profoundly thankful for the fact that her mother never got up until after she'd left; she didn't have the energy to argue about whether or not she was making herself look like a slut to attend school.

The bus stop was crowded, the thirty or so children from her year and the years above joined by five terrified-looking newcomers. Eleanor Newland, Connie's chief tormentor, sat in the middle of the bench, surrounded by people. She sneered when she saw Connie, and whispered something to her friends, who erupted into laughter. Connie turned her back on them. Any hopes that things might have blown over in the course of the summer were swiftly dashed.

The bus turned up five minutes late, by which time Connie was sick of the whispers and giggling from the group behind her. She made her way to the back of the top deck, hoping that they would stay downstairs, but they followed her, of course.

'Isn't it amazing how different people can look after a break,' Eleanor said loudly, sitting down in the seat in front of Connie. 'Some people look better, of course. And some just seem to have morphed into clowns.'

Her friends laughed, predictably. Connie kept her eyes fixed on the outside world and tried to convince herself that she wasn't paying attention.

'Then again, if *I* was a killer, I suppose I would try and disguise myself as well.' Eleanor turned around so she could look Connie directly in the eye. 'Is that it, killer? You're trying to hide from us? Because I can't think of any other reason you would voluntarily make yourself look that stupid.'

Connie didn't reply, digging her fingernails into her palms to keep herself in check.

'Of course, it might not be *us* she's trying to hide from,' Eleanor continued. 'I've heard Billy's dad's been looking to get his revenge. Apparently he's been running around the woods at night, summoning demons to avenge his son's murder.' Eleanor leaned in so close Connie could feel the heat of her breath on her eardrum. 'Is that it, hmm? Scared someone's finally going to make you pay for what you did?'

Connie's palms throbbed, but she didn't relax her hands, scared she might lose control and let some emotion flicker across her face. The rumours had been going round for a while; she'd heard them like everyone else. But everyone else didn't have to put up with the woods backing on to their garden.

Everyone else didn't have to hear the stirring of the trees, the noises of animals in the dark.

After a while Eleanor seemed to get bored, and started talking about something else. Connie tried to tune her out, but regardless of what she was saying her voice was still like a drill, boring holes into her skull. She spent the journey fantasising about what Eleanor would look like with a bloody nose, or a black eye; lying on the ground with all of her friends laughing at her.

It wasn't much, but it helped a bit.

The sight of the school building rolling into view made her feel momentarily dwarfed and powerless. As she stepped off the bus she found herself surrounded by people who were talking, laughing, catching up with friends after a long absence, and she was struck suddenly by the unfairness of it all. No one would ask her how her summer had been. No one would even have noticed if she hadn't come back.

She made her way up the path to the front doors, alone, and tried to remember what life had been like before. It felt as if it had been much longer than a year.

now

Lily's lectures were always crowded. Richard wasn't sure whether she noticed him, sitting at the back of the room, shadowed by a sea of eager undergraduates. He hadn't told her that he sometimes came to watch her, performing small miracles of revelation which might impact on ten people in the audience, or a hundred, or even, by osmosis, the whole world.

He'd snuck in before she'd arrived, found a seat at the back of the lecture theatre. She rarely looked further than halfway up her audience; he knew it made her nervous to look at people who were so much higher than her. She directed her lectures at the people in the first two rows, and so there was always competition among the students to sit as close to the front as possible, something Richard observed with pride.

'The continuum of probability falls somewhere from impossible to certain, and anywhere in between.' Her voice was strong when directed at large audiences. It would be difficult to guess how rarely it was used outside her working life.

As she talked, Richard tuned out the individual words, allowed the rise and fall of her voice to wrap itself around him. He'd heard the lecture enough times before to understand the basic concepts, but that wasn't the point. He wasn't there to learn, or even to marvel in the amount that she knew. He was there simply to listen.

She spoke for two hours, her voice expanding within a scribbling silence. And afterwards she left, without preamble, without pausing to speak to her students, without seeing him there. The room bustled, and emptied; and Richard sat in the silence, alone, until all trace of her voice had faded.

He got a call from his editor when he was on his way back to the office. There had been a house fire on the outskirts of town. No one dead, but the family dog was badly burned, the kitchen and one of the bedrooms completely gutted. The person they would usually contact to cover the story was busy; would he mind stepping in?

The photographer was already there when he arrived, strutting self-importantly through the remnants of the blaze, taking photos of things which, through the act of being photographed, he hoped to inject with retrospective poignancy. He would undoubtedly take beautiful photos, none of which would be used. The shot that would accompany Richard's story would be the standard family-stand-devastated-before-ruined-house photo. No artistry in that – nor, for that matter, in the writing that would accompany it.

'Hello, Mike.'

'Richard! What a surprise. Am I right in thinking you don't usually do this sort of thing?'

'Mmm. I suppose I've been working my way up to it.' The photographer raised an eyebrow, and Richard relented. 'Nick was busy,' he admitted. 'Someone found dead in a house in the city centre. Young girl, I think.'

'Oh, yes. I heard.' *Of course you did.* 'Have you spoken to the family yet?'

'No, no. Just arrived. Is the dog still alive?'

'Yeah – lot of fuss about nothing, actually. His fur's a bit singed but he's fine. Not even a good photograph in it.'

Richard nodded. 'Right. Well, I'll go and speak to the family, then.'

The oddest thing about house fires that had been successfully extinguished was the way the damage just stopped. The fire had indeed gutted the kitchen: black walls, food packaging reduced to ashes, the room barely recognisable as it must once have been. The flames had travelled upwards, taking out the bedroom above, and blowing out all the windows at the back of the house. But the fire door between the kitchen and the living room had been closed, creating a perfect border between the devastation of the fire and the normal life beyond. One side of the door blackened; the other standing as if nothing had happened. And, beyond, sofas, carpets, photographs of smiling children. Everything as it had been.

The family were huddled together in their living room, their space of preserved before-the-event. Mother, father, teenage daughter. It was the daughter whose bedroom had been destroyed, so she sat in tears, clutching her lightly toasted dog in desperate anguish.

Richard had never covered a story like this, but had been trained in journalism the same way that everyone else had. Knew the questions to ask, the sympathetic noises to make. He was not an intrusive reporter, he was a caring man, a defender of their truth – the man who was going to tell their side of the story. Not that there was really another side: it was a straightforward story; no arson, no foul play. A possible fault with the cooker, which he would need to be careful with, but other than that, simple. Wouldn't take long to write.

He made his way back to the office. It was buzzing as always; that irresistible atmosphere of Things Happening Right Now. Sometimes he felt rather detached. Tried not to resent the fact that he didn't get the stories, but couldn't help feeling that the news took place around him while he sat blindly in the middle, groping for a handle on the world that stubbornly refused to materialise.

But this was different. Not the biggest news in the world, but it was a story nonetheless. Something that involved people, emotion, photographable snapshots of humanity. He was a part of the machine, which was so much more to him than just a machine. It was the fabric of his universe; the place where the world was transformed from Event to Word. He was so much more comfortable with Word.

He was one hundred words into the piece when his phone rang. He picked up the receiver absently, still focused on the sentence he was halfway through creating. 'Richard Hargrove.'

'Richard, hi. It's Eric.'

It took Richard a moment to place the voice. And then it clicked: Lily's colleague.

'Eric. Hi. Everything alright?'

'Well, actually, not exactly.' Eric paused, a pause which sent a current of pure fear through Richard's nervous system. 'Now don't panic. Lily's fine, she is, but she's been taken into hospital. She collapsed a little while ago.'

'Collapsed? Do you mean she fainted?'

'She was unconscious for about five minutes.'

'Jesus. Did they tell you where they were taking her?'

Richard copied down the details, in writing which, he observed in a detached fashion, was oddly controlled. His hands weren't shaking, even though his heart was beating at about twice its usual speed. He left without bothering to shut down his computer, without remembering to tell anyone where he was going. He forced himself to walk in even strides to the door, down the stairs, out of the front door. Broke into a light jog as soon as he was outside, but did not run. No need to run, to panic. She probably hadn't eaten, or maybe she was overtired. She'd had trouble sleeping recently.

No need to panic.

Five minutes was a long time.

then

Marcus got home from work just after three o'clock, most days. The firm he worked for was surprisingly casual in its attitude to working hours; as long as he did his allotted eight hours each day, no one seemed to mind what time he arrived or left. As a result he'd been leaving the house earlier and earlier in the last few weeks, often arriving at work before the sun had fully risen, leaving Connie to get herself to school. Anna, he knew, was unlikely to get out of bed before mid-morning.

In the weeks since Christmas he'd always made it home before Connie did, to find the house empty, the space oddly deserted and ringing with silence. Anna, who didn't work, spent most of her afternoons in her bedroom, or walking in the woods, or roaming around the village; she said she couldn't stand the house when no one else was in it.

It was the silence of Lily's absence, he knew; even over the Christmas break, when they'd all been at home more often, Anna had been absent more often than not. But they rarely talked about it, and Anna had taken to acting as if Lily had never been there. He'd caught her one day, boxing up all the photos and childhood mementoes that had once had their home on a special shelf in the living room. She'd shoved them away in the top of the wardrobe in their bedroom, ignoring his protests. 'They'll keep better, away from the light,' she'd said briskly. 'You don't want to go rummaging through them in a sentimental moment and then find them all crumbling to dust in your fingertips, do you?'

He'd conceded the point, knowing that in reality she just couldn't bear to see the reminders of what their family had been, even though watching her hide them away was almost as hurtful to him as closing the door on Lily at the end of every visit. The shelf sat exposed and empty, now, and Anna's poor attempts at filling it with books and videos had done nothing to lessen its presence.

Today he arrived home to find Anna sitting at the kitchen table. The radio was on, a low, comforting babble that made him think of times past, when he would often have come home to find Anna and Lily playing together. The house would have been in disarray because Anna never thought to tidy up after herself, and it would be Marcus and Connie who picked up after them, muttering about how they were obviously the grown-ups of the family.

Now it was just Anna sitting there, a curtain of dirty blonde hair falling in front of her eyes, her mouth pursed in concentration as she moved a pen in broad, sweeping strokes across the page in front of her. Marcus stood in the doorway for a moment, watching, thinking she was absorbed and hadn't noticed him come in; but of course she'd heard the front door slam.

'Stop it, you're breaking my concentration,' she said, looking up from the page. Her expression was half-amused, half-annoyed.

'Sorry.' He took a step towards her, then stopped, feeling oddly hesitant. 'Can I – can I see what you were doing?'

She looked down, as if considering, and then shrugged and held it out to him. He took it gingerly. It was an A4 sketchbook, bound with black cardboard, the pages thick and white and substantial. On the top page was a sketch of a naked woman. It was rough, but not unskilled.

He traced the curve of the woman's body with a fingertip, gently.

'I like it,' he said finally, handing it back. 'What made you suddenly start drawing?'

She shrugged, defensive. 'I've always drawn a bit.'

'Anna, we've been married for thirteen years. I've never once seen you pick up a pencil and draw something. I've never even seen you colouring in with the girls.'

'Don't be ridiculous.' She closed the sketchbook and stood up, moving across the kitchen in two strides. 'Tea?'

'Sure.'

As she filled the kettle, he studied her back, her shoulders taut and rigid underneath her black T-shirt.

'But seriously,' he said, noting the way her muscles visibly tensed as he spoke. 'What made you start doing this today?'

'What does it matter?' She sounded annoyed.

'It matters because I love you and I'm interested,' he said, in the most reasonable voice he could muster. 'Why do you not want to tell me?'

'It's nothing. I just – ' She put the kettle in its cradle and flicked it on. 'I was speaking to a friend today, that's all. About – bereavement, and trauma, and so on. And they said it can be good to do something creative. To get the feelings out, or whatever.'

'So you drew a naked woman?' Marcus was genuinely perplexed.

'Well, apparently I don't really have *feelings* like other people do.' Her voice was bitter, and Marcus found that he wanted to step closer to her, but he wasn't sure how to bridge the gap between them.

'Darling, you definitely do have feelings.'

'You make me feel as if I don't.' She looked directly at him, then: her blue eyes, so like those of her daughters.

'How can you say that? I've never doubted that you had feelings. All this time, I've been trying to protect you – '

'I don't want to be *protected*, Marcus; I want to be *understood*.' Her eyes blazed.

'How can I understand if you won't talk to me?'

'I'm *trying* to talk to you.' She marched back to the kitchen table, picked up the sketchbook, and threw it at him. It bounced off his shoulder, one corner digging sharply into his skin before it fell to the ground. 'Learn to listen, why don't you?'

Without another word, she turned and walked out of the patio doors. By the time he'd recovered enough to follow her, she'd crossed the lawn and was disappearing into the woods.

Connie arrived home just after four o'clock. Marcus heard the click of the front door from the kitchen. He was sitting at the table, in much the same position as Anna had been when he'd arrived home an hour earlier; he'd rescued the sketchbook from the floor, and had been perusing it intently, searching for clues. He flipped it shut when Connie appeared in the doorway.

'Hey, stranger.'

'Hey.' She dropped her bag on the floor next to the table. 'Where's Mama?'

'She went for a walk.' He jerked his head in the direction of the patio doors.

'The woods again?'

'Again?'

Connie was rummaging through the cupboards, searching for food, and she didn't notice his head snap up. 'Yeah,' she said, her voice vague. 'I've seen her go walking in that direction a few times. I'd have thought it would bother her, being out there, but it doesn't seem to.'

Marcus weighed up his next sentence before speaking. 'Does it bother *you*?'

Connie shrugged, still facing away from him. 'Obviously.'

He was surprised at her honesty, but he didn't pursue it. He sat watching her while she took bread and peanut butter out of the cupboards. 'You want some?' she asked, when she saw him looking.

'No, thanks.'

'Then what are you staring at me for?'

He smiled as she slipped two pieces of bread into the toaster. 'Sorry. Just thinking. Did you have a nice day?'

'Not really.' She leaned back against the counter, and Marcus was reminded again of the similarity between his daughters' eyes and his wife's. Lily's and Connie's eyes were virtually identical – vivid blue, ringed with darker blue, flecked with grey. Anna's were only different because her eyelashes were sparser, the creases in her skin more pronounced. 'Next question?'

'What do you want for dinner?'

'Takeaway. Next?'

'What kind of takeaway?'

She smiled, her eyes scanning the ceiling as she mentally trawled through her list of takeaways. 'Chinese?'

'Hmm. I might be able to manage that, I suppose.'

'Seriously?' Connie looked genuinely excited, which made Marcus laugh. He forgot what it was like, sometimes, to not be in control of your own circumstances, to be at the mercy of older and more sensible people all the time.

'Sure. Why not? We'll have to wait till Mama gets home, though. I'll never hear the end of it if we order without her.'

'*Cool.*' Connie's toast popped up, and she set about spreading it liberally with peanut butter, looking more animated than she had in weeks. Was that all it took, then: the prospect of a meal that wasn't home-cooked? Or was it just that any change from the day-to-day routine was a welcome relief?

In the end Anna didn't come home until gone seven, so Marcus ordered without her. When she came through the door they were curled on the sofa together, surrounded by foil containers and plastic bags, a large plate of prawn crackers on the cushion between them.

'Hey,' Marcus said. His voice was controlled, purposely cheery: he was determined to be normal and not demand to know where she'd been for nearly four hours. 'I ordered you chow mein. It's in the fridge, if you want it.'

Anna looked confused; also out of breath and dishevelled, as if she'd been running. 'Chow mein?'

'Yeah. That's what you usually have, isn't it?'

'Um, yeah. Thanks. I'm not actually that hungry right now, though.'

She hovered in the doorway, awkward.

'You can sit down, you know.'

'I know.' But still she didn't. 'I might go upstairs, actually. Have a shower. I was walking for a long time.'

'Yeah, you must have been.'

She looked at him curiously, as if trying to figure out if there was a hidden meaning in what he was saying. But Marcus turned back to the TV, and she shrugged.

'See you in a bit, then.'

Her footsteps echoed on the bare floorboards; they followed her all the way to the bathroom.

Marcus went to visit Lily every other weekend. Sometimes, maybe one in three times, Connie and Anna would come with him. In theory he welcomed their presence – he thought it made the family less broken, somehow, if they were all in the same place together at least some of the time. But actually, all of them together generally meant arguments, awkwardness, discussions about the future; things best avoided. And so when

Connie said she had plans and Anna said she'd better stay home to look after her, Marcus tried not to let his relief show.

When he pulled into the driveway his father was in the front garden, digging at the borders between clumps of daffodils, and Lily was kneeling on the ground behind him, bundled up in a thick coat and fingerless mittens, sorting through a pile of stones. She looked up for a moment at the sound of him slamming the car door, then went back to her stones without acknowledging him.

'Hey, Dad.' Marcus spoke loudly, overcompensating for his father's slight deafness. The older man turned slightly and lifted a hand, but didn't stop his digging. Marcus crouched down beside Lily.

'Whatcha doing, Lils?'

She didn't look up, but continued shifting stones from one pile to another. He squinted, trying to see her logic, but it was lost on him. The usual distinguishing features – size, colour, shape – didn't seem to be of importance in whatever system she was using.

'If you can figure it out, you're smarter than me,' his father said, coming up behind them and laying a hand on Lily's shoulder. She looked up briefly, a faint trace of a grin on her face, and then bowed her head again and continued her sorting.

'How's the garden coming along?'

'Oh, same as usual, really. Not much to do this time of year. Lily's been helping me tidy up some of the shrubs while I loosen the ground a bit ready for spring planting, but then she got distracted by *this* – ' He waved a hand in the direction her stones. 'She's not been much use since.'

'Can't blame her. Sorting is more fun than gardening.'

'And both are more fun than lessons with Grandma. Isn't that right, Lily?'

Lily didn't look up.

'What do you mean? Have the lessons not been going well?' Marcus looked from his father to his daughter, both of whom stared at the piles of stones on the ground and wouldn't return his gaze.

'Why don't you go and have a chat with your mother?' his dad suggested, without looking up.

Marcus found his mother doing the washing-up, singing softly to herself as she looked out of the window. For a moment he was struck, as he sometimes was, by her age, the extra years blurring the features of a face that was almost as familiar as his own. He couldn't remember when she'd started looking like a grandmother instead of a mother.

'What are you doing lurking in doorways instead of coming to say hello like a normal person?' She didn't turn her head, still staring at something out of the window, but she was smiling.

'How did you know it was me?'

'Heard your car pull up, didn't I? Come and give me a hug; if I try and move I'll get bubbles everywhere.'

He came to stand behind her, hugging her around her shoulders. She pressed her cheek into his forearm. 'I've been watching that blackbird out there,' she said, lifting a bubble-covered hand and pointing out of the window. 'He's been bobbing around singing to himself for about fifteen minutes. Not a care in the world.'

'Well, I don't imagine blackbirds have much to get stressed about.'

'I'd like to see you build your own house every year and not get stressed,' she retorted, and then laughed and changed the subject. 'Where's that daughter of yours? Still following your father around like a lost puppy?'

'Yep. She's sorting stones into piles.'

'Ah, yes. She's been doing that for a couple of days. Got your father totally confused, trying to figure out her system.'

'And me,' Marcus admitted.

'Yes, well. You were never much good at that sort of thing.'

'And you are?' He raised an eyebrow, stepping to one side and picking a soap-covered glass off the worktop. 'Can I rinse this?'

'Sure.' She lifted her hands out of the bowl so he could run the tap. 'I'm done now anyway. And yes, for your information, I am. I figured out what she was doing straight away.'

'Really? What is it?'

His mother grinned. 'It's to do with the indents.'

'Indents?' Marcus narrowed his eyes, puzzled.

'Yes. You know? Those things that stop the stones being round and smooth?' Her tone was warm, teasing. 'She's sorting them according to the number and size of the indents. There might be some other factors as well, but that's the main thing.'

'Oh.' Marcus turned this over in his head, wondering at his daughter's behaviour. 'Right. So Dad said something about the lessons not going well?'

'They're not going at all, actually.' She pulled a tea towel out of a drawer, wiped her hands, and then picked a plate off the drying rack. 'Lily seems to have lost interest in the last couple of weeks. No particular reason, I don't think, but nothing I can do will get her to sit down with me.'

'You don't think you've upset her somehow?'

'No, I don't think so. She's still happy to cook with me, and we watch films together, and so on.'

'Hmm.' Marcus leaned back against the kitchen counter, watching his mother as she concentrated on drying a wine glass. 'Maybe she needs to go back to school. Be with other kids.'

'I thought the school recommended that she not go back until she was speaking.'

'Only because they're too lazy to deal with her not speaking.' Marcus realised his voice was unusually harsh, and he took a breath before continuing. 'We can't keep her out of school forever, can we? And they can't refuse to take her just because she won't talk.'

'Well, not necessarily because she can't talk. But they might say she's difficult, or antisocial, or what have you.'

'In what way is she difficult?'

'Oh, Marcus, come on.' His mother put down the wine glass and the tea towel. '*You* find it difficult, don't you? Having a daughter who doesn't speak?'

He shrugged, and found himself being forcibly reminded of standing in this same kitchen at the age of fifteen, with his mother speaking to him in the same tone of voice. He'd felt the same defensiveness then, and the same twinge of childish embarrassment. 'Yes,' he admitted at last. 'Of course it's difficult.'

'So how do you imagine it is for other people, who don't have the same love for her that you do? Can't you imagine how hard it is for them?'

He sighed. 'But it's not as though she misbehaves.'

'Not talking is a form of misbehaviour, Marcus.'

He glared at her, but she held his gaze, steadily. 'But she's not – it's not like that.'

'How can you be sure? How can any of us be sure, really?'

'What's your point, Mum?'

She sighed. 'I don't know. I just – I'm not sure it's working. I think maybe she needs professional help of some sort. Or at the very least a professional opinion. I have no idea whether I'm helping, or making no difference, or even doing her damage. And I'm starting to feel as if maybe I don't want the responsibility of trying to guess.'

Marcus nodded. Looked down at the floor. Noted the scuff marks on the lino that had been there since he was a teenager.

'Yeah, that's fair enough.'

'I don't want you to think I'm giving up on her.' She took his hand then, and when he looked up he realised she had tears in her eyes. 'Really. If I thought I was helping I would do this for years. But I need to know that I'm doing the right thing for her.'

He smiled, and put his arms around her, marvelling at how small she was; the top of her head rested an inch below his chin. 'I know, Mum. I'm sorry. I hadn't realised I was being so selfish.'

'Don't start beating yourself up – '

'Shh. I won't start. But I will talk to Anna about taking Lils to see someone. Okay?'

When she nodded he could feel her nose digging into his chest. He tried to remember when it had been the other way around: when she'd been the taller one, and he'd had to stretch his arms to reach around her waist. But she felt so fragile now, it almost seemed as though that person had never existed.

now

The hospital was an endless succession of waits. Waiting for tests, waiting for test results, waiting for various doctors to collate their opinions on test results. Lily said even less than usual, and spent a lot of time looking out of the window. She was at the end of a row of beds, and with the curtain drawn she could almost pretend they were alone. Richard held her hand and twitched anxiously every time someone came on to the ward.

He'd tried asking her about what had happened. 'I fainted,' was all Lily would say, her tone of voice growing more petulant with each repetition of the statement. He tried hounding doctors, hunting down concrete responses, and was met with nothing but a series of apologies.

In the end he gave up, and called Connie, who said she'd come right away.

Darkness fell early, so that the sterile whiteness of the room, and its motionless occupants, were reflected unavoidably in its wall of windows. A short while later, muffled bangs, like distant gunshots, punctuated the silence, and Richard realised it was the fifth of November. *Remember, remember,* his mind whispered. A look from Lily told him that he had inadvertently spoken aloud. The surrounding buildings were too high for him to see the fireworks in the sky, but he craned his neck nonetheless.

Connie's arrival scattered their silence irretrievably, as always.

'Do they know what's wrong yet? Have they told you anything?' She directed the question at Richard, bypassing Lily entirely, though she did sit down on Lily's other side and take her free hand.

'No. They've done scans, and blood tests. We're just waiting for the results.'

'What *happened*?' This time she did look at Lily, her badly veiled accusations fixed firmly on her sister.

'I fainted.'

'But why? What happened to make you want to faint?'

'I didn't *want* to faint,' Lily said, irritably.

'Well, no, I didn't mean that. But what was happening?'

'Nothing.'

'Was it because of Mama?'

Lily exhaled through gritted teeth, but said nothing. Richard looked at her, surprised. He didn't often see her express signs of irritation, even with Connie, who he knew irritated her intensely.

'It's a lot to take in – '

'We knew she was going to die, Connie. And I hadn't seen her for years.'

Connie looked as if she'd been slapped. 'That doesn't make it any less upsetting.'

'I think it does.'

'You're just trying to block it out. You always do this – refuse to acknowledge when something upsets you. You don't talk, you don't *let go*.'

'I'm not you.'

'I'm well aware of that.'

Richard watched as the two sisters faced each other down, silently. Struck by the similarity of their expressions.

'So if not Mama, then what?'

'I don't think anything actually happened, as such,' Richard said, trying to inject some reason into the proceedings.

'Well, *something* must have happened.'

'People faint all the time. I'm sure it's nothing serious.' He squeezed Lily's hand, encouragingly. Her response was weak, but definitely there.

'They wouldn't have her in hospital if it wasn't serious – '

'*Connie* – '

'Don't treat me as though I'm some idiot who can be placated, Richard, because I'm not. This is my sister and she was unconscious for five minutes and no one knows why. And she won't bloody tell me what happened beforehand. I'm allowed to ask questions, and I'm allowed to be pissed off.'

'Connie.' It was Lily who said her name this time, little more than a whisper. 'It's okay. I'm fine. I feel fine.'

'But you're in *hospital*.'

'Shhh.' Richard realised that Connie was crying, then, shaking with silent tears. Lily must have felt her trembling. 'I feel fine.'

Richard looked at the two of them. The swiftness with which their roles could reverse never failed to surprise him. He was sure that half of their communication passed in front of him, completely unnoticed.

He was relieved when a nurse came in, breaking the silence, prompting Connie to wipe away her tears, return to her former self. With their normal roles resumed, he knew where he stood. Could put aside the possibility that he might ever be anything except Lily's pillar of support, strong, and unshakeable in his priorities.

'Well, Lily. I think I'm right in saying you have quite a history with this sort of thing?'

The doctor couldn't have been older than twenty-two, and yet he was talking to her as if she were a child, and a misbehaving one at that. She glared at him. At her side, Richard took her hand and watched the doctor hopefully.

'You're very lucky. Nothing to indicate that you're not perfectly healthy,' the doctor continued brightly. 'But with your medical history we'd like to recommend that you take a break for a while.'

'What do you mean, her history?' Richard looked from Lily, glowering on the bed, to the doctor who looked down at her carelessly. 'I know she fainted a bit as a child – '

'Perhaps you'd rather discuss this alone?' the doctor suggested, raising an eyebrow at Lily. She shook her head firmly. 'Okay, then. Lily has been treated for various anxiety-related disorders since she was a child. Part of that was due to her tendency to collapse under stress. Part of it – ' he gave her a significant look ' – related to her refusal to speak. She was diagnosed with something known as conversion disorder.' He looked at them both, his expression bordering on scornful. 'In the nineteenth century it would have been known as hysteria.'

Richard ignored the carelessness in his tone. 'And what does this disorder involve?'

'The symptoms are wide-ranging and unspecific. It involves the conversion of stresses or traumas into physical symptoms that the body is forced to deal with. These could be seizures, tremors, fainting… loss of speech.' He looked at Lily once again. 'All of the symptoms are manifestations of mental disturbance of some kind, and, as such, should not pose any genuine physical threat.'

'You're trying to say she's making it up.'

'Not at all.' The tone was as careless as ever. 'The symptoms are very real. But they are not an indicator of a physical illness, and therefore Lily does not belong in a hospital. She should go to her GP and discuss treatments for anxiety. I would recommend some counselling.'

'I can go, then?' Lily's voice was calm.

'Yes.'

'Thank you.'

The doctor left the cubicle, and Lily began to move herself out of bed, shifting her stiff limbs slowly under the sheets. Richard tore his gaze away from the curtain to look at her.

'How could you not have told me about this?'

She shrugged, stretching her legs off the side of the bed.

'Lily, I'm serious. You knew there was something wrong and you never said?'

'*You* knew there was something wrong.' She had her back to him as she spoke.

'Not something like this. Not talking is not the same as – as collapsing, or having seizures, or – '

'I've never had seizures.'

'But you could. If you let this go untreated, who knows what things your brain could convince your body it needs to do? How could you not have told me?'

'I've had treatment.'

'And it's worked spectacularly well, obviously.'

She stood up, trying to pull her hospital gown around her so that she was fully covered while she looked around for her clothes. She didn't answer him.

'Lily, please. This is serious. We need to talk about it.'

She located her clothes on the chair next to her, and started to pull them on under her gown.

'*Please.*'

She looked at him. Looked away. Sat down on the edge of her bed to put her socks on.

'I want to go home,' she said, quietly.

He drove her home that night, amid a skyful of celebration. When they passed the fairground, the firework display was at its pinnacle, and they paused for a moment to watch the lights blazing in the sky, to hear the shouts of delight that floated through the air and landed softly on their ears.

Lily was almost asleep by the time they got home, and Richard half-carried her up the stairs to their flat, depositing her in the bed. She fell asleep immediately, without even asking for a story. He watched her for five minutes until her breathing became deep and even, and then he eased her gently out of her trousers, and pulled the duvet up to her shoulders.

The answerphone light was flashing in the living room. He thought of work for the first time since he'd left that afternoon. Realised that he'd probably screwed up. He wandered through to the kitchen, poured himself a whisky, and took a long swig before topping it up and carrying it back through to the living room. Turned on the TV, though he knew he wouldn't watch it. He flicked to the 24-hour news channel and turned the sound down.

They hadn't been able to guarantee that it wouldn't happen again. They'd asked if anything upsetting had occurred recently, and then said a reaction like hers wasn't surprising, considering the circumstances. Recommended a holiday. He'd almost laughed.

He wondered if he was doing something wrong, letting her be the way she was. Maybe it wasn't healthy. He took it for granted; tried to make it as easy as possible. Maybe he actually made her worse, letting her spend so much of her life in silence. But then, that was why she loved him.

He assumed.

As he assumed so much. Because, of course, she never said a fucking word about it.

In one motion he lifted the glass in his hand and flung it against the wall, sending whisky flying up his arm and across the room. Splashing brazenly across the wall. The glass shattered, and fell in a million pieces behind the unit which held the TV.

He breathed deeply, shakily, and waited to see if she'd wake up.

Not a sound.

He pressed 'play' on the answerphone, and listened as his boss explained in weary tones why he would never make it as a journalist.

Lily awoke to the sound of breaking glass. Lay in perfect stillness to see what would come afterwards. Nothing but the low rumble of the television and, after a minute, the electronic chatter of the answerphone, indecipherable.

She could remember lying in bed as a child, listening to her parents arguing. Breaking glass had always been followed by slamming doors. And then the agonising wail of her mother's tears. Anna had never troubled to keep quiet, never worried about who heard what.

Lily lay in the darkness, listening, but no further sound came from the living room. She waited for two hours until she heard Richard move, and then she turned over and pretended to be asleep. He crept into the bedroom, slipped under the covers with a minimum of movement. Didn't disturb her, except to lean over and lightly kiss her on the forehead.

She fell asleep with the imprint of his lips still burning on her skin.

then

The driveway went on forever. There had been wrought iron gates at the entrance, improbably high, but that had been at least five minutes ago. The comforting crackle of tyres on gravel made Lily feel as if she were coming home. But this place wasn't home. All she could see were trees, and, far in the distance, a house as big as a palace.

Her parents were talking in the front, but she couldn't hear what they were saying. The radio was on, playing a song that she knew. She didn't sing along, but she mouthed the words, echoing the tune in her head. Some of the words were unrecognisable, and she made up her own language to fit in the gaps.

They pulled up next to some stone steps, which led up to a door at least twice the size of their front door at home. There was a brass knocker, a gargoyle with a loop in its mouth that sneered down at them from above. The building was very long, with rows of windows in both directions, neatly lined up with the windows on the floors above. All the windows had bars across them.

'What do you reckon, Lils?' Her father turned round from the driver's seat to face her. She looked up, but didn't reply.

'There's no point, Marcus.' Her mother's mouth, twisted with the bitterness of her own bad luck.

'We wouldn't be here if there was no point. Come on, Lily. Let's go and find out if anyone's home, shall we?'

Her mother didn't bother waiting for Lily to answer.

'You go,' she said. 'I'll park the car.'

Her father mumbled something that Lily didn't hear and climbed out of the car, opening the rear door so that she could follow. Her mother shifted awkwardly into the driver's seat. She didn't look at the back seat.

'Come on,' her father said, reaching down to take Lily's hand. She let him, and followed him up the stairs. The car drove off behind her.

'Do you want to knock on the door?'

Lily looked up at the knocker, with its gargoyle that glinted slightly in the mid-afternoon sun. It looked more menacing than it had done from the car. She shook her head.

'Okay, then.'

Her father reached up, grasped the loop of brass firmly in his fist, and knocked three times.

The inside of the house was dark, despite all the windows Lily had seen from the outside. The hallways were wide, with black and white checked floors that stretched into infinity. There were a lot of doors, and all of them were closed.

A man – who introduced himself as Dr Hadley, though he didn't look much like a doctor – had answered the door, and was leading them through the house. There were other people around, and everyone nodded to Dr Hadley as they passed, and smiled at Lily. No one looked at her father. The further they got into the house, the more worried she became that her mother wouldn't be able to find them once she'd parked the car, but no one mentioned it and she tried not to think about it.

Dr Hadley showed them into a room that was full of books. There was a desk in the corner, with several chairs around it, and he and Lily's father sat on opposite sides of the desk. Lily went to look at the books. She was good at reading, but she didn't recognise many of the words in the titles. Some of the books were so old that the titles had faded, and she couldn't make out the letters.

'Eighteen months, you say?' Dr Hadley's voice, though quiet, carried across the room. Lily turned around, and saw that he was bent over his desk, writing. Her father had his back to her, but she could see him leaning forward, looking at what Dr Hadley was doing.

'About that, yes. Maybe a bit more.'

'Has she said anything at all since...?' His voice lowered still further, and Lily couldn't make out what he'd said. She turned back to the books. A lot of the titles had the word 'child' in them. So he was a doctor for children. For her. She wandered away from the desk, until their voices were just a murmur in the background.

At the far end of the room there was a window, without bars on. It was too high for her to see through when she was standing on the floor, but there was a low pipe running round the skirting board that she could balance on. Clinging on to the windowsill with her fingertips, she could just about see out. She'd been expecting to see the front of the house, but instead she found herself looking out on to a courtyard. It was covered with grass, and flowers, and there were people outside. Two children, not much older than her, cartwheeled up and down the grass while a woman in a nurse's uniform watched from a distance.

Lily stayed there for a while, until she felt her feet getting hot through the thin rubber soles of her shoes. She realised the pipe must be like the radiators at home. She jumped down, and rejoined her father and Dr Hadley. The doctor was talking on a telephone now, while her father stared off into the distance.

'We've been talking about you,' Marcus said, lifting her on to his knee. 'Dr Hadley thinks it might be a good idea for you to stay here for a while. Just a week or two. So that he can keep an eye on you and help you get better. Would that be okay?'

Lily thought about it for a minute. She didn't like the house much, or Dr Hadley. But she wouldn't mind more time to look at the books, and the courtyard looked nice. She nodded.

'Good girl. He's just speaking to someone on the phone, and they're going to find you a bedroom to sleep in. It'll be like a holiday. Or going to boarding school.'

Lily had always been fascinated by the idea of going to boarding school.

'I'm sure your mama will be here in a minute. Then we'll say goodbye, and go away, because we can't sleep here. But we'll come back tomorrow.'

Lily knew she should feel afraid, being left here by herself. That was why her father was explaining everything. She didn't feel much of anything.

Dr Hadley put down the phone, and looked up at them with a smile that didn't quite look right. 'We've found a room. Did your dad tell you, Lily? You're going to be living with us for a little while.'

She looked up at him. His hair was going grey, like her father's, and his glasses were too big for his face. They poked out over the edges, making him look like an owl.

She nodded, once.

Anna didn't come inside, but crouched down on the front steps to give Lily a hug. 'Goodbye, my darling. We'll come back tomorrow. Make sure you be good and do everything the doctors tell you, won't you?'

Lily tried to nod, but her mother was holding her too tightly and she couldn't move.

'Don't worry if you hear any funny sounds. You're quite safe here.'

Anna pulled back, keeping her hands on Lily's shoulders. Lily noticed she was crying.

'Goodbye, darling,' she said again, looking Lily directly in the eye. She paused for a moment, perfectly still. Waiting. And then:

'Oh, fucking forget it, then.'

now

'In the beginning was the word.' Richard was whispering, not sure if she was awake, not wanting to disturb her if she wasn't. 'And the word was...'

There was a pause, long enough for him to think that she was indeed asleep. He almost rolled over and left her to it. And then:

'Lumbered.' She was smiling, her eyes still closed. It was one of their favourites.

'Okay. Well, once upon a time, in old England, there lived a girl called Sarah. She was a servant girl, and had been all her life, working with her mother and her grandmother and her two sisters, for a family called Stephenson. They weren't a bad family to work for, despite the fact that they were very rich and very posh; they owned a house in London and another in the country, and acres of forest land, but they were always kind and never treated their servants as slaves. Sarah, as the oldest of her sisters, was in charge of looking after the two daughters of the family, Amelia and Amanda.

'Amelia and Amanda were only a year apart in age, and virtually inseparable. They were both very lively, and kept Sarah busy all day, so that by the time she went to bed she was usually exhausted, and fell asleep as soon as her head hit the pillow.

'Because they were very rich, Amelia and Amanda were constantly being given new toys to play with; and, because they got bored easily, they tired of their new toys very quickly.

Their parents were kind enough to pass on these disregarded playthings to Sarah's sisters, who were similar in age, but it wasn't long before they outgrew them, and it fell upon Sarah to find somewhere to store them.

'Luckily, there was a room in the house known as the lumber room. It was the home for all the furniture that had been broken or discarded throughout the years, and, because the Stephensons were a very old and very rich family, the room was very large. It was one of Sarah's favourite places to go, because there was so much history there. Her favourite piece of furniture was a beautiful old four-poster bed. One of the posts was broken, but it made no difference to Sarah; when the house was quiet and she had no work to do, her favourite pastime was to lie on the bed and imagine she was a princess.

'No one else ever went in the lumber room, except to put things in there; and so it came to be that Sarah knew its contents better than anyone else. Admittedly most of the things in there were broken, but she loved them nonetheless.

'When Amanda and Amelia were old enough to be thinking about finding husbands and starting their own families, the Stephensons fell on hard times. Mr Stephenson ran his own business, and in the winter of Amanda's fifteenth year the business fell apart. It was quickly revealed that he had built up a lot of debt in the course of trying to save the business, and that he now owed a lot of money to people that he wasn't able to pay back. The decision was made to sell the country house and move the whole family to London permanently, so that he could find a new job more easily.

'There were, of course, many consequences that arose from this decision, and for a while Sarah and her family were worried for their jobs. Luckily, it transpired that they were to move to London with the family, although the rest of the servants would have to look for work elsewhere.

'The most unfortunate consequence for Sarah was that the lumber room, and all its items, were to be abandoned in the country. She almost wept when she found out that the contents of her treasured room would not be coming with them; but of course there would be no space for a pile of broken furniture in the modest London house.

'Amelia and Amanda, being Sarah's friends as well as her employers, realised how much it upset her to be leaving all those memories behind. When she explained that the main thing that upset her was the thought of leaving everything by itself to rot in the lumber room, they decided to organise a sale, so that every item of furniture could find a new home. They enlisted Sarah to help with clearing the room, and they had many hours of fun sorting through all of their old toys, which of course, being young women now, they had completely forgotten about.

'On the day of the sale they laid out everything on their lawns, and invited all of their neighbours to come and see what they had to offer. Because their neighbours were very kind and they wanted to help the Stephensons, they came to see if there was anything that was worth buying, and many of them went home well pleased. But there were still several items left at the end of the day, one of them being the four-poster bed; and Sarah, though she knew there was nothing more that could be done, was very sorry to know that she had to leave it behind.

'Soon afterwards they all travelled to London to live in the new house. Sarah and her family had all been there before, although they didn't feel so at home there as they had in the country. When they arrived they made their way promptly to the servants' quarters (which, because the Stephensons were so kind, were actually just another wing of the house); and because there were fewer servants than usual, the others having lost their jobs, there was enough space for them to have a room each. The rooms had already been assigned, and Sarah made her way to her room straight away.

'She didn't know, of course, that Amelia and Amanda had arranged for all of the leftover furniture from the lumber room sale to be brought to her room for her to look after; and so she got a wonderful shock when she walked through the door to find the four-poster bed waiting for her.

'Although her young friends had tried to explain to their parents how she felt about the lumber room, Mr and Mrs Stephenson never did quite understand, and so from that point on they always referred to Sarah as having been "lumbered" with their old furniture.'

Richard told the story with his eyes closed, preferring to wait until the end to see Lily's reaction. It was worth it; when he opened his eyes she was facing him, smiling. 'I like Sarah,' she said, tilting her head forward to kiss him on the nose.

'I like you,' he replied, pulling her closer to him and returning her kiss. 'And I especially like waking up next to you and knowing we don't have to go anywhere.'

'Don't you have to go to work?'

'Nah. I told them what happened. They said take as long as you need.' He leaned in to kiss her properly, so that he wouldn't have to look her in the eye. He never had been any good at lying.

'Nice of them.'

'Well, even horrible newspapers have to be nice sometimes. So. My little invalid.' He grinned. 'What can I get you? Coffee? Toast? Pancakes?'

'Pancakes? Really?'

'Well, seeing as we have to get your strength up. With maple syrup?'

She nodded. 'And banana?'

'Done.' He laughed softly. 'Do you think all women are this easily pleased?'

'Mmm. Probably more so. But you'd have to put up with them chattering all the time.'

'Couldn't be having that.' He took one more look at her, duvet pulled up to her chin, tousled dark blonde hair poking out from under the covers, and then rolled out of bed in one smooth movement.

The house was empty by the time Connie awoke. Nathan had left her a coffee by the bed. He'd dropped the boys at school on the way to work, as he always did. Usually Connie would have been up to make them breakfast, but evidently she'd been so tired she'd managed to sleep through the alarm. She reached out a hand to feel the coffee mug, and found it cold.

They'd argued when she got home the night before. Nothing serious; their arguments were rarely serious enough to be continued from one day to the next. He thought she was overreacting about Lily, worrying too much as usual. Didn't understand. Would never understand, how it felt: as if she had to protect Lily, shelter her from the world.

Richard would have understood, of course, but there was no sense in phoning him now. They were probably still asleep. Or maybe he'd gone to work.

But he wouldn't, surely, leave Lily to look after herself.

She wanted to speak to Lily. Such a stupid thing, when you saw someone every week. How to explain that it felt as if you never saw them at all?

Hadn't seen them, in fact, for years?

She pulled the covers over her head. Considered staying there for the rest of the day. For a split second she could imagine it: Nathan's face, when he got home to find that she'd spent the whole day in bed.

He'd call a doctor, of course. One that wasn't him.

She pushed the covers back again, reached for the phone. Maybe Richard would be at work. Then changed her mind. Retracted her hand and sank back into the bed, exhausted.

Maybe she would leave it until tomorrow.

then

There were bars across the windows in Lily's room, which cast shadows on the floor of checked black and white tiles. They made an odd, criss-crossing pattern of light and dark with no symmetry which Lily tried to deconstruct, to no avail. She looked until her head hurt, and then she stared at the walls, which were plain white and required no effort on her part.

The first morning, she had awoken early, with no idea of what was required of her. She could hear movement outside the door, but she didn't dare leave the room by herself, and so when the nurse came for her she was sitting on her bed expectantly. The nurse took her hand and led her through the house, past rows of doors – open, now, and revealing the identical cells contained within – up stairs, down hallways, chattering all the way. Lily followed passively, half-listening, watching everything as she passed. There were other children here, both boys and girls, but no adults. 'You won't find any grown-ups in this wing,' the nurse said cheerfully, which Lily took to mean that they were banned, kept elsewhere.

The nurse led her to a large bathroom and shut the door behind them. She ran her a bath, gave her soap and a towel and clean clothes to change into – her own clothes, Lily realised, though she didn't remember bringing any – and then sat on a chair in the corner of the room and read a book while Lily bathed. She wasn't used to having someone watching over her, so she made as quick a job of it as possible. When she dressed herself her skin was still damp. The nurse handed her a toothbrush and a tube of toothpaste, and, when she was finished, brushed her hair for her and twisted it into a single long plait which fell in the centre of her back. Lily never wore her hair like that, preferring it loose, but she made no comment.

When they left the bathroom, there was another girl waiting outside – older, but still with an accompanying nurse, and hundreds of scratches on her forearms, some silvery, some dark, some vivid red. She didn't look at Lily, but stared straight ahead, at the door she was headed for. Lily's nurse took her to a room with lots of windows, and left her there.

That first morning, Lily had discovered there were lessons, of sorts. The number of children varied from day to day, the ages ranging from a year or two younger than Lily to girls in their late teens. There were no boys older than thirteen. This was not something she deduced, but something she was told. No boys over thirteen. No girls over eighteen. No children under five. Age was an important factor, she gathered. Age, and gender. In a place where they were defined by the aspects of themselves that were theirs alone, these were the things that bound them together, the common differences by which they were categorised.

In the morning they were all together. They were taught normal subjects, like reading and art and maths and science. There was a lot of disruption in the classes – temperamental children screamed, threw things, started fights. The girl Lily had seen outside the bathroom was prone to arguments and screaming fits, and was frequently taken out of the room to calm down.

The morning classes became something of a routine. Lily worked out that if she sat in the far corner, near the windows, away from all the cupboards that lined one wall and held the art and craft supplies, she could be left in relative peace. The other kids clamoured for art and craft – they liked chaos, mess, and the opportunity to throw paint in each other's eyes. Lily sat in the corner, reading books and solving maths puzzles, and no one bothered her.

The nurses had sometimes asked her to read to them, to which she'd responded by closing the books and putting them back on the shelves. They had persisted for a few days, until she'd stopped getting the books out altogether. She stuck with the maths puzzles, which required no verbal demonstration.

After these lessons, there was group therapy. Lily sat on the edges of these sessions, swinging her feet in the air, watching them whoosh backwards and forwards, getting closer and closer to the floor. She imagined tiny people on her toes, riding them like a rollercoaster, screaming to get off every time her feet ventured closer to the black and white sea below.

Lunch was the same as it had been at her old school: noisy, chaotic, unpleasant. Food tasteless, bordering on inedible. She chewed rubbery meat that could just as easily have been vegetable and tried not to catch anyone's eye.

After lunch she had one-to-one sessions with Dr Hadley. Lily waited in her room until a nurse came for her, and guided her back to the office she had first visited with her father. Dr Hadley would talk to her, ask her questions, note her lack of response. He generally asked closed questions, allowing her to nod or shake her head as required. When he asked open questions – forgetting, maybe, or deliberately provoking her – she simply stared at him until he rephrased them.

And after that, her parents: her mother angry, unforgiving; her father, just her father. Every day, the same.

'We've invited you here today because we've reached the end of our period of initial assessment.'

'Yes.'

Her father was next to her, holding her hand. Her mother was on his other side.

'As you're probably aware, Lily hasn't made a great deal of progress that would be immediately obvious. She is still emphatically non-verbal in her communication. However, we do feel that significant progress is being made with regard to her communication skills in general.'

'How so?' Her father again.

'These things obviously take time. Lily is gradually starting to show a willingness to participate in group activities. She pays attention to what is going on around her in a way that she didn't when she was first admitted. Even in two short weeks, she has shown a significant level of improvement in her general alertness and interaction with the outside world.'

Her father squeezed her hand. 'Is it appropriate for her to be here while we discuss this?'

'It is. We think – ' and at this point he fixed his gaze pointedly on Lily ' – that Lily listens to everything that goes on around her. And, as she is aware that her refusal to speak is not a normal or acceptable mode of behaviour, there is no need to conceal from her the fact that she is here because of that. She knows that we are trying to encourage her to communicate. Meetings like this reinforce the fact that we are working on your behalf, rather than as an independent body to which she doesn't necessarily need to pay attention.'

'I see.'

Her father fell silent for a while. Lily watched him as he watched her mother, who stared fixedly at the floor and did not move her head, even once.

'What would you recommend?' he said finally.

'I would recommend a further stay of no less than six months, with visits from you on a monthly basis.'

'We wouldn't be allowed to see her?'

'We feel that your presence is... reinforcing her current behaviour. She is essentially being rewarded on a daily basis for behaving in a way which we don't wish to reward. We think we would make progress much more quickly if your presence weren't so pervasive.'

Her father nodded, swallowed. His expression was very similar to that of her mother's. 'Would we receive regular updates?'

'One of our nurses can speak to you on the phone once a week.' Dr Hadley smiled, and leaned forward on his elbows. 'It's in her best interests, Mr Emmett. I promise.'

Her father nodded again, though he didn't look as if he agreed in the slightest.

now

'You must understand the position you've put us in.'

'Actually, no. Not really. Not at all, in fact.'

Richard shifted his hands in his lap, considered making some kind of emphatic gesture. In the end he just let them twitch, meaninglessly. Defeat was etched in his every movement, even while his words carried a promise of defiance.

'We can't employ people who act in this way.'

'My girlfriend was in hospital.'

'Yes, we understand that. But how much time would it have taken to have told us that? It was over an hour before someone realised you had actually gone. Then we had to find someone to finish your work, check the facts – and obviously we wasted time looking for you, trying to contact you – it's just not professional, to be frank.'

But to be Richard… Not the time.

'I realise that. I'm sorry. I had an emotional reaction to a situation as opposed to a professional one.'

'Sarcasm is not going to help you – '

'That wasn't sarcasm. I'm just trying to defend my position.'

'There is no defence, Richard. If the same thing happened today, you'd behave in the same way, wouldn't you?'

'Of course. So would most people, I imagine.'

'Not serious journalists. You see, this is where the difference lies. If you really cared – if it was your number one priority – then you'd understand that. But your priorities lie elsewhere.'

'With my *family*. It's not like I'm privileging a different newspaper or – or calling in sick to watch TV or whatever.'

'We're terribly sorry – '

'You're not, though, are you? You've never really thought I could make it, and now I've proved you right, and you'll be glad to see the back of me.'

'This kind of talk isn't going to get us anywhere.'

Richard looked from his managing editor, Sam, to his line manager, Ellis, and saw his hopelessness etched on their features. These were the men who had hired him five years ago, when there was some possibility that he might rise to the challenge of professionalism. They looked weary, and unsympathetic, and he knew that there was no real hope for him here.

'We're not saying there isn't a place for you here, Rich. You know it's not like that.'

'No, I'll always have a place making cups of tea.'

'You're being melodramatic.'

'Well, I've had a fairly tiring and dramatic few days, and this isn't really what I wanted to come back to.' He looked from face to face, searching for some kind of emotion, but found only flat disdain.

'You can't pretend it's a surprise.'

'To be told I will *never* write features because of *one* fuck-up? It is a surprise. Actually, it's a pretty fucking major surprise.'

'If we could try to keep the bad language to a minimum – '

'Oh, this is ridiculous.' Richard stood up and walked out, just barely managing to control himself enough to not slam the door behind him. He was trembling as he grabbed his coat. He hesitated for a moment in front of his desk, and then grabbed the photo of Lily that he kept there as well. It was a statement, he knew that. If he didn't take the photo he could pretend that he might come back, that he was just going for a walk to cool off. Taking the photo was effectively telling them that they could stick their job.

He did know that, and he did it anyway.

Five years was long enough.

Lily was sleeping when the phone rang. She hadn't been back to work yet, though she'd been doing a vague imitation of working from home: checking her emails regularly, toying with the ideas she'd been working on for the last couple of months. Nothing that could be strictly referred to as productive, but she was doing enough to keep herself afloat.

Today, though, she'd found herself wandering aimlessly through the flat, unable to settle to anything. Her head felt as though it was buzzing with ungraspable thoughts. It was the absence of Richard, she knew; his going back to work had signified a return to normal life that she wasn't entirely ready for. So she'd got up an hour after he'd left, and wandered aimlessly from room to room, carrying the scent of steaming coffee with her from space to space; and at midday she'd retreated back to bed, exhausted by her unproductiveness, and fallen into an instant, dreamless sleep.

It was deep enough that the ringing phone didn't entirely rouse her, and it was a few seconds after the caller had hung up that she realised she was awake. The sunlight – greyish November mid-afternoon almost-dusk – touched dustily on her belongings; and Richard's, of course. Their intertwined existence scattered thoughtlessly throughout the room. The rumpled space of the duvet next to her, waiting for his return.

The phone started to ring again, and she hauled herself out of bed.

It took four rings to cross the living room and pick up the receiver. Her mumbled hello was greeted with a five-second-long silence that was almost enough to convince her she'd imagined the ringing of the phone; and then she realised that there was no dialling tone.

'Hello? Who's there?'

'Lils.' Connie, sounding not like Connie, like not-Connie. 'I thought you'd be back at work by now.'

'I don't... I couldn't.' She struggled for a moment for a fuller explanation, and gave up. 'Is everything okay?'

'Sure. Of course.'

'You don't sound okay.'

'Don't I?' She laughed, a not-Connie laugh, humourless. 'I've been worrying about you, I suppose. Silly of me.'

'You shouldn't.'

'No, probably not.'

'Is there... Did you want to speak to me about something?'

Connie laughed again, and this time there really was humour there, though Lily couldn't imagine where it might have sprung from.

'I suppose I just wanted to talk.'

'Oh.'

'But of course, that's the last thing that you want to do, right?'

Lily didn't bother to respond. Couldn't see what there was to say.

'Do you ever think about Dad?' Connie asked.

'I... What's wrong?'

'Our parents are dead, Lily.'

'Yes.'

'They're dead. Gone. Don't you ever think about that? Don't you want to *talk* about it?'

'Are you drunk?'

A pause. And then: 'Oh, fucking forget it, then.'

Lily stood for a while, holding the receiver to her ear, listening to the buzz that signified Connie's departure from the conversation. Trying to remember where she'd heard that tone of voice before.

To lose. To part with or come to be without. From the Old English, *losian*: to perish. And also *forlēosan*: to forfeit.

He had lost his job, parted with it, come to be without it. Forfeited it? Yes, almost certainly. For what?

What had he gained in return?

Lily had lost her parents, lost her friends, lost her words. And he had found her – he with an abundance of words, which he gave to her, willingly. *Find*: to meet with or discover by chance, to discover or obtain by effort – which was it? Chance or design? He had found her by chance, certainly. But how had she found him? Through her own chances, or through his desire to hold on to her?

Did she make decisions, he wondered, or did she simply drift along on the tides, finding, losing, allowing other people's chances to shape her existence?

He walked the streets with no destination in mind, the photo of her in his jacket pocket, his knowledge of what he had done nestled at his breast. He felt as if he teetered on the edge of a precipice. Could see what had gone before but had no idea what was to come. Didn't know how to tell her what he'd done. Couldn't decide how to proceed.

Maybe he could just wander into the Jobcentre. Find something else. Continue as if nothing had happened.

One decision didn't have to change everything.

And yet, it inevitably did. Because what would he do? He couldn't rely on a good reference. Couldn't get another job at a paper, even if there had been one available. And what else was there? Five years in one direction, only to find you'd been driving towards a brick wall all this time. And when you got there, what did you do?

Swerve abruptly to the left?

Crash into it and hope for the best?

Or drive straight through, and discover that the wall was not made of brick after all; that you'd emerged on the other side, unscathed?

It was Connie who found him; accidentally, because of course she wasn't looking. He was sitting on a bench, watching children play on one side of a park while teenagers toyed with adulthood on the other. And, in between, parents provided the sense of a necessary order: the destination towards which the younger generations were headed.

She had Luke and Tom with her. Richard realised they were on their way back from school: both of them in their uniforms, dark blue sweatshirts with nondescript logos, Tom holding Luke's hand to keep him from running off. Luke clamouring for something – ice cream, video games, Richard couldn't tell, but whatever it was he wanted it and he wanted it *now*, please, thank you very much.

Both boys started running when they spotted him, and even Connie sped up, though she limited herself to a purposeful stride.

'Shouldn't you be at work?'

He smiled lopsidedly. 'Haven't gone back yet.'

'Don't lie to me.'

'Uncle Richard, I've got a treasure map! Look.' Luke dove into his rucksack, emerging with a crumpled piece of paper, which was indeed a crudely executed treasure map. X marks the spot, in red pen, a sharp contrast to the blues and greens of the background.

'Excellent. Did you make it?'

'Yes.' Luke nodded solemnly. 'Me and Tom are going to find the treasure. Do you want to come?'

'Definitely. Give me a minute to talk to your mum first, though.'

The two boys bounded off in the direction of the playground, and Connie sat down next to him, her eyes never leaving them as they retreated into the distance.

'How did you know I was lying?'

'Well, I rang Lily today, and you weren't there. She didn't *say* anything, of course, but I figured you'd gone back to work. And now you're here, and if you weren't at work you'd be at home looking after her, so – there you go. Also, you're a rubbish liar.' She smiled, though she didn't seem to mean it.

'I lost my job.'

'Oh, Richard.'

'It's my own fault. I walked out when Lily was in hospital. Forgot to tell them where I was going. And then I walked out again today.'

'So you didn't exactly "lose" it, then.'

'Mmm. I was thinking about that. Forfeited my job, is what I've settled on.'

Connie gave him a curious look, but didn't comment. 'So what are you going to do?'

'I have no idea.'

'Well, you'd better start thinking pretty quickly. What with Lily being in the state she's in – '

'Don't try to pretend you know what state Lily's in. She might be fine, for all we know.'

'She's not fine. You know she's not. That collapse – you know what it meant.'

'It doesn't have to mean anything,' Richard said. 'She's never been like that since I've known her. Maybe she's changed.'

'People don't change.'

'They *do*, though. Aren't you different from the way you were ten years ago?'

Connie leaned back against the bench, stretched her arms out in front of her. 'Not really.'

'Come on. You're a wife, a mother. Those are things that change you.'

'I'm still the same person, though. I still worry about the same things. I still react to things in the same way. I'm still wasting hours of my life trying to look after my baby sister when I should be devoting my energies to looking after myself.'

Richard raised an eyebrow. 'Do you really think that?'

'Of course.'

'But you don't need to look after her. I'm here for that.'

'And a fantastic job you're doing, right now.'

'Don't be a bitch – '

'It's true. You may be devoted but you don't understand her the way I do, and you never will. Every time something happens, you run to me for advice because she won't talk to you and you can't read her mind. Which is fine, I understand that, but you can't then act as though I'm completely superfluous to the whole thing. *She* might not realise how much I do for her, but you, at least, could have the decency to remember it every now and again.'

'I'm sorry. I didn't mean it.'

'I know.'

'I just feel like I've let her down. But all I was trying to do was help her.'

'Look, Richard, some people can't be helped. Lily is never going to change – and don't protest that you don't want her to, because I know that you don't, or at least you think you don't. But I for one would like it if she changed just a bit. Just enough to convince me that she was okay, so I could stop worrying about her all the time and get on with my own life. And I think it would benefit you, too.'

They sat in silence while Richard tried to formulate a response. He wanted to tell her that she was wrong, but she wasn't. At least not entirely. It was as though there was an essence of correctness about what she was saying, but it missed the mark. It wasn't how he felt.

How to make her understand that what he loved about Lily was the notunderstanding? That being with her was something akin to being in the presence of God, a being so far beyond his comprehension that he was constantly in awe of her.

Then again, maybe he was just a typical man, and she was just a typical woman, and he wanted to protect her.

'Maybe it's you that needs to change,' he said eventually.

Connie laughed; a short, humourless burst of inarticulate emotion.

Then she went to be with her children, and left him to his own devices.

then

Connie sat in the middle of a row of red cushioned chairs, slouched so low that she was almost horizontal. Her school bag occupied the seat next to her. The chairs lined the wall opposite the deputy head's office in one of the busiest school corridors, designed for maximum humiliation in between classes when the hallways boiled with students. For the moment there was no one around except a squeaky-shoed receptionist who kept walking back and forth, giving Connie a disdainful look each time she passed, but it wouldn't be long until she was subjected to the stares of every passing student.

It was nearly the end of the school year, and there was a feeling of anticipation, of general winding-down as everyone edged closer to six weeks of freedom. Sunlight streamed through the windows behind Connie and warmed the back of her neck, carrying tantalising hints of ice cream and freshly cut grass and tanned shoulders. Inside, though, the darkness was thick and dusty, as if the overall air of gloom couldn't be penetrated by mere sunlight.

The door in front of her opened, revealing a tall man, slightly younger than her father, with a tuft of dark hair that was greying at the sides. Mr Elliott's face was generally kind, though at that moment he didn't look pleased to see her. He gestured her into his office without a word, and closed the door behind them, waving his hand in the direction of a chair. 'Take a seat, please.'

She did as she was asked, and waited silently while he walked around the desk to sit down opposite her.

'Are you going to tell me why you're here?'

Connie looked down at her knees, unsure what to say. She'd never seen him look angry before, and there was a hardness in his eyes she found unnerving.

'Connie, please, do me the credit of at least attempting to explain yourself. We both know the official version of the story, of course. I'm asking to hear yours.'

She bit her lip, feeling small and childish. 'I don't know.'

'Oh, come on.' His voice was derisive.

'I don't know what they've told you. But it's lies.'

'How can you know it's lies if you don't know what they've said?'

She raised her head to glare at him. 'Because it's *always* lies. You know that as well as me. Everyone knows how they all treat me, and the school still always takes their side over mine. Every time. It's not fair.'

'Unfortunately, Connie, fairness isn't really the issue at hand here.'

'What's that supposed to mean? Isn't this my chance to tell my side of the story? To – to vindicate myself, or whatever?'

'Go on, then. Vindicate yourself.'

Connie realised she was trembling. 'You won't believe me.'

Mr Elliott sighed, and leaned back in his chair. 'Actually, Connie, I always believe you. I just think you go about dealing with things in the wrong way. I don't think it's fair that you have to deal with it in the first place, but you only make things worse for yourself.'

She glared at him, but his expression was unrelenting. 'Okay. Fine,' she said eventually. 'They stole my PE kit. And when I tried to find it they shut me in the showers, and no one realised until after the lesson, because they told Mr Bentham I'd gone home ill. So I was pissed off, and I punched Eleanor

117

in the face. And instead of punching me back, like a *normal* human being, she ran and told a teacher so I'd get in trouble, and she'll beat me up after school instead, where no one can tell her off. That's it. The whole story.' The injustice of it made her eyes sting with tears, but she wasn't going to cry. Not in front of the only teacher who didn't think she was some kind of monster teenager from hell.

Mr Elliott was still leaning back in his chair, surveying her, his face calm. His eyes had softened, but his expression was largely unreadable. Connie couldn't tell if he believed her or if he just felt sorry for her for being such a pathetic liar.

'Do you think,' he asked eventually, leaning forwards and resting his chin on his hands, 'that punching Eleanor was the best way you could have reacted?'

'Of course not.'

'So why did you do it?'

'Because she's a bully and she makes my life hell every day and I really, really wanted to.'

The corners of Mr Elliott's mouth twitched as this. 'Do you know why she bullies you? Maybe if we could get to the bottom of why she doesn't like you then we could try and fix whatever the problem is.'

'Why does there have to be a reason?'

'There's always a reason.'

'No, there isn't. Plenty of people get bullied just because they're – short, or they have – I don't know – ginger hair, or whatever. Those aren't real reasons. They're just things that bullies make up when they've decided they don't like someone.'

Mr Elliott nodded. 'And does Eleanor ever give you a reason like that? Does she think you're short?'

He was smiling, now, and Connie looked at him sharply, trying to figure out if he was mocking her.

'No.'

'Does she say anything?'

'What does it *matter*? Nothing she says is true. She knows it isn't true. She just says it to be mean.'

'But maybe she believes it to be true.'

Connie narrowed her eyes. 'She knows she's lying.'

'But what if she doesn't, hmm? How do you know what she thinks? If she genuinely believes something about you – something awful – then maybe her behaviour is slightly more understandable.'

'If you know what it is, then why are you making me tell you?' Connie folded her arms over her chest, defensive.

'I don't know anything, Connie. I've just heard rumours, like everyone else, and I've read newspapers, like everyone else, and I think you know exactly why Eleanor doesn't like you but you'll do anything as long as you don't have to talk about it.' His voice was even, and free from accusation.

'They're just rumours.'

'I believe you.'

'Then why aren't you taking my side? Why isn't she in here, if you know I'm telling the truth?'

'Because I don't *know* anything. I believe you, that's all. Fact is, I've still got a pupil who's been punched in the face and says you did it. And you're not denying it, so what am I supposed to do? I can't be seen to condone your behaviour.'

'But you can be seen to condone hers?'

'Are you going to officially complain to me about her behaviour?'

Connie looked at her feet, and said nothing.

'Thought not. Look, Connie, I want to help you. Really, I do. But the only way this is going to get resolved is if you talk to these girls. Tell them what happened when you were younger. Isn't it possible that this is all a misunderstanding – that these girls are actually scared of you because of what they think happened out there?'

Connie snorted. 'If they were scared of me they wouldn't be constantly trying to beat me up.'

'Sure they would. That's what I do when I'm scared of people.' Mr Elliott smiled and, reluctantly, Connie smiled back.

'Thanks for the pep talk,' she said. 'So what's my punishment?'

'Is that all you have to say for yourself?'

She nodded.

'Fair enough. I think a week's worth of detention ought to do it, don't you?'

The house was warm and slantingly sunlit when Connie arrived home. She could see all the dust, highlighted at odd angles by the shafts of light, thickening the air around her. Her footsteps echoed in the hallway, and she placed her bag on the floor next to the rows of shoes, listening carefully. There was no sound from inside, though she could hear distant voices in the garden.

She toyed with the idea of going straight upstairs, but she knew it was inadvisable. Her parents would know something was wrong regardless, so she might as well get the worst of it over with.

She found them in the garden, digging up the flowerbeds. Her mother was dressed in jeans and a T-shirt, her long hair swept back from her forehead and fastened in a red scarf Connie had never seen before. She was kneeling in the dirt, her hands plunged into the earth, and Connie's first thought was that she looked happier than she had in months. She wasn't smiling exactly, but there was a lightness to her expression which reminded Connie of earlier times. Of Life Before Billy.

Her father was on the other side of the lawn, wielding a spade, shovelling wood and weeds into a pile for a bonfire.

He was the first to notice Connie, and he lifted his hand in a wave as she stepped out on to the patio. 'Hey, stranger. What's going on?'

'I was just about to ask you the same thing,' she replied, smiling faintly. 'What's all this about?'

'Oh, nothing major. Just a general tidy-up that's long overdue.' He lay the spade down on the grass and walked over to give her a hug. 'How was your day?'

She shrugged. 'Day-like. Are we having a bonfire?'

'Yeah, I thought I'd light it tonight. You want to help?'

'Sure.' She wandered over to the pile, prodding it experimentally with a toe. 'It's been ages since I've been out here.'

'Well, I think we've all been neglecting it a bit.' Marcus hesitated, as if he might say more, but decided not to. 'Your mother's going to do some planting over the next couple of days.'

'Isn't it a bit late in the year for that?'

'For most plants, yes.' Anna stood up, brushing dirt off her jeans as she did so. 'There are some things we can plant now. Might not see much activity until next spring, but at least if we make a start now then we know it's there.'

Connie nodded. This seemed to contradict most of what she knew about gardening, but she chose not to say anything, not wanting to test the boundaries of her mother's newfound good mood.

'We were thinking,' Anna continued, her eyes wide and slightly unnerving, 'that we might go on a holiday at some point soon. Nothing major. Just get out of the house for a few days, go somewhere peaceful. What do you think?'

Connie hesitated. 'With Lily?'

'Not this time.' Her father jumped in before Anna could. 'The institute won't let her leave at the moment. But that doesn't mean we can't get away for a bit, does it?' He reached out a hand and squeezed her shoulder. 'I think we could all do with a break.'

'We need to stop putting our lives on hold,' Anna said bluntly. 'We can't just sit here, waiting for Lily to come back.'

We could have just not sent her away in the first place, Connie thought, but didn't say it aloud. 'No,' she said instead. 'I guess we can't.'

She went back inside after a while, leaving her parents to it. She picked up her school bag from the hallway, remembering as she did so the letter that was inside it, advising her parents that she was in trouble again. She had promised Mr Elliott that she would give it to them, and for a moment she felt bad about betraying his trust, when he'd expressly said that with any other student he would have put it straight in the post. But then, surely he shouldn't be putting her in that position? Giving her the responsibility of bringing about her own downfall?

She hesitated, and then went back to the patio doors. Stuck her head out of the door until she could see her father. 'Dad?'

'Yeah?'

'Can I stick some stuff on the bonfire?'

Lily, as Connie remembered her. Eight years old, tiny, blonde, almost ethereal in her pale insignificance. Voice just a whisper:

– *Connie please **take me with** you I **want to come** don't leave me behind* –

In the dark, in a room with bars on the windows. The institute.

Shadows behind her, shifting but never quite resolving into an image Connie could identify. Black on black, indecipherable.

– *Only crazy people live in a place like that* –

The walls of the room blended into the trees outside so that they were surrounded by grasping tree fingers. Twigs snapped underfoot. Lily on her bed, suddenly very far away. Calling to Connie, but Connie couldn't hear what she was saying.

The bed seemed to be moving. Alive?

*– Help me don't leave **me** here please **hush** it's all in your imagination **but** it's not it's **not** I **didn't** make it up I swear –*

'She's insane, you know, didn't you know that, I thought we told you?' The voice, much closer. Connie turned to find her mother standing next to her.

'You're supposed to care about her.'

'I'm just telling you the truth.'

'If you really cared you'd help me get her back.'

'Don't you know? No one comes back from there.'

Her mother took a step forward, and vanished into the trees.

Or became them. They felt alive, but Connie didn't want to touch them to find out.

A brief flash of teeth, the faintest glimmer of claws.

No way forward, no way back.

Connie took a step, hesitantly, but even if she ran it would be too late. Lily's bed was getting further and further away, and Lily was sinking into it, so that her legs were already half-gone, and it was impossible to tell where Lily ended and the bed began.

She screamed her name, and abruptly found herself in her own bed, heart pounding, drenched in sweat, the shadows around her making a fleeting effort at looking menacing before they receded into the normal darkness of her room.

She took a deep breath, and lay back down, counting her breathing, two seconds in, two seconds out, until her heart slowed to its normal rate. She didn't go back to sleep.

now

Lily sat at the kitchen table, letter in one hand, the other curled around a steaming mug of coffee. The warmth in the palm of her hand was keeping her almost-grounded in the present moment, though she still found herself drifting. It was the words, she thought, frustrated. They were blurring on the page in front of her. Rearranging themselves into senseless sentences. Sentences without sense. *Tenc. Cent.*

Oh, for pity's sake, not now.

The university letterhead hovered above it all, the one thing that seemed to Lily concrete and understandable. The rest of the words were too small and close together.

Dear Ms Emmett...

Richard was at work. He'd only been back for five days, but already Lily had settled into a routine. She got up when he got up, checked her emails, went back to bed an hour later, slept until mid-afternoon. Then she got up and toyed with some work until he got home. She mostly paced from room to room, scribbling on her graph pads, covering them in scrawls that Richard wouldn't understand.

He believed her to be doing work. He always thought the best of her.

The phone rang, but it was distant, otherwhere. She didn't answer it.

In light of recent events, we would like to offer you...

She traced the words on the page with one finger. It was a horrible font, she observed, distantly. Richard would hate it.

All angular and computery. He was a fan of serifs, flourishes, things that looked old-fashioned.

A sabbatical. Wasn't that supposed to be a good thing? She'd heard people talking of them as something to be earned, something exciting. Time off to do research, wasn't that basically it? So why did she feel like she was being fired?

Time to rest. Well, she certainly didn't need that. If anything she needed less time. Her days were filled with time. All she had, in fact, was time, which she filled with sleeping and remembering and forgetting and not a whole lot else.

It couldn't be right. Richard would be home soon. He would sort it out.

Richard tried the home number again, but hung up after five rings. He didn't want it going to answerphone. Didn't want to leave a message and then spend the next hour or two waiting for her to ring back.

At least if he could keep ringing it would give him something to do.

He'd spent five days pretending. Leaving the house at the usual time, coming home at the usual time. Wandering from café to park and back again. Getting buses to random villages and strolling around them.

Today, he'd come back to Drayfield.

It hadn't been intentional. He'd decided to go further afield, having grown tired of the local scenery, and happened to look up as the train he was on passed through the nearby town. Figured he might as well get off and catch a bus to Drayfield: at least he'd be wandering around somewhere with some significance to it. All villages blended into one another after a while. He wasn't sure how many more quaint white cottages he could stand to look at.

Drayfield was a fairly modern village, all things considered. It had expanded from a small cluster of houses (all quaint and cottagey) to a relatively sizeable collection of streets, housing about a thousand people. It had a couple of pubs that didn't look like terrible places to spend time in, a church that was rarely more than half-full, and a small high street with all the necessary shops and a couple of souvenir places that seemed to exist in the optimistic expectation of some future tourism. Although it didn't have a school, the one in Farnworth, the nearby town, was known to be good, so plenty of families with young children lived here. All in all, Richard reflected, not an awful place to be.

The house where Lily and Connie had grown up was right on the outskirts. The front garden looked considerably more overgrown than it had done a few weeks ago, with weeds invading the gravel driveway, and the bushes almost obscuring the front gate. But it was still a nice house. Although he didn't have the keys, he walked around the back and peered in through the patio doors. The kitchen looked dark, less welcoming than it had done last time he had been there. But that was just because he was looking at it from the outside, of course. Once they were inside, and once they'd decorated a bit...

He tried to imagine Lily's expression. Whether she'd say anything at all. Would she tell him, if she didn't want to come? Or would she just go along with his wishes, thinking that she didn't have a choice?

He knew Connie had been worrying about what to do with the house. And he knew Lily had been restless ever since they'd visited it. Richard thought of the effect it was having on her psyche; the things that were going undealt-with, her separation from her past. She wasn't just passing out for random reasons. There had to be something going on there. And there was Connie, of course. Constantly worrying about her sister. Connie was right. Richard had been wasting his time, selfishly wishing that Lily wouldn't change. Refusing to face up to the fact that it would be better for all of them if she did.

Well, maybe not for him. But better for her.

Even though she might not see it that way.

She was asleep on the sofa when he got home, the TV projecting silent images across the room, her half-drunk coffee sitting stone-cold on the table. She didn't even stir when he walked in. It was only four-thirty, but it was already dark, the room lit by the greenish glow of the lamp in the corner.

He surveyed the room, looking for other clues. He knew she'd been feeling low since he'd gone back to work. She'd faked productivity, but he wasn't an idiot. He might not understand maths, but he'd spent enough time watching her from the sidelines to know what real work looked like. Besides, she was different when she was occupied with a problem. There was usually an insurmountable distance between them which felt like some kind of force field. At the moment, she might be far away, but he could still get close enough to touch her.

He paused by her side, brushed silvery strands of hair away from her face; she huffed in her sleep, scowling, and he smiled to himself and pulled his hand away. Walked through to the kitchen, to find the post disordered on the table. The letter from the university, resting neatly on the top.

He read it through twice, trying to find words which belied anything but concern. There were none. They weren't firing her; they knew how precious she was. They were just giving her some time off to preserve whatever it was that made her who she was.

He smiled, went back into the living room, and tucked himself under her legs. She moaned softly, but didn't wake up.

Connie was putting the boys to bed when the phone rang. Nathan was out, attending some work do that she hadn't been in the mood for. He'd grumped at her for not going with him, but conceded the fact that he would have a better time by himself than with a miserable wife in tow.

She left Tom in charge of tucking Luke in, and caught the phone just as the answerphone clicked on, whirring and announcing itself in its ridiculously patronising female voice. 'Hello?'

'Hey, it's Richard.'

'Oh.' She waved a hand impatiently in the direction of the answerphone, as if that might in some way silence it.

'Everything okay?'

'Yes. Sorry. Putting the boys to bed; the answer machine's going haywire... Can I ring you back later?'

'Well, actually, I was just wondering if you wanted to go for dinner tomorrow.'

His voice was hushed, Connie noted. 'Just the two of us?'

'Yeah. I've got some things to discuss. And, er, probably an apology to make, after the last time I saw you.'

Connie laughed. 'Don't worry about that. You had just lost your job. And I haven't been the most cheerful person of late. I'm sure we were both overreacting.'

'Even so...'

'Dinner would be lovely. Actually, Nate's out tonight so that works out perfectly for us. He can do child duty tomorrow. Usual time, usual place?'

'Excellent. See you then.'

They hung up, and Connie went back upstairs, not sparing a moment to wonder what he might want to talk about.

then

'You do realise, don't you, that everything is just meaningless? Life, I mean. There's no point to any of it.'

Lily looked up from the page that she had been working on. Esmeralda, the girl with the scars on her arms, was curled up in the armchair opposite Lily. She was supposed to be reading, but she kept putting the book down and looking out of the window, or looking around the room and sighing loudly.

'Of course, *you* know. That's why you don't talk.'

Lily wondered if she was being given permission to get back to her work, and decided that she probably wasn't. She continued to watch Esmeralda, until the older girl turned to look at her directly.

'The nurses know as well. They're just trying to brainwash you. Like they were brainwashed when they were younger. It's all just some big fucking... conspiracy. It's crazy. The whole world's a conspiracy. And we're all just robots.'

Lily watched as Esmeralda chipped the purple polish off her nails, flicking tiny flecks of colour on to the table between them, revealing the bare nail colour beneath. Esmeralda's skin, Lily had noticed before, was paler than anyone else's she had ever seen. Almost translucent. As though she was gradually fading out of the world, ceasing to exist in stages.

'I mean, take this place. They've got us all in here to make us better, but there's not even a name for what's wrong with us. We're just... casualties of life, or some shit. There's nothing medically wrong. They can't actually make it better. They're just keeping us here so we don't infect the rest of society. I mean, like you, for example. What's wrong with you? You don't talk – so what? Lots of people would be better off if they didn't talk. The world might be a better fucking place if people did a bit less fucking talking.'

Out of the corner of her eye, Lily saw one of the nurses sit up, take notice. They didn't like swearing.

'But no, just because you're not like *everybody else*, there's something *wrong* with you. You need to be fucking *fixed*. It's just – it's fucking – '

'Okay, enough.'

One of the nurses – taller than the rest, with thick eyebrows and a mouth that never smiled – appeared next to Esmeralda, and took her by the hand. 'I think it's time you came with me.'

'That's ridiculous. We're just talking. I was going to start reading my book in a minute.'

'I heard you. Swearing. Lily's only nine; you think she needs to hear you swearing at her? No, I don't think so, either. Come on, we'll take you somewhere quiet. You can have a rest.'

Esmeralda tried to pull her hand away from the nurse's. 'I don't *want* to fucking rest, I feel better in here, with people, I don't want to go – '

But the nurse was unrelenting. 'Up you get, dearie.' The cheerful tone could have almost obscured the forcefulness of her pull on Esmeralda's arm. Another nurse joined the first, and together they left the room, Esmeralda's smothered protests stalking their progress.

Lily watched the door for a moment, until the sound of Esmeralda's voice had faded completely. Then she returned to the worksheet in front of her. She had settled into a rhythm now. It had been nearly six weeks – she had been counting the days off on a chart on the bedroom wall. A nurse had suggested that she might like to do that, to know how she was progressing.

They only had a limited supply of maths worksheets; after all, it was not a proper school and children were not supposed to stay in residence for long periods of time. She had started with the ones designed for eight-year-olds; although Grandma had been teaching her, her maths was patchy and Lily was lacking in some areas of vital basic knowledge. In a week she had progressed to the nine-year-olds' worksheets, and a week later she'd completed those. She worked on little else. The nurses insisted that she spend at least an hour each day doing something other than maths, so she rotated between art, science and music, all of which she could do without having to speak. They didn't like the fact that she wouldn't read aloud to them, so she left the books alone for the most part, though she missed reading.

Esmeralda usually sat next to her while she was working. Often she read; sometimes she would draw, or play guitar. While she drew she would talk constantly, quietly, whispering the incomprehensible secrets of the universe into Lily's ear. Lily rarely understood, but she liked the company all the same.

In the past week Esmeralda had been taken away on three separate occasions for talking too much or too loudly. Lily had been to visit her in her room after one of the occasions, to make sure she wasn't lonely. She had managed to stay there for almost an hour before a nurse tracked her down and took her back to the common room.

The institute was a strange place, full of unstated rules and unspoken schedules, but Lily didn't mind it. She liked the feeling that there was some kind of order to everything that was done: someone, somewhere, knew what was supposed to be happening and directed things accordingly. There was a plan, and someone other than Lily was co-ordinating things.

All that was required of her was that she exist.

The corridors had come to seem familiar over the course of the last few weeks, the black and white tiles casting comforting patterns that resonated warmly in her mind. The windows looking out over the courtyard were glimpses of a world that she spent no time in, but liked all the same. Occasionally she managed to sneak out of class when one of the other children was being particularly difficult, and she always came to the same corridor, where all of the windows looked out on to the same view.

She didn't like the windows on the other side of the house. They looked out on to fields, trees. A view which stretched out into the ether, infinite and unstoppable. When she walked past those windows with the nurses, she kept her eyes on the floor and counted tiles until they'd passed.

She had no memory of how she'd got outside. Usually the doors were locked. Only allowed out at break times, in groups, with supervision. That was the way things were. Some things were so intrinsic to the running of an institution that they didn't even need to be classified as rules; they were just the laws that operated beneath everything, the underlying ecosystem upon which the organisation lived and breathed.

Yet, she was outside.

The driveway at the front was gravel, all crunch and no spring. The courtyard was dried-up grass, oft-trodden mud, flowers that didn't die easily. She'd never been out the back before; had no idea how she was here now. Her bare feet sank into the grass, but not through. Like walking on a cold, slightly damp trampoline.

Walking away from the building, she felt rather than saw its looming presence, its many eyes on her back. The sun was setting behind it, and so she was in its shadow. Paling into even further insignificance.

There was no sound. Or at least that was how it seemed. Deafness, numbness all around. Like being in a dream, where nothing existed except for what was immediately visible to you, and even that could never be trusted, was liable to disappear, transmogrify, with no warning whatsoever.

The woods, which skirted around the right-hand side of the house, sneaking up on the windows and reaching out branch-thumbs to graze the panes, sloped downwards away from the house. There was an expanse of neatly cut lawn directly in front of them, like an ocean which Lily must cross in order to get to the safety of the other side. She ran, bare feet thudding on open lawn, but once there she found there was no safety.

When the nurses found her, she was curled up on one side, eyes closed, thumb in mouth, and she would not open her eyes when they said her name. She shook violently for hours, long after she'd warmed up, and the only sound she emitted was the tiniest of murmurs, with not a hint of language underlying it.

now

Nathan always said he hated going to parties without Connie. It was the polite thing to say, he assumed; it would hardly be right to admit that actually he preferred going alone. Enjoyed the chance to speak to people who weren't her. Enjoyed the opportunity to feel like someone other than a husband, a father, and a doctor.

Of course, it was a party full of doctors. But they were doctors pretending not to be doctors. Just as half of them were husbands pretending not to be husbands. Middle-aged men pretending to be young men.

Relatively sober men, pretending they were still capable of drinking a bar dry.

It was someone's retirement do, and all the local practices had combined to give him a good send-off, despite the fact that the majority of them had never worked together and rarely socialised together. The result was that the room was full of people Nathan didn't really know, and he found that he was actually enjoying himself.

'I bet you earn a fortune,' one girl was saying, laying her hand on his arm, practically panting the words in his direction. He laughed, feeling somewhat uncomfortable in the position of Attractive Rich Available Man. Perhaps because it was so utterly ridiculous that he should have been placed in that position.

'No more than anyone else here,' he replied easily, shifting himself slightly so that he could drop her arm from his without causing offence. He managed it, but probably only because she was drunk enough to be struggling to stand up, let alone notice the subtleties of body language.

'Oh, but I've heard of you,' she said. She sounded as if she was barely aware of what she was saying. 'You own your own practice, don't you? You must be *loaded*.'

'Well, there are other things in life. And I'm not sure "loaded" is quite the term.' He looked around the room for an exit from the conversation. The girl was pretty, well turned-out, vacuous – exactly the kind of girl he didn't find remotely interesting. He briefly wished for Connie's presence at his side: she had a certain way of turning a phrase, vicious and yet sugar-coated, so you couldn't quite tell where the sting had come from. She would have been rid of this girl in a second.

'Of course there are other things in life.' Her hand was back on his arm again, blood-red fingernails – talons, he couldn't help thinking, such a striking difference from Connie's neat red toes – and he was less subtle in removing it this time, shaking her off impatiently.

'Sorry, but I have to go to speak someone over there.'

He left too quickly for her to formulate an objection, walking swiftly to the other side of the room.

He got a whisky from the bar – his third, and he was starting to feel the effect, a pleasant buzz just beneath his skin. He leaned back against the bar, scanning the room for people he recognised. There were a few people from his surgery by the buffet table, but no one he particularly wanted to talk to. A couple of people on the other side of the room, but they were too close to the girl he'd escaped from. She was still standing in the middle of the room, scanning it determinedly, presumably for a glimpse of him. He noticed the door to the balcony, and slipped out of it as surreptitiously as he could, closing it gently behind him.

The night air was warm for November, and his suit was just about sufficient to keep him at a reasonable temperature. The balcony was bigger than he'd expected – by the looks of it, it stretched around the entire building. They were only seven or eight storeys up, but it had the feel of an American tower block: very cosmopolitan. Or perhaps that was just his conception of such things. He preferred life on a smaller scale.

'Nate.'

He turned to the right, and spotted his only real friend from work, waving a cigar in his direction, beckoning him over. He obliged, reaching out for a handshake as he approached.

'James. Good to see you.'

'You too. Enjoying yourself?'

'Mmm, actually, I am.' Nathan grinned, and raised his whisky glass by way of explanation. 'Some girl in her twenties has just been propositioning me. How about you?'

'Yeah, not too bad.' James waved his cigars in Nathan's direction, and he took one with a nod of thanks. 'Which girl?'

'In there.' Nathan gestured in her direction. 'Blonde, fingernails like talons, can barely stand up on her own.'

'Oh, her. Yeah, she's been chasing people around fairly indiscriminately, I believe. As long as you're rich and not physically disfigured she'll give it a go.'

'I thought she might be one of those. It was the repeatedly asking if I was loaded that gave her away.' Nathan grinned, and lit his cigar with a flourish.

'Subtle. So where's Connie tonight?'

'Oh, she's not been feeling great recently. You know, with her mum dying, and her sister being a nut job, she's not had much of a break.'

'Oh, come on – Lily's not a nut job. She's always seemed normal enough whenever I've met her at your place.'

'Maybe not. But she's going to turn Connie into one if she carries on the way she's going.'

'That bad?'

'Well. Maybe. Where's Angela?'

'We split. About two weeks ago. Didn't I mention it?'

'Oh, you might have done. I've been pretty distracted... not that that's an excuse. What happened?'

'The usual. We liked each other, we had a nice time, she brought up marriage, I stopped having a nice time.'

Nathan laughed. 'That does sound pretty standard. Maybe you need to address your commitment issues, or whatever it is that women refer to them as?'

'Maybe. Or maybe I just need to find a girl with no fucking interest in getting married. Is that really too much to ask?'

'Apparently so.'

They stood in silence for a minute, smoking, looking out over the town below. They could hear the music from inside, and the dull murmur of conversation from around them, but despite that the night felt strangely peaceful.

'Maybe you should take that girl home,' Nathan suggested, only half-joking.

'Which girl?'

'The one who's been propositioning everyone in the room.'

'Oh, no. I couldn't bear to steal her away from you.'

'Funny.'

'Seriously, you're not really worried about Connie?'

Nathan paused for a moment, considering. 'Yeah, I suppose I am.'

'In what sense?'

'Well, she doesn't get out of bed. She doesn't talk about anything, except Lily and how worried she is about her. And that blasted house.'

'What house?'

'Her mother's house. Connie's childhood home, actually, but she moved out when she was young and never went back.'

'How come?'

'Oh, some weird stuff happened there. I never really got to the bottom of it. Connie just said there were bad memories. Lily doesn't speak about anything unless she has to. I assume it has something to do with their dad dying – they never really talk about that either.'

'Sounds mysterious.'

'It's mostly just irritating. I don't think there's any huge mystery there. Just a general refusal among everyone to talk about things in a normal way.'

'So you don't think maybe there's a reason they don't talk about it?'

'I think Connie would trust me enough to tell me, if that was the case.'

'Hmm.' James raised a knowing eyebrow. 'Don't be so sure. Women are strange creatures. They work in mysterious ways.'

'Huh. I doubt it.' Nathan took a long slug of his whisky, and winced slightly. 'As far as I can tell, they just like us to believe they do, so they can get away with more.'

Another hour and a half, and Nathan was drunk enough to be pleasantly unsure of where he was or who the people around him were. He'd gone inside for a while, but found the crowds and the noise confusing: people kept veering out in front of him when he was trying to walk in a straight line. He grabbed two drinks at once to save himself a second trip inside, and retreated back to the balcony, where James was talking to a redhead in her early thirties. She smiled warmly when Nathan approached, and he couldn't help but smile back.

'Nate, this is Andrea. We used to work together at the Park Surgery. Andrea, this is Nathan, one of our more esteemed doctors.'

'Nice to meet you.' Nathan went to hold out a hand for her to shake, realised that both of his hands were full and, shrugging apologetically, offered her one of his drinks instead.

'Thanks, but I don't do whisky.'

'Why ever not? Nectar of the gods, you know.'

'Mmm. My stomach doesn't agree.'

'How unfortunate. Can I get you something more palatable?' He grinned, fully aware that he was going out of his way to be charming, but feeling no particular inclination to stop.

'Actually, I've got a drink. But thanks.' She was polite but firm – a gentle rebuke, he felt, and took the hint.

'Fair enough. I think I might go in search of a bathroom. I'll catch up with you later.' And with a nod to them both he retreated inside.

Once inside, he found that there was nothing for it but to actually go in search of a bathroom. He wasn't having too much difficulty walking, though putting his drinks down when he got inside proved something more of a challenge. He exchanged cheery nods with a man who was leaving as he came in, and took advantage of the empty room left by his retreating back to check his reflection in the mirror. He nodded approvingly while straightening his tie, and almost winked, though held himself back just in time. He wasn't sure he was drunk enough to excuse that sort of behaviour.

He was aware that he was having a good time, and that he should probably be heading home fairly soon. He knew it was nearly midnight, and that Connie would be pissed off. Also, he had work in the morning. And he didn't want to wake up the boys by coming in too late.

On the other hand, he couldn't remember the last time he'd been wifeless. Childless. It wasn't an opportunity he allowed himself very often.

He checked his phone, and realised that Connie had tried to call him over an hour ago. She'd then sent a text, which simply read, *Going to bed now. Don't wake me up xx*. The kisses were a good sign, he assumed. She'd sounded annoyed earlier, but she was obviously somewhat more cheerful now. Or, if not cheerful, at least slightly more forgiving.

With a mental shrug, he downed the remainder of one of his drinks. Sod it. He would go home soon. What was the point in having an understanding wife and not using it to his advantage?

He arrived home around three am. Connie didn't wake when he came in; didn't even stir when he almost fell over trying to take his trousers off, though he knocked several items off the dresser while doing so.

He crawled into bed beside her. Slipped a hand around her waist, under the T-shirt she chose, unfathomably, to wear to bed. Marvelled, as always, at how soft her skin was, how delicate she felt. Kissed her neck, and felt her murmur, almost inaudibly, in her sleep.

Never another like you, he thought, drunkenly, not entirely sure where the words had come from. Then passed out.

then

The drive took place in near-total silence, interrupted only by Marcus's occasional comments about the landmarks they were coasting past. They left around four on Friday, just making it past the motorway by the time rush-hour cars started dribbling on to the road. Marcus had plotted a 'scenic' route for them to take – one which avoided most of the traffic and took almost twice as long as it could have done. They arrived at the caravan park just in time to pick up the keys; five minutes later and the office would have been closed. They hauled their cases into the caravan as the sun was setting, and tried not to notice that there was no one else around, that the caravan was dark and poky and that the three of them, plus suitcases, filled all of the available space without difficulty.

'It's only a few days,' Marcus said, too heartily, trying to rearrange the cases so that there was enough space for them to sit down.

There was only one bedroom; Connie would sleep on the sofa-bed in the living area. She took this in without comment. She and her mother sat on the sofa and looked around the room, taking in the predominantly beige décor, the TV in the corner which looked as if it had been around since the nineteenth century. Marcus fussed with water and gas and electricity, eventually combining his efforts in all three areas to produce a pot of tea, which he placed proudly on the table. 'Not too bad, eh?' he said, still using his over-cheerful voice, producing plastic mugs with the sort of flourish which might more commonly be reserved for groundbreaking scientific discoveries. Connie and her mother accepted their tea without comment.

The sun set too quickly for them to get a good look at their surroundings, and none of them wanted to venture outside in the dark. They spent the evening in front of the TV, which crackled and fizzed its way in and out of focus, and Connie wondered how many other families would travel two hundred miles to sit in a living room less comfortable than their own, watching the same programmes they could watch at home on a smaller television set.

They went to bed early, and slept little; the creaking of the caravan kept Connie awake until the early hours, and she lay staring at the front door in the dark, half-expecting someone to come bursting through it.

Esmeralda had stopped leaving her room. Lily went to visit her most days, but the nurses didn't approve of this, so she had to do it in secret. She usually went in the evenings, the time when the order of the house seemed to break down and the nurses were likely to forget what they were supposed to be doing and who they were supposed to be looking after. The advantage of her silence was that her disappearance generally went unnoticed; no one really registered the absence of nothing.

Lily spent her evenings sitting in the chair in the corner of Esmeralda's room, wordlessly watching over her patient, who was often so out of it she didn't notice anyone was there. When she was awake and alert – when, she informed Lily with delight, she had managed to avoid taking the drugs they'd been trying to slip her – she talked endlessly about the conspiracy to keep her locked up, about the pointlessness of existence, and about her parents, who became more demonic with every passing day. She knew the truth, and they were determined that she wouldn't have the chance to tell anyone. But she knew. And, some day, she would tell the world.

The red welts on her arms blazed her fury.

When they had succeeded in drugging her, she was either delirious, or virtually catatonic. It was the latter that worried Lily the most: when her friend, who was usually so alive with something (even if it was just the misery of her existence) stopped speaking, and sat motionless in her bed, staring at the wall without seeing a thing.

Sometimes the nurses came in to check on her. They would fuss around her and tell her what a good girl she was being, how she'd be out soon if she just continued to behave herself, while Lily hid under the chair and held her breath until they'd gone.

One day they found her. 'So this is where you've been running off to,' one of the nurses said, clamping her hand firmly around Lily's wrist and leading her back to her own room. 'It won't do either of you any good, you know. Esme needs to rest and you need to spend time with other people.'

She didn't clarify who these other people might be, and, when they got back to Lily's room, she left her there alone.

After that they kept a close eye on her. Escorted her to visit Esmeralda once a week, but always when she was asleep. Lily took to sneaking out of her room in the middle of the night. Esmeralda was usually awake in the night, and Lily would sit on the end of the bed and listen to her whispered confessions. Sometimes she would fall asleep there, curled up with Esmeralda's arm draped sleepily over her, but she always woke up in her own bed.

One night she woke from a nightmare to find the whole house silent and dark. Aware of the monsters lurking under the bed, she leapt off the mattress, landing a good two feet away, clear of grasping claws. She ran the distance from her room to Esmeralda's, shadows chasing her all the way. Burst into the room, shutting the door quickly but silently behind her. Pressed herself against the door, breathing heavily, until the danger had subsided. No monsters here.

Esmeralda was asleep, eyes shuttered by lids which glowed white in the moonlight. Lily took a step forward, and then stopped, registering the odd way in which she was positioned. On her back, arms spread wide. And stains on the sheets.

Blood blacker than the dark.

Lily turned and ran.

She didn't know where the nurses slept, had no idea where she was heading, but she hurtled blindly in the direction of the common room and was relieved when she found a light still on, a glowing orb of safety in the thick black of the corridors. One of the nurses sat behind the desk, immersed in the flickering of the TV in front of her. She looked up as Lily approached.

'What are you doing out of bed?' she asked, her voice reproachful.

Lily gestured in the direction of Esmeralda's room, breathless, hoping the panic in her face would be enough.

'Did you have a nightmare, sweetie? It's okay, you know. It's not real.'

Lily shook her head, reached out and grabbed her hand, trying to pull her in the direction of Esmeralda's room. The nurse wouldn't budge.

'You need to tell me what it is, Lily,' she said. 'I'm not playing guessing games at this time of night.'

Lily stamped her foot in frustration.

'Okay, okay.' The nurse stood up reluctantly. 'Lead the way.'

She refused to quicken her pace, despite Lily pulling on her hand, and so they walked sedately back to the room,

Lily's insides screaming all the way. 'You're not supposed to have been here,' the nurse said, when she realised where they were headed. 'Didn't we tell you to stay in bed?'

Lily glared at her, and pushed the door open.

Connie awoke the next morning with the sun in her eyes and the dawn chorus ringing in the trees outside. The curtains didn't reach all the way to the corners of the windows, and shafts of bright light zigzagged their way across the room, illuminating the dust in the air and making Connie squint.

She hauled herself out of bed and got dressed as quietly as she could, aware that every movement caused the caravan to shake on its foundations. She went into the tiny bathroom and splashed her face with water, noting her reflection in the tiny mirror above the sink. She was paler than usual, and dark circles ringed her eyes like bruises. She pulled her hair back into a ponytail without brushing it, leaving a bunched collection of knots trapped with elastic.

She unlocked the front door and slipped out, not bothering to leave a note for her parents.

The sun, still not fully risen, was surprisingly warm. There was a chill in the shadows, though, and Connie was glad she had thought to bring a jacket. She paused briefly outside the front door, taking in the view that she had barely registered last night. A mountain, densely forested, rose directly behind her. Ahead, through the trees, she could see the steep drop of the ground falling away into valley. There were three other caravans in the clearing, only one of which had a car parked outside it. Connie moved on, not wanting to run into anyone if she could help it.

A wide gravel path veered off in one direction, leading back to the road they had driven in on. She walked the other way, plunging into the trees on a path which was just too narrow for a car to drive down. She was enclosed in darkness immediately, but she could see space ahead where the trees cleared and the sun had forced its way through.

She could hear nothing except for birds chattering in the trees and a distant rush of water. She was used to the quiet – Drayfield was hardly a hive of activity in the evenings – but she could usually hear the distant conversation of her neighbours in their gardens, or of people walking up the lane. Here there was no human noise at all. Her footsteps, crunching on the gravel, seemed loud and out of place.

The path took her through a clearing, where daisies pushed their way through the grass and birds hopped freely along the ground. Then she rounded a corner and found herself facing water.

The mountainside on her right had gradually opened out, becoming less densely wooded as she'd walked, and now it was open and rocky, sparsely littered with dry-looking bushes. Water darted over the rocks in a series of waterfalls, which opened out into shallow pools and finally spread across the path in a stream which was just too wide to leap across, though it was dotted with flat rocks that could easily be used as stepping stones. The pathway she was on continued upwards alongside the stream, becoming a series of steps as the mountainside got steeper, and she decided to follow the path and see how high it would take her.

As she climbed, she allowed herself to wonder what Lily was doing at that moment. It had been three months since she'd been sent to the institute, and Connie had only been allowed to visit her once. She had worked hard to pretend that she didn't find the place disturbing; they'd sat in the common room and played wordless games, and Connie had tried not to pay any attention to the other children who watched them from every corner. One of Lily's doctors had taken her into his office before they left and quizzed her about the night Billy died, but when Connie said she couldn't remember he had left it at that.

More and more, in recent months, she had found herself consciously pushing Billy to the back of her thoughts, especially when other people were around. She was systematically forgetting their friendship. With Lily gone and her parents silent on the subject, she could almost pretend she'd imagined the entire thing.

Except for the others at school, taunting her with what they believed she'd done.

Connie climbed higher, her footsteps following the water back to its source, and tried to imagine what life would be like if Lily never came back. Would the accusations fade over time? Would everyone forget, if Lily no longer existed? Or would they blame her for that too?

And was it okay, to want to sacrifice an already-broken sister in exchange for a happier life?

She paused by a pool in the stream, taking a seat on a large, flat rock which had been baking in the early-morning sunshine. Connie was hungry now; she must have been walking for well over an hour. She wondered if her parents were up yet, if they'd be wondering where she was. She felt a savage pleasure at the possibility of them being anxious about her.

She looked up the mountainside, considered climbing higher, then decided against it. If her parents were awake then they'd almost certainly be concerned about her. And besides, she was hungry.

She made her way back to the caravan.

Connie's parents were frantic by the time she got back, and for a moment she was half-sorry and half-pleased; she couldn't remember the last time they'd worried about her.

Then they spoke, and she realised it wasn't her they were worried about at all.

'We have to go home,' her father said as soon as she stepped through the door. 'There's a problem with Lily.'

He explained as they carried their things out to the car, Connie thinking it was just as well they hadn't had time to unpack. 'A messenger came down here about an hour ago, said he'd got a phone call for me from the institute. It seems one of Lily's friends has hurt herself.'

There was something about the way he said this which implied she hadn't fallen over in the playground.

'Lily's very upset. Her doctors think it's inadvisable for her to stay where she is, for the moment. I've got to go and take her back to Grandma's.'

Connie stared at him, disbelieving. 'Why can't you just bring her home?'

'Well, we don't think she's ready for that yet.'

'But that's ridiculous! Being away isn't helping her, is it? Has she even spoken one word since she's been gone?'

'Well, no, but – '

Connie threw the bag she was carrying on to the ground. 'Do you think you can just send her away and bring her back when someone else has made her all better? What she needs is her family, not some random strangers.'

'Her grandparents are her family,' her father said quietly.

'Yeah, but they're not her *parents*, are they? They're not you. They're not *me*.' Connie glared at him, eyes filling with furious tears. 'Didn't it ever occur to you that we were down there together that night? That maybe it would be better if we got through it together?'

'Connie, please, we're just trying – '

But Connie didn't hear what they were just trying. She stomped over to the car, climbed into the back seat and jammed her Walkman's headphones firmly in her ears. As they drove home, she could see her father turning round, trying to talk to her, but she stared stubbornly out of the window and didn't hear a word he said.

now

Connie, as she had been then, first strains of womanhood pushing through childish limbs. Face-paint streaked across unblemished skin; careless clothing, which inadvertently revealed youth along with too much flesh. That sense of brash arrogance, combined with an awkwardness within her own skin. A smell of too many combined beauty products: moisturisers, shampoos, perfumes. And, underneath it all, the scent of someone who was well cared for: still a child.

She was standing on the banks of the river, in the village where she had grown up. Billy was in there somewhere, though she hadn't seen him. There was the odd ripple, a shadow under the water. A presence that hung in the air. Expectation.

Dread.

She shifted, was awake; saw Nathan's face in the moonlit glow of their bedroom. She felt feverish, unsure.

Back on the riverbank.

The water shifted, held out its arms to her. As if Billy stood there, inviting her to join him. The clouds above darkened, boiled in the sky, and behind her was nothing: empty space and no time at all.

She was on her knees and unable to move. The ground bit into her skin, gravel-like. She tried to push her hands forward, but all was mud and resistance, and she slid and fell, face-first. Something pushed down on her from above; she couldn't move.

And still that feeling. Something above and something below. Nothing behind.

'Okay?'

A murmur, reaching out to her from somewhere, but it was too far. She couldn't push against the current – the tides – the whatever it was that was pushing her down –

'Connie.'

It was Billy, she knew; Billy calling her home. She pushed forward, trying to reach him. Held out her hands, met nothing but air. She was too late, he was gone, and she couldn't breathe, was being crushed, would die here, alone; and she deserved it, that was the worst thing of all –

With an effort, Nathan shook her awake. Her screams filled the house, woke the children; and even after Nathan had got them settled it was hours before she managed to get back to sleep.

'Do you not think maybe you should stay home tonight?'

'Because I had a bad dream?' Connie's eyebrows were raised in disbelief. 'Perhaps I should also leave the nightlight on? And wait for you to tell me a bedtime story?'

'There's no need to be a bitch.'

'I'm not. You're being a patronising arse. I don't need babysitting.'

'You know full well I'm not trying to treat you like a child. I'm just worried about you. That wasn't a normal dream.'

'No. It was a nightmare. Probably brought on by you stumbling in at, what, four in the morning?'

'Three.'

'Oh, much better. And where were you until three o'clock this morning? You told me the place shut at midnight.'

She was working hard on keeping her voice low; the boys were upstairs playing and she didn't want to disturb them.

Nathan had conveniently avoided any discussion about the time he'd come home by being worried about her, and then being at work. As a result, she'd spent most of the day quietly stewing about it.

'I was with James. We went to a casino.'

'Oh, fabulous. Gambling. An admirable pastime.'

'I can't speak to you when you're like this. Forget what I said. Please do go out, and leave me in fucking peace.'

'Oh, that's right. Turn it round on me.'

'I was just trying to show you some concern, Connie. Just worried about your mental health. You know? Because your sister's driving you crazy and you've just lost your mother and you spend more and more of each passing day in bed, thinking I won't notice as long as you get up in time to pick the boys up from school? Don't make me out to be the bad guy here.'

'If you were that worried, why were you out all night?'

'Because I was having fun, and I was drunk, and I felt like it. It's not as though you didn't know where I was, and it's not as though you weren't invited to come along. You chose not to come with me.'

'Because I was tired.'

'No, because you were depressed. There's a difference, you know.'

'Oh, yes, I forgot. What the doctor says must be correct. I can't just be tired and in a bad mood, like any other overworked mother. It has to be *depression*. Why does there always have to be a name for everything these days?'

'Stop it. *Stop this*. You're being ridiculous.'

'Am I?' Her voice was shaking, partly out of annoyance at having such a weak comeback. But she felt utterly defenceless. How was it that he could spend so much time creeping around, cat-like, absorbing details but never bothering to share them with her? And all the while she'd just assumed he wasn't paying attention.

'Look, I don't want to fight with you.' His voice was gentle, conciliatory. *Because he knows he's won,* she thought, spitefully.

'Don't tell me what to do, then.'

'Okay, okay.' He held up his hands: surrender. 'Do whatever you want. Go and discuss whatever it is that Richard wants to discuss. Have a lovely time.' He leaned forward and kissed her, softly, on the cheek. 'Please. Please have a lovely time.'

She nodded; touched the place where his lips had brushed her cheek; nodded again. And left.

Richard was already there when Connie arrived, ten minutes late and slightly flushed from the cold outside. She babbled apologies as she pulled off her coat and sat herself down opposite him, and Richard could see that her eyes were red and swollen, though he didn't comment.

'How are the kids?' he asked, once she'd got herself settled.

'Oh, fine, you know. Getting on okay at school. Tom's boring us all senseless with stuff he's learning about the environment. "Did you know, Mummy, that in 1987 an area of the Amazon rainforest the size of Britain was burned?" and so on.' She smiled to herself. 'I love the way kids assume they're the first generation to have ever learned anything.'

'Yeah, it's great. They can teach you all the things you've spent the last thirty years forgetting.'

'I'm not sure there's enough room in my head for all that stuff any more.' Connie poured herself a glass of water from the pitcher on the table, then looked around for a waiter. 'Don't suppose you've ordered yet?'

'I ordered wine. I felt it would be presumptuous to order food. Also, I wasn't sure how long you'd be.'

'Yeah, sorry about that. Nathan's being a pain.'

'Really? Why?'

Connie drank half of her water in one go. 'Oh, I don't know, really. He's pretending he's all worried about me because I've not been sleeping that well and so on, but then he went out last night and stayed out until three in the morning, so he couldn't have been that worried, could he? It's just irritating me.'

'Nathan was out until three in the morning?' Richard's eyebrows were furrowed in concern.

'It was a work thing.' She laughed at his expression. 'It's fine, he invited me along but I don't really like that sort of thing. I just wish – you know – I wish he'd be a bit more responsible, sometimes. Around the house, I mean. Obviously I know he's responsible at *work*.' She spat the word across the table with an expression of distaste.

'He's got a tough job.'

'Yeah, I know. It doesn't exempt you from responsibility in all other areas of life, though, does it?' She sighed. 'Anyway, enough about me. How's Lily? Have you told her about losing your job yet?'

'Um. I haven't had the chance, actually.' Richard explained briefly about Lily being given a sabbatical. 'I really think it'll do her good, you know? She obviously needs to take a break from it all, and she's just blocking everything out and getting on with work instead.'

Connie looked sceptical. 'Thing is, Richard, Lily's never been particularly good at dealing with things. She just shuts down and carries on as if nothing's happened.'

'I realise that. But maybe this will be her chance to sort herself out a bit.'

'Right. And what do you propose? Are you going to start counselling her, now that you've both got some spare time?'

'Oh, come on, Connie, I'm being serious.'

'Sorry.' She was contrite. 'What did you have in mind?'

'Well – ' The waiter appeared at his side, and he stopped talking abruptly. They both sat in silence as the waiter poured the wine.

'Can I take your orders?'

They ordered the same food they ate every time, and the waiter departed, wending his way through the tables towards the kitchen. Connie watched his progress, sipping her wine and barely tasting it.

'So I thought we might move into your mother's house,' Richard said, his voice rushed and nervous.

Connie stared at him blankly. 'You – what?'

'I know it sounds crazy, but I think we both need a break. I think some new surroundings – and for Lily some familiar ones – might be just what we need. And also,' he continued quickly, before she could say anything, 'now that I've lost my job we're going to need some extra money, and, seeing as the house is just sitting there at the moment, we could live there rent-free and let out the flat.' He paused, looking at her closely, trying to read her expression. 'If you don't mind,' he prompted.

'Um, I – sorry, I'm just really surprised.' She smiled faintly. 'I don't mind at all, but have you spoken to Lily? That house, it – it's got a lot of history for us, you know?'

'I know there's a lot of history with your parents – your dad dying and your mum being, well, the way she was – but I thought maybe if Lily was back there she could confront some of it. It's like the doctor said,' Richard said, his voice speeding up again. 'She's got these physical symptoms because she's not dealing with the emotional trauma, and if she goes back there then she'll have to deal with it all and then – she might – well...' He stopped, feeling foolish.

'Get better?' Connie suggested, raising one eyebrow.

'Yeah. I suppose. It's not so far-fetched, is it?'

Connie shrugged. 'No, I suppose not. Has she ever spoken to you about that house? Or... er, our parents, or – anything?'

'Not really.' Richard took a long sip of his wine. 'I know she was really close to your dad. And I know your mum was institutionalised and – well, you know – the depression. But she doesn't really talk about your childhood.'

Connie nodded. 'You know about her not speaking, though? I mean, really not speaking?'

'Yeah, of course. She said about you guys being bullied, and – well, I'm not stupid, Connie. I know there are things she isn't telling me and I know you guys had a difficult childhood, but I really think she might get past it better if she faces it. Don't you agree?'

Connie looked at him. He looked so earnest and so hopeful, staring up at her as if she had all the answers, and she wondered how her sister had managed to find this man who wanted nothing more than to make her happy.

It didn't matter how she'd found him, of course. It mattered that he was there.

'I don't know,' she said finally. 'But I think it's worth a go.'

'Really?'

'Yeah. Anything's worth a go, really, isn't it?' She grinned, and raised her glass in a toast. 'To confronting the past,' she said, and their glasses met across the table with a gentle clink.

Lily was in a field. It was dark – no, not dark: twilight. Dark enough that she couldn't help but stumble over things in her path. Light enough that she could see the horizon, blurry blue-black. There was a silvery light in the air, which was not light, but an absence of dark.

She couldn't see the ends of the earth, but she could feel them, on all sides.

Creatures whispered through the grass at her feet, brushed her bare toes, making her tense. She would not scream.

She could feel the presence in the air, the someonethere, though who it was she couldn't be sure.

She took two steps forward, and fell through the earth.

The fall wasn't a long one, but she felt all the breath leave her body as she plunged downwards. Adrenaline shot to her extremities, a tingling so pervasive it was painful. She landed in a cavern, fully dark, underground, underworld. The floor was dirt, the hole she'd fallen through just large enough that she could make out walls.

And that sense, still. Someonethere.

She held out her hands. Scrabbled in the dirt for a way out. Panic setting in as she realised the hole was too high for her to reach, and there were no doorways in the walls; and even if there had been they would have led further into the earth; no way out: she was trapped, and struggling to breathe through dirt-clogged airways.

Think. Calm. Must be some way out. Something.

The walls were briefly illuminated, perhaps by lightning, and the panic intensified. Words all over the walls. Silvery scrawls.

get out get out get out getoutgetoutgetout

Esmeralda's body on the ground, two feet away, the same silvery scrawls covering her arms. Her blood, of course.

And her face, half-eaten by maggots. But still she was smiling.

And the approach, from behind, of something as yet unseen.

Finally, Lily allowed herself to scream.

She was awake by the time Richard got to her; breathing heavily, but starting to calm down. The bedroom was dark, the green flashing numbers on the alarm clock casting an odd, uneven glow across her face. She'd been crying in her sleep.

'What was it?'

She shook her head. He sat down next to her, put his arms around her, felt her heart pounding next to his steady pulse. Her breath, short sharp gasps, warm on his neck. She breathed deeper, steadied herself.

'It was just a dream,' he said, quietly. She nodded into his neck.

'Where were you?' she asked, pulling back, lying back down.

'I needed to talk to Connie about something.' She looked at him, questioningly, but didn't say anything. 'And now I need to talk to you about something. But I think it can wait until the morning, don't you?'

She nodded. Too tired to be curious. Already slipping back into unconsciousness.

He lay down beside her, fully dressed, and held her close as she fell asleep. Thinking, if he held her tight enough, if he cared enough, then maybe he could take control of her dreams. Force them down the right path, soothe her splintered unconscious, and give her a restful night.

then

In the end, Marcus went on his own to pick Lily up from the institute, dropping Connie and Anna at home on the way. It was mid-afternoon by the time he arrived, and Lily was waiting for him on the front steps, her bag packed, a nurse keeping watch from the doorway.

Lily stood up when the car pulled up in front of her, but she didn't step forward until Marcus got out of the car.

'Hey, stranger. How long have you been sitting there?'

Lily just stared at him. It was the nurse who answered, her voice flat and businesslike. 'It's been a couple of hours. Once she was packed she wouldn't go back inside.'

'I'm so sorry. I got here as quick as I could, but we were on holiday – '

'Yes, I heard.' Dismissive. 'Would you mind coming inside? There's some paperwork to sign. Won't take long.'

'Sure.' He crouched down next to Lily. 'Do you want to wait in the car? I won't be a minute.'

She nodded, and he opened the back door for her, letting her scramble on to the seat before closing and locking it behind her.

The inside of the building was cool and airy, and there was no one around. Marcus's footsteps echoed in the empty corridor. The nurse was waiting for him, perched at the reception desk, a pile of paper in front of her.

'If you could just sign here,' she said, pushing a pen into his hand.

'Would you mind giving me a bit more detail? About what happened?' He scanned what he was reading as he signed, only half-concentrating.

'It was as I said on the phone. Lily's friend attempted suicide. Lily was the one who found her. She was – very shaken up, understandably.'

'Don't you have people watching out for that kind of thing? Why was the girl not being watched?'

'There'll be an investigation,' the nurse said smoothly.

'Right.' Marcus handed her back the pen. 'Well, I wouldn't mind knowing the outcome of the investigation. If it's not too much trouble.'

'I'm sure that can be arranged.'

'And I'll be ringing Dr Hadley next week to discuss Lily's requirements going forward.'

'I'll let him know.'

Her voice was textureless, her face bland to a fault. He watched her for a moment, to see if her expression would flicker, but she remained frozen in place. He spun on his heel and went back out to the car.

Lily was sitting in the chair behind the driver's seat, facing straight forward, her seatbelt done up. Her rucksack was on the seat next to her. She didn't move when he got in.

'Sorry to keep you waiting for so long,' Marcus said. He turned in his chair to face her, but she didn't meet his eye. 'It must have been a long day.'

Nothing.

He turned back to face the windscreen, and turned the key in the ignition.

'I'm going to take you back to Grandma and Grandpa, as it's closer,' he said. The roaring of the engine half-obscured his words, but he wasn't sure she was listening anyway. 'And then tomorrow we're going to make a decision about what to do next. Okay?'

He looked at her in the mirror, but she was still staring straight ahead, her face motionless.

He talked to himself as he eased the car out of the driveway. He wasn't sure if she was listening or not, but he found it comforting, hearing the sound of his own voice. After a while he realised she was asleep; her eyes were closed, head tilted to one side, mouth drooping slightly.

He smiled, and continued talking to himself for the rest of the journey.

'What does Anna say about it all?'

Marcus sat at the dining table, his parents seated opposite him like an interview panel. Lily was upstairs; she'd gone straight up to her room when they'd got home, closing the door behind her. He'd considered going in anyway, exercising his rights as a parent. But in the end he decided she deserved some time to herself, and retreated back down the stairs to where his parents waited for him, carefully non-accusatory.

'She says nothing, most of the time,' Marcus admitted, running his fingers through his hair until it stood on end, sticking out at odd angles from his face. 'She acts as though she feels I've made all these decisions without her, so I might as well carry on making them.'

'Does she want Lily to come home?'

'Who knows? She's barely at home herself.' He stopped, realising he was being unfair. 'That's not true, actually. She's been a bit better the last couple of months. But she spends most of her time in the garden. Barely speaks to me, or to Connie.'

'Where was she before? If she wasn't at home?' His mother's voice was careful, but Marcus knew what she was asking.

'I could hazard a guess,' he said. 'But I'd rather not go there.'

'Fair enough. Well, the way I see it, you've got two options.'

'Which are?'

His mother was all practicality. 'Leave her here, or take her home.'

'I can't keep leaving her here with you,' Marcus said, his voice tired. 'I feel like I'm failing her as a parent. Connie said something to me today, about shipping her off and expecting someone else to make her all better. And you know what – she's right, isn't she? That's exactly what I'm doing. Waiting until she's fixed before bringing her home.'

'Son, you're being too hard on yourself.' His father's voice was stern, commanding. 'Keeping the balance in a family is always hard. And, after everything your family has been through, it was the right thing to do: giving Lily some space, taking her away from that house.'

'I want to move,' Marcus admitted. 'But I don't think Anna will agree.'

'Why not?'

He didn't reply, and his parents didn't push it.

'Do you think Lily would be able to cope with going home?' his mother asked, her voice gentle.

'How should I know? She's not likely to give me a straight answer, is she?'

'She might. When was the last time you tried asking her?'

Half an hour later he climbed the stairs to Lily's room, which had once been his room. He knocked gently, and pushed open the door without waiting for a response. She was sitting cross-legged on her bed, a collection of pieces of paper spread out in front of her, and she didn't look up when he came in.

'Hey, Lils,' he said softly, not really expecting a response. She was focused on the paper in front of her. He looked over her shoulder, and was unsurprised to see it was a collection

162

of photocopied pages from a maths textbook. He scanned the page, seeing if there was anything he recognised, but it was a blur of meaningless equations.

He pulled the chair out from under the desk and sat down in front of her, so he would be directly in her line of sight, if she ever looked up.

'I've been talking to your grandparents. Trying to figure out what you might like to do now. And it occurred to me that no one had asked you.'

He paused, waiting. No response.

'I know you're not going to want to talk to me. But if you could just let me know, somehow, whether you'd rather be here or at home. I don't want to keep making decisions without your input.'

She stared stubbornly at the piece of paper, and said nothing. He leaned back in his chair, watching her face. She had turned ten last month. Her face was becoming more like Connie's, and even Anna's; mouth pursed, blue eyes narrowed, she looked more adult by the day.

It struck him, suddenly, that he was missing her entire childhood. It wasn't enough to see her every other weekend. She was growing up and he hadn't even noticed, still framing her in his mind as an eight-year-old shadow of her sister. When was the last time Anna had seen her? How long would it be before she ceased to be recognisable as the child she'd once been?

'I want to take you home,' Marcus said. His voice was quiet, but she looked up at that.

'Do you want to come back with me? Live with us again? You'd have to go back to school, there'd be no grandma to teach you, but you could be with Connie again. Be with all of us. What do you think?'

She looked at him for a long time. Her eyes were unreadable, but he felt like she was trying to communicate *something.* 'Please,' he said eventually. 'Please just tell me. Do you want to come home?'

Her voice, when she spoke, was less than a whisper: it was the hollow outline of a word, no substance at the centre.

'No,' she said.

part two

then

'We should move away from here. At least move Connie to a different school.' Connie, standing behind the kitchen door, heard the pleading note in her father's voice.

'Fighting and bullying are a way of life in secondary school. That's not going to stop just because we move her somewhere else.'

'But maybe if they didn't know the history... She's not such a weird kid, is she?'

Connie noted the implications in the silence from her mother, and wasn't at all surprised.

'Things could be different,' her father implored. 'At least if we get away from this *house* – '

'I love this house.'

'Really? Because you never seem to spend any time here.' There was a pause, and then Marcus's voice, softer. 'Think of Connie. And Lily will be coming home soon.'

Connie froze, as if the words had paralysed her. Was it true? Or was her father just being his usual optimistic self, blindly assuming that some day Lily would come home and everything would return to normal?

It had been nine months since they'd removed Lily from the institute, taken her back to their grandparents' house. It should have become normal by now, but sometimes Connie still felt as if she was standing still, just waiting for Lily to return so her life could pick up where it had left off.

'Where would we go?'

'I don't know. We don't have to go far. A couple of villages away, even.' His voice became low, coaxing. 'Lily's getting better, Anna. I know you don't want to believe it, but it's true. What if coming back here undoes all that good work?'

'Why wouldn't I want to believe it? You think I want my daughter to be stuck like that forever?'

There was a long pause, and then, 'That's not what I meant.'

'Well, *what*, then?' Connie noted the hysterical note in her mother's voice.

'I just meant that you don't believe it. Because you – I don't know. Maybe you're scared to believe it. But it is true. I promise you.'

There was a long pause, and Connie held her breath, waiting. It went on for so long that she thought maybe they'd stepped out of the back door without making any noise. And then her mother's voice. 'Well, she's still never said a fucking word to me.'

The slam of the patio door reverberated in the silence she left behind her.

Connie waited five minutes, listening for her father's movement and hearing nothing, and then pushed the door open, to find him still sitting at the kitchen table, head in his hands. He lifted his head as she approached; turned, tried to smile. All he really managed was a curious deepening of the creases in his skin.

'You been home long?'

'Just got back. I went for a walk after school.'

'How was school?'

'The usual.'

Her father nodded and said nothing. She liked the fact that she didn't have to lie to him. Her mother was fragile; you had to protect her from the truth. Her father might bend under the weight of his responsibility, but he wouldn't break.

'Is Lily really going to come home soon?'

Marcus looked up in surprise. 'Yes.' He must have seen the disbelief etched on her face, because he took her hands in his. 'Really. I mean it. She's almost back to her old self.'

'But it's been so long. How will she remember who her old self is?'

'Do *you* remember?'

It had been nearly three years. In some ways Connie had become used to being an only child, had forgotten what it felt like to share her day-to-day life with someone else. But, when she did think of her, what did she see? Photographs, snapshots, mismatched snatches of conversation. An eight-year-old who worshipped the ground Connie walked on and cried every time she was mean to her.

But it wasn't just that. The secrets they'd shared. Using Morse code to tap out messages on the wall between their beds when they were supposed to be asleep. Passing notes between their bedroom windows.

She didn't remember ever feeling lonely before Lily had gone.

'Sort of.'

'How about you come and visit her with me this week-end?'

Connie had been less willing to visit recently. The last time had been, what, three weeks ago? Her mother only went once a month, after all, and Connie had started to think that maybe she'd have a better chance of making friends at home if she wasn't spending most of her weekends visiting her sister.

Her *mental sister*, as the people at school never failed to remind her.

'I don't know,' she said, hedging. 'Will Mama be coming?'

'I hope so.'

'She hates it, doesn't she?'

169

Marcus sighed, and stood up, gathering the mugs that were dotted around the kitchen table. 'It's complicated,' he admitted. 'But yeah, she doesn't like it much.'

'Does she want Lily to come home?'

'Of course.' He lied so smoothly that Connie wasn't even sure he was aware it was a lie. 'We all want her home, don't we?'

Connie, studying a sticky ring-shaped shadow left behind by a mug on the table, didn't reply.

Lily came home two weeks later. They tiptoed around each other, like two cats that weren't quite sure whether they were friends or enemies, fighting for the same share of the food. Estranged people, who had once shared something that had not quite disappeared. Connie felt she existed simultaneously in the present and the past, with this creature who had not been part of her life for nearly three years, but who had always been part of her life, in the background; perhaps the most important part.

At home silence reigned: even the conversations were just interrupted silence. The family took their cues from Lily. The girls spent much of their time in their respective bedrooms, with the doors closed. Their parents still fought, but quietly, on the edges of their awareness. Mostly they were in separate rooms, doing separate things, existing on separate planes.

Connie wasn't sure what was worse: the anxiety that things might change when Lily returned, or the slowly dawning realisation that they hadn't.

now

Lily stood in the room that had given spatial context to her formative years, staring mutely at the walls. They seemed all wrong from this angle: she was too tall for them. The window was too low, and the vines on the wallpaper twined into the drooping plaster of the ceiling to give a sense of the world caving in on itself. The view from the window was not the same as it once had been, and her gaze skimmed over the tops of the trees, seeking the fields beyond.

Richard was downstairs; she could hear him moving.

It felt the same as it had when they had been here a few weeks ago. The house seemed like a living thing that grew around her and clawed its way into her consciousness, dulling her mind and making her sluggish. She couldn't form thoughts properly; found herself distracted by the patterns in the dust on the floorboards. Everything was subtly wrong – too small, too colourful, too empty – and she couldn't separate the real from the remembered.

There wasn't much left of the room as it had been. A single bed-frame cradling a dusty mattress. A desk, far too small to be of any use now. Everything else had been tidied away, shuffled off into boxes, stowed away in attics or cellars or wherever these things were kept. They had done some half-hearted tidying when they'd been here last, putting some boxes down in the cellar, but she didn't think much of it would have been hers. She'd been shunted around so much as a child, she wasn't sure where any of her possessions had ended up.

171

They'd arrived at midday, after an uneventful two-hour drive. Richard had been talkative in the car, but she hadn't been in the mood, so they'd turned the music up and sung along to the Smiths for most of the journey. Their belongings – those deemed too important to go into storage – had been piled up on the back seat, and when Richard braked sharply they'd heard things dislodging themselves from the mass and tumbling to the floor. They'd pulled into the driveway accompanied by the clatter of falling cutlery.

For the past few hours Richard had been resolutely upbeat, unpacking and organising and sweeping dust and shadows to one side with fluid, easy movements. Lily had trailed behind him, hoping some of his demeanour would infect her, but she felt drained of energy and she couldn't concentrate. After a while she'd mumbled something about making up the bed, and made her way up the stairs, sinking into the shadowy gloom of the house.

The staircase was a tiered passageway, walled in on all sides and lit by a single, bare bulb. It opened out at the top on to a landing with four doors: three bedrooms and a bathroom. Her parents' room to the left, looking out over the front of the house. Bathroom straight ahead. And her and Connie's rooms to the right, side by side, windows overlooking the back garden and the forest behind.

They'd already decided that they would sleep in her parents' room – aside from any other considerations, it was the only one with a double bed – but she couldn't resist sneaking a look at the other rooms. And that was how she had come to find herself staring at the walls, unable to believe that this was a real, physical place rather than just somewhere she had imagined. Had she really been a child here? Had Connie?

She heard Richard coming up the stairs behind her, and told herself to snap out of it. She reached the doorway just as he got to the top of the stairs.

'Which one's ours?' he asked. He was carrying two large suitcases.

She pointed to her parents' room, and watched as he lugged the suitcases through the door, dropping them with heavy thuds on the bare floorboards beyond. 'God, it's dusty in here,' he said, reappearing in the doorway. 'We're going to end up with respiratory infections.'

Lily smiled faintly, but said nothing.

'Is that your old room?' He indicated behind her, and she nodded. He walked over, so she had no choice but to go back in with him. He stood beside her, surveying it all with interest.

'I like the wallpaper,' he said, reaching out to run a finger down it. 'It's a bit like being inside a forest, isn't it? And with the trees outside – ' Lily flinched as he pointed, but he didn't notice, too busy looking around him.

'Can we see Connie's room too?'

Dutifully Lily led him next door. He noted the way the beds met at the wall with a smile. 'Could you talk through the walls?'

Lily shook her head. 'We used Morse code.'

'You knew Morse code as kids? That's pretty impressive.'

She shrugged. 'Dad taught us.'

Richard looked at her curiously, but she didn't say anything else, and he didn't push her. After a minute he put his arms around her, lifting her face so he was looking directly into her eyes. 'I'm glad we came,' he said, his voice soft and serious.

Lily kissed him, then pressed her face against his chest, so she wouldn't have to answer.

then

'Are you absolutely sure you're ready to go today?'

Lily nodded, impatient.

'Because you can wait a couple more days, if you want to. It's no problem.'

'Dad, stop babying her. She's fine.'

Marcus looked from one daughter to the other. Couldn't help smiling at the identical stubbornness of their expressions. They had always looked so similar, both thin and pale, like two blonde ghosts who flashed in and out of existence. Lily looked almost exactly the same as Connie had three years ago. It was almost as if she'd gone away Lily and come back Connie.

Except, of course, that Connie was still there.

'Okay. You'll look after her? Show her around?'

'Yes, Dad.' Connie rolled her eyes, something she did frequently these days. It made Marcus laugh, the affectation of grown-up gestures, though he struggled not to show it.

'Good. And don't forget – '

'Oh, shut *up*, Dad, we'll be fine.'

Connie took Lily's hand, dragged her out of the front door. Marcus thought he heard Lily's pale goodbye trailing after them, waif-like. But maybe it was just an echo of Connie's.

As soon as they rounded the corner, Connie dropped Lily's hand. She started to walk faster, not intending to outrun Lily, but always keeping one step ahead of her.

'You know I can't really look after you, right? You have to make your own way in these places. Otherwise people won't respect you.'

Lily said nothing, her eyes fixed straight ahead. Connie wasn't even sure she was listening.

'I'll be there if you need me,' she added, her voice slightly more gentle. 'But I can't babysit you. You understand?'

Lily nodded.

Connie watched her for a second, waiting. Then stopped dead, grabbed Lily by the shoulders. Her voice was a low hiss in her sister's ear.

'And you know, it would be really fucking sensible if you started talking once in a while. I've had just about enough of being the sister of a freak.'

Her grip on Lily's shoulders disappeared as abruptly as it had arrived. Lily stood still, the imprints of her sister's fingers burning lightly on her skin, and watched as Connie stormed away into the distance, leaving her in the street alone.

It had been three years since Lily had been in a proper school, and back then she had been at primary school – small, gentle, entirely focused on making learning fun, rather than just making it happen as quickly and with as little fuss as possible. The institute had been another world, and Lily had slotted into it as best she could; the fact that they expected you to behave oddly meant that she had never felt particularly out of place when she was there.

Secondary school was different.

It was bigger than anywhere she had ever been. There seemed to be a constant level of background noise, a buzz that filled her ears and made her feel dizzy. People barged into her and didn't even think to say sorry. She found she was constantly fighting just to keep hold of her books.

The corridors weren't dissimilar to the institute's, though they seemed much bigger. They had the same tiles on the floor, black and white squares. She counted them as she walked from place to place. This made her walk slowly, but she found it easier to breathe when she was counting.

The doors were all wrong, though. They led to rooms she didn't recognise. And the windows looked out on to unfamiliar fields – huge, empty expanses of grass with goal posts dotted at seemingly random intervals.

When she was counting squares she couldn't count door numbers, so she spent most of the first day getting lost. She walked into rooms late, time after time, and received dirty looks from teachers and students alike. They washed over her, meaningless.

She didn't speak a word.

now

They attacked the house together the next morning. Threw open windows, expelled dust from every corner, wrestled territory away from spiders and ants and other creatures that had invaded in the absence of people. The little that remained in the way of traces of prior occupation was carefully and quietly removed by Richard, stowed away in the cellar to worry about later. Lily noticed, but said nothing, glad that he was taking charge so that she didn't have to think about it.

Lily concentrated her efforts on the front of the house: their bedroom, the living room, the bathroom. If Richard noticed that she stuck close to those rooms, steered clear of windows that overlooked the back garden, then he chose not to comment.

They pushed out long-distant memories with the collected possessions of their shared life. Spread their familiar duvet on the bed where her mother had once given birth. Ate dinner off their own plates, watched their TV in the living room, while the ghosts of Connie and Lily's childhood selves, oblivious, played games to fill the space.

The collected unspent breath of every conversation that had never taken place textured the air around them, but they breathed their way through it. Feigning indifference.

At night, Richard filled the silent space with stories, whispered Lily into sleep with his own personal etymologies. Quietly rebuilt their own private world over the top of the house's history.

On their third day, they ventured into the village together. The sun blazed cold, the air crisp, their cloudy exhalations colouring the air. Lily held on to Richard's hand, walking half a step behind, like a reluctant child. She stopped from time to time, to stare at seemingly unremarkable buildings. Richard wondered what she was seeing. Superimposing the old on to the new. Reshaping her childhood.

'We should go to the high street,' Richard suggested. 'Have a look at the shops. They've probably changed quite a bit, you know.'

'Mmm.'

'The newsagent's looks as though it hasn't changed for about a hundred years, though.'

'Cook's,' Lily said, absently, her eyes on some flowers by the roadside. She dropped Richard's hand to crouch down beside them. 'Isn't it the wrong time of year for flowers?'

'Depends what kind.'

'What are these?' Lily reached out a finger, brushed the red-black petal, softly.

'Hellebores,' Richard replied, leaning down beside her.

'Can we grow some? In the front garden?'

'I don't see why not. We could have a whole winter garden, if you want.' Paused. Tentative. 'There'd be more space out the back.'

She didn't respond. Brushed the petal one more time, then stood up and resumed their walk.

'So Cook's was there when you were little?'

'Mmm. The window displays looked like a doll's shop. All dusty and full of old tins. And they had jars of sweets behind the counter.'

'They still do.'

Lily nodded, smiled almost imperceptibly. 'Good.'

They walked hand in hand down the high street, peering into all the shops. It was a strange juxtaposition of old and new: a bookshop with so many piles of books it was as if they'd forgotten what shelves were for, nestled next to Boots, with its clinical white modernity. There weren't many people around. Pensioners ambling towards the post office. Parents pushing buggies with no particular destination in mind. They went into Cook's, and Lily smiled to see the seemingly immortal Mr Cook, timeless, ageless, still working away behind the counter. They bought humbugs in paper bags and walked in the direction of the river.

There wasn't much Lily remembered, really. So much of her childhood had been spent elsewhere, and she'd never returned after the age of twelve. But there was something in the texture of the place. She was trying to fit her adult's feet into child-sized footprints; reshaping the edges, smudging the exterior lines.

The river was a perfect countryside river, tripping its way over the tops of the rocks and pebbles beneath. There was a bridge – stone, crumbling, story-like. Lily could remember playing Poohsticks with her father and Connie. On the other side of the bridge, outskirts, woodlands. And farmland. A few abandoned structures, tool sheds, stables. Not worth exploring, at least not today.

They took off their shoes and scrambled down the riverbank, out of sight of the path above, not that there was anyone around to see them. They walked for a few minutes until houses had been replaced by trees, fields, absence of civilisation. Lily jumped from stone to stone, shoes dangling from one hand, the other held out to steady herself. Richard followed at a gentler pace, testing each stone before committing his weight to it.

They sat down on a rock at the water's edge and dipped their toes into the freezing water, giggling as it teased their toes. They sucked humbugs, and realised their mistake as the mint made the cold even sharper on their tongues. Sat arm in arm, watching the sun on the water. Thought of nothing, as their new home drove out the old one, making space for change.

'In the beginning was the word.' Richard's whisper, in the blanket darkness of their bedroom, not penetrated by street-lamps or civilisation. 'And the word was...?'

'Hellebore.' He could hear the smile in her voice. Couldn't help smiling back.

'Once upon a time, in ancient Greece, there was a plague of madness which spread through the village of Argyn. It only affected the women; it caused them to run naked through the streets at night, weeping, screaming, calling down visions of hell upon everyone around them. Their fathers and husbands did what they could to restrain them – tying them to their beds, locking them in their rooms – but all their efforts proved futile. The women couldn't control themselves, and no number of chains could keep them from breaking free. The men called in priests, and witch doctors; they tried bleeding them, and feeding them sedatives; but nothing had any effect. Every night, the women would run free, and no one in the village could sleep for the racket that they made.

'One of these women was called Helena, and she, like many others, did all she could to prevent her own descent into madness. With the help of her brother, a goatherd named Melam, she secured a prison for herself beneath their home. They built a concrete tomb, not unlike a mausoleum, and every night Melam would lock her inside. The strength of a hundred men would not have been enough to move the walls of the fortress, and, though Helena fought to break free, she was never successful. During the day Melam would let her out, and she would run the household while he did his daily work. In this way, they continued in some semblance of a normal life, though they never stopped looking for a cure for Helena's condition.

'Several priests passed through the village, offering their opinions on the condition that afflicted the women. One claimed that it was the god Dionysus who was to blame: he had infected the women, forcing them to exhibit their most reckless tendencies. But, no matter how many explanations the priests offered, they could not provide a cure, and one by one they left, and life went on.

'Melam spent his days on the hillside, tending his herd, and gradually he began to notice that they, too, exhibited certain signs of the madness that was afflicting the female population. In fact, all the animals that roamed on the hillside – the goats, the squirrels, the foxes and the badgers – seemed to suffer from similar symptoms. They would run around, wild and untamed, sometimes foaming at the mouth, sometimes howling uncontrollably. They were never actually violent, but they seemed unable to control their physical impulses. The only animals that seemed completely unaffected were the deer.

'Melam spent several weeks examining the behaviour of all of the animals. He watched where they went, what they came into contact with, and, most carefully, what they ate. After a month of careful observation he concluded that the only difference between the deer and the rest of the animals was their fondness for eating a certain flower.

'The idea of plants as natural medicines had of course been around since time immemorial, but Melam could not recall any particular usage ever having been made of this plant. Quietly – not wanting to build false hope within the community – he gathered some of the flowers and took them home with him at the end of his working day. While Helena was locked up in her tomb, screaming and desperately trying to escape, he worked through the night to reduce the plants into a concoction that might be drinkable.

'In the morning Melam served the medicine to Helena with her breakfast, claiming that it was a plant derivative, just discovered, which would be good for her digestion. Because she loved her brother dearly, Helena did not question him; Melam did not tell her the truth, lest the potion didn't work. And so both of them went about their day as normal, and when Melam returned home in the evening he locked her up as he always did.

'He waited outside the door for several hours, but the usual rantings and ravings that could be clearly heard even through the layers of concrete failed to materialise. Melam didn't dare open the door until morning, just in case the potion had in some way rendered Helena silent while failing to cure her madness. But when he opened the door in the morning he found her quite well rested, and thoroughly surprised.

'He told her what he had done, and gave her the same potion again that morning; and the next night he decided to risk leaving her free of her prison. Again, she slept soundly; not a touch of madness could be detected in her sleeping countenance. And so, the next day, he brewed up as much of the potion as he could, and he took it into the village.

'The villagers could scarcely believe their ears when he told them what he had discovered, and, certainly, few of them were willing to leave their wives and daughters unchained the first night. But within a week they were declaring Melam an earthly god, and demanding that the flower be named after he who had discovered it.

'Melam, though, being the humble person that he was, did not feel worthy of having any article of nature named after him, and so, he suggested a different name. It is from him that we get the name of this flower that for so long was thought to be a cure for madness: from *hellos*, or "fawn", and *bora*, "food of beasts".'

then

Connie arrived home from school first. She'd got off the bus without waiting for Lily for the third time that week, walking away fast so she couldn't catch her up. She tried to convince herself it was an attempt to get Lily to break free, start making friends with other people. What was it they called it – 'tough love'? It didn't automatically equate to being a bad sister.

Lily hadn't yet complained. And it wasn't as though she was completely incapable of talking, these days. If she had a complaint, she could raise it like anyone else.

The house was quiet. Her father would be out at work, she knew. Her mother was out in the garden: Connie could see her from the kitchen window, crouched in the flowerbeds, her headscarf blowing in the wind. It was almost dark, but Connie knew that was unlikely to stop her; she rarely came inside before it was pitch-black these days, and when she did she went straight to her room and didn't come downstairs all evening.

Connie knew that it was unnatural for a mother to spend so much time avoiding her family, but she found that it wasn't something she could bring herself to care about. Tried to explain it away, as though maybe if she started caring then she would care too much and she wouldn't be able to stop.

Not just: she didn't care. Was incapable of caring. Had lost that part of her brain, somewhere.

Behind the sofa, never to be seen again.

She made herself a sandwich and ate it at the kitchen table. The kitchen was dim in the fading light; it had been grey all day, never properly brightening, in that way that felt close and uncomfortable, as if the edges of the world had shifted that few million miles closer. As if all that existed was what could be seen out of the window. And even that was dampened, shrouded in mist.

Lily came through the door just as Connie was washing up her plate. Stood at the counter, eyes accusing, but didn't say anything. Just stood there.

'What? Speak, if you want something.'

'Why?'

'Why what? Why speak?'

Lily shook her head, impatiently. 'Why leave me?'

'Because you need to learn. I told you, I can't baby you forever. You need to make friends.'

Lily considered this. Tilted her head to one side, a demonstration of thought. She had got used to acting things out, so that people waited for her. 'Friends like yours?'

Connie had no answer to this, and turned to walk away.

'Were they mean to you?'

Connie stopped in her tracks. Looked down at her little sister, so much younger than her in age, but so much the image of what she herself had once been. 'Are they mean to *you*?' she asked.

'Yes.'

Connie reached out a hand. Found it suspended in mid-air, didn't really know what to do with it, and placed it on Lily's shoulder as gently as she could.

'They were mean to me. They are mean to me. But you get used to it.'

Lily nodded. She moved away, started making her own sandwich, and Connie understood the conversation to be closed. It was the longest conversation they'd had in three years.

'Do you ever think about what it would be like to live in a place like this?'

They were doing the rounds of local National Trust properties, at Marcus's insistence, and Lily had been standing at the first-floor window, nose pressed against the glass. Connie's voice beside her made her jump, echoing her thoughts exactly, and Lily nodded. The imperfections in the glass added a hazy sheen to the scene in front of her, as if it were swimming in sea mist.

'You'd be a princess. Or friends with royalty, anyway,' Connie continued.

Connie was wearing a short skirt and knee-high black boots with high heels, and looked out of place in the stately home with its period furniture and wooden floors. Lily had been envying the boots in the car – she'd not seen them before. Marcus had scowled when Connie had left the house wearing them, but he hadn't said anything.

An elderly couple came to stand next to them, and in wordless agreement Connie and Lily moved on into the next room, which was long and empty, nothing but a hallway full of pictures. A volunteer stood in the corner, a man of about sixty, who looked as though he was about to say something to them and then thought better of it. They came to stand in front of the biggest portrait in the room, of a young girl who looked sad and overdressed.

'You never see them smiling,' Connie muttered, almost to herself. And then, 'She looks a bit like you, actually. Don't you think?'

Lily shrugged. She didn't see the resemblance, but she didn't want to contradict Connie.

'I heard somewhere that every human is related to every other human. Or almost everyone, anyway. So maybe this girl was our great-great-great-grandmother, or something.'

Lily looked at the girl's face, which looked the same as all the other faces on the walls: oily Victorian features, marred with old-fashioned seriousness. 'Maybe,' she said eventually, her voice a whisper. Connie looked as if she was about to continue talking, and then their parents came into the room, and she fell silent.

Marcus was keeping up a constant stream of conversation while Anna trailed slightly behind him, like a disgruntled child. Neither of them noticed their daughters at the other end of the room, and Marcus's words carried across the empty space, echoing uncomfortably among the hushed whispers in the rest of the house. 'Lily's been doing pretty well at school, but we keep getting letters about Connie – she's bunking off all the time, never does her homework – '

'Why are you telling me this as if it's new to me?' Anna asked wearily. 'I've read the letters too, you know.'

'Well, I wasn't sure. You've seemed pretty – distracted, recently.'

'Distracted, hmm? How tactful of you.'

'Well, you know, by the garden, and – '

'Yes, I know what you meant.' Her voice was harsh. 'What do you propose to do, then? About Connie?'

'I don't know. We could at least try having a word with her. See if there's any reason she doesn't want to go to school.'

Lily looked up at Connie. Her mouth was set, and she stared directly at their parents, as if challenging them to notice she was there. They carried on talking, oblivious.

'She's always hated secondary school,' Anna said, her voice dismissive.

'I think the other kids have been picking on her. Maybe we should talk to the school, get them to intervene – '

'I don't think us storming in there telling everyone to be friends with her is going to help matters, do you?'

'Well, it's better than doing *nothing* – '

Marcus stopped talking abruptly. The clicking of Connie's heels as she stormed out of the room had alerted him to her presence.

'Oh, brilliant.' He sighed, and looked over at Lily, still frozen to the spot. 'Did she hear everything?'

Lily shrugged. She caught her mother's eye, but Anna looked away immediately.

'Guess that's something else I'll have to apologise for later,' Anna muttered, to no one in particular.

'Oh, were you planning on making apologies, then?'

Lily flinched. Her father's voice was more venomous than she had ever heard it before.

'Well, you obviously think I need to. What should I apologise for? Attempting to make the best of a bad situation? Trying to be a family even though you've made it abundantly clear that you don't want me to be part of it?'

'I'd *love* you to be a part of it. Unfortunately, you never seem to be around for me to include you.'

'Never around? I've been here the whole time.'

'In the garden. Or walking in the woods. Or hiding upstairs in our bedroom, refusing to talk to anyone.'

Lily realised they'd forgotten she was there again. Or maybe they just didn't care any more. She clenched her fists and watched the blood drain out of her knuckles, but not the gaps between them. No matter how hard she clenched, she couldn't make the white patches spread any further. She could feel the half-moon imprints of her fingernails in the soft flesh of her palms.

'I don't *refuse* – ' Anna began, but Marcus cut her off.

'Don't try and deny it. You're never around, you never spend any time with them – or with me, for that matter; no one has any idea what's going on in your head and no one can get close to you. In what way are you here, really?'

There was a pause, in which Lily stood very still, watching her parents breathe.

'Fine,' Anna said eventually. 'What do you want me to do, then? Should I talk to Connie?'

'I don't really see what you could say that would make any difference, given that it's you she's angry with.'

'Has she said as much? She seemed pretty pissed off with both of us just now.'

'Yes, alright, she's angry with me too. But that's different.'

'Oh, right, I see. Different.'

'Anna, please.'

'I'd just like to know how it's different, that's all.'

Lily moved closer to the windows, edging forward slowly so as not to draw attention to herself.

'She thinks you don't care about her.'

'I'm her mother. How could I possibly not care?'

'Well, in case it slipped your notice, Anna, refusing to spend time with the people around you tends to make them think that you don't care.'

Lily closed her eyes and started counting. *If I count to one hundred and they're still arguing, I'm just going to leave.*

'I'm having a hard time, okay, I don't know what to do. I know it's stupid but it's not fair to punish me when I'm trying my hardest – '

'What do you mean, *punish* you? I haven't punished you at all. In case you hadn't noticed, I've been pretty damn forgiving.'

'You mean you've acted that way so you can take the fucking moral high ground.'

Sixteen. Seventeen. Eighteen.

Lily wondered if she could slip out without them noticing.

'It's got nothing to do with any moral high ground! I'm just trying to keep our family together. I've got a wife who spends her life hiding in the garden, one daughter who won't speak to me and another who only speaks to me to tell me to fuck off. Explain to me what I'm supposed to do to make this situation more bearable, *please*.'

Twenty-seven. Twenty-eight. Twenty-nine.

'Maybe, instead of sitting there feeling sorry for yourself, you should take a look at the underlying problems. Maybe there's a reason why all of this is happening to you. And I don't just mean that you're unlucky, or, or, I don't know – '

'That my children have got your bad genes?'

'Oh for fuck's sake, Marcus, why does everything have to be my fault? It's not like you're Mr fucking Perfect, is it?'

The last thing Lily remembered thinking was *forty-nine*, before she slumped to the floor, the room darkening around her.

An hour later, Lily sat in the waiting room at the emergency doctor's office, next to her father, who chewed on his knuckles and darted his eyes nervously around the corners of the room. There was only one other person present, an elderly man who looked as if he was struggling to breathe. He closed his eyes every time he inhaled, as if the effort involved in making his chest move consumed all of his available energy, with none to spare for trivia such as sight.

Lily had been unconscious for less than a minute. She'd woken up to find her parents on either side of her, her mother's fingers clutching desperately at her shoulder. She didn't remember fainting, but she remembered waking up and feeling trapped, pinned to the floor by her parents' anxiety.

'Not long now,' her father said, his eyes on the clock above the door. She looked at him, then looked away when he didn't meet her gaze. She wondered how he knew.

She had been here before, once, when she was five or six.

It hadn't changed. It wasn't like the usual doctor's office; there were no toys and no windows, and only one receptionist, who looked bored and sullen. She had eyed them without interest as they'd explained why they were there, and waved them towards the hard plastic chairs that lined the room before returning her attention to the radio in the corner.

Eventually a doctor appeared in the doorway and called them through.

His office was almost the same size as the waiting room, and felt much more welcoming, with posters on the walls and the afternoon light streaming through the window. He gestured them into chairs with a smile, and then sat down opposite them, his gaze fixed on Lily. 'What seems to be the problem?'

Lily stared back him, wide-eyed and solemn.

'She doesn't speak much,' Marcus offered.

'Okay. We'll let Dad do the talking, then, shall we?' The doctor turned his gaze to Marcus.

'Lily collapsed. I suppose she just fainted, but, well, she's never done it before and – I – I think it might be stress-related.'

'Really?' The doctor had an expression of carefully measured patience on his face. 'What makes you think that?'

'There have been some family issues. Lily's been – well, check her records: she's had problems with not talking and – '

'Yes, I can see that from her notes. She's been at Dr Hadley's institute?'

'Yes, just for a while – '

'And he wasn't able to help?'

'No, he did help, but she had to leave before she was ready. They – there was an incident.'

The doctor eyed him, his expression sceptical. 'I have to say, if the problem is mental, you'd be better off discussing further treatment options with Dr Hadley.'

'He was treating her until recently, but he didn't seem to think she needed anything further.'

'Well, then, maybe it's worth looking into possible physical causes. I can schedule some tests. If you like.' The doctor's voice was sceptical, but Marcus nodded.

'If you think that would be helpful.'

'Well, it's good to explore different options, I suppose. I can give you some leaflets as well, about psychiatric services in the area.'

Lily tuned the conversation out. She watched people walking past the windows, and realised the glass was half-mirrored, so that people looked like shadows as they walked in front of it, grey and not quite fully formed. She wondered what it looked like from the other side.

'I'll request those tests, then. Someone will be in touch. Ask at Reception on the way out about those leaflets.'

Marcus thanked the doctor and stood up, taking Lily's hand as she did so. Looking up at him, she thought he looked exhausted.

She looked back at the doctor as they left the room, but he was already buried in his paperwork, and he didn't look up.

now

There was a distance between Connie and Nathan. A remoteness, an estrangement, a standing apart. A sense, real or imagined, of a space between them: unbroachable, unencroachable. Their paths seemed to circle around each other but never cross; there was no moment where they met in the middle.

Even when the children were around, they couldn't seem to communicate in any meaningful way. They were civil and almost friendly: they discussed dinner arrangements, future plans, schools and work and their neighbours. But there was something missing. An absence of feeling. In the evenings Connie went to bed early and read, or sometimes just lay there for hours, feeling as if a chasm had opened up somewhere inside her. Nathan sat downstairs, listening to his music, reading back issues of *New Scientist*, wondering where his wife had gone.

Wondering if it was his fault.

He couldn't think of a time when he'd ever felt so estranged from her. He was a private man, and used to keeping himself to himself, to a certain degree, but Connie had never been like that. She was a woman with Opinions. She liked to discuss things. She wanted everything out in the open, dissected, analysed, shared. He'd always assumed it was some kind of adverse reaction to having Lily for a sister.

He wanted to recommend some form of help. Counselling, perhaps. But he couldn't seem to broach the subject. She was the woman with whom he'd always felt comfortable talking about anything, and suddenly he was finding it difficult to discuss the logistics of cleaning the bathroom.

He knew she had a lot on her mind. Knew she was still coping with the death of her mother, knew she was worrying about Lily, probably even missing her, though considering the nature of their relationship he found it hard to understand why. He guessed that she was missing Richard, too. And it wasn't as though he thought he could fill those holes in her life. But he wanted to help.

Unfortunately, tact had never been his strong point. He was direct, forceful, to the point. He could tell her what to do to make herself feel better, and she would resent him for it, and do the opposite of whatever he told her. And so they coexisted, quietly, meaninglessly. When the children weren't around, a sleepy silence descended over the house, and thickened, almost imperceptibly.

He sat up at night, thinking about being there, thinking about not being there. He thought about where he could be, if he wasn't sitting alone in his house, like an absurd and ineffective guard dog.

She was always asleep when he finally went to bed.

'Are we going to see Uncle Richard? I made another map and he promised to come and hunt with me for treasure.' Luke was hopping from foot to foot in the hallway, looking like a miniature Michelin Man in his shiny blue padded jacket. Connie, hunting through her handbag for her keys, looked up distractedly.

'Um. Not today.'

Connie shook the bag in irritation to see if it jangled. Somewhere, deep within, it did.

'Why not?'

'Because Uncle Richard and Auntie Lily have gone to live in Grandma's old house for a while.'

'Why can't we go and see them there?'

'Well, er...' In frustration she turned the bag upside down and dumped the contents on to the post table. Wallet, phone, wet wipes, chewing gum, receipts, loose change and a whole plethora of random objects that Luke had found and insisted on keeping. And, finally, her keys. 'We can. But not today.'

'Why not?'

'Because Daddy's taken the car.'

'We could get a bus to Grandma's house,' Tom suggested. He was perched on the stairs, tying his shoelaces, similarly insulated against the late November weather.

'Yes, we could, darling, but we've got other things to do today, I'm afraid. Mummy needs to go into town and buy some things. And you both need new shoes.'

'I don't want new shoes,' Luke said, sulkily. 'I want to see Uncle Richard.'

'How are we going to get into town if we don't have the car?' Tom asked.

'We're going to walk. You do both remember how to walk, don't you?' Connie started shoving objects back into her bag, fighting to keep her temper. Intoning the mantra that she couldn't help reciting every time she saw all the calm, collected, permanently in-control mothers she came across at school. *I am a good mother; losing my temper does not make me a bad mother; they are all just lobotomised gibbons and I am a real person.* On reflection it wasn't a particularly good mantra, but it had a calming effect all the same.

'I can't remember how to walk,' Luke said, predictably, dropping to the floor and beginning to crawl towards the front door. 'We're going to have to crawl into town.'

'Well, I suppose at least you won't need new shoes if you're going to be crawling everywhere. Right, are we ready? Tom, have you finished with your shoelaces yet?'

Tom held out his shoe-clad feet for inspection, proudly.

'Good boy. Right. Come on, then.'

Saturdays were usually family days. For the last few weeks they had been the only days that Nathan and Connie had managed to communicate with any semblance of normality, generally because they were around Richard and Lily – or, more often, just Richard. Lily, who had always taken genuine pleasure in spending time with her nephews, had abruptly stopped coming with him. Richard explained that it was nothing personal; that she was struggling to do much of anything.

Connie felt like saying that she knew exactly how she bloody felt. This week, with Nathan away at a conference and Lily and Richard still settling into the house, Connie had felt somewhat at a loss. She loved spending time with her sons, of course, but she felt so generally unsettled that the disruption to her routine was entirely unwelcome. She wanted to spend time with Nathan, pretending that things were fine. She wanted to watch Lily communicating with her sons in the only language that seemed to come naturally to her. She wanted to talk to Richard, to know that he was okay, that they were both okay.

She wanted a distraction from thinking about herself.

The fifteen-minute walk into town was relatively peaceful. Tom enjoyed taking charge of Luke when they were out and about, holding his hand when they crossed roads, instructing him to wait for the green man. Connie watched them and tried to savour snapshots of memory. She wanted the image, forever, of her two boys looking out for each other, mittened hands clasped together, on a nondescript street on a grey winter's day.

She wanted, inexplicably, to cry.

It was how she'd felt for weeks: a constant veering from perfect normality to utter despair. Nathan would say it was grief, of course, and not to worry about it. She would heal in her own time. She needed to talk about it, to bleed the wound or squeeze the pus from the memory or whatever the fuck else it was that he had been advising lately. He would tell her, in his calm and unintentionally patronising doctor's tone, about all the other patients he'd seen who were suffering from grief. He'd almost certainly embark on a conversation about the five stages and drive her to the point of suicide.

This was why she couldn't communicate with him; this was why they'd been feeling like disparate elements of a thing that had once been a whole concoction. Because he saw her as a set of symptoms, as a patient. The same as any other. And that was probably the sensible way for him to look at it, if she was honest with herself – it was better that he look out for her mental health objectively than try and involve himself in it.

Except that she didn't need a doctor. She needed her husband. She needed someone who didn't know the scientific ins and outs of grief and depression and the official stages of mourning. She needed someone who would hold her and tell her that it didn't matter that insanity ran in her family because she had turned out fine, she was okay, she would be okay; that everything, basically, would be okay.

Her sons stopped to cross the road, and she bent down abruptly and wrapped an arm around each of them, squeezing them to her. They wriggled when she tried to kiss them, saying that the cars had stopped and that they needed to go before they started again, and she released them, gently, keeping a hand on each of their shoulders. Keeping them close to her.

Hoping against hope that, whatever other failings she might have as a mother, she would not bring them up to be the same as the rest of her family.

Richard had gone out. Lily had forgotten to ask him where. No idea when he'd be back. It didn't matter, much.

The shadows of the house closed around her, but she couldn't bring herself to turn the lights on.

She was in the kitchen, which had been Richardified: he'd made it into a place unrecognisable from its previous life. There were all their belongings, neatly lined up on the counters: the tea and coffee jars with their colourful striped patterns, the notice board which advertised the public parts of their life. The calendar, with his distinctive scrawl filling in all the important details. The things Not To Be Forgotten.

She seemed to be forgetting everything, lately.

Funny, how the recorded things, the Important Things, the Appointments and Events and Birthdays, were the things that you least needed to remember, once they had passed. Was it possible to keep a calendar to record the things that you really cared about?

She could keep a diary. She'd tried, once. Hadn't got much further than *Dear Diary, Today I went to school and...*

She'd found there wasn't much she'd wanted to keep, then.

But how useful it would be. If she could remember things as they'd actually happened. If things appeared in her memory correctly, with Cause and Effect being the way round that they were supposed to be, so it was all ordered, organised, collected. If she could dip into her narrative and remember what day an event had happened, what had preceded it, what had followed it. Instead of this random collection of things which were contradicted by all common sense.

Like the bar stools. She remembered it one way. Knew it was another. Connie probably remembered it differently from that. And that was just one detail. Completely irrelevant.

She didn't know whether she kept going back to it because of the discrepancy, or because of the fact that they were no longer there. Where had they gone? And why?

Why didn't she just ask Connie?

She paced from one side of the kitchen to the other, frustrated. Tried not to look at the patio doors while doing so, but her eyes kept flicking towards them. The dark smudge of the patio, with the sprawling lawns and the borders beyond. All overgrown now; lavender rendered colourless by winter, intermixed with weeds, and the remnants of her mother's once lovingly tended flowers. And, beyond, the darkness of the woodland, trees hulking over the house and casting shadows on the lawn.

She was forcing herself to stay there, to face it down. No, she wasn't doing anything of the sort. She was pretending it didn't exist.

To pretend. To profess, assert, maintain, originally. The playful aspect of the word didn't exist until the nineteenth century. How did Richard's knowledge get inside her head like that? She absorbed him. Did he do the same with her?

Did it matter?

She slammed her hand down on the breakfast bar. Felt the pain, blunt but still searing, shoot up her arm. A slight relief, nothing more. A reminder that she was still alive, awake.

That there was more to existence than just the darkness creeping in from the patio doors.

Richard would be home soon. Maybe she could talk to him. Tell him what was bothering her.

Or maybe not.

then

The Christmas holidays were a subdued affair in the Emmett household. Connie, who had coursework due in the first week back at school, spent her time in her room, blasting music so loudly that the walls shook. Anna disappeared into the garden for long stretches of time, sometimes wandering into the woods and not coming back for hours. Lily sat in her room and tried to do the advanced work her maths teacher had sent her to keep her going, but she found the noise distracting, and after two days of suffering through it she retreated downstairs. She found her father sitting in the living room, watching a war documentary on TV. He looked up and smiled as she hovered in the doorway.

'You can come in, you know. I won't bite.'

She sat down next to him on the sofa, nudging his arm until it came to rest on her shoulder.

'Have you learnt much about the world wars yet?'

Lily shook her head, following the flickering pictures on the screen with fascination. She recognised some of the faces, though the only one she could name was Hitler. 'Grandpa told me a bit,' she said quietly.

'Yeah, your Grandpa's pretty knowledgeable on that subject.'

They watched in silence for a while, letting the low, calm voice of the narrator wash over them. Lily thought of Christmas at her grandparents' house, with tinsel sparkling on every surface and strings of cards decorating every wall. Her father had tried, but something about the house seemed flat and lifeless, as if even the decorations weren't in the mood to celebrate.

'Will Mama be making Christmas dinner?'

'I don't know, sweetie.' Her father's eyes were still fixed on the TV. 'She might not feel like it. But, if not, then we can make dinner for her, can't we?'

That wouldn't be so bad, Lily thought. The three of them could do dinner for Anna. Maybe it would cheer her up, to see them there, still acting like a family.

'We could make cake,' she suggested. 'And Connie could help.'

'Of course. If she wants to.'

They sat quietly for a while. Lily watched the scenes flicker across the screen: a black and white parade of soldiers, and the billowing dust clouds of years-distant explosions.

'I had something I wanted to talk to you about, actually.' Marcus's voice was hesitant, and Lily looked up, curious. 'I was talking to your headteacher, before the holidays. She said she's interested in you seeing a doctor when you go back to school. What would you think about that?'

'Like Dr Hadley?'

Marcus nodded. 'Similar. It would just be someone to talk to. If you felt like talking, obviously. They wouldn't force you.'

'Why does she want me to see a doctor?'

'They just want to make sure they're doing everything they can to help you.' Marcus's eyes were on the screen as he spoke, and Lily couldn't read his expression. 'Do you think you'd be okay with that?'

Lily shrugged. 'I suppose so.'

Marcus squeezed her shoulder.

'Good girl.'

They fell silent. The programme changed to a soap opera that Lily struggled to follow, and an hour later her father went to bed.

Contrary to the atmosphere of the previous week, Christmas morning was genuinely festive. Marcus got them all up at the crack of dawn, insisting that it was 'tradition', though it had been so long since they'd spent Christmas together that it was hard to remember whether they'd ever even had traditions. They put on a tape of Christmas hits, opened the living room windows so that the house was flooded with cold air, and sang along so loudly that the few dog walkers who passed the house turned back to stare.

'People will think we're mad,' Marcus said, sounding delighted.

'They'd probably be right,' Anna said dryly.

'Surely everyone goes mad at Christmas, though?' Connie said. 'All that time locked up with their families?'

'Who was it who said "hell is other people"?' Marcus was grinning.

'I dunno. Some philosopher. Do you think they meant all people, or just the ones you're forced to be around every day?'

'Like us? Are we your idea of hell, Connie?'

'Have I looked like I've been enjoying myself lately?' But she was grinning too.

They opened their presents, and then they made dinner together, Connie and Anna chopping vegetables alongside one another as if they did it every day, Marcus stuffing the turkey with slightly too much enthusiasm. Lily hung back a little, hovering around the table, not quite sure where she slotted into the scene. 'You can come and help,' Marcus said, encouraging, but there was nothing to do that wasn't already being done, and she ended up standing awkwardly at his side.

Once dinner was in the oven they sat on the living room floor and played games. They started with Scrabble, but Anna quickly grew frustrated, not being able to get beyond four-letter words. Connie decried the game as 'stupid', and Lily said nothing as they packed it away and got out Monopoly instead. She didn't enjoy Monopoly much – it was difficult to play without a lot of talking – but she joined in half-heartedly, pushing her silver dog round the board and handing over baffling sums of imaginary money. She lost quickly, and sank into the background with relief; she was much happier watching.

They ate dinner in the late afternoon, the sun setting over the garden as they pulled crackers and read out awful jokes. The enthusiasm was starting to wear off slightly; Lily could see Anna withdrawing back into herself, Connie getting short-tempered. Marcus was over-bright, still trying to draw everyone together, but there was a desperation behind his gestures that indicated the attempt wasn't working. 'Cake,' he said, too loudly, once everyone had finished eating. 'Who wants cake?'

It was shop-bought, dry, and not quite as it should be. Lily could vaguely remember the days when they would have spent hours in the kitchen preparing for Christmas Day, Anna directing two flour-dusted children in the proper methods of stirring and sieving while Marcus was at work. Her grandmother had been the same, last year: up to her elbows in cake mix, cheerfully conducting Lily's movements around the kitchen as if she were an orchestra. This cake had been put into production silently, out of sight, and Lily didn't quite trust it. She picked the pieces apart so that she ate the fruit cake, then the icing, and then the marzipan, saving the best for last, because marzipan was always shop-bought, and therefore couldn't be ruined. Connie saw what she was doing and laughed.

'I remember you doing that when you were five.'

'Really?'

'Yeah. Except in those days you didn't bother with the fruit cake at all. You used to give Mama your cake and just eat the icing and the marzipan.'

'I remember that,' Anna said, laughing. 'We used to do a swap. I gave her all my marzipan in return for all of her cake.'

'I think Lily got the better end of the deal,' Marcus observed.

Lily tried to remember. She had snatches of memory: her mother in the kitchen, or in the garden, towering over them, picking them up when they fell over. She was never involved, though. Lily couldn't imagine her doing something as frivolous as swapping cake for marzipan – something that brought her down to their level.

After dinner was cleared away they retreated back to the living room, and Marcus put on a film. Lily stayed just long enough to ensure that everyone was suitably engrossed, that she wouldn't be missed, and then she slipped upstairs to her room.

She felt separated from the rest of them, in a way she couldn't put her finger on. As if there was something going on behind the scenes that she couldn't quite grasp. All the false cheer, which only that morning had seemed so genuine. As if they had all discussed it the night before and decided that, for one day only, they were going to be a real family – happy, carefree, pretending they liked each other – and then, when the darkness drew in, all would be allowed to return to normal. Lily lay down on her bed and pulled her covers over her head, enjoying being cocooned in the darkness. What was the point? she wondered. If they had no intention of carrying it on into the future, then why was this one day so important?

There was a soft knock at her bedroom door. Lily froze under the covers, taking care not to move her chest when she breathed in and out. Another knock, and then the low creak of the door being pushed open. 'Lils?'

She exhaled at the sound of Connie's voice, and pushed back the covers so her head poked out of the top. Connie pushed the door closed behind her, then sat down on the end of the bed, careful not to crush Lily's feet. 'You okay? They were asking after you.'

Lily nodded.

'Sure?'

She nodded again. Connie reached out a hand, found the lump of her ankle under the duvet and squeezed it, gently.

'You know they'll have stopped all this happy families crap by tomorrow, don't you? We just have to get through one day. Pretend we all like each other. Then back to normal.'

Lily watched the outline of her sister in the dark, expressionless, and said nothing.

now

'Excuse me. Hey. Excuse me.'

It was a few moments before the voice penetrated Richard's consciousness, and he realised that it was speaking to him.

'Sorry, fella. You look like you were having some pretty deep thoughts there.'

'Deep? No, not really.' Richard laughed uncomfortably, caught off-guard. He'd been leaning against the low stone wall of the churchyard in the centre of the village, looking at the headstones within its perimeter. Mostly tilted at angles, crumbling limestone with once elegantly chiselled lettering, now faded to illegibility. A few were better cared for, brighter white, upright: recent. Some even had flowers. But most were memorials which commemorated nothing but the very presence of absence in the world.

The man was probably thirty years older than Richard, and dressed casually, in farmer's clothes: sturdy boots, worn jeans, oiled jacket for keeping out the elements. He had a whiskery beard, and dark eyes which gave little away. His smile seemed genuine enough, though, as he stepped off the path and came to stand beside Richard.

'Well, seems to me that if you're standing outside a churchyard you're going to be thinking about either death or religion. Both of which qualify as deep, in my book.'

'Hmm. I suppose I was thinking about death, in an abstract way. Nothing serious.'

He laughed, then stopped when the man didn't laugh along with him. 'Flippancy doesn't do you any good in the long run, you know.'

'Nor does dwelling too much on things you can't control.'

'Absolutely right.' The man clapped him on the shoulder, abruptly approving. 'My name's Ed.'

'Richard. Nice to meet you.' They shook hands, vigorously.

'You've just moved into the Emmetts' old place, right?'

'Yeah. Well. Still the Emmetts' place, technically. My girlfriend Lily grew up there.'

'Really? When was the last time she was there?'

'Oh, years ago. I'm not too clear on the dates. Did you know her mother?'

'No, not really. Just heard rumours about the family, you know how it is.'

'Yup.' Richard grinned.

'So what are you two doing here, then? Just fancied a change of scenery?'

'Well, actually, I lost my job,' Richard admitted. 'And Lily's taking some leave from her work, because of her mother dying, so... I suppose we thought a change would do us some good. Well. *I* thought that, anyway.'

'And it's not working out?'

'Oh, I don't know,' Richard hedged, not wanting to divulge too much to a total stranger. 'Too early to tell, really.'

'I hear that house is full of memories, you know. Ghosts.'

Richard looked at him curiously. 'Yeah, well, I thought if Lily could face them...'

'Not just hers.' Ed's voice was rough, forceful. Like a dog's bark: a warning. He reverted to syrupy softness so quickly that Richard wasn't sure if he'd imagined it. 'So are you looking for work?'

'Yeah. I'm not sure what I want to do, though. I was an aspiring journalist, but it didn't really work out...' He trailed off, shrugged. 'I don't suppose there are many jobs in a small village like this. I could drive into town, but I haven't wanted to leave Lily alone too much.'

'You care about her a lot.' The tone was approving, but there was something else unidentifiable.

'Yes, of course.'

'Glad to hear it. Hey, here's an idea. Have you ever tried bar work?'

'Sure, back when I was a student.' Nonplussed.

'Well, a good friend of mine runs the pub in the centre of the village. He could use a hand in the evenings. It's not the kind of pay you're used to, I imagine, but it'll provide you with some spending money while you're looking for something more permanent.'

'I don't know. It's been a long time,' Richard hedged, politely. Tiptoeing around the words *please God no*.

'Oh, you never forget. It's a good way to meet people, you know. Integrate into the community.'

Richard laughed. 'You make it sound like I've just got out of prison.'

'Heh. Well. This place can be a bit like that. We're not so good with outsiders, you know?'

'People seem friendly enough.' Even as he said it, he knew it wasn't true. It had been almost a week and no one had spoken to them. Their neighbours might not have been next door in the sense of being attached to the side of their house, but they were still close enough that a visit to say hello wouldn't have been out of the question.

'Come on. Give it a go. What have you got to lose?'

Richard's most hated of all trite phrases: the rhetorical question with a million different answers. Everyone, always, had something to lose.

And yet, the asking of the question had the same effect, every time.

He shrugged his shoulders, laughed uneasily, shrugged again. 'Sure. Why not?'

There was a soap bubble in the sky. Lily stood, nose pressed against the glass of the patio doors, following its drifting progress. It lurched suddenly higher, and glinted, rainbow-bright in the sunlight, before popping soundlessly into a shower of drizzly fragments. Stillness inside the house, and out. The years-distant echo of childish voices in the air.

*– Can we play in **the garden** Mama please **everyone else** is outside and Billy's **got a** water gun –*

The voices receded, along with the hazy summery quality of the light, and Lily stared at the garden through her adult's eyes. Visibly withering into winter. She could see it all at once. The faded yellowy patches on the grass, worn threadbare by the sun's relentless attention. The crystals of frost that had clung to the blades of grass that morning, making them simultaneously fierce and astoundingly beautiful. And as it was now: dull, fading into early dusk, and utterly dead.

The force of her parents' absence hit her, abruptly, as it sometimes did, making her dizzy. She lowered herself to the floor. Took deep, shuddering breaths. Looked around the kitchen in its fading half-light, feeling the cavernous space of the empty house around her.

An eleven-year-old Connie, a smudge of white in the doorway, peered down at her, childishly. As if she was trying on her condescension for size, feeling her way into it. Lily remembered that look so well.

Eight-year-old Lily, just behind. Running to catch up.

*– Connie **won't you** play with me Mama won't let **us outside and** I want someone to **shut up** shithead I'm going outside and **you're not** coming –*

At the kitchen counter, Connie perched on one of the red bar stools. Lily below, scrambled to get up, but she couldn't reach. Always three steps behind.

Connie scattered breadcrumbs on the kitchen floor. An offering, the carelessly discarded remains of something she only kept out of spite. A trail, perhaps, for Lily to pick up behind her, when she followed her into the woods.

then

The first day back after the Christmas holidays, rain fell from the sky in thick sheets. The bus was more crowded than usual, crammed with teenagers who would ordinarily have cycled, and Lily got on first and had pushed her way to the back before realising that there was no space for Connie to follow. She turned around, about to head back, but Connie waved her away and took a seat halfway up the bus, in the midst of a group of girls from her year. She sat down and stared straight ahead, and Lily, left with no choice but to do the same, sank into her own seat among people she didn't recognise.

The moment the bus pulled away, Lily saw one of the girls lean in to say something to Connie. The words were lost in the howl of the bus's engines, but the laughter of the group carried up the aisle. Connie gave no indication that she'd heard anything, but Lily thought she saw her grip tighten on the bars of the headrest in front of her.

The bus bounced its way through the countryside as Lily watched her sister. The girl who had spoken had now leaned back to her friends, and was talking loudly while watching Connie for a reaction. The girl was tall, with long, curly hair and dark, narrow eyes. She wore a lot of make-up, and Lily realised where she had seen her before, loitering in the aisles of the Drayfield branch of Boots on Saturday mornings, trying out testers and pouting at herself in the mirrors.

Lily watched as the girl leaned in towards Connie and pinched her arm, viciously. Connie flinched but still she didn't look around, keeping her eyes on the road ahead. Lily thought she looked well practised at pretending nothing was happening.

The bus pulled to a stop outside the school. 'Minster Street,' the driver called over the loudspeaker, and there was a general murmur as people started to move towards the front of the bus.

Lily moved forward too quickly, thinking only of getting to her sister, and found herself face to face with the girl who had been tormenting Connie. 'Don't think we won't get you as well,' the girl hissed, and she jabbed an elbow deep into Lily's ribs, before turning and sweeping away.

For some reason Lily couldn't fathom, they rarely seemed to actually touch her. She thought maybe the silence disconcerted them. Convinced them she really was a killer. Connie was just an easy target, someone to pick on when life got tedious. Lily, they weren't so sure about.

Maybe she actually deserved it.

She heard the whispers, but, like so much other background noise, she filtered them out without too much difficulty. It wasn't that she didn't care. She'd just grown so used to the idea of being alone that she couldn't see any other way forward. It was a form of resigned acceptance.

They had other ways of getting to her, though. Even if they didn't dare physically touch her, they would crowd around her. Trap her in corners when no one was looking. Hiss insults and half-truths at her, viciously; glancing blows which left invisible puncture wounds beneath the skin.

If she couldn't see an escape route then it was harder to shut out the words.

She still counted floor tiles between classes. It had a calming effect. The black and white grid stretched out before her, endless, timeless, hundreds of footsteps click-clacking their way over it without ever pausing to think how it all fitted together.

Lockers lined the walls here and there. Not used as often as she'd expected from American TV programmes. Fewer classes per day, fewer textbooks; *ergo*, no real need to continually stop at one's locker to empty and refill one's bag. It was disappointing, in a way she couldn't identify. The ideals of television, brushing up against the way things really were. Condensed into something much more humdrum.

Still, the clanging sound of the lockers echoed pleasingly, from time to time, in the way she felt they should. Bouncing from wall to wall as they disappeared up the corridor.

She slipped into her classroom behind another student, wraith-like. There was no dip in the general level of noise to indicate anyone had noticed her entrance. She headed for the usual table at the back, slipped into her seat. Caught the eye of the boy opposite but didn't smile. It had been nearly five months, and she still hadn't learnt more than a handful of names.

She had been moved into the year above for maths classes. Her fellow students were largely indifferent to her presence, beyond resenting her slightly for being a younger student who invaded their classes and often performed better than they did.

'Right, come on. Books out, bags away.' The voice of Ms Beecham – loud, nasal, authoritative – cut through the general hum of conversation and silenced the room instantly. Lily was fascinated by the woman's power to call people to order. It made her think of the nurses in the institute, and how they'd always failed to get even one child to obey them.

'Today we're going to be making a start on probability. You're going to be doing your coursework on this, so I recommend you pay attention.'

There was a moment of shuffling as everyone opened their exercise books, found their pencils, shoved their bags under their desks.

'Probability is one of the more practical areas of maths, in the sense that all of you should be able to name some of the ways in which it is used in our society. Does anyone want to suggest any ways?'

Several hands went up. Lily listed the answers silently in her head, her eyes on the window straight ahead of her. *Genetics. Finance. Artificial intelligence. Gambling.*

She tuned out the discussion. She had no interest in *talking* about maths; she just wanted to get on with it. Outside the window she could see another class doing PE. The girls were playing hockey, looking strangely timeless in their pleated skirts and long socks. The boys were presumably inside doing something more manly. It was Connie's class, Lily realised, recognising some of the girls. Minus Connie, who had found her at lunchtime to tell her she was going home. A headache, she'd said. Lily had wanted to offer to go with her, but she hadn't dared.

It had been raining solidly for the past three days. Even now the grey clouds hung low in the sky, threatening to merge seamlessly into the darkness of night. The playing fields were almost entirely mud, and within minutes the girls were covered with dark splatters, the bare patches of skin on their thighs covered in a protective dark coating. It looked like an intense game; Lily could see, even from this distance, the ferocity on the girls' faces. One after another they fell, sliding in the mud, rising almost immediately to continue. Sky darkening blue-black around them. A distant rumble of thunder.

Lily recognised the girl from the bus. She didn't know her name, but she was unmistakable in the way she held herself: head high, dark hair flying out around her face, that expression of self-assured authority. She was directing the other girls around the field, a blur of constant movement, waving her arms this way and that. Team captain, officially or not, it didn't matter. No one was going to question her.

Watching her, Lily felt the sudden, crushing weight of what Connie was up against. How she must feel, faced with that, every day. The girls in Lily's year were mean: they taunted her, avoided her, laughed behind her back. But they had no leader, no one to mobilise them. They were just reacting to rumours, none of them wanting to be the first to admit that they didn't really care about what they had heard.

Connie was up against someone who was really willing to fight to bring her down.

Lily watched, captivated, as the girl charged up and down the field, her voice, silent but easily imaginable, carrying across the school grounds. There was no teacher in sight; this girl was the only authority they had. And, when one of the girl's team members made a mistake, there was no one around to stop her from raising her hockey stick and giving her a thwack which seemed to resonate in Lily's own cheekbone.

Silently, she turned her head away from the window. Back to the brightly lit classroom, not quite bright enough to chase away the shadows from outside. While the rest of the class worked, Lily calculated the probability that, had she been there, the girl on the receiving end of that thwack would have been Connie.

now

Nathan snuck through the waiting room on his way to lunch, staring pointedly ahead, waving politely but with sudden, unaccountable deafness at Mandy as she waved papers at him and tried to call him back. He had been in back-to-back surgery from nine that morning, and he had precisely thirty minutes until he was supposed to be back for the lunchtime meeting. For once he was determined to try and spend those thirty minutes away from Mandy and her towers of paperwork.

The air outside was bitterly cold, the sky bright and clear. Nathan stretched his arms out to his sides, revelling in it after a morning of being shut in an airless space, and nearly punched a passing woman in the face. She gave him a reproachful glare as she hurried past, and he called an apology to her retreating back, trying not to laugh.

The sun was low in the sky, and so bright he struggled to see where he was going. The surgery was in the centre of town, and the pavements boiled with office workers, restless housewives, children in school uniform enjoying a brief escape. Nathan picked his way through the crowds, moving fast, muttering apologies to those he bumped into. He hated crowds, particularly in town; hated the way they dawdled, seemingly purposeless, in the middle of the street, wandering into shops at random and stopping for no reason whatsoever. If he had his way, he would live out in the sticks and have a quiet village surgery with a few hundred patients, all of whom he would know by name.

Connie would never agree to that, though. Whenever he'd suggested it she'd made protests about the schools, about the boys having to travel by bus every day, but really he knew she just couldn't stand the quiet. She liked being all crammed in together, found safety in numbers, and he couldn't resent her for it. He'd known when he married her that he was probably consigning himself to a lifetime of city dwelling.

Though he had found himself wondering, recently, whether there might be a chance of a different life for them. Maybe, if Lily and Richard managed to make a go of it in Drayfield, Connie would come round to the idea of living somewhere smaller. Quieter. It didn't have to be the same village, or even anywhere nearby. But somewhere that was at least slightly disconnected from city life.

Lost in thought, he walked straight into the back of the woman in front of him, who spun around, her expression furious. Her features relaxed into confused recognition as she realised who he was. 'Nathan?'

'Andrea! Hi.' He grinned widely, hoping to disguise the discomfort he felt at seeing her standing there, right in the middle of the street, as if she were a real person and not part of some drunken fantasy that he should never have followed through on. 'How's tricks?'

She raised an eyebrow at his enforced casualness, but let it pass. 'Good, thanks. Just been out doing some house calls. Thought I'd grab a sandwich before heading back. You?'

'Oh, yeah, busy, you know. Been in surgery all morning, just needed to get some air before the partners' meeting.' He was aware that they were standing in the middle of crowds of people, who muttered as they pushed around them, but he felt as if he was glued to the spot. 'It's good to see you,' he said, stupidly. She laughed.

'Oh, is it? From your expression I had assumed it was mostly just awkward and uncomfortable.'

He laughed. 'I'd forgotten how blunt you could be.'

'I'm amazed you remember anything at all about me,' she said, without spite. 'You were pretty far gone that night.'

'Yeah, I know. I'm sorry, about...' He stopped, realising it was pointless.

'Don't be. It's all forgotten.' She reached out a hand, squeezed his elbow, briefly. 'Are you, uh... How are things with your wife?'

'Yeah, not so bad, thanks.' He attempted a careless grin, but it ended up as more of a grimace. 'Well, you know how it can be.'

'Sure. That's why I'm not married.' Andrea's smile was kind. 'How about we go for a coffee some time? You look like you could use someone to talk to.' Seeing his expression, she added, 'I promise I'm not going to try to tempt you into bed by means of caffeinated drinks and slices of cake.'

He laughed. 'I didn't expect you to try. Coffee would be nice. I'd say now, but I've got to get back and everything...'

'Yes, me too.' She rifled in her bag for a minute and produced a business card, which she thrust in his direction. 'Give me a call some time?'

He put the card in his pocket, and nodded. 'Sounds great.'

She reached up to kiss him on the cheek, and then she was gone, as quickly as she'd appeared, absorbed into the crowds around him. He stood there for a moment, feeling almost dazed, unsure what had happened. Then he continued on his way, his fingers brushing the edges of the card in his pocket.

He arrived home shortly after seven, pausing just inside the doorway to listen out for any indicators as to what kind of day it was. If it was a good day, Connie and the boys would be playing a game, or the boys would be playing while

Connie made dinner. There would be noise, chatter, smiles when he walked through the door.

Bad days generally meant silence, with the boys shut upstairs in their rooms, playing out of earshot of their mother.

Nathan could hear the low chatter of the TV in the living room, from which he deduced it couldn't be an entirely bad day. He kicked off his shoes, dropped his keys in the dish in the hallway – the one that Connie, for reasons he couldn't fathom, flatly refused to use – and walked through to find the boys curled up at opposite ends of the sofa, eyes glued to a cartoon Nathan didn't recognise. 'Hey, dudes. What're we watching?'

'You're too old to say "dudes",' Tom said, giggling.

'I'm your father and I can say whatever I want,' Nathan retorted, leaning over and lifting Luke out of his seat, holding him high above his head so that he squealed and wriggled. 'Don't you agree, Luke?'

'Dad! Put me *down*!'

'Not until you agree with me.' Nathan shook him menacingly, and he shrieked.

'I agree! I agree!'

Connie appeared in the doorway just as Nathan dropped him back on to the sofa.

'Trying to get them worked up before bed, I suppose?' she said.

'Oh, don't be like that. We were just having a bit of fun.'

'It's after seven.'

'I know. My magical time-telling device told me.' He waved his watch in her direction, grinning, making the boys laugh. She glared at him and turned and walked back into the kitchen. Tom looked at Nathan, eyes worried.

'She's right,' Nathan said with a shrug. 'I shouldn't have been messing around when you guys are on your way to bed.'

'We're not going to bed *yet*. And you were only playing.'

'It doesn't matter. I should know better.' Nathan ruffled his hair, and waited until he had gone back to focusing on the TV before following Connie into the kitchen.

'Are you okay?' he asked, suppressing the urge to start a fight.

'Fine.' She didn't look at him. She was hunched over the cooker, stirring something, the back of her neck radiating tension.

'I'm sorry.'

'It's fine.'

Nathan decided to ignore the tone of voice, which clearly stated that it was not fine. 'I've been thinking,' he said, carefully.

'Makes a change.'

'Ha, ha. I've been thinking about Christmas.'

He saw her stiffen, almost imperceptibly. 'What about it?'

'Oh, come on. You don't have to say it like that.'

She stopped stirring. He thought she was going to shout at him, but she simply put down the spoon, turned to face him. She folded her arms across her chest, eyes glinting with exhaustion. 'What about Christmas?'

'I thought we could spend it with Lily and Richard.'

She kept eye contact, unblinking. Nathan felt his eyes begin to water as he fought to not blink either, and then realised he was being ridiculous. 'Well?' he prompted, when she didn't respond.

'Here? Or at Drayfield?'

'Whichever you prefer. I don't mind. I just thought it would be nice to all be together.'

'We've never done Christmas together before.' Her face and voice were equally expressionless; he had no idea what she was thinking.

'Yeah, it'd be a change. But wouldn't it be nice? Especially this year, with things having been so difficult…'

'What things?' She was instantly defensive, resentful.

'Oh, come on.'

'No, really. What things?'

'Your mother dying. Lily being seriously ill and being forced into taking a sabbatical. Richard losing his job. Are any of these things a good enough excuse?'

He saw her soften slightly, and realised she'd thought he'd been talking about their relationship. 'Oh,' was all she said. Her voice was quiet, childlike. He knew she couldn't think of anything to say.

'It's been a tough few months. Don't you think it would be nice to end the year on a good note? And the boys would love it.'

Connie nodded. 'You're right. I'll talk to Lily and Richard about it.'

'Yeah?'

She smiled. 'Yeah.'

then

Dr Mervyn had met up with Lily once a week since she had returned to school after Christmas. The other students watched her go, assessing, deciding for themselves what it meant. She felt their thoughts, directed at the slump of her shoulders.

When she had first started seeing the doctor, they'd rarely spoken. He'd explained that he knew as much as anyone else about her history, and didn't need to know more, unless she cared to share it; that he understood that she chose not to speak, rather than being physically unable to, and therefore felt no particular need to pressure her into it; and that she should use her time with him in the most productive way she could think of. She mostly did homework, or drew pictures of whatever was outside the window.

Over time, they'd started speaking, just because it was natural to do so if you spent enough time in a room with only one other person. Dr Mervyn didn't start the conversation, and he didn't ask open questions. Because of this, she knew he wasn't trying to trick her. He didn't engage her in games to try to get her to talk, or treat her as if she were incapable of making her own decisions. Over the course of three months they built up an unconventional, not-quite-doctor-patient relationship, borne mostly out of mutual respect for each other's privacy.

'My mama's been talking about starting to work,' Lily told him, after she'd spent ten minutes idly doodling on the pad in front of her. She'd started drawing a bird that was perched on a branch outside, over and over again, but she couldn't seem to get its head right. Maybe the beak was too big. She frowned, and made adjustments to her latest attempt.

'Yes? That's good news.' Dr Mervyn had been flicking through a book of psychoanalytic theory, as he often did when they were together, but he placed the book on the table when she spoke. Sometimes he read passages to her, though she didn't understand a great deal.

Lily nodded, and scribbled over the bird. Turned the page, started again.

'I don't know if she should.'

Dr Mervyn waited to see if she'd say more. When she didn't, he said, 'Don't you think it's a sign that she's feeling happier?'

Lily shrugged. 'Not really.'

'I see. Have you mentioned this to your father?'

Lily shook her head. Sketched the outline of the bird, in big strokes, confident. Frustrated. If she lifted the page, she knew, she would be able to trace the indents on the other side of the page with her fingertips, like Braille.

'Do you think you should?'

'No.'

Dr Mervyn picked up his book again, flicking through it idly. Still listening, but not waiting-listening. Not expectant-listening.

'People thought Esmeralda was getting happier,' Lily said, finally. Quietly. There was a pause while Dr Mervyn thought about this.

'Did they really, though? From what you've told me, they were keeping her in her room, away from other people. That's not a sign that they thought she was getting better.'

'They told me she was.'

'Are you sure?'

222

Lily looked at him. Confused. No one had ever questioned her recall before.

'Of course. I remember.'

'Sometimes we remember things differently from how they actually happened, though. I bet there are things that you and Connie remember differently about being little. It doesn't mean there's anything *wrong* with your memory. But, as you get older, you rationalise things, and when you think about things that have happened you sometimes change them by accident, to bring them in line with a more rational view of the world. Maybe you imagine that the doctors told you Esmeralda was getting better, because you can't understand why they didn't help her if they knew she was getting worse.'

Lily was quiet for a long time. Her pen hovered above the page, hesitating where it had been sure a moment ago. The as-yet-undrawn bird hesitated too, flickering in and out of tentative existence.

'What if I don't remember something at all?'

'You mean a complete blank?'

Lily nodded.

'Well, that can mean lots of things. Mostly it happens at times when the brain is under great stress. It means that all our extra blood and adrenaline and so on is sent to the places in the body that need it most, so some of the less essential parts of the brain stop functioning for a short time. As far as the body's concerned, memory isn't very important, so that's one of the first areas that shuts down.'

'So it doesn't really mean anything?'

'Well, it means that you were in an emotionally heightened situation, and that your brain thought you might need to run away.'

'But it doesn't mean you're shutting out anything really bad? Like, um, whatsit – ' she waved her pen around vaguely ' – that thing you told me about. Repression.'

'No, not necessarily. There could be all sorts of reasons. Situations where the brain actively hides things from us, like when we repress a memory, aren't very common at all. It's much more likely to be a perfectly normal physiological reaction.'

'Physio...?'

'Physical. Rather than mental.'

Lily nodded. Lapsed into silence. They sat for a while, contemplating.

'You know, if it is repression, then sometimes you can prompt yourself to remember,' Dr Mervyn said. He watched her steadily from behind his notepad. 'There are things we could do together, if you were interested in trying.'

'Like what?'

'Certain exercises. I would present you with things that might trigger something in your memory. It would all be done here,' he added quickly, seeing the look on her face. 'I don't mean re-enactments, or anything like that.'

'Would we need special sessions?'

'No, I don't think so. We should be able to do it in our normal time.' He paused, giving her a moment to think it over. 'What do you think? Does it sound like something you might like to pursue?'

She nodded, slowly. 'I think so.'

'Great. I'll draw up some plans, then, and we'll talk about it in our next session. Does that sound okay to you?'

Her smile was faint, but definitely there. 'Yeah. It sounds okay.'

now

Lily and Richard ate dinner in silence. They sat in the kitchen – Richard had started to insist on this, without really knowing why – and Lily was facing away from the patio doors, eyes on her plate, pushing her food around in circles. Halfway through, Richard stood up, strode across to the kitchen counter and flicked the radio on. He sat back down without saying anything, but he'd made his point clearly enough.

'Did you do any work today?' he asked eventually.

Lily shook her head.

'Well, I might have found a job. For what it's worth.'

No response.

'Don't you want to know what it is?'

'The job?' Her voice was vague, and she didn't look up from her plate.

'Yes, the job.'

'Of course I do.'

'It's bar work. In a pub in the village.'

'Oh.' A pause, while she contemplated all the possible responses to this. 'I didn't think you liked bar work much.'

'I don't. Not much. But we could do with the money.'

She nodded. 'Do you want me to get a job?'

'You have a job.'

'Oh. Yes.' Could you still have a job if you weren't doing any work?

'I think it'll be good to work somewhere in the village. We could meet some people.'

Lily said nothing.

'Well, it'll be good for me, anyway.'

'Yes. You're right.' She looked up, forced herself to make eye contact. Smiled, sort of. 'Maybe I could come and visit you at work.'

'I'd like that.'

'Good.'

Silence fell again, gradually. It grew between them like a fungus, obscuring everything else, until it was the only thing in the room.

Richard went to bed first. He left Lily in the living room, staring out of the window at the animals that moved surreptitiously through the front garden. Hedgehogs mainly; she could hear their slow shuffling, though they remained hidden in the bushes. There were cats, too, but they stalked the open air, proud and defiant, eyes glinting in the reflected light from the window.

After a while she turned the light off. The equality of the separate darknesses, inside and out, made it easier to see from one to the other. She no longer saw her own face ghosted back at her in the glass.

The darkness away from town was different, somehow. There was no orange undertone to it, of course, no street-lights except in the very centre of the village. But it was more than that. The darkness was thicker, more malevolent. There were things that lived in it.

Inside and out.

She moved through to the kitchen, half-heartedly clearing the plates that they'd left out earlier. She kept the lights off, but the moon was bright at the back of the house, easily casting enough light to see by. She could see its silvery shadows, picking their way across the lawn towards her.

Something caught her eye as she carried the plates back to the sink, and it took a moment for her to work out what it was. Something in the landscape had changed.

The lavender, she realised. Two days ago it had been wild, abandoned. Now it was all cut back, drawing her eyes more firmly to the trees beyond.

Had Richard done it? When had he even been out there?

But, if not Richard, then who?

Two child-size ghost-shadows lurked in the doorway, whispering stories that she couldn't understand.

And, outside, the church bells chimed once, calling the midnight hour across the sleeping village.

Richard lay awake for a long time, listening to the low rustle of the house as it settled itself around him. He wondered what Lily was doing. He couldn't hear any sounds from downstairs, no hints of her movements. It was silence accented by not-silence; the creaking shuffle of the house seemed to draw attention to the lack of sound from its occupants.

He turned over familiar etymologies in his mind, treading oft-travelled paths through the history of language. *Silence*, deriving from the Latin *silentium*, among other sources: a state of being silent, an absence of sound. A largely uninteresting etymology, indicating a passivity, a state of being that just *was*, with no intent or foresight on the part of the object rendered silent. It hadn't been used as a verb until the sixteenth century, and yet, if you dug deep enough, there were hints of something more deliberate: the Latin *desinere*, meaning to stop, suggesting the silence was embedded in the act of ceasing something else. When Lily was silent, was it a natural state of being, or was it because she actively ceased creating noise? And, if it was active, then what was the purpose behind it?

And then there was the Germanic *anasilan*: the ceasing of the wind. A less purposeful stopping, simply the gradual cessation of external noise, the return to stillness. Was that what she was aiming for? A form of meditation, perhaps: external silence in an attempt to grasp at internal stillness?

A nice idea, one that brought him comfort, sometimes. But then there was the nagging voice at the back of his head: what if he was looking at it from the wrong angle? What if the silence was not hers, but being wrought upon her? *To silence* – to prohibit or prevent from speaking: to hush.

What if her silence was not a choice, but something that had been thrust upon her?

And, if it was, what was he supposed to do about it?

then

The four of them were at home on a Saturday afternoon, two weeks after Easter. There was still a chill in the air, though winter had lost its edge, leaving longer days and lighter skies in its wake. It was light when they got home from school now, and Connie had taken to sitting in the garden in the afternoons, wrapped in a blanket. Lily, so quick to follow everywhere else, did not follow her there, though she sometimes watched from the safety of her bedroom window.

Anna had spent the morning walking in the woods, and had returned more energised than she had been in weeks. She was sitting at the kitchen table, sketching, lost in her own world. Lily and Connie were sprawled side by side in the living room, staring at the TV. Marcus was pacing from room to room, restless, too cheerful, trying to encourage communication between the two rooms.

'Come on, girls. What a wonderful day. Why don't we all make lunch together? Or go for a walk? When was the last time we all went for a walk together?'

Dutifully they pulled on boots and coats and hats and scarves, wrapping layers around themselves to give the appearance of being more substantial. Lily had bought a new coat a few weeks ago – bright red, pillarbox-red, like a signal, or a warning – and she looked odd next to the rest of the family in their wintry blues and greys.

They walked out of the village, across the fields, down towards the river which connected them, meanderingly, to the rest of England. Their exhaled white clouds filled the air around them as they followed the water through back streets and common land, which looked strangely deserted without its summer coating of cows. Lily and Connie trailed behind their parents; the girls did not speak, but watched the water and thought separate thoughts about how cold it must be.

The sun was low in the sky, an orb of half-hearted light against a blanket grey backdrop. There was a heaviness to the air, the promise of rain, perhaps. The people they passed walked quickly, heads down against the cold, bare skin muffled by mittens and woollen hats. Quietness pervaded, contemplative; even the dogs which trotted obediently beside their owners did so in silence.

Connie slowed her pace, almost imperceptibly, and Lily followed suit. There was a junction in the pathway up ahead: one fork continued along the riverbank, while the other veered sharply to the right and abruptly disappeared behind lines of bushes. By tacit agreement they fell back as far as possible from their parents so as to make their disappearance less noticeable, and then slipped away up the right-hand path.

'Run,' Connie hissed, as soon as they were out of sight. Connie had longer legs, but Lily was more energetic, and they kept an even pace, panting as the cold air hit the back of their throats. 'The park,' Connie said, her voice low and determined. They kept their eyes on the distance. Their absence probably wouldn't be noticed for a few minutes, but there was no point taking chances.

They burst through the gate into the children's playground, which was mercifully empty. There was a whine as the gate swung shut behind them, and then the dull clang of metal on metal. There was a slide in the corner of the park, with a castle at the top, enclosed by red wooden walls. Connie climbed up the ramp first, and shifted along inside the castle to make room for Lily to squeeze in beside her. They sat in opposite corners, feet resting lightly on graffiti-scrawled walls.

'Have you tried smoking yet?' Connie pulled a crumpled packet from her pocket, along with a pink plastic lighter. She proffered the packet in Lily's direction; two left, one upside-down in the pack, bits of tobacco poking out of the top. Lily shook her head.

'You've got to try it some time,' Connie said with a shrug, taking one out and putting the packet back in her bag. 'You can have a few drags of mine, if you like.'

'Okay.'

'You probably wouldn't be able to smoke a whole one on your first go, anyway.'

Connie lit the cigarette with a sharp inhalation, and then exhaled slowly, savouringly. The cloud of smoke filled the air around them with carcinogenic acridity, the only scent that Lily could make out against the clarity of the cold air.

'When did you start smoking?'

'When I was your age.'

Lily nodded. Acknowledged the implied challenge. 'Does Dad know?'

'He's caught me a couple of times. He told me off, but not very seriously.' Connie inhaled, punctuating. 'I don't think he's really got the energy for disciplining us at the moment.'

'Because of Mama?'

'Not just that.'

'Me?'

'Yes. And me.' Connie held the cigarette out for Lily to take. 'I think we're all wearing him out.'

Lily held it between the tips of her fingers, the way she had done with fake cigarettes, once. Admired the strange extension to her hand, simultaneously so out of place and so natural.

'Do you think he'd ever kill himself?'

If Connie thought the question strange, she didn't say anything. She shook her head. 'He's stronger than that.'

'Good.' Lily lifted the cigarette to her lips. Inhaled, tentatively. Coughed, predictably.

'You have to inhale properly. You breathe in, to get the smoke in your mouth, and then you breathe in again. Like this, look.' Connie took the cigarette from her sister, did an exaggerated demonstration of inhaling, and then passed it back to Lily, who followed suit awkwardly.

'You'll get the hang of it.'

She wasn't sure she wanted to, but she nodded, obediently.

They sat in silence for a while. Lily took a couple more drags of the cigarette and then passed it back for Connie to finish. A man with a dog entered the park and sat on a bench near the entrance. The two of them went as still as possible, and stayed that way for ten minutes, while the man sat on his bench, oblivious. Lily focused on the graffiti that was scrawled across the walls in stark black marker pen. Eventually, the clang of the gate signified the departure of the man.

'Can I tell you a secret?' Connie was smiling, eager, though there was something not quite right about her smile. Lily nodded.

'I'm going to run away one day.'

'Run away where?'

'I don't know. Anywhere. Just away.' It was the look in her eye which wasn't right, Lily realised. As though she was trying to communicate something which was not being said.

'Forever?'

'Probably not. I just want to go somewhere where no one knows who I am for a while. Then I expect I'll come back.'

'What about Mama and Dad?'

'They'll be fine. It'll give Dad less to worry about.'

A pause. Then Lily's voice, smaller than before. 'What about me?'

Connie smiled and leaned forward to ruffle Lily's hair. 'You won't need me for much longer.'

'I'll always need you.'

'Nah. You'll be doing your own thing soon. Having me hanging around will just cramp your style.'

'GCSEs?'

'I'll probably stay to finish them. I don't mean I'm going *right now*.' She laughed. 'I need to wait until I'm sixteen anyway. I won't be able to get a job until then.'

Lily said nothing, turning it over in her mind.

'Look, don't worry about it. I shouldn't have said anything. It won't be for ages yet. I just thought you might be excited for me, that's all.'

Lily nodded. Then shook her head. The effect was something along the lines of a confused spasm, and it made Connie laugh.

'Come on. Let's go find Mama and Dad, before they completely freak out and think we've gone to join the circus or something.'

They scrambled down the ramp, one after the other, then set off at an easy run, bounding across the deserted grass. Frosty blades of grass crunched underfoot, and their footsteps were loud on the frozen ground. Their blonde hair streamed out behind them like May Day ribbons, and when, in mid-stride, they caught each other's hands and smiled, they almost looked like children playing.

now

The pub was a ten-minute walk from the house, wedged between the Co-op and the post office, spilling its picnic benches across the pavement in an attempt to claim as much of the street as possible. The Golden Lion, one of three pubs in the village, and probably the busiest, from what Richard had seen on his late-night walks. Despite its inherent old-mannish quality, with its hideously patterned carpets, hunting memorabilia plastered all over the walls and the fire that burned constantly regardless of the outside temperature, it was the only one of the three that managed to attract a mixture of all ages. It was a family pub during the day, a place where teenagers weren't ashamed to be seen on a Friday night, and a sanctuary to the collection of elderly men who propped up the bar on any given day of the week. All in all, if Richard was going to regress to his student days and earn a living assisting in the inebriation of strangers, this wasn't a bad place to be doing it.

Ed had told him to show up at eleven on Saturday morning. The landlord, Tim, had been out of town all week, but he hadn't missed a Saturday night in his pub for twenty-one years. Ed had reported this fact with some amount of pride. Richard had tried not to let it depress him too much.

The front door was open when he got there, but, stepping over the threshold, he got the distinct impression that the place wasn't open yet. For one thing, half the lights were off, and the watery sunlight outside hadn't done much to penetrate the gloom within. For another, there were boxes and suitcases all over the floor, and not a single person in sight.

He hesitated in the doorway. Considered calling out, but found himself muted by some instinct or other. He took a step forward, then another, stopping to look at the boxes on the ground. A delivery, he assumed; but the boxes were all mismatched, and some were clearly falling to pieces, held together with metres of masking tape. It was more like someone moving house. But moving in? Or out?

He walked up to the bar, and leaned over to see if anyone was lurking out of sight. He realised he could hear a radio, very distant: upstairs? Only the faintest traces of it carried to the bar, disembodied voices whispering their way through the rows of waiting pint glasses. Behind the bar, deeply coloured bottles seemed to shimmer in the dark light. He caught his eye in the mirror behind the bottles, and saw a flicker of movement behind him.

''T'fuck d'you think you're doin'?'

Richard turned so fast he nearly fell. A painful jolt of adrenaline spurted outwards to his fingers and his toes; he had to gasp to keep from shouting out. 'Sorry,' he said quickly, breathlessly. 'I wasn't sure if anyone was around – '

'We open at half-past.' The man was huge, with shoulders that were roughly twice the width of his own, and the voice was somewhere between a growl and grunt. His eyes were sharp, though, glinting deep within a face which was mostly beard.

'Yes. Sorry. It's just, I was told to come here at eleven.' The man stood motionless, waiting. 'By Ed,' Richard continued, feeling smaller and more inarticulate by the second. 'He said you might have a job going?'

The man continued to watch him, silently, as if waiting for some sort of sign. Then abruptly he nodded, and thrust his hand in Richard's direction. 'Tim. Nice to meet you.'

'Richard.' They shook hands, Richard relieved to be back on familiar conversational ground.

'Have you done bar work before?'

'Yeah. Not for years, though.'

'It doesn't change much. Help me carry these upstairs?' Tim indicated the boxes on the floor.

'Uh, sure. Of course.'

Richard crouched down to lift a box, awkwardly, finding himself unable to get a proper purchase on it. For someone so large, Tim was all fluidity – he lifted two boxes in one smooth movement and was halfway up the stairs before Richard caught up with him.

The stairs were narrow, uncarpeted, and dark; they led down to the cellar as well as up to the flat above the pub, and they smelled of damp and sweat and old beer. Tim took them two at a time, negotiating the tight corners with ease while Richard struggled awkwardly behind, and they emerged into a small but brightly lit kitchen, where the radio blared invitingly. A tall red-headed woman was cleaning the window above the kitchen sink, her hair held back from her face with a green silk scarf. She turned and smiled when they entered. 'Hey, who's this?'

'This is Richard. He wants to work for us.' Tim dumped his boxes in the middle of the floor, and Richard followed suit, observing that there was ten per cent less grunt in Tim's voice when he spoke to the woman. 'Richard, this is Rosa. You might have seen her behind the bar.'

'Actually – ' Richard began, thinking to explain that he'd never actually been inside the pub before today, but Rosa interrupted him, stepping forward and holding out a translucent hand for him to shake.

'Lovely to meet you. Are you new here?'

'Sort of. My girlfriend – ' he began, and then found himself halting awkwardly, as a teenage girl shuffled into the kitchen, all ginger curls and pubescent sulkiness. She had none of Rosa's projected good nature, but nevertheless the resemblance between them was startling. She turned wide green eyes briefly in Richard's direction before dismissing him as irrelevant.

'Mum, there aren't enough plug sockets in my room.'

'I know, darling, Tim's going to find you a multi-socket thing. There should be one lying around somewhere.'

'Well, I need it now.'

'Okay, give us a few minutes, will you? We've got company.'

'But I need to straighten my hair.'

'Well, that only requires one socket, surely?'

'Yes, but *Hollyoaks* is on and I'm talking to Gina online. And I need to straighten my hair *now* because I'm meant to be meeting people in half an hour and I'm not going out like *this*.' She yanked her curls away from her face in a demonstration of their abhorrence.

'Okay, okay. Tim? Can you go see if you can find it? There's one in our room she can borrow for now if needs be.'

Tim grunted, and left the kitchen, with the miniature Rosa trailing persistently behind.

'Sorry about that. That's Ella – daughter from my previous marriage, you know – her father's being a total *arse* and buggering off to Spain for a year so she's coming to stay with us and she's not happy about it at all, as you might have noticed.' All this was divulged cheerfully, through the back of her head, as she filled the kettle with a thundering hiss. 'Tea? Coffee?'

'Er, yes. Tea would be great. Thanks.' Richard looked around for somewhere to sit down, but all the chairs were already occupied, by boxes or by haphazardly draped clothing. He leaned against the dresser instead.

'So what brings you here?' Rosa asked, darting a glance at him over her shoulder.

'My girlfriend grew up here. Her mother died a couple of months ago, so we've moved into her old house.'

'Oh, the Emmett place?'

Richard nodded, feeling slightly uncomfortable. 'Does everyone know everyone round here?'

Rosa laughed, delightedly, as she rifled through cupboards looking for tea bags. 'Well, I know more people than most. But actually I only know about the Emmetts through vague gossip. No one's lived in that house since I've lived here.'

'Yeah, it's been a while.'

'Are you doing it up? Or just in need of a change?'

Richard shrugged, not sure how much he wanted to say. 'Just a change, really. I just lost my job, and Lily's on a sabbatical from work.' He shifted awkwardly, casting about for something else to talk about. 'So this job, then. Was Ed just making it up, or do you really have a vacancy?'

She laughed. 'We really do have a vacancy. Though I'm afraid it would only be a few shifts a week. I just need someone around so I can spend some time with Ella, and Tim doesn't really want to spend more hours here than he already does.'

'Fair enough. Part-time sounds great, actually. That way I can still look after Lily.'

'Does she need you to look after her?' Rosa's question was casual, her attention directed at filling cups with boiling water, but Richard still noticed a hint of defensiveness creeping into his voice.

'She's not been well recently. Stressed out by her mother dying, I imagine. It would be good if I was around.'

'Fair enough.' Rosa placed a mug of tea in front of him. 'What's she doing while she's on sabbatical?'

'Research, I guess.' Rosa raised an eyebrow, and Richard continued, 'She's a university lecturer. They've given her some time off, you know, because of her mother.'

Rosa nodded. 'What does she lecture in?'

'Maths, unless she can avoid it.' At Rosa's quizzical look, he added, 'She doesn't really talk, most of the time.'

'She's a lecturer who doesn't speak?'

Richard laughed. 'It's not that she doesn't speak at all. More that she only speaks when she deems it necessary. Obviously, in order to carry on her research it's necessary to be a lecturer, so it's necessary to speak. But at home her conversation is mostly functional.'

'Is there any particular reason?'

Richard laughed again, uncomfortable. 'Probably too many to go into right now.'

'Sorry. I'm prying, aren't I? Tim's always telling me off for asking too many questions. I think it goes with the job.'

'Yeah, you must get a lot of drunks pouring their hearts out to you.'

'Mmm. Something like that.' She took a sip of her tea. 'Well, you've passed my initial tests. And I doubt Tim would have invited you upstairs if he wasn't in some way inclined towards giving you a job. How about we start you off with a trial shift tomorrow night?'

'Sounds great.'

'I can't promise much excitement, I'm afraid. Thursday nights are darts nights, so the place will be mostly full of bickering old men.'

'Excellent. I love darts.'

'You do?' Rosa lifted an eyebrow, sceptical.

'Sure. Throwing sharp objects at walls. What's not to love?'

They laughed. 'In that case, welcome aboard,' Rosa said with a smile, raising her mug and clinking it gently against his.

When he got home Lily was sitting on the floor of the living room, leaning her back against the sofa. The TV was on, silent pictures flickering in the corner of the room, but her gaze was directed out of the window, looking at something Richard couldn't see. 'Hey.' He dropped a kiss on the top of her head and sat down on the floor next to her. 'How's your day been?'

'Fine.'

'I got that job I was talking about.' Lily didn't move, eyes still focused on the outside world. 'I start tomorrow night. Should be okay, I think. The people seem nice. You want tea?'

Lily looked at him then, as if suddenly realising he was there. 'Please.'

He shuffled off into the kitchen, still talking, his voice trailing like a banner behind him. 'The landlord was a bit grumpy with me at first, but the landlady, Rosa, she was really friendly. Apparently she needs to cut back her hours to look after her daughter, so she wants me to do a couple of shifts a week. Could be just what we need.'

Lily could hear him moving around, filling the kettle with water, taking cups out of the cupboard. 'As you said, maybe you could come down and visit while I'm there? Getting out of the house might get your brain moving again.'

'My brain.' She said it to herself, too quiet for him to hear. He appeared in the doorway almost instantly.

'You say something?'

'Oh, just – my brain. It is moving.'

'Well, I didn't mean to imply you'd been lobotomised or anything.' He tilted his head, smiled. 'I just know you haven't been able to concentrate properly. I was wondering if it was because you're spending too much time in this house.'

'You wanted to move here.'

'I know that. I'm not criticising. I just want you to be happy. And I want you to go back to work. At some point, obviously, when you're ready.' He caught himself, babbling. Made his mouth stop.

'I'm not an invalid.'

'Sweetheart, I didn't say you were.'

'We've only been here two weeks.'

'I know, Lily. I know that.' He came and sat down next to her again. Lifted her fingers, which were clenched white-knuckled around her knees, and pulled her hand into his lap. 'I'm not trying to rush you or make you do anything you don't want to. And I think it's great for you to have some time out, some time to adjust to everything. But I worry about you being in this house.'

'You brought me here.' She looked confused. As if she couldn't work out what he was getting at.

'Yes, because I had to. Because we don't have any money and there didn't seem to be any other option and because I thought it might help. But it's not helping, is it? You were better off at home.'

Lily didn't respond. Didn't have any idea what she was supposed to say.

'I know you don't want to talk about things, and I know you don't want to make life harder for me, but if you're really unhappy here then please, please just tell me. I'll find another job; I'll do whatever I need to do to make you feel better. I just want you to be okay.'

'I am okay.' She flexed her fingers, and then pushed them through the gaps between his larger ones, until their hands became one interlinked limb.

'Really? You're not just saying that?'

'I promise.'

He smiled, and leaned over to kiss her cheek. She turned her head, and her eyelashes brushed his nose, her lips meeting his.

'You want me to tell you a story?'

Her mouth curved beneath his, and she nodded. Squeezed his palm in wordless thanks. Then closed her eyes and let his words wash over her.

then

'Before we start, there are some things I need to make you aware of.'

Lily nodded. She felt oddly exposed, sitting across from Dr Mervyn without her usual pen and paper. He had set his notebooks to one side, and there was a clear space between them, like a pitch or a playing field. The desk was smooth mahogany, so clear that Lily could see her own face reflected back at her.

'Firstly, I have spoken to your parents about the fact that we're going to be doing this, so they might ask you some questions. Please bear in mind that everything we discuss in this room is confidential, so you are under no obligation to share anything, *but* if you do want to talk to them you're very welcome to do so.'

Lily nodded again. She felt as if she was being placed under arrest and Dr Mervyn was reading her her rights.

'Secondly, because we know exactly what it is you're struggling to remember, I can be very specific in the triggers I present to you. This may be upsetting. You need to understand that I am not trying to upset you; I am only ever presenting you with information in the hope that I will be able to help you.'

He paused to allow her to nod again.

'Finally: this exercise is for your benefit, and you are here voluntarily. As such, you can stop this exercise *at any time*. If you feel upset, or in any way unnerved by anything that I show you, we can stop and you are under no obligation to start again at any point. It is absolutely essential that you understand that I'm not going to pressure you on any aspect of this, okay? If you want to stop, we stop. It's as simple as that.'

Lily nodded again. Took a deep breath. She found she was shaking slightly, and stretched out her fingers on the desk to stop them from trembling. She looked up to find Dr Mervyn looking down at her with concern.

'Are you really sure you want to do this?'

'Yes.' Her voice was a whisper.

'Absolutely? One hundred per cent?' He smiled faintly.

'Yes. Absolutely definitely.'

'Okay. So. I'm going to present you with a series of objects, one at a time. You can look at as many or as few as you like today, and you can go back to previous objects at any time, but I will only put one object on the table at a time. It's best to take things slowly with this: look at the object on the table, think about what it conjures up. You can try to connect it with what you know about what happened, or just think generally about what this object means to you. Usually I would ask you to describe for me what you see and feel, but, because speaking is not your favourite method of communication, I'm going to ask you to write it down unless you feel particularly driven to speak. Does all that make sense?'

'Uh-huh.'

'One thing I must make clear is that I would like to be able to read everything you write down, unless you specifically choose to cross it out so I can't see it.'

'Why?'

'It will help me plan future sessions,' he said simply. 'Now. I'm going to bring out the first object. Are you ready?'

Lily nodded. She realised she was holding her breath, and let it out in a rush. Dr Mervyn reached into a box under the desk and pulled out an object, which he placed on the desk between them. It was a photograph.

Lily leaned forward, looking at it closely. It was a photo of her and Connie in the garden, when they were very young, before the incident with Billy. Neither of them was looking at the camera; they were playing with something on the ground. Lily squinted, but she couldn't make out what it was. Behind them, the trees loomed, casting shadows across the grass.

'I remember,' she murmured, barely aware that she was speaking. 'Connie had this thing. A Bug Jug. She was catching insects in it.'

She stared at the photo. Remembered the feeling of jealousy, watching Connie playing with something that she wanted. And feeling terribly sorry for the bugs, trapped by the glass walls, running from side to side, encased by something they couldn't see. She had tried to join in, she remembered, and Connie had refused to let her; and then, when Mama had intervened and forced her to share, Connie had decided she was no longer interested, and left Lily alone to play by herself.

She stared. Why had her mother taken this photo? Was this an example of them playing nicely together? Lily didn't remember it as being nice, but maybe it was as good as things had got between the two of them.

Lily scribbled some words, disconnected sentences about childhood feelings. Nothing about Billy, yet. Though she could feel his presence, trapped in those trees.

'Okay. Next object.'

Dr Mervyn took away the photograph, and replaced it with a marble. Lily realised with a jolt that it was Billy's. 'Where did you...?' she began, but trailed off. It didn't matter where he'd got it from.

The marble was distinctive: green glass, with a perfect yellow orb in the middle of it. Lily had never seen another one like it – would have known it anywhere. She remembered lying on her stomach in the grass, the sun warming the soles of her bare feet, and Billy's face right in front of her. There had been a gap between them, she knew, but in her memory they were nose to nose; she could feel his laughter as if it were her own. They'd been rolling the marble back and forth for hours, it seemed, watching it glide through the grass between them. Connie on the sidelines, grumbling; left out. And Billy, pleading with her: 'She hasn't got anyone her own age, Connie, can't you just be nice to her?'

'She's got plenty of things of her own; she just always wants to steal *mine*...'

Lily scribbled down the memory. It had been, what? Six months before he died? No, because it had been summer, the sun so hot it had felt as though it was falling out of the sky, and he had died in September... So it couldn't have been more than two months before the end.

What had they done, that summer, except lie in the grass and eat ice cream and play marbles?

And what had Connie done, except sulk and complain and shoo Lily away?

Lost in thought, she barely noticed what she was doing as she gestured for Dr Mervyn to remove the marble, replace it with something else. She looked away; stared out of the window, at the pools of afternoon light that lapped at the grass outside. She could feel exactly what it would be like to lie on that grass. The same as lying on her own lawn, back then. The slight dampness, the springiness of the grass beneath her limbs.

The smoothness of the strands between her fingers.

She looked back at the table, at the next object. And found herself staring straight at Billy.

Lily was shaking when she left Dr Mervyn's office. Billy's face was imprinted on the inside of her eyelids; if she closed her eyes, he was right there, in her head. She balled her fists into her eye sockets, trying to scrub him out, but it just seemed to push him further in.

She walked without thinking where she was going; she didn't return to class. Down the corridors with their black and white checks, which she found herself counting almost without thinking. All the doors were closed, no one was around, and the corridor felt too wide, too high, and she was just a tiny speck in a sea of tiles and fluorescent strip lights. The veins in her forehead thumped against her skin and made her dizzy.

She hadn't said anything. She felt guilty that she hadn't said anything. Or even written anything down. But the sight of his face... She should have been expecting it. Should have known that among a list of objects that might remind her of that night would be Billy: his face, or his name, or his belongings.

But it wasn't that night she was remembering. It was just him.

She hadn't even realised she'd forgotten him. You noticed when people first died. She'd never spoken about it, of course, never had any way of communicating it to anyone, but she'd thought about him every day for months. For years. During all her time at the institute he had been with her, her big sister's best friend, her older brother, the first boy she'd ever loved. He'd been her silent companion, and she'd been silent with him, and in that way they'd been together, somehow. And she hadn't noticed when she'd started being silent by herself; that was just the way it was.

How would you notice the absence of a thought? It was only when you thought of it again, and suddenly realised, it'd been weeks since you'd thought of him. Months. When did he become part of your past, rather than your every day?

When did he stop occupying every waking minute?

It was a shock when you realised that people were right: that time did heal all wounds. That you did move on, eventually.

And it was even more of a shock when you realised later that you never really had.

When she got to the bus stop Connie was already there, staring in the other direction. Lily sat down beside her. Connie looked down, surprised, and then shifted slightly, in acknowledgement. 'Shouldn't you be in class?' she asked.

'Shouldn't you?' Lily retorted. Connie smiled.

They sat quietly for a while, watching the traffic roll past. It wasn't a busy road, most of the time, and there weren't that many cars. There were trees on the other side, behind a fence: the back border of the private boys' school. The trees were thick enough to obscure the building entirely.

'Did you see Dr Mervyn today?'

Lily looked up, surprised. 'How did you know?'

'Dad mentioned it. He wanted to know if I still had any of Billy's stuff. He said you were trying something out.' A pause. 'He said it might upset you.'

Lily nodded. There was a trail of ants on the ground, picking their way across the concrete in an awkward line, and she watched their progress without really seeing what they were doing.

'Did it? Upset you?'

Lily shrugged. 'I guess.'

'Well, you left school early. You don't usually do that, right?' Connie looked down at her, scrutinising her. 'Or are you secretly as bad as me?'

'No.'

'So it did upset you.'

'He showed me a photograph of Billy.'

Connie's face became strangely expressionless. Almost as if someone had momentarily immobilised all her features. 'Oh.'

'I'd forgotten his face.'

Connie nodded, slowly. 'Yeah. That happens.' She had tried to sound blasé, as if it didn't really matter, but her voice caught and she looked away.

'Do you still miss him?'

There was a long pause before Connie answered. Lily noticed the ants had picked up a crumb of biscuit and were carrying it between four of them like a palanquin.

'Yeah,' Connie said eventually. 'Yeah, I still miss him.'

The bus turned up, and they got on, sitting at opposite ends of the back seat so they could stretch their legs out into the middle. Halfway through the journey they shifted so that they were sitting side by side, and Connie lifted her arm so that Lily could lean into her, and gripped her sister's thin shoulder in her white-knuckled fingers all the way home.

When they got back their father was out, but Anna was in the kitchen, propping up a newspaper at the table. She looked up as they came in. 'You girls are back early.'

'There was a fire alarm. It wouldn't stop going off, so they sent us home.' Connie's lie was so smooth Lily could almost hear the ringing of bells, the inward shrug of the teachers as they resigned themselves to the inevitable and let them all leave.

'Oh.' Their mother's interest was more fleeting than a butterfly, and she disappeared back behind her newspaper. Connie and Lily made their way upstairs.

'Have you seen any of Mama's photos?' Connie's whisper trailed up the stairs after Lily.

'No.'

'Come with me.'

Connie grabbed her by the hand and led her into their parents' room. It was dimly lit; the sun set on the opposite side of the house, and this side was always gloomy in the afternoons, shadows stretching out from corners and creeping from under furniture. Connie didn't switch on the light, though. They tiptoed across the room, instinctively imitating the silence of the house, and Connie eased open the wardrobe door, and stood on tiptoe to reach the top shelf. She pulled out a shoebox.

'Come on. My room.'

They slipped back out of the room, into Connie's room, and closed the door behind them. Connie flicked on the radio, and a warm chattering filled the silence. Lily felt properly calm for the first time since she'd left Dr Mervyn's office.

'Mama thinks I don't know about these,' Connie said, her voice almost a normal pitch now, knowing Anna wouldn't hear them above the radio. 'I found them when you were away. She hid everything, you know. Our entire childhood.'

Lily, who still had part of her childhood tucked away at their grandparents' house, said nothing.

'Anyway, she went out one day and she'd left them on the bed. So I went through them. There aren't loads – well, you know, she wasn't ever that much of a mother – but there are – well, have a look.'

Connie pulled off the lid, and revealed a stack of maybe a hundred photographs.

Resting on the top was a photo of the four of them: father, mother, two daughters. Connie a toddler, chubby and round but standing proudly upright; Lily just born, swathed in blankets, clutched in her mother's arms. Anna looking more peaceful than Lily had ever seen her, and their father, smiling, arm slung casually around her shoulders.

It looked like someone else's family. Lily was fascinated.

She lifted the picture, and found another, and another; year after year of them growing older, becoming different people. In different poses: at the park, at their grandparents' house, at Christmas, on Lily's birthday. Connie wrapping herself in tinsel, grinning with no front teeth. Lily covered head to toe in flour, wielding a rolling pin. Snapshots of a childhood Lily could barely remember; certainly not one she would imagine had looked so happy, so varied.

And then came the shots with Billy. Connie and Billy on the swings at the park; Lily standing at the side, looking on, trying to join in. Then Lily on the swing, and both of them trying to push her. Lily sitting between Billy's legs, going down the slide. The three of them in the paddling pool in the garden. Lily standing over them, waving her arms, directing the action. Then building the swing in the garden. Billy's father sawing the wood for them. Their own father, tying the rope to the tree.

So straightforwardly, easily happy.

And their mother off-camera, framing their childhood from behind the lens.

'Do you remember this?' Connie said, holding different photos under Lily's nose. 'What about this? And this?'

And each time, Lily nodded. *Yes. Yes, I remember that.*

Somehow, when it was Connie holding out the photos, it didn't seem to hurt nearly as much.

now

It was just after twelve, and the coffee shop was almost deserted – just one elderly man in the corner, propped up behind a newspaper, and a youngish guy with long hair and glasses that were too big for his face, stirring sugar into his coffee so violently that drops of coffee were flicking over the table in all directions. Nathan chose a table near the back of the room, with a clear view of the door. He was five minutes late, but obviously not quite late enough to be fashionable.

The waitress ambled over, took his order without much interest. Nathan sat back and watched the people walk past outside. The street, which would have been bristling with people an hour ago, was now virtually deserted. A mother with her toddler stopped outside the window, peering at the menu, but walked on a moment later, obviously not finding what she was looking for. Two teenage girls in school uniform came in and took a table in the corner, looking furtively around them, making sure there was no one there who might recognise them. The waitress deposited Nathan's coffee in front of him and then went to greet the teenagers; Nathan guessed from the way she spoke to them that they were regulars.

Andrea appeared a minute later. She was talking on her phone, visibly harassed, but still uncomfortably beautiful. Nathan tried not to notice the way her hair seemed to glow in the light from the window.

She finished her conversation as she sat down opposite him, muttering, 'Uh-huh, yep, I'll call you back, okay? Bye, then.' She snapped the phone shut, and placed it on the table in front of her. 'Sorry,' she said, smiling at him. He wondered when Connie had last smiled at him like that: as if she were actually happy to see him. Then dismissed the thought as childish.

'No problem,' he said easily. 'Coffee?'

'I'll have a tea, actually, if you don't mind.' The waitress appeared and took Andrea's order, and then disappeared, leaving silence in her wake. Nathan took a sip of his coffee; it was too hot, scalding his tongue and making him wince.

'So,' Andrea said eventually. 'You rang?'

'Well, you suggested meeting for coffee,' he replied, grinning half-heartedly.

'Forgive me for saying it, but I got the impression this might be more than just a casual get-together.'

'Why do you say that?'

'Well, for a start, you asked me to meet you on a day when we're both supposed to be at work.' She looked at him shrewdly. 'I guess you're supposed to be doing house calls?'

'Mrs Mitchell's very ill,' he said gravely. 'She needed my immediate attention.'

'You should probably go and see her, then.'

'She also has Alzheimer's. She won't remember that she called, so I've got at least an hour, I'd say.'

Andrea shook her head, smiling despite herself. 'You're terrible.'

'Not really. I'll drop round on my way back. She calls about once a fortnight, and she's always surprised when I turn up.'

'Does she have any family?'

He shook his head. The waitress appeared, set Andrea's tea down in front of her, and vanished again.

'So what's so urgent, then?'

Nathan shrugged. Now that he was here he felt faintly ridiculous. 'I suppose I just wanted to talk.'

'To someone who's not your wife?'

He shrugged again. Nodded. 'Yeah, that's pretty much it.'

Andrea looked at him steadily, sizing him up. 'Do you want to have an affair?'

He laughed. 'God, you really are blunt, aren't you?'

'I don't see the point in beating around the bush. If that's what you're here for, I'd like to know sooner rather than later. Also, I'm not a marriage counselling service.'

'Do you think that's what I want from you?'

'Well, it's an odd time of day for an affair.' She smirked. 'Unless you were planning on blowing off Mrs Mitchell altogether, of course.'

'I don't think I want an affair. I also don't think I want marriage counselling.'

'Well, then, I'm at a bit of a loss as to what I'm doing here.'

'Hmm.' He leaned forward slightly, resting his elbows on the table, cradling his coffee between the palms of his hands. 'To be honest, I think I just wanted a friend.'

'Am I not a bit of an odd choice for a friend? I mean, you can't exactly go home and tell your wife, *Hey, I made this awesome new friend today*, can you?'

He laughed. 'That's kind of the point, I suppose. I don't want to have to tell Connie about you.'

'So you want to have an affair without actually having an affair?'

'Can you stop making me sound so sordid?' He was annoyed, and it made her laugh.

'Sorry. But isn't it kind of like you just want to have a secret? Something that makes you feel better when you're fighting with her?'

'It's not just that.' He sat back from the table, irritated. 'I also like you.'

She softened slightly. 'I know. But that doesn't mean we can be friends.'

'Why not?'

'Because. Because I'm single and female and you find me attractive. Or at least, you have done at some point. What if she found out about me – what would you say? *Oh yeah, that's my friend, I met her when I went back to hers after a party one night?*'

'That's not – it's not like that.'

'It's like that a bit.'

'Stop being difficult.' He glared at her for a moment, and then they both laughed. 'See, I like you because you make me laugh. Because you don't – I don't know, scowl at me every time I walk into the room. Is it really that wrong of me, to want to spend some time with someone who treats me like a human being?'

'No, I suppose not.' She sipped her tea, thoughtful. 'Are things really that bad?'

He shrugged. 'I don't know. We just don't seem to communicate at the moment. I have no idea what she's thinking any more. But you probably don't want to hear about it.'

'Not particularly,' she admitted. 'But it sounds like you need to talk about it.'

'Can we have dinner one night this week?'

She laughed. 'Will you tell your wife where you're going?'

'Sure. Dinner with a colleague. That's what we are, aren't we?'

She laughed again and shook her head. Stood up, leaving her tea on the table, half-drunk. Dropped a kiss on his forehead, and left without another word.

He sank back into his chair and watched her go.

then

'Sir, Cassie's away.' Eleanor's voice carried across the gymnasium.

'I'd noticed.' Mr Bentham, busy digging out enough footballs for all the boys to have something to dribble with, was monumentally unconcerned with how many girls might be bunking off PE to spend time with their boyfriends and/or smoking behind the bike sheds.

'That means we've only got one midfielder.'

'Isn't there anyone else who can step in?'

'The only other girl is Connie.'

Eleanor, eyes wide, the picture of innocence, her dark ponytail bobbing childishly with every movement of her head. And yet, there was something distinctly un-childish in the cling of her hockey shirt, the way her skirt flounced when she walked.

Connie had claimed an overwhelming love of football early on in the term, the instant she'd realised that playing hockey would mean being out on the field with twenty-one girls hell-bent on hurting her and no adult supervision. Mr Bentham, keen to demonstrate his lack of sexism, had positively welcomed her into the fold. Fortunately she had proven to be relatively skilled and had therefore been allowed to carry on playing football with the boys.

This was different, though. Boys couldn't be made to play hockey when there was a girl available to step in.

'Connie!'

She had been watching the exchange from twenty feet away, and knew it was pointless to argue. If Mr Bentham got wind of the fact that she didn't want to join in with the other girls, he would more than likely force her to do it every week to teach her the value of teamwork. 'Yes, sir.'

'There's a space on the hockey team that needs to be filled.'

'Yes, sir.'

She followed Eleanor's ponytail as it bounced its way on to the playing fields.

Connie pulled on her bib, and joined the ranks of reluctant players. There were perhaps six of them – Eleanor, of course, and her closest allies – who actually enjoyed spending their time in this way. Everyone else did it under duress, though there were the odd one or two who actually might have enjoyed the game, in more cheerful circumstances.

Eleanor, as team captain, called the shots. Connie obeyed the sound of her whistle, breaking into a light jog where necessary, trying not to involve herself in any actual running. The air was freezing, making the back of her throat ache. What had been a light drizzle for most of the afternoon became heavier spots of rain – not enough of a downpour to call them inside, but enough to cause damp clothing to cling uncomfortably. Wherever sticks hit the grass there were showers of cold mud; some, inevitably, were deliberately aimed in Connie's direction. Within five minutes she was soaked, and counting down the seconds until the end of the lesson.

Across the fields, the windows of the school buildings glowed invitingly: people learning lessons more valuable than how to keep yourself upright when the world was conspiring to make you fall over. Somewhere in there, Lily was in a classroom, surrounded by people who were mostly indifferent towards her, and teachers who would step in to protect her. Connie felt searing jealousy, tinged with a certain relief.

'Connie! Get back in formation!' The shrill of the whistle punctuated Eleanor's words, and Connie pulled herself back to the game. Tried to find the ball in the semi-darkness, but all she could see were indeterminate shapes, with curved stick appendages. She jogged in the direction of the others, trying to give the impression of purposefulness.

The rain grew heavier, until it was a steady downpour, the clouds thickening into darkness. More lights flickered on across the field; teachers giving up any pretence that it was still daylight outside. Connie tried to stay attached to the game, but she seemed to float alongside it, unable to find a purchase. She could follow the movement but not the purpose, as if she'd forgotten how to play.

'That's it, ladies!'

The voice of Mr Bentham carried easily across the field, though he was barely visible in the distance, a mere shadow against the looming background of the school buildings. Eleanor blew her whistle – always had to have the last word – and, in one movement, twenty-two sticks dropped loosely to the side, and the girls began trudging back towards the school. Connie fell behind, not wanting to be too close. Not realising that Eleanor was behind her.

The first blow was so hard and so sudden she didn't even manage to formulate a cry in response, just a shuddered gasp as she dropped to her knees. The second caught her on the nose, releasing a torrent of blood on to the wet mud beneath. She fell to all fours, choking on shock.

The third blow was an explosion of stars. They pulled her roughly on to her side, to ensure she didn't choke on her own blood; then left her unconscious in the darkness.

By the time she came to, the moon was high in the sky, and the school buildings were locked, so she couldn't retrieve her belongings. She walked home in a daze, covered in blood and mud, her face already uncomfortably swollen. She concocted elaborate stories as she walked; stories which didn't involve other people.

As it turned out, she didn't need them. Her parents were waiting in the kitchen when she got home, impatient, anxious – a parental unit such as she wasn't sure she'd ever seen before. It threw her off guard. And confused her: how late was she, for them to look so worried?

She understood a moment later. In the split second between the time it took for them to register her face, exhibit their shock and swallow it: and for them to look behind her, for the younger sister who also hadn't returned home when she should have done.

now

Richard was at work, and Lily was in her childhood bedroom, which she had transformed into an office over the course of the morning. It didn't look very different from how it had done when they'd first arrived – still the same undersized furniture, the same crawling green wallpaper – but she had rearranged the furniture, clearing a space on the floor big enough to spread out all her notes. She had never been able to work with traditional filing systems, preferring to spread everything out around her so it was easily accessible, but sharing an office had made that a less than viable option, and Richard wouldn't have appreciated her doing it in the flat. For the first time since they'd arrived, she could see that there might be some benefit to living here; could imagine learning to work in this space.

If she stood at the window she could see the garden, with the woods stretching out behind it, but she found she didn't mind so much from up here. She could also see into the neighbouring garden, and it was a comfort to see people pottering around – a young couple, probably the same age as her and Richard, and their toddler. She had never spoken to them. She wondered whether Richard had.

They were out there now, or at least the mother and the toddler were. The mother hung out washing while the toddler dug around in the flowerbed. Every now and then she would pull out something which was unmistakably a worm, and bring it to her mother, her face proud and excited. Her mother's cry of 'No, Miriam, you *mustn't*,' carried clearly through Lily's open window and made her smile.

She could feel fragments of less unpleasant childhood memories creeping up on her. Things that usually got suppressed along with everything else, because they all blurred into one, became interchangeable. But there were good things, she knew. Like the swing she and Connie had built for one of the trees – just a plank of wood and some rope, long since rotted away, but still. It had kept them occupied for an afternoon. She remembered finding the wood, their father helping them tie it to a branch. Billy had been there, and his father. Lily could remember swinging out over them all as they sat in the garden, the swooping in her stomach as she reached the top of the swing's upward curve, and everything ahead of her just feet and sky.

Billy and his father had been around a lot. She could remember them all spending time together in the garden, having barbecues, playing games. Could hear snatches of shouted conversations. See Connie's face, ducking behind trees. Billy's chin, resting on his elbows as they lay next to each other on the grass. Her mother's face, laughing: different.

The garden had been the most peaceful place in the world, then.

She watched her neighbours playing and thought that maybe nothing had really changed.

She spent a couple of hours steadily working, only occasionally distracted by noises from outside. It was easier up here in her old room; the noises were further away and she didn't feel obliged to pay attention to them. Her childhood desk had proved too small and she was sitting on her floor, back to the window, facing the door, which was slightly ajar; she could see the hallway, dim because all the other doors were closed and no sunlight touched it. Shadows flickered there occasionally, but they were harmless and she tried not to notice them.

She had arranged her paperwork around her, in her preferred fashion – books to the left, then stacks of notes on her own ideas, then stacks of notes on other people's ideas. She had been sifting through, trying to bring herself up to date with what she had been working on a few weeks ago. Marianna had forwarded her some photocopies of recent journal articles – things that she'd noticed and thought would fit in with Lily's research – and Lily had been scanning them, picking out the ones that seemed useful, putting the others aside for future reference. She had found herself wondering for the first time who was teaching her classes, how the students were getting on in her absence. The undergraduates would be fine, of course, but she felt guilty about the PhD students. She was supposed to be looking after them. She wondered whether she should email them, let them know she was still around, if they needed her. Though of course she wasn't, not really. And was she allowed to be in touch, if she'd been removed from the university? Wouldn't they all have found new supervisors, ones who weren't liable to collapse at a moment's notice?

She couldn't help feeling that being cut off from the academic world was causing more problems than it was solving. Though it was nice to have the space to get some work done. Some real work, without all the lecturing and marking getting in the way.

The phone rang downstairs. She could hear it, but it sounded distant, other-worldly. Maybe it was next door's phone? But no, it was definitely the sound that their phone made – the same one that had been there when she was a child, with its round dial and clumsy handset. A shrill, impatient ring, quite unlike any modern phone. It was a sign of how little contact her mother had had with the outside world that she'd never bothered to update it.

She considered getting up to answer it. But then the ringing subsided, and she inwardly shrugged, and settled herself back on to the floor. She couldn't think of anyone she would want to talk to anyway. People who knew her would ring her on her mobile.

Someone was shouting outside. It was the neighbours again, now having some sort of argument. Lily could hear the child crying, the mother scolding her. Amazing how quickly games could turn sour.

She resisted the urge to go and watch them from the window. Picked up another journal article, scanning the opening paragraph for hints that it might be useful to her. She could only pick out a couple of words before the shouting distracted her. She put down the article, got up and went to the window, irritated with herself for being unable to resist her curiosity.

The daughter was kneeling on the ground in tears. Her mother stood over her, fist raised. For a moment Lily was worried, and then she realised the fist was clutching a worm; the daughter's kneeling was pleading, rather than afraid. 'Don't hurt Wormy,' she screamed, screwing up her face until her bright red cheeks looked as though they might burst.

The mother's response was quieter, and Lily couldn't hear it from so far away. Nevertheless she pushed herself forward, pressing her nose to the glass, trying to hear what they were saying.

And saw a flicker in her own garden, just out of her range of vision.

She flinched, drew back instinctively; then gathered herself, leaned forward. The flicker had been over to the far right, on the patio, near the doors. If she pressed the left side of her face right to the glass she could see the whole patio, but there was nothing there, just a pool of weak sunlight blinking through the trees.

The phone rang again and she pulled herself away from the window, the cries of the child outside dying away as she stepped out of her room and into the hallway. She felt more than saw her way down the stairs, edging through the gloom towards the phone. The sound stopped when she was two steps into the kitchen, leaving a thumping silence in its wake.

The room was so still she could hear the dust move.

And then ghost-Connie was at her feet, as if she'd been there all along.

She looked different this time: less of a flicker, more like a real child. She was still pale and ethereal, but there was a solidity to her centre, just blurring at the edges when she moved. Lily crouched down, to look at her more closely, expecting her to vanish. Instead she giggled, and moved nearer to the patio doors.

Lily stood up and followed, tentatively, inching forward step by step. A flicker on the other side of the glass made her flinch, but it was just ghost-Lily, come to join her sister. The two girls stood for a moment on opposite sides of the glass, hands pressed together through the panes. Then Lily opened the door and ghost-Connie went bounding out onto the lawn, her younger shadow just a blur in her wake.

Lily took a step outside, trying to shake her sense of unease. The quiet conviction that she had seen something more substantial than the shiverings of her own mind.

Took another step, and another, confidence growing as the ghost-children beckoned her forwards.

And then another flicker, to her right: too tall to be a child.

Bit back a scream, seeing the man striding towards her across the lawn.

then

It was dark where Lily was.

She'd lost track of how much time had passed. At first she'd been concentrating on keeping as quiet as possible – they'd told her she had to stay quiet, otherwise they'd come back and shut her up for good. They were bluffing, of course. But that didn't mean they weren't capable of hurting her.

After a while the noises outside had faded, and she'd deduced that most of the people in the building had gone home. She'd tried banging on the door and calling out a few times, thinking that maybe there would be cleaners around. But there had been no answering noise. No squeak of rubber shoes on plastic floors. Everyone was gone.

Just her, for miles.

The darkness was absolute. She held a hand out in front of her face, experimentally. Nothing. Not even shadow superimposed on shadow. All she could see were odd white flashes if she closed her eyes, and then of course she wasn't really *seeing*, because her eyes were shut.

At least if she couldn't see then neither could anything else.

She pushed herself further into the corner she'd chosen as her area of refuge, and pulled her knees up to her chest. She knew there was nothing *in here*, at least. She'd seen it when they pushed her in, for a start. And also she'd had a quick grope around, once she'd had a minute to get her bearings. She was in a cupboard of shelves, in the space between the floor and the lowest shelf. If she sat up straight her head rested against wood. There wasn't enough space for anything to be in there with her – if she stretched out her legs she could touch the opposite wall.

It was just a cupboard.

It probably wasn't even locked, but, because the shelves went right up to the door, and the door handle was higher than the bottom shelf, she couldn't get to it to let herself out. Badly designed, really.

The silence was scaring her. She could sense the emptiness of the whole building, settling around her. Three floors above, at least one below. Corridors stretching out in every direction. Sleeping classrooms. Curtainless windows, looking at nothingness, both inside and out.

The figments of her imagination, unfurling to fill the empty space.

She had been in the maths department when they'd found her. She often stayed behind for a few minutes after class – Ms Beecham liked to recommend exercises for her to do at home. She already referred to Lily as her 'star pupil', though not in front of other people.

The department had been quiet when Lily left the classroom, so they hadn't had difficulty cornering her. One girl in front, hand clamped over Lily's mouth. One girl behind, arm around her waist, pinning her hands to her side. Pulling her by the hair with the other hand. Lily, too disoriented to even try to scream, had weakly followed.

They'd pushed her into the cupboard, kicking her to make sure she didn't try to escape. By chance they'd got her face; she could still feel the ache in her jaw. Invisible bruises blooming in the dark.

Then they had slammed the door shut and left her.

She wondered if she'd still be here in the morning. She was hungry, and she needed the toilet. She didn't know how much longer she could sit here, expecting someone to turn up any second. It was clear there was no one nearby. She would have been able to hear them.

It got harder to breathe the more she thought about it. The closeness of the space. If she stretched out her hands and feet she could touch all four walls without difficulty. Sitting up straight only reminded her that there was no room overhead.

There was an agitation in her limbs. As if her bones were itching. Her muscles made cramping protests. She wriggled, raising her feet higher on the wall, until she could almost stretch her legs out properly. But it wasn't enough. She could still touch the walls. It was as though the darkness *was* the walls. Or as though the two had combined to become one solid, suffocating blanket.

She wanted out.

Reluctantly, humiliatingly, she succumbed to the fact that no one was coming to find her. Felt the damp warmth spread beneath her, and wondered where on earth Connie was.

'Tell us again.'

'Mama, there's nothing else to tell. I think we should look for her. Or call the police.'

'I'll do that.' Marcus stood up, uncurling himself in a movement which appeared to take all his energy. 'Tell your mother again what happened.'

'Dad, I'm not going to sit here all night waiting for the police to show up.'

'You're not going out there again by yourself.'

'Well, bloody hurry up and come with me, then.'

'Connie – '

'Marcus, she's right.' Anna's voice was quiet, but strong. 'Lily could be seriously hurt. Those girls knocked Connie unconscious; God knows what state Lily's in. I want to go and find her.'

Across the table, Connie's eyes met her mother's. For the first time in years, she felt something pass between them. The realisation that she was indeed her mother's daughter.

'We should call the police too, though. It can't hurt to have more people looking.'

'Quick, then.'

Marcus left the room. Anna stood up, walked to the sink. Opened the cupboard underneath and pulled out a clean cloth. She ran it under the tap, wrung it out until it no longer dripped. Then crossed the room to crouch down next to her daughter and gently wipe the blood from her face, as if she were a six-year-old. 'How long has this been going on?' she asked, the steel in her voice in sharp contrast to the gentleness of her movements.

'Forever.' Connie winced, and tried not to flinch away from her mother's touch. 'You must have known.'

'It may have escaped your notice, but I've not been the most attendant of mothers.'

'Even you couldn't have paid that little attention. We're still your children.'

Anna said nothing for a moment. She pushed Connie's hair away from her face and tucked it behind her ears, stroked her cheek. But Connie turned her head away.

'I didn't stop loving you.' Anna's voice was sad, but not pleading.

'Right. So you – what, just couldn't summon the energy to look after us?'

'Something like that, yes. You might understand one day.'

'I fucking hope I never do.' Connie stood up so fast her chair fell over, but she made no move to pick it up. She was shaking, though whether from rage or exhaustion she wasn't really sure.

'You're being childish.'

'Yes. I'm still a child, in fact. You haven't been absent for *that* long. Yet.'

'You're fifteen.'

'Oh, you kept count?'

'Don't make this out to be my fault – '

'You were all about the apologies a minute ago. Now nothing's your fault again? You're a fucking joke.'

'You've got a mouth like a sewer.'

'And whose *fucking* fault do you think that is?' Connie couldn't remember ever having been so angry. Tears burned at the corners of her eyes, her lip trembled, her jaw ached from clenching it so tightly. White-knuckled, with half-moon cuts on her palms.

And her father in the doorway, his disappointment dousing the room like cold water.

'Is this really the time?' he asked, his voice quiet but carrying like a stage whisper.

Connie looked from one of them to the other, and walked out of the kitchen. Stormed out of the house, slamming the front door so hard that she heard one of the tiny glass panes fall from its frame and splinter on the concrete below. She didn't turn around.

now

Connie had assumed that things would be simpler, with Lily living further away. In some ways they were: she didn't feel a constant obligation to pick up the phone and check how her sister was getting on. She wasn't arranging clandestine meetings with Richard to sort things out. Although her concern for Lily was a constant prickling in the back of her mind, it was no longer her responsibility. There was nothing she could do, and she just had to accept that.

But, if she wasn't focused on Lily, then there was nothing to focus on but herself.

Life, it seemed, operated around her, virtually without her input. She'd never noticed it before. She was a good mother, of course: she participated, she picked the boys up from school, she played with them, she helped with their homework. She arranged activities and cooked nutritious dinners. But it was as if she just slotted into a prearranged set-up, without really having to think about it, all the important decisions having been made earlier, at a point when she had been in some way useful.

She couldn't put her finger on what it was that made her feel this way. Nathan earned all the money, yes, but he always had. He paid the bills; he kept their lives running, essentially. The logistics of their life went on behind her back, out of sight, and that made her feel in some way childlike. But it had to be more than that. More than just a lack of control over her financial situation.

Perhaps it was the fact that he got the boys up in the morning. That, if she chose – and these days, it seemed, she often did – she could lie in bed all day and no one would notice, as long as a certain amount of washing was done and food for dinner had been purchased. The fact that dust was gathering like clouds before a storm and she hadn't hoovered for six weeks and the plants hadn't been watered seemed immaterial to the running of the household.

Connie, in fact, seemed immaterial to the running of the household.

The only times she felt as though she truly mattered were weekends. When there wasn't a set schedule; when she could do something with the boys that wasn't just picking them up from school or dropping them off at whatever activity they were supposed to attend that night. The rest of the time she merely existed, floating from room to room, trying to find some place for herself in a life which seemed to regard her as largely useless.

She didn't know whether it was the sudden removal of responsibility for her mother, or for Lily, or whether it was the distance between her and Nathan – the feeling that he was operating in a space that was separate from hers. It could even just be that the boys were growing up. But, whatever it was, she couldn't continue like this forever, barely existing.

She needed a purpose.

She was wandering half-aimlessly through Sainsbury's – she knew that she needed to buy something for dinner, but not what she wanted or which aisle she might find it in – when her mobile began to ring. The number was unknown, but that didn't mean much – most of her phone calls came from school, or Nathan's work, or random businesses trying to sell her things; the numbers were almost always blocked.

'Hello?'

'Yes, hello. Is that Constance Emmett?'

'Not for a few years,' she laughed, 'but yes, that was me. Who am I speaking to?'

'My name's Lewis and I work at Farnworth Manor Hospital. We have your sister here with us?'

Connie felt her blood turn to ice, at the same moment that she wondered why on earth he was posing the sentence as a question. 'Lily?'

'Yes. We have two contacts here, you and a, er, Richard Hargrove?'

'That's right, yes. What's happened to her?'

'Well, we've been trying to contact Mr Hargrove, but we can't seem to get through to him – '

'I'll contact Richard,' Connie said, firmly, her voice considerably calmer than her hands, which had begun to tremble. 'What's wrong with Lily?'

'First of all, she's in a stable condition, so please don't panic. We're not too sure what happened. It seems she's had a fall and hit her head. If you could come to the hospital – '

'I'll be there as soon as I can.' Connie hung up the phone on the middle of his sentence, picked up her bag, and abandoned her trolley in the middle of the aisle, causing an old woman to shoot her a dirty look. Connie, momentarily forgetting that she was now a mother in her thirties who wore sensible shoes and obeyed *No Smoking* signs, took great pleasure in giving her the finger as she marched past.

Connie followed the signs for the ICU, and emerged from the lift into a wide corridor lined with individual rooms. The nurses' station was at the end of the corridor, and bustling with activity. One of the nurses led her to Lily's room, where an almost unrecognisable shape lay, swathed in blankets and bandages, hooked up to machines which Connie couldn't identify. A doctor, in his thirties with a pale smattering of ginger hair, came by a short while later.

'She had a nasty fall,' he explained, 'but actually she's been extremely lucky. She's sprained her wrist, so we've bandaged it up for the time being, and there's some bruising, but we've given her a CT scan and there doesn't seem to be any damage from hitting her head. We've not yet seen any signs of her waking up, but that's nothing to worry about at this stage.'

'And what if she doesn't wake up?' Connie asked, her eyes not leaving the unconscious figure in the bed.

'That's extremely unlikely,' the doctor said, smiling his most reassuring smile – which Connie found more patronising than reassuring – and moving on to his next patient.

A welter of bruises darkened Lily's forehead and left cheekbone. Her left wrist was swathed in bandages and the visible part of her hand was swollen and unrecognisable. Wires connected her to machines that monitored her heart rate and brainwaves, and, whatever the doctor said, this seemed much more serious than any time she had collapsed before. She'd never been unconscious for more than five minutes.

'Hey, Lils,' Connie murmured, lowering herself into the chair next to her sister, and pushing her fingers inside the curled fist of Lily's right hand. 'What are you sleeping for, huh?' She squeezed her hand, hopefully, but there was no corresponding pressure.

She wondered where Richard was. Whether she should call him again. She'd left two messages on his answerphone on the way here and it seemed pointless to leave a third, but she couldn't imagine where he could be that would prevent him from picking up his voicemail. Especially now, so soon after Lily's last collapse. Wasn't he on permanent standby? Weren't they all? She wondered fleetingly if he was ignoring his phone because he'd gone somewhere he shouldn't have. Was Richard capable of cheating? It seemed unlikely. As far as Connie knew – and she thought she knew better than anyone else – Richard's entire life revolved around Lily.

But, if that was the case, then where was he now?

Connie chewed on her lip, debating what to do. Her instinct was to find Richard and bring him here to her sister. But then there was the chance that Lily would wake up and find neither of them here. That would be unacceptable.

After a moment's thought, Connie rang Nathan and asked him to pick the boys up from school. Then she settled more comfortably into the chair, to wait for her sister to wake up.

It was Richard's third shift at work, and he was getting used to the rhythms of the place. Rosa seemed to expect very little of him, and so he was generally free to chat to the regulars, do the crossword, ease himself into village life. Rosa kept him entertained with stories of her daughter's misdemeanours while he picked apart cryptic clues absent-mindedly, his mind tripping over hidden meanings as she talked.

He'd left his phone at home, something he hadn't realised until he was halfway to work, and although a vague worry was nagging at him – what if something happened and he couldn't be reached? – there was also a part of him that was enjoying the relative freedom.

Ed had been in earlier, to see Tim and Rosa and to check how Richard was getting on. 'I suppose I could stop for one,' he'd said with an easy smile, when Richard had waved a pint glass at him. 'Mine's an Abbot, thanks.'

'So I thought I'd have seen you around before this?' Richard had said, hoping he didn't sound accusatory.

'Yes, sorry about that. I meant to come in and have a word, talk you up, you know. But it's been a hectic couple of weeks. Haven't known whether I'm coming or going, really. How are you getting on here? Settling in okay?'

'Yeah, actually. It's been good. I've been making friends.'

'With Rosa, right?' Ed had laughed easily. 'She's the only friend anyone needs in this place. Keeps the whole village going, if you ask me. And how's that girlfriend of yours getting on?'

'Oh, you know.' Richard had shrugged, smiled half-heartedly. 'She's doing okay, I think. Spends most of her time at home.'

'Alone?'

'Yeah. Well, when I'm not there. She's doing a lot of work, I think.'

Ed's smile was sympathetic, though Richard hadn't been trying to invite sympathy. 'Is she there now?'

'Yeah.'

'And where's that sister of hers? Does she come to visit?'

'Not yet, but I'm sure she'll turn up soon enough.'

Richard was grateful when Rosa came over to talk to them, deflecting the conversation away from his personal life, and Ed had left shortly afterwards. Richard had been scanning the headlines of the paper ever since. He was fascinated by local newspapers, by the things they considered to be news. *Man Feeds Pet Chicken to Dogs. Locals Outraged by Trolley Debacle.*

At four o'clock the pub closed for a couple of hours – another wonder of village life: the fact that the pubs shut in the middle of the afternoon so everyone could go home and rest up for the evening – and Richard wandered home, pausing to pluck a sprig of holly from someone's bush. Lily loved holly bushes, especially when it was close to Christmas. She would tie bunches above all their picture frames, attaching tiny red beads if there were no genuine berries.

The house was quiet when he walked through the door,

but that was nothing unusual. It took him several moments to realise that something wasn't right, and a minute more to work out what it was. It was something in the air that felt wrong, like a scent of something unfamiliar.

It was when he walked into the kitchen and realised that the patio doors were open that he began to worry. Lily hadn't been out the back of the house since they'd moved in there. She'd barely even spent any time in the kitchen unless he was there, as far as he could tell. She'd set up camp in the living room.

He stepped outside, into the rapidly darkening evening, squinting into the trees in the vain hope of seeing something moving. Other than trees stirred by the breeze, there was no sign of movement whatsoever.

'Lily?' he called, his voice pointlessly quiet, subdued by the shadows and the feeling of wrongness. And then, louder, realising he was being ridiculous, 'Lils?'

No response. He felt his insides tighten, as if his stomach was attempting to migrate into his lungs.

He stepped back inside, pulling the door shut behind him, though he didn't lock it, in case she was outside and beyond his earshot. He ran up the stairs, darting into all the rooms, trying to tell himself he was being ridiculous. She'd obviously just gone for a walk. She'd been shut in the house for days; it was perfectly reasonable for her to want to go out. Maybe she'd gone round the corner to buy a pint of milk.

But then, why had the patio doors been open?

The upstairs of the house was deserted. He made his way back into the kitchen. Spotted his phone lying on the kitchen counter, and felt a jolt of terror as he noted the missed calls. Six from Connie. A couple from an unknown number.

Heart thumping uncomfortably in his throat, he listened to Connie's voicemail.

Then grabbed his car keys and headed for the door.

then

Connie caught the bus back into Farnworth. It was dark outside, and the bus was almost entirely empty – just one middle-aged man who sat near the driver and stared straight ahead. The driver grunted at her as she waved her pass at him, and drove off without waiting for her to sit down, so that she stumbled in the aisle and fell into the nearest seat.

The darkness meant that she had to press her face right against the glass to see through to the outside. She watched the familiar scenery, as the countryside shifted into lamplit streets, with clusters of large houses set back from the pavement. The houses blended into rows of terraces, nestled tightly together, fighting for space; and finally into shops and public buildings, large and glass-fronted and impressive.

She got off at the usual stop and set off in the direction of the school, with no clear idea where she was going. The school grounds were dark and tightly locked against intruders; there was no point trying to break in, when the police would be able to get access legally. So she walked around the back of the building, searching the alleyways that she had avoided since her earlier run-ins with Eleanor and her gang.

The streets were deserted; she was surprised by just how quiet it seemed. She had expected the town to be much busier than the village at night, but, although it was more brightly lit and there was a sense of activity somewhere in the air, the streets themselves were quiet, almost eerie. Her footsteps echoed unnaturally loudly, the sound bouncing off bricks and garage doors.

Connie knew it was pointless being out here. Lily would have walked from school to the bus stop; she knew better than to hang around outside school, inviting trouble. And so the only places she could possibly be were inside the school grounds, or somewhere unguessable: somewhere she wouldn't normally go. As Connie couldn't explore either of those, there was no point in her being out here.

And yet, she felt so useless sitting at home. Discussing the possibilities while Lily could be lying God-knows-where... Connie forced the thought out of her head, walking with renewed vigour back in the direction of the school.

Perhaps there would be a gap in the fence. Or maybe she could find a caretaker, or even the police – surely they would be here soon, once they had finished taking statements? Then Connie would be able to help them look – she could point them in the direction of Lily's classrooms, guide them around the school. She could be helpful, unlike her parents, who sat at home awaiting their daughter's return.

Connie walked the perimeter of the school, searching for signs of life, but saw no one. Surely the police should be here by now? It had taken her twenty minutes to get into town; they could have driven here from her parents' house in half that time. Or was that it? Had they already been and gone?

Maybe they had found Lily straight away – if she was trapped somewhere she would be making some amount of noise, presumably. Clamouring to be found. If she was conscious, of course. So maybe that was it – they had come here already, found her, and now Connie was wandering around in the dark for no reason?

She stopped at the gate, peering through the bars in the hope of catching a glimpse of light or movement, but there was nothing.

That had to be it, then. They had found her. Taken her home.

Connie turned round and walked back to the bus stop.

Lily wasn't sure if she'd fallen asleep or simply stopped thinking. Either way, she found her situation reasserting itself after a while, awareness of where she was slowly pushing its way back to the surface. Her trousers were still damp, and now cold. The hard surface of the floor felt as though it was bruising every inch of skin that rested upon it. Her muscles ached from being bent into awkward positions for too long.

She thought she could hear noises outside.

How long had she been here now? Three hours? Four? Not long enough for it to be morning. Would anyone be wandering around the school in the middle of the night?

Maybe, if they knew she was here.

She raised her first, banged on the door a few times, paused. Listened intently for any hint of movement on the other side of the door.

Nothing.

She banged again, but without really meaning it, then slumped back against the wall.

The house looked the same as it had when Connie left, still half-lit behind the drawn curtains. She crept around the side, not wanting to announce her presence just yet. There was no police car parked outside, so they had obviously left, but her parents' car was still there. So Lily must be home, then, because if not then surely they would have taken the car to look for her? Or maybe they were both still sitting at home, leaving the job of searching up to the police. Or would one of them have gone with the police in their car?

Connie peered in through the window at the side of the kitchen. The glass was blurred and impossible to see through, but she didn't want go and look through the patio doors; she would be too visible, and she wanted to see them before they saw her.

She could see two shapes at the kitchen table. Both looked adult-sized, so no Lily: maybe she was upstairs in bed? Surely not, though. It had barely been an hour since Connie had left; Lily couldn't have returned home and been put to bed in that space of time.

So she was still missing. And her parents sat at the table, sharing a coffee, doing absolutely nothing to find her. She saw them lean into each other, exchange a kiss, and she felt her anger flare again. How could they be so uncaring? Did they perhaps believe that there was no real danger? That Connie had exaggerated her own experience, made it seem worse than it was? Or did they truly think they could help matters by sitting around doing nothing?

She peered through the glass again, and felt the first twinge of unease, the feeling that something was not quite right. When was the last time her mother had looked that relaxed, that carefree? When was the last time her parents had shared any physical contact? They had their backs to her, but they were sitting much closer together than they usually would be, and there was a relaxedness to their posture which seemed all wrong, especially now. What was going on? Had it all been an act – the fighting, the unhappiness? What would be the purpose of such an act?

She crept around to the patio doors, trying to get a closer look, through glass that wasn't blurred. She crouched down so that her face would appear at foot-level, hoping they wouldn't notice it.

It took a moment to work out what was wrong. Then she realised: the bulk of the man's back, the T-shirt he was wearing, the broadness of his shoulders: this was not her father.

While he was out looking for his youngest daughter, her mother was kissing another man in their kitchen.

The man turned his head slightly, and with a jolt of shock which was almost painful, Connie realised who he was. Why this scene held a disturbing note of familiarity.

Not pausing to think it through, fighting against a flurry of half-remembered images, she turned and fled.

The sounds outside were growing closer. Lily banged on the door, but the noises outside were too loud. Footsteps. Whistling. Doors swinging open and closed. It was definitely methodical. They were checking for something.

Someone.

They had to be looking for her. She banged again, her arms weak and useless.

When they opened the door at last, she almost didn't have the energy to react. It was a man, she noted dimly. Maybe the caretaker. She couldn't tell. He shone his torch inside, caught sight of her in the back, crouched down. Shone the light into her eyes, searching, making sure. Then lowered it, realising he was hurting her eyes.

'Oh,' was all that he said.

And behind him, just visible, another man, his outline much more familiar.

Her father, come to bring her home.

now

Connie was still perched by Lily's bedside when Richard arrived. She barely looked up as he came into the room: the slightest inclination of her head, to confirm that it was Richard and not a doctor. Then she went back to studying her sister's sleeping face, still clinging to her undamaged hand, as if she could drag her back into consciousness.

'Took your time,' was all she said, but it was an expression of exhaustion rather than a reprimand.

'I'm so sorry. I was at work.'

He took a step forward, hesitated, then sat down in the only other chair, on the opposite side of Lily's bed.

'You can't take your phone to work?'

'I forgot it. Please don't make me feel worse than I already do.' He reached out a hand to touch Lily's face; she was cool to the touch, pale and still, shrouded in avocado-coloured wool. 'Has she woken up at all?'

'No. The doctors say they don't know when she will.' Connie looked at him then, and he realised she'd been crying, a rare enough sight.

'But she definitely will?'

Connie turned away, looking back at Lily. 'They think so.'

'Think so?'

'They – ' Her voice caught in her throat, and she took a breath, visibly steadying herself. 'They said it's impossible to tell, with head injuries, but they aren't worried at the moment.'

Richard stared at Lily's expressionless face. She had been fine less than four hours ago. He'd heard her pottering around in her old room, shifting paperwork about. She'd even been humming to herself. Watching her now, he felt cold and numb, as though the blood was flowing more slowly in his veins, not quite reaching his extremities.

'Do you know what happened?' he asked eventually.

Connie shook her head. 'She fell, apparently. I don't know how they found her, or... well, anything, really.'

'You mean it wasn't you who found her?'

Connie looked at him blankly. 'How would I have found her?'

'I don't know. I just assumed...' Richard trailed off, confused. 'How did she get here, if it wasn't one of us?'

'I have no idea. The doctors didn't say.'

Connie's expression was helpless, which snapped Richard out of his numbness. Clearly it was his job to get some answers.

'Okay. I'll go and ask them what happened.' He reached out a hand, trying to find a part of Lily which looked undamaged enough to touch, but Connie was clinging to her only good hand. He settled on running his fingers along her jawline. Then he stepped out of the room, back into the corridor, which felt crowded and oppressive in comparison to the quiet surrounding Lily's bedside.

There weren't many members of staff around. He wandered down to the nurse's station and found a harassed-looking middle-aged woman, her cheeks flushed with her own sense of responsibility. She shuffled paperwork for several moments before looking up at him.

'Can I help you?'

'I'm with Lily Emmett. She came in a couple of hours ago, I think? Over there.' He pointed, uselessly – his finger indicated the entirety of the corridor.

'Emmett. Emmett.' The woman muttered to herself, pulled out a file. 'Oh, yes. Are you her husband?'

'Partner. We're not married.'

'Are you her next of kin?' she asked, with a tone of barely concealed exasperation, as if she were talking to a five-year-old.

'Yes.'

'Good. I can stop trying to phone you, then.' She laughed humourlessly at her own joke. 'What can I do for you, Mr Emmett?'

'No – I'm not...' He gave up, realising she really couldn't care less about the details. 'I'd just like to know how she's doing. Connie – her sister – said she hadn't been given much information.'

The nurse flicked through Lily's file. When she spoke, her voice was brisk and efficient. 'Her vitals are still fine. These things can be unpredictable, I'm afraid. It could be a few minutes, it could be a day. But we're monitoring her closely.'

He nodded. 'And is there any danger she won't wake up?'

The nurse looked at him with the first hint of compassion he'd seen since he arrived. 'I'm afraid I'm not the best person to be discussing that with you. I can get her doctor to come and talk to you as soon he's free?'

'Yes. That would be great. Thank you.' He turned to walk away, and then remembered what else he was supposed to be asking. 'Do you know how she got here? She should have been at home alone.'

The nurse glanced down at the notes again. 'An ambulance was called to the house. The person who called it had disappeared by the time the paramedics arrived.'

'Male or female?'

'I really don't know, sir. I'm afraid you'll have to ask your wife when she wakes up.'

Richard went in search of coffee. He could feel the nurse's eyes watching him all the way down the corridor.

He returned with two flimsy paper cups that held a substance which looked like coffee but bore little resemblance to it in taste. He handed one to Connie, and for the first time since he'd arrived, she looked at him properly as she thanked him.

'What did they say?'

'Not much. Someone called the ambulance to the house, they don't know who. They still don't sound too worried.' He tried to sound confident, ignoring the fact that Lily looked utterly lifeless, her mouth slack at the corners instead of set in its usual stubborn lines of sleep. 'The nurse said she'd send a doctor round to talk to us soon.'

Connie nodded, and turned back to watching her sister, holding her drink absent-mindedly in one hand.

'Where are the kids?' Richard asked.

'Nathan picked them up.'

'Is he coming here?'

'No.' Connie took a sip of her coffee and winced. 'How do they manage to make this stuff so horrible?'

'I imagine they infuse it with bodily fluids.'

Connie grimaced. 'Delightful thought.'

'So what's your plan? Do you need to go home? I'm happy to stay here by myself, you know, if you need to – well… get on.'

'It's fine. Nathan can handle it.' She caught Richard's look, and added, 'He is their father, you know.'

'Yes, I realise that.'

'I'd rather be here when Lily wakes up.'

Richard nodded, knew there was no point in arguing. 'I'm sure she'll appreciate that.'

'Don't.' Connie's voice was abrupt, surprising him.

'Don't what?'

'Don't go diplomatic on me.'

'What? What did I say?'

She didn't say anything for a moment, staring into her coffee.

'It's what you're not saying,' she said, and then, 'Forget it. I'm being stupid.'

'Connie, if there's something going on – '

'It's nothing.' She put her coffee down on the bedside table, and reached again for Lily's hand. 'Nothing we need to talk about now.'

Richard watched Connie for a while, but she said nothing further, and in the end his eyes drifted back to Lily's sleeping shape. The soft rise and fall of her chest contrasted with the unnatural noises of the machines that watched over her. He cradled his coffee in his palms and watched her until darkness fell outside, pushed gradually aside by artificial light; and all the while Connie sat beside him and said nothing.

Later, after the doctors had been to visit and decided that Lily wasn't showing any signs of waking up any time soon, Connie agreed to go home and get some sleep. Took a few steps towards the door, then stopped. Turning back to face him, her eyes sharp and glinting with tears, she said, softly, 'You know, I think he's having an affair.'

Richard said nothing, and she left, closing the door quietly on the words; leaving them in the room for him to do with them as he wished.

He sat down next to Lily, picked up her good hand. Ran his thumb over the indents in her knuckles, willing her to wake up. The lights had been extinguished now, and the hospital seemed much quieter, just the odd squeak of footsteps in the corridors outside.

'In the beginning was the word,' he whispered, half-expecting someone to come into the room and tell him to shut up. Nothing. 'And the word was...'

Lily slept on, oblivious.

part three

now

There was a shifting in the distance, a sound Lily could hear but not quite get a grasp on. She stood in a garden of uncut grass, which she saw growing surreptitiously out of the corners of her eyes, clawing its way towards her knees. The garden was a perfect square, the edges fenced off by pure blackness; you could drop off the edge and fall into nothingness. Lily wanted to go and look, to see what was beyond the edge, but when she tried to move there was a resistance similar to pulling a rooted plant from the ground; as if her feet were not resting on the grass but were part of the undergrowth itself. She looked down, but she couldn't distinguish her feet in amongst the greenery.

'One, two, three,' a voice counted, solemnly, sounding unaware of her presence. Lily pulled at her feet until she stood on tiptoes, but she couldn't see where the voice was coming from. 'Four, five, six, seven – '

Lily spun her head from side to side, but she couldn't see who was making the noise. 'Who's there?' she asked. Her voice was hoarse and scratchy, not her voice at all. It felt as though she was exhaling words directly from her throat, rather than letting them seek out their consonants in the grooves of her tongue.

'Who's there?' she asked again, and her voice worked a bit better this time.

'You made me lose count,' the voice reproached, but still she couldn't see where it came from. It was male, childlike.

'I'm sorry. I can't see you.'

'But I'm right here.' The child was on the floor in front of her feet, and she knew he had always been there. 'You made me lose count.'

'What are you counting?'

He laughed, curling one hand into a fist and shoving it into his mouth in an attempt to control his mirth. 'You know what I'm counting,' he said, rocking slightly on the ground. He looked familiar, but she couldn't place his face. The voice was all wrong. Or maybe the voice was right and the face was wrong?

'What are you counting?' she asked again. It was very important, she knew. Everything hinged on this.

'You're silly,' he said, shaking his head, but he showed her anyway. He lifted up his hands, revealing a pile of dead insects. And, on the ground, the glass dome he had caught them in.

The one he had used to drown them.

'Bugs went swimming in the Bug Jug,' he said, laughing again, and abruptly the blackness around them started to shift, to ripple and swirl in a way that made Lily feel dizzy. She could see colours in the dark – foggy impressions of colours, like pictures of deep space with its swirls of orange and blue – which gave a sense of depth to something that had previously seemed like an ending. If she stepped off the edge, she knew, she would fall forever.

'You need to wake up now,' the boy said, his laughter gone as quickly as it had come.

'No, I don't. There are still things I need to know. Things I need to see.'

'You can see them when you're awake, if you look hard enough.' The childlike voice was diminishing, being replaced by its adult counterpart. 'Lily. Please. You need to wake up.'

'I don't want to,' she said, steeling herself against it, already feeling her dream-self slipping away.

'But I need you to,' adult Richard said, and suddenly he was there in front of her, the child vanished as quickly as he had appeared.

Lily was lucid but disorientated when Connie arrived, about an hour after she received Richard's phone call, having broken half a dozen traffic laws in her haste to be back at her sister's side. She was breathless, frantic, and Lily laughed at her, sleepily. 'You didn't need to rush,' she mumbled. 'I'll still be here in a day's time, I'm sure.'

'I wanted to be here when you woke up,' Connie said, aware even as she said it that she sounded childish, petulant. As if she'd been denied the ice cream flavour that she'd asked for.

'I know.' Lily's voice was soft, soothing, and Connie felt calmer.

'I'm sorry,' Richard said, reaching out quickly to take her hand. They were all connected in a line then, with Richard in the middle, holding both their hands. It felt wrong. Connie dropped his hand without trying to be obvious about it, and moved around the bed to touch Lily's shoulder. 'I should have called sooner,' Richard continued. 'But I didn't want to get you here unnecessarily, and she woke up so quickly... I am sorry.'

'It's okay,' Connie said, not looking at him. 'How are you feeling, Lils? What happened, for Christ's sake?'

Lily shrugged. 'I don't remember.'

'You must remember something. Were you with anyone? The ambulance crew said they found you outside. What were you doing outside at this time of year? Or at all? That garden...'

'It's fine.' Lily's voice was abrupt, dismissive. 'The garden's fine.'

'You can't possibly mean that.'

'It's just a garden. There's no reason to be afraid of it.'

'Lily, you know as well as I do that it's not "just" a garden, not to you – ' Connie realised Richard was watching their exchange with interest, and stopped talking abruptly.

'I don't know what happened,' Lily repeated, her voice unusually firm. 'So there's no point asking me.'

The three of them fell silent. Connie lifted a hand to stroke Lily's hair, but Lily shifted away, wincing.

'Sorry,' Connie said. 'I just – I was really worried about you.'

'I know.' Lily let go of Richard and reached out towards her sister.

'You were unconscious for two days, did Richard tell you that?'

'Yes.'

'That's not normal, Lils.'

'It's a head injury. I expect they're usually unpredictable.'

Connie nodded. Squeezed Lily's hand. And, meeting Richard's eyes over the top of Lily's head, found her own expression of disbelieving concern mirrored back at her.

The kids were on their way to bed by the time Connie arrived home. Pyjama-clad and clutching novelty hot water bottles (Tom had Spider-Man, Luke an unbranded blue teddy which he would probably abandon as not suitably cool in a year's time), they rushed to greet their mother, with Nathan protesting in the background that they were supposed to be going to brush their teeth.

'How's Auntie Lily?' Tom asked, his voice very serious. When Luke joined in – 'Auntie Lily, where's Auntie Lily, 'where?' – Tom shushed him, and said sternly, 'She's in hospital and Mummy's very worried about her.'

'She's fine,' Connie replied, trying not to smile or, worse, cry. Resisting the urge to gather her children into her arms and never let them go. 'She's awake now and she's doing very well. The doctors say she may be able to go home soon.'

'Can we visit her before she goes home?' Luke asked hopefully. Weirdly, he loved hospitals; when Tom had had his appendix out a year ago, Luke had been thrilled by the machines, the very hungry caterpillar that crawled its way down the wall of the main corridor in the children's ward, the nurses who showered attention upon him and made him promise to look after his big brother. He was always disappointed to hear that someone had been in hospital and he hadn't been able to go and visit them.

'I don't know, darling. It depends how she's feeling.'

'So we'll wait and see?' Luke said, making both Connie and Nathan laugh. It was one of their most oft-used expressions.

'Yes, we'll wait and see. Now, boys,' Connie said, standing up and guiding them gently back towards the stairs. 'I believe Daddy was in the middle of putting you to bed?'

They disappeared up the stairs, chattering about which story they were going to have. Nathan followed them, dismissing several story ideas on the basis that they were too long or too lively for this time of night. 'There's no such thing as too *lively*, Dad,' Tom said dismissively. 'They're only *stories*.'

Connie smiled to herself and wandered through to the kitchen, shedding outer layers as she went: shoes kicked off in the hallway, coat draped over the sofa, bag dumped on the dining table. She flicked the kettle on, felt reassured by its answering roar of activity. Pulled two mugs out of the cupboard – matching, unpersonalised, sensible mugs – and went about making tea automatically. Her thoughts, such as they were, seemed to scrabble over themselves and couldn't quite get a handle on anything solid. She worried for Lily, for herself, for Richard. For her children who thought that stories were only stories.

By the time Nathan came back downstairs she was on the sofa, mugs on the table in front of her, television mutedly displaying scenes of today's horror from around the world. The headlines tripped across the bottom of the screen, the usual selection of war, protest, political entanglements. She let it wash over her, barely seeing it. Her sense of disconnection from the rest of the world seemed to grow by the day.

'So how was Lily really?' Nathan asked, sitting down next to her, gently linking one arm through hers. She let it stay there, though it felt odd: as if they were forcing a contact which was not quite natural.

'She's okay. She doesn't remember what happened, so we're still none the wiser on that front. For all we know, someone bashed her over the head when she wasn't looking and we're all just carrying on as if she's mental and brought this on herself.'

'Do you really think that's how you're carrying on?'

'Well, you know what I mean. She's got a history of collapsing, so we're assuming it's just another collapse with much worse consequences. But what if it's not that? What if someone actually wants to hurt her?'

'Why would anyone want to hurt her?' Nathan's voice, even and reasonable, grated on her already raw nerves.

'How should I know? She doesn't bloody speak to me about anything.'

'Connie – '

'Don't, okay. Just leave it.'

'I think you should examine the reasons why you think Lily might have been attacked.'

Connie turned to face him, baffled. 'She was unconscious in hospital for two days with a sprained wrist and a head injury. What the hell else am I supposed to think?'

'But she has a history of collapsing, you said so yourself.'

'But not like *this* – '

'Not the point, Connie. There's nothing to indicate this is more sinister than anything that's happened in the past. So I think you should focus on *why* you think Lily might have been attacked.'

'For fuck's sake, Nathan, I really can't see what you're driving at.'

'Fine. I think you're using Lily's problems as a way of avoiding your own, and I think you should get counselling.' He didn't look at her as he said it, but watched the TV screen, his face as expressionless as his voice.

'I'm worried about my sister, so you think I should get counselling?'

'No, that's not the reason, but yes, I think you should get counselling.'

Connie was quiet for a moment, trying to swallow the angry retorts which threatened to burst past her lips. Finally: 'Are you having an affair?'

Nathan looked at her for a moment. Then he unlinked his arm from hers, and walked in measured paces to the front door. She heard the rustle in the hallway as he gathered his coat, checked he had his keys, slipped his shoes on. He was careful not to slam the door on the way out.

then

The house was generally quiet when Lily got home from school. Her mother had barely left her room since Connie had run away; the garden had been abandoned, weeds springing up all over the place. Marcus, who had once seemed to have an endless amount of patience, seemed to have run out of it in recent weeks: he avoided being at home, working longer and longer hours, sometimes not arriving back until Lily was thinking about going to bed. The evenings were consumed by silence and loneliness, and Lily spent more and more time working on the advanced maths problems her teacher had been giving her, and reading books on mathematical theory.

It was three weeks since Connie had left, and they hadn't heard a word from her.

Lily sometimes wondered, half-heartedly, what her class-mates did when they got home in the evenings. Or what she would be doing if Connie were around. Instead, she was making dinner every night and taking it in to her mother on a tray, trying not to feel horrified at Anna's appearance, at the smell of her room. She missed Connie most at these moments, wishing she had someone to share them with, to lessen the horror of the experience.

She stepped through the front door into stillness, picking up the envelopes on the floor as she did so; Anna never bothered to look at the post these days. She closed the front door quietly, and stood for a moment, letting her eyes readjust to the dim light. It was bright outside; spring was working its way optimistically towards summer, and the days were gradually lengthening, extending orangey fingers into the dark evenings. Inside all was dark and quiet, as usual. Only the kitchen was bright as she walked in, the wall of south-facing windows flooding the room with light.

Lily put the post on the table and paused, listening for movement upstairs. There was none. It had been a week since Lily had seen her mother out of bed for more than a few minutes.

She poured herself some juice from the fridge, and checked the cupboards for food. There were basic supplies – enough for spaghetti bolognese, or something similar. She would have to go shopping tomorrow.

She took her bag through to the living room and ploughed through her homework. They were doing *Romeo and Juliet* in English, a play she found herself utterly unable to connect with. She'd started to become concerned, that other girls in her class seemed so focused on the idea of boyfriends, love, marriage. She'd felt the odd flicker of interest, but she couldn't imagine spending that much time with one person. Couldn't even begin to imagine the intricacies of a physical relationship. She'd searched the play for clues as to what she should be feeling, but there was nothing there. The idea of someone touching her didn't just fill her with fear, it left her utterly perplexed.

Nevertheless, she wrote two hundred words on Romeo's passion for Juliet. Then she wrote up the notes on a science experiment they'd done that day. The only sounds were her breathing, and the scribble of pen on paper.

When she'd finished, she put her books away and went into the kitchen to make dinner. It was just starting to get dark outside so she flicked on the lights, and the reflection of the bulbs bounced back at her in the windows, making the room over-bright and harsh. The windows had wooden blinds, and the patio doors had thick curtains which she pulled across, shutting out the darkness of the garden. She flicked on the radio, and listened to the chattering of the DJs as she made dinner.

She took Anna her dinner on a tray, knocking as she entered the room. Anna was propped up in bed, and the lights were on: an improvement on the last few days. She smiled wearily as Lily entered the room, and put aside the photo album that she'd been looking at. 'Hey, sweetheart. How was your day?'

'It was okay.' Lily handed her the tray, making sure she wasn't going to be able to spill it. Anna was wearing a white T-shirt which was spotted liberally with food stains. Lily longed, for a moment, to rip it off of her and throw it away.

'Are you learning anything interesting?'

Lily shrugged. She found it harder to talk to Anna than most people, perhaps because she found her vocalised parental interest so at odds with her behaviour.

'Bet you have lots of homework, right?'

Lily nodded and, taking this as permission to leave, went back downstairs, closing the door behind her as she went.

She ate dinner at the kitchen table, sitting with her back to the patio doors. As she ate she sifted through the post, and was surprised to see her name, stamped across one of the letters in a semi-familiar scrawl: *Miss L. Emmett*. She opened the envelope carefully, and unfolded a single sheet of cream notepaper.

Dear Lily,

I'm so sorry it's taken me this long to write to you. I was going to call, but I thought Mama or Dad might answer the phone, and I'm not ready to talk to them yet. You can let them know I'm okay, though, if you want. I suppose they've been imagining the worst.

I'm in Germany at the moment. I hitched most of the way. Not sure why Germany – it just seemed like the easiest option. I was predicted an A in my German GCSE after all! It's harder speaking the language here than it was at school, though.

I'm sorry I left without saying goodbye. Stuff just got a bit weird – I'll tell you about it when I get back. I did make sure you were okay before I left the country. You'll have to tell me what happened when I see you next.

I'm sure I'll see you soon, once I've sorted out my head a bit. I'm working as a farm labourer at the moment, but that won't last forever. I expect I'll come back when my money runs out.

Give my love to Dad. And to Mama if you want, I suppose. But keep most of it for yourself.

Lots of love,
*   Connie xxxx*

now

Lily drifted in and out of sleep for a week and a half, dreaming fitfully and disconnectedly of things that might have once been real. Richard appeared often, sometimes alongside Esmeralda, whose arms were still striped with silvery blood, and child-Connie, who watched sternly and dispassionately from a distance and never spoke. When she awoke, frequently, to find Richard at her side and Connie on the end of the phone, she found herself unable to separate the two of them from their dream-selves, and struggled to talk to either of them.

She woke once to find Connie in Richard's usual chair. Richard was on the other side of the room, staring out of the window, and didn't notice her wake up. 'Hey, sleepyhead,' Connie said, squeezing her hand. 'We were just talking about coming to spend Christmas with you. What do you think? Proper family Christmas? We could get a tree.'

Lily squinted at her, confused. Trying to remember the last time they'd spent Christmas together. 'But we don't do Christmas.'

'Don't be silly. I've always done Christmas.'

'*I*' *is not* '*we*', Lily thought, but she didn't dare say it aloud. 'Where?'

'At your place. Mama's place.'

Probably the last place they had done Christmas together, in fact. 'Okay. Sure.'

'Really?'

'Yeah. We're not doing anything else. Are we?' She looked up at Richard, who was still looking out of the window.

'Huh? Oh. No. Definitely no other plans.' He smiled, but his face looked odd. As if the smile had shaped his face into a slightly irregular position. 'We could get a tree.'

'Yes. Connie said.' Lily looked from one of them to the other, trying to work out what was wrong with the conversation. 'Are the boys coming?'

'Of course. I wouldn't spend Christmas without them.'

'No, I meant here. Today.' She watched her sister's face, but Connie was carefully composed, not even a twitch from her facial muscles.

'Maybe later. They're at school at the minute.' She looked at her watch, constructed her face into an expression of surprise. 'Actually, I should probably make a move. It's just gone two.'

'Nathan not picking them up?'

'No, not today.' Connie leaned over and kissed her on the forehead. 'I'll bring them with me later, if you like. They'd love to see you.'

Lily nodded.

'Right. I'll see you both later, then.' She hugged Richard, and then disappeared with a backwards wave to both of them.

A child-shaped shadow followed her out of the room, unseen by Richard, and Lily closed her eyes to stave off the image.

'They said you can go home tomorrow,' Richard said brightly, crossing the room to sit next to her. 'That'll be good, right?'

Lily nodded again.

'Unless you don't want to?'

'Don't want to what?'

'Go home. Well, you know. Back *there*.' Richard eyed her intently. 'Would you rather go back to our flat?'

An image, so sharp she could have reached out and touched it, of them playing Scrabble in their flat, exchanging words like gifts. Of the room glittering in tinsel and flashing multicoloured lights. Last Christmas, then. Lily with her feet tucked under a blanket, Richard next to her on the sofa, bottle of ruby wine nestled between them. Yes, she would like to be back there. But she shook her head, thinking practically of the tenants. 'The house is fine.'

'Even the garden?'

'It's winter.'

'Well, it won't always be winter. And you seem to have been out there the other day.'

Lily touched the bandage on her head. Had she really been out there? She remembered unlocking the door, trying to catch the girl-shaped shadows on the grass. Or not *catch*, because of course she knew they weren't real. But to follow them. To see where they might lead her.

It must have been then that she collapsed.

'It's fine. We can go back.'

Richard smiled, lifted her hand to his lips. 'We'll make it nice. For when the others come to stay.'

Lily closed her eyes, and tried to imagine the house full of people talking, laughing, having a nice time. Maybe that was what was needed, to finally expel all the ghosts.

Connie took the boys to visit Lily straight after school. They bought cheap burgers from the canteen downstairs and ate them at Lily's bedside while she drifted in and out of sleep. Connie and Richard carefully avoided any mention of Nathan. Instead they focused on holiday plans and abstract discussions of the future. There was talk of going abroad in the summer, a trip away for all of them, which Richard tactfully did not mention he couldn't afford.

When Connie got home, it was to find that Nathan still hadn't returned.

She put the boys to bed, leaving Tom in charge of Luke, and switched the radio to Radio Two while she half-heartedly tidied the kitchen. They played songs she knew the words to, even though she couldn't identify the song or the artist. Every third or fourth track they played something Christmassy, and she tried not to find the songs desperately sad.

Tidying done, she poured herself a glass of wine and switched off the radio. Silence descended as soon as she sat down. There was no shifting around upstairs, no creaking as the boys tiptoed into each other's rooms. She would check on them in a while, and they would be buried in blankets, soft-haired sleeping heads protruding tentatively into the night.

She realised that this was what it would be like if Nathan never came back. Silence, stretching across everything. Only the chatter of anonymous voices on the TV and the radio to keep her company.

She would die of loneliness.

Dismissing the thought, she dug around in her handbag until she found the notebook she carried everywhere. It was her book of lists, and it was currently filled with Christmas-related collections of words and names. Her card list – almost all crossed off, now, with only two weeks to go. Her stocking-filler lists – the already-bought and the to-be-bought – the first of which would not be crossed off until each item was wrapped and in its proper place. Her food lists, which would now have to be altered to include six – impossible to think that Lily would provide the food or do the cooking, though Richard was usually enthusiastic enough. They had never spent Christmas together, but they always spoke on Christmas Day, and Richard was always in the kitchen when they did.

She went through, making alterations here and there, feeling measurably calmer the more organised things became.

She wondered how she had come to this point, this level of adulthood, where she thought about events more than ten minutes before they happened and felt happier for doing so. She tried to remember what it had been like to vanish into the world, with no one looking out for her and no idea what might happen next. Tried to remember the enjoyment that had come from not knowing, not being able to plan, and from having no one to care about or be responsible for.

It was gone, now. Eroded by the intervening years. Her life, without responsibility for other people, would be no life at all.

At nine o'clock she tiptoed upstairs to check on the children. Both slept peacefully, heads turned to one side, arms splayed above their heads. She wondered if she'd ever told them that they slept, separated by two walls and an ocean of unconsciousness, in identical positions. She wondered if they'd care.

At half-past ten she drained the last of the bottle of wine and went to bed, falling asleep instantly. Two hours later Nathan slipped into bed beside her, and she didn't stir at all.

They took the bandages off Lily's wrist and head at nine the next morning, exposing the bruised skin beneath, and pronounced her fit for discharge. Richard half-carried her to the car, placing her in the front seat as if she were a porcelain doll. He drove considerably slower than the speed limit all the way home, and Lily didn't comment, watching the countryside crawl past the window in silence.

They arrived home to find the house a mess, dishes piled on the sides and life debris scattered across the furniture. It had been two weeks since Lily had been there. Richard had been home every day, but only to sleep, and once to go to work. With normal routine suspended, there hadn't seemed much point in things like cleaning.

Now, though, Richard regretted not having done something about the place sooner. He'd had whimsical thoughts about them tidying the house together, abolishing the dirt and the remnants of the last few weeks in much the same way as they had when they'd first moved in. But of course she wouldn't be capable of it. Of course she wouldn't be able to do anything except lie down, watch TV, put her feet up.

He settled her on the sofa and went to make a cup of tea. While the kettle boiled he collected dirty cups and plates from the table, opened old post, tried to create some semblance of order. He remembered the first time he'd been in this kitchen, months ago, laying out their tea bags, kettle, mugs, in an attempt to claim it as their own. Did it feel as though it belonged to him any more now than it had done then? Probably not.

The thing that was missing from this house, he had come to realise, was Lily. She was just not *here* in the way she had been in their flat. Of course her *things* were here and there, scattered about, but she didn't seem to use any of them. He had once spent his days deciphering her moods from the clues she left him, reading her scribbled mathematical notes while she wasn't looking, flicking through the books she read when he wasn't there. There was even a kind of joy in reading her half-finished crossword puzzles; seeing the answers that had come to her easily, the ones that were elusive to her. Trying to work out why she knew some things and not others.

Now, there was nothing. She didn't seem to do anything with her days, and so there was nothing to decipher. When was the last time she'd done any work? Read a book? Read a newspaper, even? If she did any of these things then it was secretly, out of his sight. She no longer left him any clues.

Was it because she didn't want him to know? Or was it, contrarily, because she did? Did she want him to talk to her instead of figuring her out on his own?

Or was it simply that there was not as much to figure out as there had been before?

He made the tea, absent-mindedly selecting their favourite mugs: hers a chipped white mug with cartoon rabbits on it (a present from her childhood, she'd told him once, though she didn't remember from whom), his a dark brown mug with a blue flower on one side. He carried them through to the living room, thinking that maybe if they spoke, if he asked what was wrong rather than respecting her right to silence, then she would give him the answers he required. Find her way back into her life, and into his.

In the time it had taken to make the tea, though, Lily had fallen asleep. Her delicate head rested on one arm of the sofa, blonde hair splayed across her face. Her hands were clasped tightly together in her lap, and, on the TV in front of her, Dick Van Dyke was solving murders in silence.

then

'Do your parents ever talk to each other about anything, except to argue?'

Lily had been with Dr Mervyn for half an hour, and neither of them had spoken until now. Since Connie had left, their sessions had resumed their old format – they'd made no further forays into Lily's memory, at her request. There was a change, though: since Connie's departure something seemed to have been released in Lily, and she had found it easier to talk. This had made it easier for Dr Mervyn to ask questions, and their sessions had come somewhere close to resembling normal counselling sessions.

Lily considered her answer for a minute, thinking back over the conversations she'd overheard recently, then shook her head. 'No.' She hesitated, wondering if she should offer more, and then: 'They only talk about Connie, and they can't talk nicely about her.'

Dr Mervyn nodded. Presumably this was the answer he had been anticipating. 'Do you talk to them at all?'

Lily shook her head. She had been toying with maths homework for the last half-hour, in between bouts of staring out of the window, but now she turned the sheet of paper over and began sketching the bare branches of the tree outside. Dr Mervyn (or, more likely, the school) had installed new blinds recently, so the world outside the window was interrupted, cut into segments by harsh black lines. She focused on trying to get the three-dimensional effect of the lines being in front of the rest of the picture, rather than just periodic strike-throughs of the image.

'Do they try to talk to you?' Dr Mervyn asked. Again, Lily shook her head.

They fell silent for a while, both of them occupied with their separate tasks. Outside the door, two women were having a loud and unnecessarily raucous conversation about the hopelessness of their husbands' respective behaviour. The words filtered into Lily's mind, though she didn't want them there. Drunkard. Layabout. Waste of space.

If someone was wasting your space, wasn't it your own fault for having that space available in the first place?

'Do you have any idea where Connie might be?' Dr Mervyn's voice intruded on her thoughts again. She considered the question.

'No. She sends me letters, but she doesn't say where she is.'

'Do your parents know that she's safe?'

Lily nodded. 'I showed them the first letter.' A pause. 'Not the others.'

'And do you know why she left?'

Lily looked at him. Measuring. She had not discussed Connie's departure with her parents, except to let them know she wasn't dead. They had never asked, given that she'd been locked up at the time Connie left, and she'd never mentioned the conversation they'd had in the playpark. She wondered now whether it mattered, and decided it probably didn't: either way, Connie was gone, and Lily didn't know where she was.

'She told me before that she wanted to run away,' she said eventually. That day, how many months ago? Barely two. Not even sixty days had passed since they'd shared a cigarette and talked about the distant future when Connie would abandon her here.

She had never imagined it would be like this.

Dr Mervyn's face had an alertness to it now, though he was careful not to change the pitch of his voice. 'Did she? When was that?'

'A while ago. I don't know.'

'Did she say why?'

Lily didn't reply, and Dr Mervyn stopped asking questions. He knew that Lily didn't respond well to anything she perceived as pressure. As if she would only talk when she thought people weren't interested in the response.

They passed the rest of the hour in silence, and when the time was up Lily packed away her things and thanked Dr Mervyn for his time. He in return thanked her for hers, and they concluded the session in the usual way.

With her hand on the doorknob, Lily turned back, to see him engrossed in his notes, oblivious to her now their time was up.

'She wouldn't have just gone like that, if nothing was wrong,' she said quietly. 'Something must have happened. Otherwise she would have said goodbye.'

By the time Dr Mervyn had begun to formulate a response, Lily was out of the door and halfway down the corridor.

She didn't return to class after their session. She felt too unsettled, her thoughts skipping from one subject to the next, unable to make connections between them all. Her parents – Connie – the cupboard – Connie's classmates – her parents' sadness. All jumbled, blurring into one another, one thing refusing to stand out above the rest. Connie had been her protective layer, sheltering her from the outside world. She didn't need to think when Connie was around, she merely *did*; Connie steered her in the right direction while she acted in whatever way felt right at the time.

Now that was gone, and the world was crashing in from all directions. She craved the silence that had once been so easy to find.

She walked across the fields, idly thinking she might find someone with a cigarette, try smoking again. Maybe she could grow to love the acridity in her mouth. Connie had enjoyed it, after all. Or maybe she could take up drinking. Make friends with older kids. Sneak out in the middle of the night, smash wing mirrors and graffiti the walls of the playground. She didn't know what, but something needed to be done.

Now Connie was gone, she was in danger of spending the rest of her life alone, listening to the walls of their house crumble to dust in the silence.

now

Richard had carried Lily up to bed at midnight, and placed her as carefully as he could on the bed beside him, folding the sheets around her for protection. She awoke five hours later to darkness, and the faint sound of his snores. She was disorientated, and it took almost a minute to figure out where she was and how she had come to be there.

The glow of the moon outside the bedroom window cast odd, silvery shadows across the room. She was almost never awake when Richard wasn't, and the house felt strange, the noises unsettlingly loud and unfamiliar. Her head ached fiercely, her wrist slightly less so. She wondered if there were painkillers in the house.

He didn't stir as she rolled out of bed and tiptoed across the room. Shadows darted around her feet, but she looked straight ahead, refused to acknowledge them. Reflections and distortions of light and mind, and nothing more. Ahead of her, more solid ghosts led the way.

*– You know I **don't like** the dark I don't want to go out **there** shut up okay you said **you wanted** to come you can't change your **mind now** –*

Ghost-Connie held out her hand, insistent, and her pale sibling slipped down the stairs in her wake.

Lily kept her eyes straight ahead, unwilling to watch them as they disappeared through the kitchen and out of the back door. What had happened had happened. Going over and over it wasn't going to change a thing.

She could almost feel Connie's reproachful gaze, and she turned her back on their past selves, refused to engage with them. She tried to argue with her in her head. *It's worse at night, you see. They're too real and I don't know what they'll try and make me do. Can't you understand that? Tomorrow it will be different.*

Connie stood in silent and distant judgement, and refused to answer.

Lily found what she was looking for on the kitchen table. Hospital-related paraphernalia: her discharge papers, after-care instructions, and a small pharmacy's worth of painkillers and sedatives and God-knows-what-else. She found the least intimidating-looking painkillers, and took two with a glass of ice-cold tap water. She wondered vaguely if the painkillers were strong enough to make hallucinations worse, but found she didn't care enough to check the leaflet inside. It was unlikely she'd be trusted with anything that strong, even with Richard at home to watch over her. *Too risky, my dear. You're not exactly someone we can trust, are you?*

The voice sounded vaguely familiar. Perhaps one of the nurses from the hospital? The patronising tone definitely sounded nurse-ish.

Ghost-Connie was back at the patio doors, watching her, like a cat waiting to be let in. Her shadowy sister was nowhere to be seen. Lily turned away, trying to reason with herself. She wasn't really there. She was just an instrument of memory, trying to help Lily figure out what had happened. It was Lily's fault she was there. Lily, who stubbornly refused to remember anything by herself. Was it any wonder her brain had to conjure ghosts to nudge her in the right direction?

Behind ghost-Connie, the ever-shifting landscape of the garden was spread out in the moonlight. Something about it seemed wrong. Everything was tidier, the weeds sparser, the borders more organised. Richard keeping himself busy while she'd been in hospital, perhaps? But hadn't he been at her side the whole time? Hadn't the state of the house when she came home been testament to that?

She walked through to the living room, leaving her ghosts behind, hovering outside. She knew where they wanted to lead her, but there had to be another way. Something else that would trigger her memory, something that didn't involve going back.

It was about time she found it.

For the first time in weeks she felt motivated. It just wasn't tolerable to spend so much time being stalked by a past you couldn't remember. It was one thing to have a few ghosts, the odd memory-blank, but to let them affect your health? To collapse over and over again under the weight of what was hidden from view? She was no longer shielding herself from the past, but residing permanently within it.

There were memories enough in this house, without having to go into the woods. In the hallway between the kitchen and the living room was the door to the cellar. Lily had barely looked at it since they'd first moved in; they had hidden everything down there and then locked it away. Out of sight. Out of her mind.

Not any more.

She pulled the door open carefully, remembering its slow creak, careful not to wake Richard. The light-switch was to her right, dusty and covered in cobwebs. She flicked it on, and the bare bulb above her head shivered into dim, orangey illumination. Another, at the bottom of the stairs, created a circle of light on the concrete floor. The staircase between the two, with its ladder-like wooden stairs that left ankles vulnerable to grabbing from below, flickered with shadows.

Ridiculous, her inner voice said firmly, shoving her downwards. The cellar was no more of a danger now than it had been when she was five years old, regardless of how scary it might appear.

Ghost-Connie watched her from the top of the stairs, saying nothing.

The boxes were lined up against the far wall, just as they had left them when they'd tidied them away. Her mother's belongings on one side; her father's, the little that remained, on the other. And Connie and Lily in the middle, wedged between the two. Much of their stuff had already been down here, thrust out of sight by their mother years ago.

Lily selected a box at random. Connie's things had been all jumbled together with her own, and neither she nor Richard had felt inclined to try to separate them. Their individual histories, like their current lives, wouldn't exist without the other to give them perspective.

She wanted to take the box upstairs, but her wrist was still aching, and it was too awkward to try and move it one-handed. The cellar was cold and empty in the greyish pre-dawn half-light, and the floor was scattered with dirt. She could *feel* the shadows around her, as if they were tangible, as if they breathed her exhalations; but she was being ridiculous, of course. There was nothing more sinister in this room than twenty years' worth of dirt. She forced herself to sit down on the floor, pressing her back against the wall so that nothing could sneak up behind her.

The box was a seemingly random collection of the half-remembered and the completely unknown. Lily picked out the first object that came to hand: a blue bear, fur half-gone on one side, one eye coming loose and giving it a slightly demented expression. She recognised it as Connie's, though Lily felt it was probably she who was responsible for the damage to the eye. She couldn't remember if it had a name.

She placed it to one side, picked out the next item. A pink plastic digital watch, the battery long since dead, displaying nothing but the blank grey of unaccountable time. She tossed it to one side. She remembered the last time she'd worn this.

She pulled out object after object, some striking flickering, half-heard chords in her memory, others confusing in their unfamiliarity. Even back when they were kids, there had been parts of Connie's life she hadn't known. White tennis shoes, size eleven. When had she ever had those shoes? And why had her mother kept them?

Of course, they could have been from afterwards. Lily often had to remind herself that there was a large chunk of their childhood that had not been shared.

As she pulled out objects, examined them, held them, discarded them, two pairs of eyes watched unblinking from the top of the stairs. Ghost-eyes, empty, and yet, they seemed to *know*. Knew what she was looking for, even though she didn't. Would know when she'd found it, even though she probably wouldn't.

And behind them, another pair of eyes, supposed to be sleeping: instead, searching for just a glimpse of sense in silent, unfathomable behaviour.

Richard called Connie from work later that day, not wanting to be overheard by Lily. The pub was deserted, and likely to stay that way, for an hour or so at least. Rosa had disappeared into town with Ella, and Tim had been out every day that Richard had worked there. On the phone Connie sounded distracted, but there was enough concern in her voice for Richard to continue the conversation without feeling guilty about the questions he wasn't asking.

'What sort of things was she looking at?'

'I don't know. I didn't look too closely, and she put it all back as soon as she realised I was up. It looked like toys and things.'

'I didn't think Mama had kept any of that stuff.'

'Really? Don't all mothers?' Richard was baffled, but Connie laughed.

'I know Lily doesn't talk much, but she must have given you some idea of what our mother was like? She didn't exactly cherish the memories of our childhood.'

'Maybe she did, and was too shy to show it.'

'More likely she shoved everything in a box after Dad died and just couldn't be bothered to chuck it away.'

Richard could hear her clattering in the background, as if she was tidying. 'Are you sure now's a good time to talk?'

'Yeah, it's fine. I'm just getting everything sorted for Christmas.' There was a pause, and Richard, lost in thought, didn't realise a response was expected. 'We are still doing Christmas, right?'

'Of course. Absolutely. Lily can't wait.'

'You mean *you* can't wait.'

'Connie, don't. She really does love you. And the boys. It's going to be great to have a proper family Christmas for once.'

'If Lily can get through the day without collapsing and Nathan can manage to stay in the house for more than ten minutes at a time.'

'What do you mean?'

Connie sighed, a loud crackle in Richard's ear. 'It's just that he keeps having to go and see patients. Or so he says. I know it's that time of year, and lots of home visits are required and all that, but he's supposed to have booked this week off work. Surely even if you're a doctor you're allowed to have holiday?'

'Don't, Connie.'

'Don't what?'

'Don't jump to the conclusions you're jumping to. He's always had a strong work ethic. And he's never booked time off over Christmas before. This is probably why.'

'But if he has holiday during the summer he never has to go into work.'

'Maybe he's volunteering to do more than he would normally, because it's Christmas and because he doesn't want to stay at home when things between you two are so hard. But that doesn't automatically mean what you think it means.'

'I asked him, you know. He didn't even reply. And he hasn't spoken to me since.'

The front door to the pub opened, and Ed walked in, looking unnaturally large in the low doorway. He lifted a hand in greeting, and made his way to the far end of the bar, not quite out of earshot.

'He might have just been shocked,' Richard said, trying to be reasonable. 'Anyway, Connie, I've got to run. I've got a customer.'

'Okay. But Richard, can I ask you a favour?'

Only a slight hesitation. 'Sure.'

'If you get a chance, can you speak to Nathan? See if you can get anything out of him? Christmas will be miserable otherwise.'

'I don't know if it's really my place.'

'He knows we talk; he knows I will have told you what's going on. It would be weird, wouldn't it, if you didn't want to get his version of events?'

'Connie, it's one thing getting his version of things. It's quite another getting his version and then reporting back to you. What if he tells me that you're right? Am I then supposed to keep his secret, or tell you what he said?'

'You're supposed to be a friend.'

'Yes, but to *both* of you. I'm sorry, Connie, but I can't take sides on this one. I already feel like I'm betraying Nathan half the time, because I spend so much time talking to you these days. You understand that, don't you?'

There was a pause. Richard could hear Connie shuffling things in the background, thinking it over. He gestured an apology to Ed, who brushed it away with a wave of his hand.

'I do understand,' she said, finally, reluctantly.

'Thank you. I will talk to him, though, and tell him how worried you are. How's that?'

'Okay. Thank you.'

'No problem. I've got to go. Speak to you soon.'

'Yup. Bye.'

The pub rang with the old-fashioned ding of the receiver as Richard replaced it in its cradle. 'Sorry about that. How are you today?'

'Not bad, thanks. Everything okay?' Ed gestured unnecessarily in the direction of the phone.

'Yeah, it's fine. Just family stuff.'

'Is Lily okay? I heard about the fall.'

Richard had never lived in a village before, and still found it unsettling, the way news travelled among people he probably wouldn't give the time of day to in the street. 'She's recovering. I brought her home yesterday.'

'That's good news,' Ed said, nodding.

'Yeah, it could have been much worse. Anyway, I'm being a terrible barman today. Can I get you a drink?'

'Just a half, please. I've got to drive into town in a bit. Is Rosa about?'

'She's gone out with Ella.' Richard leaned down, groping under the bar for the half-pint glasses. His fingers brushed the shelf underneath the glasses, and came away covered in sticky residue. 'Urgh. Sometimes I wonder why Rosa doesn't make me give this place a thorough cleaning, rather than just standing around doing nothing all day.'

'I think she's worried that if she makes her staff do anything then they won't be willing to work for peanuts any more,' Ed replied, laughing. 'Is the place that bad?'

'I've worked in worse.' Richard examined the glass closely, then rinsed it in the sink for good measure. 'It could do with some general maintenance, though.' He pulled half a pint of the ale Ed had had last time, hoping he wouldn't object to the presumption. It was the kind of pub where people expected not to have to be too specific about what they were ordering, if they were in frequently enough to be recognised by the staff, and Richard didn't want to stick out as the new man by constantly asking people what they wanted.

'Well, I'm sure Rosa wouldn't object to you giving it a good going-over when you're not busy. I imagine the flat and the cellar could benefit from it, as well.'

'You're probably right there.' Richard placed Ed's drink in front of him. 'So what brings you in here, anyway? Were you after Rosa for anything in particular?'

'Nah. Just thought I'd drop in and say hello. I haven't seen much of her since Ella's been here.'

'Ella does seem to keep her busy. That's teenagers for you.'

'I guess.'

'You don't have kids, then?' Richard realised he had never asked before. Though presumably Rosa would have mentioned it.

'No.' Ed started to say something else, then stopped, and shrugged expansively.

'Sorry. Am I being nosy? I'm told it's the barman's prerogative.' Richard grinned.

'No, not nosy. It's just that my wife left, and my son, when he was a boy.'

'God, Ed, I'm sorry.'

Ed waved a hand in the air. 'Don't be. It's been a very long time.'

'Have you had any contact at all?'

'Not really.' He looked uncomfortable. 'I don't even know where she is.'

Richard shook his head. 'That's awful.'

'Yes, well, I probably wasn't the greatest husband.' He shrugged. 'Still. Twenty-five years, you'd have thought she'd have got over it by now, wouldn't you? Nothing in life longer than a woman's memory, that's what I say.'

Richard laughed, feeling awkward. 'I guess I'll find out, if I ever do anything to invoke Lily's wrath.'

'You two seem pretty happy together.'

'Yeah. We don't really fight, or anything.' Richard laughed again. 'Lily doesn't talk enough for us to fight, I suppose.'

'There must be advantages to that. Wish I'd married a woman who could keep her mouth shut.' Ed took a long swig of his drink. 'Do you ever feel like some of the passion's missing, though? I used to love a good argument to get the juices flowing.'

'Really?'

'Sure. How do you know what really matters to you both, if you don't ever get passionate about anything?'

'I don't – ' Richard stopped, confused. 'I don't think we're lacking in passion.'

'I'm sorry, son. I'm not questioning your relationship. You're obviously good together.'

'Yeah.' Richard nodded. 'Yes, I think we are.'

'Just be careful you don't leave her at home on her own too much, eh?' Ed laughed, and downed the rest of his drink in one gulp. 'Anyway. I've got to be off, I'm afraid. But I'll swing by again soon.'

'Sure.'

'Tell Rosa I said hi, will you?' Ed stuck a hand across the bar for Richard to shake.

'I will do. Bye.'

Ed ducked his head as he disappeared through the door.

then

Lily and her father sat in silence outside the head teacher's office. Lily stared at the closed door, with its dark wood and bronze nameplate, stamped with the name: *Mrs Julia Brennan*. Marcus stared at the floor, occasionally shifting in his chair, lifting his head to glance down the corridor. Secretaries fluttered around them like bees, drawing near and then floating away, with no apparent purpose. They had been there for fifteen minutes when the door swung open.

'Sorry to keep you.' Mrs Brennan was brisk, efficient, waving them inside, gesturing them into seats and closing the door behind them. Dr Mervyn was already there, with his notepad and a warm smile for both of them. Marcus did not smile back, but simply nodded, radiating tension.

'Thank you for coming in today.' Mrs Brennan directed the remark towards Marcus; Lily, of course, would have been there regardless.

'It's a pleasure,' he replied, his voice blank.

'Did Mrs Emmett not wish to join us?'

She speaks to him the same way she speaks to us, Lily realised. *Like he's a child. Like he's stupid.*

'She sends her apologies. She's unwell.'

Anna hadn't left her room for weeks. Lily had crept past the door every day, careful not to let the floorboards announce her presence. She preferred it when the door was shut, when her mother couldn't fix her with her strangely unfocused stare, as if she'd forgotten who she was.

'How unfortunate. Please send her my regards.'

Both of their voices were carefully expressionless.

'As you know, it's been over six months now since Lily started seeing Dr Mervyn. We thought it would be best to have a meeting so we could discuss her progress.'

'I'm very pleased with her progress,' Marcus offered. He laid a hand on her shoulder, protective. 'She's improved enormously. Wouldn't you say the same, doctor?'

'Absolutely.'

Lily tuned out the words. They discussed her as if she wasn't there, touching on her behaviour in lessons, her attendance, her socialisation with the other students. How she'd been since Connie's disappearance. It was Mrs Brennan's opinion that Lily had acquired confidence in Connie's absence; that she was more willing to speak up for herself, now that Connie was no longer around to do it for her. 'She still doesn't seem to want to make friends, though,' she said, as if Lily were four years old.

'I'm not sure any of Lily's classmates have shown any indication of wanting to be friends with her,' Marcus said evenly.

'I feel certain that if she just gave it a try...'

And on, and on. Lily kept a list of things that were not mentioned: Connie being attacked. Lily being locked up in the school overnight. Eleanor being expelled for bullying behaviour.

All in the past, now, of course. *And we want to put the past behind us, don't we?*

'Dr Mervyn is of the opinion that he may be contributing to Lily's ostracisation,' Mrs Brennan said. 'Because the children are aware that she sees him, of course. And that other people don't. He thinks that it marks her out as different.'

More different than not speaking for years, or being accused of murder at the age of eight... Lily looked at Dr Mervyn, disbelieving. She couldn't imagine him saying anything of the sort.

'He also thinks that she's ready to make a go of it on her own. Without him, I mean.'

Lily noticed her father's hands, which were clenched into fists on his lap. 'Really? Her progress is that good, is it?'

'You must have observed yourself, Mr Emmett, that her speech is almost entirely normal now.' Dr Mervyn's voice, carefully expressionless.

'Yes. I had.' A pause. 'Thank you.'

'That's what I was brought in to help her with, as you know. I feel that we're getting to the point where I can no longer be of assistance.'

'You've cured her, then.'

Dr Mervyn laughed, without humour. 'Psychiatric illnesses aren't that simple, of course. Lily has had a difficult start in life, and she would benefit from ongoing support. I would love to be able to provide her with that, but the school has limited resources and it is their view that I have done what I set out to do, namely improving her conversational skills. They feel that ongoing treatment is optional, rather than a requirement.'

'She meets your minimum requirements, then?' Marcus smiled blandly at Mrs Brennan.

'I'm not sure what you mean,' she said carefully.

'When we first discussed Lily seeing Dr Mervyn, you requested that she get treatment because she wasn't meeting the school's basic requirements. I assume the purpose of this discussion is to inform me that those basic requirements have now been met, and Lily is as fit to attend school as any other pupil?'

Lily watched Mrs Brennan's face. She looked furious, though Lily wasn't sure why. 'Yes,' she said, eventually. Reluctantly.

'Great. Thank you for your time. And thank you, Dr Mervyn, for all your help.' Marcus stood up, held out a hand for Dr Mervyn to shake. 'Come on, Lily. You need to get back to class.'

now

They arranged to meet in the same café as before. Nathan arrived late this time, and Andrea was already there when he walked through the door. She was leaning over the counter, elbows on the glass, looking at something on the back shelf. 'Hazelnut,' she said, unaware of Nathan standing behind her. The man behind the counter nodded curtly – *an excellent choice, madam* – and plucked the hazelnut syrup off the shelf on his way to the coffee machine.

'What's the occasion?' Nathan's voice made her jump. He found it oddly satisfying, managing to catch her off-guard when she was usually so collected.

'Does there need to be an occasion?'

'Guess not. Just seems a bit extravagant for nine in the morning.' He grinned, then called over the counter, 'Two of those, please.'

The waiter waved his hand in acknowledgement. 'Take a seat. I'll bring them over.'

They sat at the nearest table, Andrea leading the way. Nathan would have preferred a seat further in, where there was less chance of them being spotted, but he said nothing, following her lead.

'I wasn't sure you'd want to meet me,' he said, still grinning, trying to conceal his awkwardness.

'You sounded upset.'

Nathan shrugged. 'I guess.'

'Well, never let it be said that I won't help a man in need.'

Andrea smiled faintly. 'I can't stay long, though. I need to get to work. As do you, I assume?'

'Actually, I'm on holiday.'

Andrea raised an eyebrow. 'Shouldn't you be lounging around in bed, then?'

'Is that an invitation?' He tried a rogueish grin, but it fell flat. 'Sorry. I've been pretending I'm at work.'

'To get out of the house?'

'Yeah.'

'Why?'

'Because Connie asked me if I'm having an affair.'

Andrea nodded, and they said nothing, for a while. The waiter brought their drinks over, and they leaned forward slightly in their seats, the scent of hazelnut blending invitingly with the aroma of freshly brewed coffee. Nathan ran a finger through the foam, lifting it to his lips before he registered the expression on Andrea's face.

'What?'

'You're just like an overgrown child really, aren't you?'

He licked his finger and smiled. 'Not at all. Connie thinks I'm Mr Sensible Doctor. She thinks I'm pretentious because I listen to classical music and read literature as opposed to books.'

'If you refer to it as "literature" then you probably are pretentious.'

He laughed. 'Yeah, maybe.' He lifted his teaspoon, stirred the rest of the foam into his coffee. 'Better?'

'Much. So, what did you say when she asked you?'

'Nothing.'

'Nothing?'

Nathan took a sip of coffee. 'Yeah. I walked out.'

'Ah, yes. I can see why she thinks you're so grown-up and sensible.'

'Fuck off – what would you have done?'

The words were said defensively, with no malice, but Andrea flinched nonetheless. 'Don't swear at me.'

'Sorry.' He was instantly contrite. 'Seriously, though. What would you have done? I needed some time to think.'

'About what? Whether you were having an affair?'

'No, you've made it pretty clear that we're not having an affair.' He smiled wryly, and she smiled back, despite herself.

'Glad to see you got the message.'

'I did have to think about what I wanted, though. With you, I mean. Because if I wanted an affair then that's as bad as having one, isn't it?'

'I don't think it's as straightforward as that.'

'But I'd have to tell her, wouldn't I?' He leaned forward, his voice urgent. 'I can't just pretend that everything's the same as it was and I'd never thought about sleeping with you?'

Andrea sighed, and took a long sip of her coffee before answering. 'Why are we here, Nathan? Am I just here to soothe your conscience?'

'I don't know. I just felt like I needed your input.'

'I told you I don't want to be your marriage counsellor.'

'That's not what I want.'

'Then *what*?' Her eyes flashed, suddenly irritated. 'You keep dragging me out of work for these weird chats, you have no idea what you want, I've told you that *I'm* not interested and yet you keep calling me. Why? I want to help, but I don't want to involve myself in your failing marriage.'

'My marriage isn't failing.'

She laughed. 'Well, there's your answer, then, isn't it?'

'What do you mean?'

She shook her head. 'You'll figure it out.' She downed half of her remaining coffee in one swig. 'For what it's worth, I don't think you should lie to her. But there are ways of telling the truth which don't involve telling her every single thought that's passed through your head. You know what I mean?'

He shrugged. She finished her coffee and stood up.

'I hope you work things out, Nathan. Really.' She leaned down, kissed him on the top of the head. 'Could you please never call me again?'

He laughed humourlessly. 'If you insist.'

'Thank you.' And she was gone.

Lily wasn't sure how long it had been since Richard had left. She had gone upstairs when she'd heard him moving about, eaten breakfast with him, evaded his questions about what she'd been doing in the cellar. As soon as he'd gone out to work she was back downstairs, sifting through the boxes, searching without any object in mind.

It had been getting steadily lighter over the course of the morning. There were windows near the ceiling, slim horizontal bars of natural light nestled within the dense brickwork. The cellar was more shadowy than the upstairs of the house, but the menace of the darkness had faded with the rising of the sun. The ghost-children were barely visible now, and Lily paid them no attention, focused on the contents of the box in front of her.

It seemed to be made up entirely of items that had once belonged to Connie. She recognised some of them – toys, items of clothing – and there were other things, such as schoolbooks, which had Connie's name printed on the front in childish letters. She flicked through a few of them, making a mental note to show them to Connie when she came for Christmas. She wondered if it was different looking at items from your childhood when you had children of your own. Did you see yourself as part of an endless cycle, age producing youth, with your own childhood memories gradually dispersing in amongst those of your children?

She lost herself in the box for a while. And then a shadow flitted past one of the windows near the ceiling. Lily looked up, but she couldn't see anything. She felt uneasy, realising suddenly that the ghost-children had gone, that the silence had thickened around her as she sat sifting through old memories.

She stood up, abandoning the box as it was, items scattered all over the floor. Took the steps two at a time and emerged into the relative liveliness of the house: she could hear the fridge humming, a clock ticking in the living room, the chatter of people as they walked up the lane.

She felt restless. Wanted to carry on searching, but didn't want to go back down to the cellar. She climbed the stairs to her old room and went to her desk, opening and closing drawers at random. There was nothing there except a few pens, ink long since dried out, and a scattering of paperclips.

She sat on the floor, surrounded by paperwork, casting around for something to distract her. And then caught sight of the skirting board.

There had always been a gap, just under the window, where the wood had come loose. She had used it for storing paper-thin secrets: notes, drawings, pictures.

Letters.

The gap was obvious if you knew where to look, widened by the bundle of letters stuffed inside, the paper poking out above the wooden edge of the skirting board. She pulled them out, and recognised Connie's handwriting on the envelopes. The letters she'd sent from Germany. There hadn't been many – you could only say so much in a one-way correspondence where you were trying not to reveal your location or talk about the past – but Lily could remember receiving them all. She traced her fingers over the German postmark, smiling, remembering how exotic it had seemed back then, how distant and strange.

She removed the elastic and shuffled through the letters, odd sentences jumping out at her from the letters which had lost their envelopes. *It's been snowing for three weeks and I don't remember my feet ever being so cold... The hostel where I'm staying is nice, they've been giving me language lessons in the evenings... I wish you were here, it would be so nice to have someone to talk to, even though I know you wouldn't talk back...*

She sat on the floor for a long time, sifting through every word. It might not help her remember, but it was still a relief to know that not every aspect of her childhood had been lost: that, somewhere in their past, there was a Connie who had sent kind words across continents, and a Lily who had waited to receive them.

then

Lily arrived home from school to find her father sitting at the kitchen table. He had a pile of leaflets spread out in front of him, and he sat with the *Yellow Pages* at one elbow and the phone at the other. He looked up and smiled when she entered.

'Hey. How was the rest of your day?'

'Fine.' She sat down opposite him at the table, dropped her bag on the floor. 'What are you doing?'

'Research.' She picked up a leaflet. *Counselling Services in Your Area.*

'Where did you get these?'

'I popped into the doctor's on the way home. There are a lot of options, you know. I'm just trying to find one that's affordable.'

She tried to trace the thought processes that had got him to this point. It took her a minute. 'You think I still need help?'

He looked up from the *Yellow Pages*, surprised. 'You don't?'

'Dr Mervyn said I was okay.'

'That's not exactly what he was saying, sweetie.' Marcus leaned forward, looking her directly in the eye. 'He was saying that the school wouldn't pay him to help you any more. Because you're much better than you were, and they only have a limited budget. But he still thinks someone should be working with you, to make sure you carry on getting better.'

'So can't I just see him outside of school?'

Marcus sighed. 'Unfortunately he's pretty popular, and he doesn't have any spaces at the moment.'

Lily nodded. Said nothing.

'But look, there are lots of other options. How about this one?' He held up a leaflet entitled *Dr Mason's Children's Services*. A woman of about fifty smiled down at Lily. 'She looks friendly, don't you think?'

'She looks a bit like Mrs Brennan.'

'You think?' Marcus looked at the leaflet again. 'I suppose she might. Well, how about this guy, then?' He held up another one. Lily didn't bother looking at it.

'Whatever you choose will be fine.' She stood up, picked up her bag again.

'You going upstairs?'

'Yeah. Homework.'

She climbed the stairs slowly, feeling exhausted. Her mind screamed a protest against seeing another doctor, though she wasn't really sure why. It wouldn't be any different from seeing Dr Mervyn. It would probably help. But she had no interest in seeing anyone else. If he couldn't help her, then she didn't want to be helped.

Her mother's door was shut as usual, and she knocked on it lightly as she passed. She didn't really expect an answer, but she heard a low murmur from inside, which might have been, 'Come in.' She pushed open the door, slowly, cautiously.

It was dark inside: the curtains were drawn and there were no lights, not even a bedside lamp. Lily could see a shape stirring under the covers, and she went in, pushing the door closed behind her. 'Mama?'

'Connie?'

'No, Mama. It's Lily.' She put down her bag and padded across the room, coming to stand next to her mother's head. She could see her eyes, peering blearily into the darkness, trying to make out the shape of her youngest daughter.

'Is Connie still away?' Anna reached out a hand, and Lily took it. Her mother's palm was warm and dry.

'Yes.'

'You've spoken to her?' Anna's voice was suddenly urgent, her grip tightened.

'No, Mama. She wrote to me. You know that.'

'Oh, yes.' She relaxed again. 'If you speak to her, tell her I love her, won't you?'

'Of course I will.'

'Come and lie down.' Anna shifted over to make room, and lifted the covers so that Lily could crawl in with her. It was uncomfortably warm, and the sheets smelled musty and unwashed. 'How long has it been, since we were all together? Hmm? You remember when we used to be a proper family?'

Lily thought about it. She wasn't sure she could.

'I've tried, you know. For so long I tried. To hold it all together, to keep us from drifting apart. And your father just keeps on messing with it all, making us all argue.'

'Dad?' Lily said. The heat and the dark made her head swim, made everything confusing.

'Yes. He doesn't love you girls like I do, you know. Doesn't understand what it's like, to be a mother. To have your children ripped away from you, ripped right out of your body, and then sent away, both of you sent away, and me left here with nothing…' She drifted into incoherence, her words blurring together until they were nothing but sounds trying to catch the attention of other sounds. Lily lay very still.

'You, though…' Anna said. And then stopped.

'What, Mama? Me what?'

'You're the wrong one,' Anna said simply. 'I never wanted you.'

But she continued to hold on to her until she fell asleep, and Lily listened as her soft snores filled the room.

now

Connie was wrapping presents in the bedroom, listening to the squeals of the boys as they played in Luke's room next door, when she heard the front door close downstairs. It was the first time in four days that Nathan had been home before everyone was in bed, and Connie felt herself freeze, hands poised in mid-air above the present she was wrapping. The boys responded instantly, thundering down the stairs like a herd of miniature elephants, screaming 'Daddy! Daddy!' at the top of their voices.

'Hey,' she heard him say, laughter in his voice, as if their reaction was a surprise. As if he'd only been gone ten minutes. 'What's all the fuss about?'

Connie sat motionless as the boys exclaimed over his absence, told him about everything they'd been doing throughout the day; smiled as they told him that they'd been 'sooooo bored' because Mummy had been wrapping presents 'allllll day'. They moved into the living room, their voices fading to a low murmur beneath her, so that she could no longer distinguish the individual sounds.

School had broken up three days previously, and Connie had been hoping that the constant presence of the boys might mean Nathan would be inclined to spend more time at home. He'd been just as distant, though, leaving before Connie got up and coming home long after she'd fallen into a fitful sleep. The boys hadn't really questioned it, used to Nathan's long working hours and his 'I'm a doctor and people rely on me' speech, so things had felt almost normal, except that there was an absence in the household that only Connie was aware of, a silence at her side where usually she would have felt support.

Tomorrow was Christmas Eve, and they were due to be with Lily and Richard by lunchtime. Connie had been starting to wonder if Nathan would even remember it was Christmas, let alone that they were going away. She couldn't imagine how they would spend the holiday period together: how they could be in the same house for even a day and pretend that nothing was wrong. It had been a week since their last conversation.

She had been thinking, idly, about the first Christmas she had spent on her own. It had been nine months after her abrupt departure, and she'd found herself in a largely empty hostel in Berlin, with only a handful of other tourists for company.

One of them, an American girl who couldn't have been more than a year older than Connie, had invited her to join their attempt at Christmas dinner. Germany in general did their present-giving on Christmas Eve, but, as Connie didn't have anyone to give presents to, it hadn't really made much difference to her. The hostel had provided a roast dinner for what had seemed like an unfeasibly cheap price, complete with candles and decorations and a generous amount of wine. There had been snow on the ground outside, and Connie could remember the excitement of waking up to her first ever white Christmas. It hadn't mattered that her family were miles away. For a few minutes, watching the sun rise over a whitewashed Berlin, she'd felt the tingle of genuine Christmas magic.

The feeling had returned after dinner, when the Americans, the couple who ran the hostel and a Swiss couple who had been passing through made their way out of the front door one by one. When she joined them, curious, Connie had found them pelting each other with snowballs, accompanied by a group of children who had already been in the midst of their own snowball fight. For a while Connie was content just to stand on the edge and watch, feeling oddly blessed, as if she had left home at exactly the right time. She refused to think about the reasons for leaving, or, worse, what she had left behind.

It was a long time since she'd spent Christmas alone, Connie thought now. It would be her twelfth year with Nathan, her eighth year as a mother. Every year since she'd returned she'd visited her mother on Christmas Day, though Lily never joined her and her mother seldom thanked her for it. Her attempts at seasonal family reunions were generally halted when Lily refused to pick up the phone.

Despite that, she'd always viewed herself as lucky, knowing that so many people didn't have anyone to spend the holiday with, knowing the feeling of isolation it could bring, being cut off from the rest of the celebrating world. But she'd also forgotten how liberating it could be, when your family weren't providing the solid foundation that they were expected to provide. She had forgotten that camaraderie, that sense of sudden and instant love that could spring up between people who were stranded together. Had found herself longing, idly, for that feeling again.

She was immersed in her thoughts, and didn't notice the sounds of movement in the hallway until there was a knock at the door. The knock was too light, too calm, to belong to one of the boys. 'Come in.'

Nathan poked his head round the door. 'Hi.'

'Hi. You don't have to knock, you know. It's your room too.'

'I thought you might have things out you didn't want me to see.' He gestured at the packages scattered across the floor. 'Or have you decided I don't deserve anything this year?'

'You can't just joke this away, Nathan.'

'I know.' He stepped into the room, moving around the presents to sit on the bed. 'I'm sorry, Connie. I shouldn't have been gone for so long.'

She nodded, but said nothing. She didn't really trust herself to speak.

'Things have been... Well. You've been here, you know how they've been.'

Connie nodded again, eyes fixed on the present she was wrapping.

'I felt as if I was making you worse. I know you keep saying you want a husband and not a GP but I don't know how to be one without the other. I can't think about you being depressed without wanting to try to sort it out.'

'Counselling isn't the answer,' Connie said.

'Okay. I'm sorry.'

There was silence, as Connie wondered whether he would answer the question that had caused him to leave in the first place, or whether he would force her to ask it again. The words sat in her mouth, fat and sour, making her feel faintly nauseous.

He caught her eye, and he understood.

'The affair thing...' he said, and she steeled herself against whatever was to come, rigidly holding her body in one place so it wouldn't betray how she felt. 'I didn't have an affair. I have genuinely been going to work all this time. But there was – ' He saw her flinch, and paused, but forced himself to continue. 'There was one night. I went back to another woman's house. I didn't sleep with her, but I did kiss her.' He waited until she looked up and met his eyes before he said, 'I'm really sorry.'

Connie found that, though her heart was beating so fast it made her blood feel as if it was fizzing, her voice was calm and steady. 'Why didn't you sleep with her?'

'Because I was very drunk and neither of us really wanted to go there.'

'Have you seen her since?'

'Not like that.'

'But you have seen her?'

He looked at the floor, nodded. She felt the muscles in the pit of her stomach twist with understanding.

'You know her from work?'

He nodded again. Connie wondered where her tears had gone. She felt breathless and dry-eyed. 'Right,' she said, eventually, not really knowing what she was saying. 'I see.'

'Connie?'

'Yeah?'

'Are you going to leave me?'

She looked up at him, and realised that her tears were in his eyes. He looked at her as if she held his entire life in her hands. Which, she supposed, she sort of did.

'I don't think so,' she said, slowly.

'No?'

'I need some time to think. This is – well.' She thought it over for a minute, chewing absently on the side of her forefinger. 'I guess it's not as bad as I'd feared. But it's worse than if you'd never done anything. So I'm not really sure how I feel, now.'

He nodded, looking down at his hands. He looked lost, and she realised she almost never saw him looking unsure of himself. It made her want to put her arms around him, but she held herself in place.

'Why did you put me through the last few days? You could have just told me. Walking out, it – it made me think it was true. Or that I'd pissed you off. But I had a right to ask, didn't I? It wasn't completely unjustified.'

'I walked out because I didn't know how to answer. I stayed away for the same reason. I couldn't stand to lie to your face, but I didn't want to tell you and ruin our marriage over something that was insignificant and stupid to me.'

'But you did lie to my face. At some point you must have lied to me, told me you were in one place when you were somewhere else.'

'I know. I know it doesn't make sense, but it was different, when you were actually asking me a straight question.'

'That's just childish logic, Nathan.'

'I know.'

'And you know how I feel, about – affairs, and – ' The tears were here now, as she thought about it, the injustice of it, of what her mother had done to her father and Nathan had done to her and everyone in the world did to everyone else in the world on a daily basis. He leaned forward, reached a hand out and clasped it around hers.

'I *know*, Connie. I didn't think; I forgot, and I was drunk, but it's no excuse. I do know, and I really am so sorry. But it's not like your mother.'

'How do you figure that?'

'It was just once. It wasn't *here*. I haven't lied to you for years, I realised what I did was wrong, and I stopped it before it went anywhere. Please. I promise you it's not the same.'

She removed her hand from his and pushed herself a few inches away from him. She found it was an effort to raise her head to meet his eyes, so she looked at his knees, encased in black cotton that hung loosely around the flesh and bone beneath. They sat in silence for a long time, while she thought about her parents, and what the other woman might look like, and what the kids were doing downstairs, and whether she could carry on with this new, different Nathan at her side, and whether she could carry on without him. Tears trickled down her cheeks and dropped off the end of her chin, but she paid them no attention. Nathan watched her, waiting, hands clasped so tightly in front of him that his knuckles had turned white.

'I need some time,' she said eventually. Her voice was clogged with tears, and she cleared her throat, feeling inelegant and dramatic.

'Do you want me to stay here over Christmas?'

'No. The boys would find it weird. And Lily and Richard – Lily's been through enough lately. I want to give her a normal Christmas.'

'You are allowed to have your own problems, Connie. Hers don't always take precedence.'

'Yes, they do.' She stood up, and found her legs had cramped from sitting in the same position for so long. 'I'm going to put the boys to bed.'

And she left him, sitting on the bed, looking unavoidably exposed: the uncertainty of everything laid out all around him.

then

Marcus drove Lily to the doctor's office. She went in alone, leaving him to wait in the car. The waiting room was largely decorated in shades of beige, and there were standard posters taped all over the walls with slogans like MENTAL HEALTH IS NOT A GAME and IS FEAR HOLDING YOU BACK? A large middle-aged woman with tight red curls sat behind a reception window on the far wall, and she smiled at Lily as she walked up.

'Can I help you?'

'I have an appointment. With Dr Robinson?'

'Certainly. Your name?'

'Lily Emmett.'

The receptionist ran her finger down a list in front of her. Nodded, once. 'Take a seat, dear, and we'll call you when we're ready.'

Lily chose a seat in the far corner of the room. There were about twenty chairs, and none of them was occupied. She looked around the room. Found herself regretting telling her father to wait in the car. The low murmur of the radio filled the room, a song she recognised but didn't know the words to.

'Lily?' The doctor appeared in the doorway. 'Are your parents not with you?'

Lily stood up. 'In the car,' she said, nodding in the direction of the door.

'Okay. Do you want to follow me, then?'

Lily followed her into a small room with two armchairs, separated by a low table topped with an ageing plant and a box of tissues. The doctor waved her into one of the chairs, and settled herself in the other one. She didn't look much like a doctor; her hair was tied loosely with a headscarf, and she wore a long patterned skirt and jewelled hoops around her wrists. She resembled an old-fashioned fortune teller.

'I'm Dr Robinson,' she said, pulling out a notepad and placing it on her knee. 'We're just going to have a brief chat today, Lily, just to see whether we get on. Is that okay?'

Lily nodded. There was something about the pitch of her voice that grated. An unnecessary elongation of the words, as if taking the time to speak more slowly made her appear more caring.

'Your father said you have trouble talking sometimes, is that right?'

Lily shrugged. 'I'm getting better. My other doctor said.'

'But you're not completely better, are you? There are still some things your father would like us to go over, as I understand it?'

Lily shrugged again, and said nothing.

'I understand you've had some difficulties in your past. A lot of disruption, is that right? A lot of unfortunate events?'

Lily stared at her, wondering which of the events in her life would be classed as merely unfortunate.

'Talking about things is one of the ways we get past them. A lot of people find that talking about events helps them understand what happened, and their feelings about what happened. And sometimes they come to counselling to talk about things in a safe place, because they find it difficult to talk at home, to people who know them well.' Dr Robinson gave her a significant look. 'Did you talk about things with the doctor you were seeing at school?'

'Sometimes.'

'And did you find it helpful?'

'Depends.'

Dr Robinson looked at her, waiting. Then: 'You can talk to me, you know. This is a safe space. I'm not connected to anyone you know, I'm not going to tell your parents about anything you say. This is a place where you can just be yourself, talk about anything.'

Lily watched her. Waiting to see if she had anything else to offer. When it became clear that she didn't, Lily stood up. 'I'm sorry, Dr Robinson. I don't think this is going to work.'

She left.

They didn't speak much on the way home. Marcus hadn't asked too many questions, but he'd been surprised that she hadn't taken longer to make her mind up. 'It wasn't right,' Lily had said, not seeing what further explanation was needed.

'But couldn't you have given it a bit more time?' he'd asked.

She'd looked at him blankly. 'Why?'

When they got home she went straight upstairs. She listened outside her mother's door, but heard no sign of movement. And then, tiptoeing, she crept down the corridor and into her own room.

The room was dark. She eased the door closed behind her and flicked the light on, wincing at the sudden harsh illumination. She moved quietly through the room, not wanting her parents to hear her. Got down on her hands and knees and crawled under her desk. Groped with a hand until she found what she was searching for: the loose skirting board, the rustle of paper beneath her fingers.

She pulled out a bundle of letters, maybe four or five of them, still in their envelopes. She held them for a minute, pressing them against her face. Then carried them to her bed; sat cross-legged in the middle and spread the letters around her. They were all from Connie, all with the same neat scribble on the envelope, the same exotic postmark. She picked up the most recent one, which she'd only received two days ago. She hadn't told her parents about it. She didn't see the point any more: they both knew Connie was alive, and the letters were private.

Lily read the letter twice. In tone, it was exactly the same as all the others had been. It was light, detached, not meaningful. No mention of why she'd gone. No mention of when she was coming home. And no hint that she might be missed – that maybe her selfishness had directly impacted on the situation at home, had made things even worse.

Lily found it hard to decide whether she missed her or whether she wished she'd disappear for good.

now

When Richard awoke on Christmas Eve, it was to find the bed empty, and Lily's imprint on the sheets still warm. He curled into her space for a moment, burying himself in her pillow; let the rays of sunshine that would usually wake her through the gap in the curtains creep across his face. He'd never even noticed the gap before, and he marvelled, momentarily, at the strangeness of familiar things seen from an unfamiliar perspective. He realised that Lily must wake like this every day, with sunlight brushing her eyelashes and coaxing her into consciousness.

He could hear her moving downstairs; hear the kettle boiling, the familiar clattering sounds of the kitchen being used. He wondered why it sounded so strange, and then realised: she hadn't been in the kitchen alone since they'd moved here. Or at least, not when he'd been around to hear it. He hadn't realised how much he'd missed the sound of cupboards swinging open and shut, water running, crockery tapping cordially together. It reminded him of childhood somehow; of waking up to find the world already going, his parents making breakfast and the radio chattering in the corner: a swirl of activity, all ready for him to slot into. And it made him think of the rare times he had awoken before anyone else: of creeping around downstairs in the dark, afraid to turn the lights on, feeling sure he would be caught out, sent back to bed. He'd had no place in the world that was his, then; everything he had was given to him by his parents.

He swung out of bed, pulled on jeans and an old wool jumper, and went in search of socks. They still hadn't got round to covering the bare floorboards with anything more than a scattering of rugs, and the floor was freezing in the winter morning air. Lily frequently wandered around barefoot, making him shudder; he hated being cold. She'd laughed at him when he'd first mentioned this, and said her feet must have been hardened by spending her formative years in a carpet-free environment. For some reason her mother had been obsessed with the idea of bare wood.

He bounded down the stairs, and then hesitated in the doorway to the kitchen, watching her. She hadn't heard him, and she was side-on at the sink, facing slightly away: his movement in the hallway had gone unnoticed. She was humming to herself quietly, up to her elbows in soap bubbles, her dark blonde hair swept away from her face but escaping in clusters from its tie. A row of bubbles gathered in the front strands of her hair, where she'd brushed them away from her face with the back of her wrist. She was focused entirely on the job at hand.

He stood silently for nearly a minute, watching her, wondering. And then she looked up, and smiled, and the spell was almost broken. But not quite.

He walked up behind her and slipped his arms around her waist. She hugged him awkwardly, with her elbows, trying not to get bubbles all over his clothes. Turned her head slightly, so he could kiss the side of her mouth. Richard squeezed his arms closer around her waist. Buried his nose in her neck. And knew that there was nothing in his future but her.

'Lily?'

'Mmm?'

'Will you marry me?'

She laughed, turning her head as far as it would go, but not taking her hands out of the sink. 'Really?'

'Yes.'

'Why?'

He shrugged. 'Because I love you and I can't imagine life without you.' He slipped a hand into the water, and found Lily's hand. Entwined his fingers around hers, causing her to let go of the plate she was holding. Squeezed her hand in a familiar sequence: one short, one long, two short.

I love you.

She smiled. *I love you too.*

He leaned closer, so close he could feel strands of her hair slipping between his lips when he spoke. 'So?'

She tilted her head, demonstratively thinking. And then smiled. He felt her answering squeeze in the lukewarm water.

Yes.

The boys had been awake and driving Connie up the wall since six. Nathan, with his irritating ability to sleep through any amount of noise, had stayed in bed until nine, and so the majority of last-minute things that Connie had been planning to do hadn't been done. There were Post-it notes flapping at her like little yellow hazard signs from every surface: *take these, cook this, DON'T FORGET THESE!!*, and so on. But there was none of the sense of calm she had hoped to cultivate through the illusion of being well-organised, and by eleven o'clock they were still nowhere near leaving.

'Why don't you go and have a shower and I'll get the boys ready?' Nathan suggested, his voice exaggeratedly calm and reasonable. Connie was flushed and wide-eyed, covered with flour from her early-morning attempts at Christmas baking (the boys had joined in with enthusiasm, and nothing much had been achieved), and she was concentrating so hard on scribbling things in a notepad that at first she didn't hear him.

'Hmm?'

'I said, why don't you have a shower? I'll get the boys ready. You'll feel much more prepared once you're properly dressed.'

'I need to take the mince pies out of the oven in a minute.'

'Did you set the timer?'

'Um...' Connie chewed her bottom lip, still concentrating on her notebook. 'I think so.'

'Then it will go off when they're done, won't it? And I can get them out of the oven.'

'True.' She crossed something out, scarring the pad with a deep black line.

'There's really no need to worry, you know. It's not as though they're expecting us at any particular time.'

'I told them we'd be there at lunchtime.'

'Ah. That most specific of meeting times.'

'Fuck off, Nathan.'

Nathan looked up at the boys automatically, but they were deeply involved in a computer game, and didn't notice their mother's unusually harsh language. 'The kids?'

'They weren't listening.'

'Even so...'

'You swear in front of them all the time, so don't get all sanctimonious on me.' She finished writing whatever it was that she'd been concentrating on, and put the notebook down on the table. 'I'll go and shower, then.'

'Thank you.'

Connie glared at him. 'For what?'

'I don't know. Being reasonable. Not shouting at me and telling me you don't need a shower. I...' He stopped, seeing the look on her face. 'I'm sorry. You're just all agitated and it's Christmas Eve and I want you to be happy.'

'Why? So we can pretend everything's fine and not upset anyone?'

'Well, kind of. Yes.'

'Things can't just go back to normal because it's Christmas.' She picked her notebook up again, as if she was considering using it as a shield. 'In our family, especially so.'

'What do you mean? Why our family particularly?'

'Oh, I didn't mean *you*.'

Nathan's features bunched in towards his nose, furrowing in confusion. 'Why... Oh.' His eyes widened as he realised what she meant. 'Shit. I'm sorry.'

'It's fine.'

'No, it really isn't. I've just been really distracted, with everything that's been going on between us... I didn't think.'

'It really is fine. Honestly.'

'But – '

'Shh.' She walked over to him and placed a finger on his lips. When she looked up at him there was sadness in her eyes, but also warmth, without the glimmer of anger that had almost become a permanent resident. She looked, almost, like the Connie he had fallen in love with.

'I'm sorry I've messed everything up,' he said softly.

'Yeah, you should be.'

'Do you think we'll be okay?'

She looked down at the floor, exposing the top of her head, with its dusting of flour. He brushed her hair, lightly, and a sprinkling of white dust flew into the air around her face.

'I don't know yet,' she said, talking to his shoes and not to him.

'Sorry. I shouldn't have asked.'

She tilted her head up, and there was a half-smile on her face, an expression of not-quite-sadness. He moved his hands on to her shoulders, feeling the fragility of her bones beneath the skin, and squeezed lightly, wanting to take her in his arms but not sure she'd allow it. 'Truce, then?'

She laughed, suddenly, out of nowhere. 'Like the Christmas armistice?'

'Sort of, I suppose.'

'And we can go back to killing each other on Boxing Day?'

He laughed. 'If you really want to.'

'Okay, then.' She twisted her head and kissed his knuckles, softly, before heading upstairs to have a shower.

then

Both Lily's parents were already up and making coffee in the kitchen when she got up on Christmas Eve. Her mother had been almost her old self for the last couple of weeks: out of bed every day, making dinner, demanding conversation. It was unnerving, to see such an abrupt return to normality: as though she'd just swept the past six months under the carpet and was no longer going to talk about it. Marcus was following suit, acting as if everything was suddenly fine again. Neither of them mentioned Connie.

They turned in her direction when she entered the kitchen, festive smiles plastered across their faces. 'You're up,' her father said, pointlessly. She nodded.

'Do you want breakfast?' her mother asked. 'I was going to make pancakes.'

'Sure.'

They ate in near-silence, cutlery clinking deafeningly on plates. Lily wrapped her pancakes into sausage shapes and drowned them in lemon juice, floating them in sour yellow pools and then dissolving spoonfuls of sugar into the liquid. Her mother watched with an expression of distaste, but said nothing. It was Christmas Eve, after all.

After breakfast they sat in the living room. It felt oddly overcrowded with the three of them sitting there. Lily read while her parents watched a film. Every few minutes her mother would lean over to inspect the book, or nudge her and say, 'It's good, is it?'

'It's fine,' Lily would reply dully, not looking up from her book.

After the third time this happened, Marcus turned round and snapped, 'If you're so interested, why don't you read it yourself?'

'I'm just trying to engage with my daughter. Involve myself in her life. Is that a problem?'

'No, it's fine. Would you mind doing it more than once a year?'

Anna gasped. 'How *dare* you?'

Marcus muted the TV. 'What do you mean, how dare I? You've barely left your bed in months.'

'I've been ill.'

'Yes, I realise that. But you haven't done much to make yourself better, have you?'

'I can't believe this. I'm finally improving, starting to feel like a normal person again, and you're attacking me. Why?'

Marcus glared at her. 'Because you're talking to Lily like she's an idiot.'

Lily shrank in her chair as both of her parents turned to look at her. 'Is that true?' Anna demanded. 'Do I talk to you like you're an idiot?'

Lily looked from one to the other, with no idea what to say. She shrugged.

'*Speak*, for pity's sake. Do I talk to you like you're an idiot?'

'Sometimes,' Lily said eventually. Then she stood up and walked out of the room.

The sound of their shouting followed her up the stairs. She closed the door on the noise, and heard her mother storming up the stairs a few moments later. She froze, expecting her to knock on the door. But there was only the sound of her mother's own bedroom door slamming.

Two minutes later, her father knocked quietly, then poked his head around the door. 'Want to go for a walk?'

They put on coats and hats and scarves, and bundled out into the cold. The sky was low and grey, the streets silent. They turned right and headed down the lane, towards the fields that clustered around the house. The air was dry, biting at Lily's gloveless hands and the tip of her nose. She plunged her hands into her coat pockets, finding an assortment of old tissues and loose change. She scraped a nail along the bottom seam of the pocket, and brought away a small cluster of fluff, which she balled up and threw into the air. It flew briefly, before tumbling to the ground behind them.

'Do you know why Connie ran away?' Marcus asked, without preamble. His voice was quiet, and Lily was surprised that he'd asked. She'd thought they were still pretending nothing had happened.

'No,' she replied, truthfully. She was quiet for a moment, and then a thought occurred to her, and she asked, 'Do you?'

'No.' His voice was heavy, and he sounded older than usual. 'I wish I did. I just thought she might have told you something.'

Lily said nothing, waiting.

'Sometimes I think this family is cursed,' Marcus continued, his voice absent-minded, as if he wasn't really concentrating on what he was saying. 'Ever since that day…' He trailed off, suddenly realising who he was talking to.

'Dad?'

'Mmm?'

'Do you know what happened?'

Marcus looked at her sharply, but didn't stop walking. Lily kept her eyes on the distance, where the expanse of fields was broken by a line of trees. 'No,' he said eventually. 'Do you?'

She shook her head, not trusting her voice.

'So. Your mum's theory that you're silent because you're keeping everyone else's secrets is shot to hell, then,' he said, laughing bitterly.

'She thinks that?'

He nodded, and sighed. 'Yes. I told her you wouldn't keep quiet about things that were important, but she thinks you're stubborn enough to take everything to your grave.'

Lily pondered this. 'Is that why she's angry with me?'

'Partly. She's also angry because she thinks she's failed as a mother.'

'Why would she take that out on me?'

'Because if she tried to take it out on herself she'd end up in hospital.' His voice was harsh, and sad, and there was a bitterness that Lily had never heard before. She knew they were angry with each other, but she hadn't realised her father could sound so unkind.

'Dad?'

'Yeah?'

'Do you wish you weren't married to her?'

There was a long pause, so long Lily thought he wasn't going to answer, as he looked at the sky with an expression which seemed to hold all the sadness in the world. 'Yes,' he said, finally, looking down at her with an apology in his eyes. 'I wouldn't give up you or Connie for the world, but I don't want to be with her any more.'

Lily nodded, and they walked on in silence. After a while she pulled her hand out of her pocket and placed it in his, finding his much larger hand clenched around his keys. She peeled his fingers away from the metal until they relaxed, and then pushed her hand inside his, folding his fingers around her smaller ones. She kept it there until they got home.

The atmosphere in the Emmett household was just as tense on Christmas Day as it had been the day before. Anna had spent most of the day in her room, not talking to either of them. Lily and Marcus had combated the atmosphere by turning the radio up and cooking dinner with the aid of Christmas songs and exaggerated dancing. Marcus sang along tunelessly, proffering wooden spoons and spatulas in Lily's direction to use as microphones, in case she got the urge to join in, though she didn't take him up on the offer. Mariah Carey was being drowned out by Marcus's warbling when Anna came downstairs, her features arranged in her standard expression of irritation.

'I was trying to sleep,' she said, by way of greeting.

'And we were trying to enjoy Christmas,' her husband replied, recklessly. He'd opened a bottle of wine, and was halfway through his second glass by the time Anna appeared. He never drank much, and his cheeks were unusually flushed, his eyes over-bright. Lily stood back, blending into the background as best she could.

'Well, I'd enjoy it a lot more if I'd had a decent amount of sleep,' Anna said.

'And we'd probably enjoy it a lot more if you just stayed upstairs,' Marcus retorted. 'You don't always get what you want.'

'Why are you being such an arsehole today?'

'I'm not. I was just in a good mood, and as usual you've ruined it just by walking through the door. Me and Lily were having a lovely time – ' He gestured in her direction, and she drew back further, pushing her shoulder-blades into the wall.

'I'm not trying to stop you having fun, for God's sake. Maybe if just *once* you'd let me join in instead of feeling like an outsider – '

Their voices rose, until all illusion of communication was gone: they were merely shouting their own grievances over the top of each other's words. Lily waited until she was absolutely sure they weren't paying her any attention, and then slipped into the hallway and up the stairs to her room.

She closed the door behind her, and then went to the window, throwing it open and trying not to wince as the cold air slapped against her bare face and hands. She stuck her head as far out as she could, gulping freezing air, feeling it rush down her windpipe and constrict her insides with cold. If she leaned out far enough then their voices were just a distant murmur against the noise of the birds in the trees, and she couldn't hear the words they said.

Two houses down, a family were out in their back garden: a father and son dragged wood into a pile while the mother watched, unwilling to join in, but smiling nonetheless. She pointed to bits of wood with hands gloved in orange wool, directing them on the best methods of construction. The son, not much older than seven or eight, kept trying to pick up logs that were too big for him, determination etched on his young face.

Lily smiled as she watched them, enjoying the simplicity of the scene, the cordiality with which all members of the family treated each other. When the boy dropped a piece of wood on his foot, and neither parent had been watching closely enough to prevent it, they didn't scold each other, they just made sure their son wasn't injured and then carried on as normal.

From her position half-inside and half-outside the house, Lily heard the front door slam. She waited, her breathing as shallow and quiet as she could make it without it hurting her lungs, for sounds from which she could deduce what had happened. Ten seconds passed, and then the car beeped: the door opened, shut. A further ten seconds, and the engine roared to life. The car itself sounded angry as it sped away, far more quickly than it usually would have done.

There was no sound from within the house. It was impossible to guess which one of them had left. She realised she was almost impressed, that they could upset each other so much in such a short space of time. It had been less than five minutes, all told.

She pulled the window closed quietly, not wanting to draw attention to herself, and then tiptoed across her room and opened the door as carefully as she could. She could hear no sound from downstairs: whoever remained had shut off the radio, and they weren't moving. That was if either of them remained, of course. What if they had left at the same time, disappeared in different directions? Would she be expected to sit here quietly, have dinner ready for when they got home?

The stairs creaked as she walked down them, despite her attempts to place her weight evenly and not disturb the looser floorboards. She was well practised at creeping around the house; she half-believed that it was the prevention of this that kept her mother from investing in carpets, but she and Connie had often snuck around in the middle of the night when they were young, while their parents slept on, oblivious.

She thought of the last time they had crept out together, and shivered, involuntarily. Over four years, and it still felt as if the legacy of that day perched on her shoulder and watched her.

Her mother was in the kitchen. She sat on the floor, legs curled to her chest, head resting on her knees, shaking silently. Lily waited for a moment, watching her. She looked exhausted. Emptied. When Lily came to stand in front of her, she stirred but didn't look up. Lily felt her strain to even out her breathing, her body racked by deep, shuddering inhalations as she tried to steady herself.

'I'm sorry I ruined Christmas,' she said, sounding as forlorn as a child. Lily knew she should feel angry, or at least irritated. But all she felt was sorry, that this was what her family had come to: that, out of all them, she was the one who seemed to have the best grip on reality.

She sat down next to her mother. The floor was cold, and she could feel the numbness seeping through her jeans. 'Where did Dad go?' she asked.

'I don't know.'

'He took the car.'

'Yeah, I know.' Anna paused for a beat. 'He was really angry with me, Lily. He told me he wanted to leave me.'

Lily nodded, but didn't reply.

'Do you think he'll ever forgive me?'

Lily shrugged. Noticed a piece of thread that was coming loose from the bottom of her trousers, and tugged it, sharply. 'He was drinking earlier. He shouldn't be driving.'

'He'll be okay. He's just trying to get my attention.'

Maybe you should pay attention, then. But Lily didn't say it aloud.

'Dinner will be ready soon,' Anna said after a while.

Together, they stood up, and carried on making dinner, as if they had been the ones who had started it.

The knock on the door came hours later. Anna had dished up the food, and they had eaten, quietly, Lily eyeing the space at the table that was the source of their silence. Anna looked resolutely ahead throughout the entire meal, staring at a spot on the wall that Lily couldn't see. Afterwards, Lily went through to the living room while Anna washed up. She turned the main light off, draping the room in early winter darkness. Then she got on her hands and knees and groped behind the sofa, searching for the switch, and, finding it, sat back to admire her work. The darkness was gone, swept away in a twinkling of Christmas lights. The lights winked on and off, playing hide and seek behind the green plastic branches. Lily was so involved in watching them that she didn't notice someone walking up the path, just outside the window.

But she heard the knock at the door.

There was only one policeman, and she remembered, later, being surprised at that: on TV there were always two of them. He was about the same age as her dad, but he was balding, and his face was etched with deep creases that she longed to poke a finger into.

'Is your mother in?'

Lily sized him up, and decided he was probably not a danger to either of them. She'd seen enough policemen when Connie had left to be able to recognise their general type, regardless of whether or not they were in uniform. 'Sure. Come in.'

She led him through to the kitchen, where they found Anna elbow-deep in soap bubbles. Her expression changed from exhaustion to surprise when she saw who it was, and then, almost instantly, to trepidation. 'Hello,' she said, guarded.

'Good evening. Sorry to barge in on you like this. Mrs Emmett?'

'Yes.' She pulled her arms out of the sink, and dried them hurriedly on a nearby tea-towel. She started to hold out a hand to shake, then seemed to think better of it.

'Jack Latham. Police constable.'

Anna nodded, uncertain. 'Would you like a cup of tea?'

'No, thank you. Could we sit down?'

'Sure.'

Anna led him into the living room. Hesitated. And then closed the door, leaving Lily in the hallway by herself.

now

Lily awoke early on Christmas Day. She could see through the gap in the curtains that the sky was still shrouded in darkness; the day had not officially begun. She rolled over, and realised Richard was awake, watching her in silence. 'Morning,' she whispered.

'Morning,' he whispered back. His eyes were glimmers of light in the darkness as they darted around her face, taking her in. He ran a hand up her back, slowly, and his fingers were warm and dry, and gentle, as they explored the network of muscles beneath her skin. She pushed her face into his chest so she could no longer see him, but she could feel his heart beating in her forehead. My fiancé, she thought, and allowed herself a moment of shivering pleasure, before remembering what day it was.

Richard kissed the top of her head, teasing strands of hair away from her scalp with his nose, burrowing into her. They lay quietly for a while, his arms clasped around her back, her palms pressed against his chest.

'In the beginning was the word,' he said, after a while, his voice still hushed in the darkness. 'And the word was...?'

'Marcus,' she replied, her voice barely a whisper.

'Ah, well. The name Marcus is said to originate from the Roman god Mars. So I suppose our story must start in Rome, with a nameless young orphan who had worked all his life and received nothing more than bread and water for his trouble.

'This orphan had always belonged, in a sense, to a middle-aged couple with too many children of their own. They had allowed him to sleep in their barn and to share the scraps of food that the whole family had to live on, but they could not afford more generosity than this, for they were starving themselves. No one knew how he had come to be with this couple: he had simply been brought to them one day, as a baby. At the time the couple had been preoccupied with other babies and other worries, and so they had not had time to spare him a name. Because of this, he had spent his life being known as Puer, or "boy".

'Puer was not an unhappy child, despite the fact that at first glance he had much to be unhappy about. The other children in the family treated him like a slave; his work was hard, and he rarely received thanks for doing it; he was severely malnourished, and had little hope of ever receiving more food than the minimum needed to survive. Despite all this, he was happy in the animal friends with whom he shared his barn, and he took satisfaction in performing his work to a higher standard than was expected of him. And so it was that, on his eleventh birthday, the father of the family, Aulus, took him to one side, and bestowed an honour upon him.

'"Up until now we have always asked you to tend the animals," Aulus said, his voice grave. "But we have seen how hard you work, and we are having trouble with other aspects of our farm. We wondered if, now that you are old enough to be trusted to do it, you might help us with our crops, so that we might all be more prosperous."

'Puer agreed immediately: it was a great honour to be asked to work in the fields. And so the next day Aulus took him to work with him, and showed him the rest of the farm.

'The farm was huge, and Puer, even with no farming knowledge, could see that it was being badly managed. But he said nothing; he allowed Aulus to show him around the whole farm, and then he was put to work in one field. He worked hard all day, doing exactly what Aulus had told him to do, and by the end of the day he had done far more than any of the other children who worked there.

'The next day was the same, and the next, and the next. For a year Puer worked tirelessly, and his field produced more crops than any of the others, and at the end of the year Aulus had a celebration in his honour.

'Naturally, Aulus's other children were not pleased about this. They didn't understand why someone who wasn't part of the family was being given such honours; they felt sure that Puer must be cheating in some way. And so they started a campaign to get rid of him. Over the course of the next year they attempted to sabotage his crop, but to no avail. Everything they did seemed to backfire. They couldn't understand how Puer seemed to be able to predict what they were going to do, or figure out things that they had done that should have been unnoticeable. They didn't realise how closely he was watching them, how deftly he deflected their attempts, without ever saying a word to their father about their betrayal.

'After a year, when his field was still the most successful on the farm, Puer approached Aulus about the possibility of working on more of the fields. It wasn't hard to convince him that it was a good idea: Aulus's sons had put so much energy into sabotaging Puer that their own fields had fallen into disrepair, and their crop harvest was noticeably poorer than the previous year.

'So it was that Puer began the work of transforming the farm into a more successful enterprise. He shifted things around, reorganised and rebuilt, upsetting many of his fellow workers as he did so. There was an uprising, at one point: all of the workers laid down their tools and refused to work in the way that Puer was asking them to. But Puer simply carried on regardless, doing the work that he could on his own, asking Aulus for help when he couldn't manage. Within two years they were the most successful farmers in the local area, and all of Aulus's sons were guilty and ashamed at their behaviour, now that they could see how much more prosperous they were thanks to Puer.

'When talking among themselves one day, Lucius, the oldest of Aulus's sons, admitted to the others that he felt they needed to do something by way of apology. "Puer has done nothing but help us," he said to his brothers, "and we need to give something back in return. He has put food on our table; he has made our father a legend among farmers. What can we do for him, to return the favour, and apologise for being so ungrateful before?"

'All the sons racked their brains for a week, but they couldn't think of anything fitting. The things that they thought of – gold, food, part-ownership of the farm – were not theirs to give, and they didn't want to admit to their father how awfully they had behaved. And then eventually the youngest brother, only just eleven years old, stepped forward.

'"We could give him a name," he suggested.

'"But he has a name. He has been Puer all his life. Why change it now?"

'"Puer means *boy*," the youngest son said, "and he is now a man. Why don't we give him a name that reflects this?"

'They all agreed that it was a good idea, and went away to think of a suitable name. After a week, they returned with their suggestions. A few names were tossed around, though none seemed fitting, somehow. And then Lucius said, "What about Marcus?"

'The boys looked at him in surprise, for it was not yet a common name. But Lucius continued, "Think about it. Marcus comes from Mars, the god of war. But Mars is not just a god of war. He is a god of war that delivers peace – and that is what Puer has done. He is also a god of agriculture. He has assured peace and prosperity in this family for years to come. This is a fitting name for him."

'They all agreed, and so they went to their father, and explained what they wanted to do. Aulus thought it was a wonderful idea, and later that night, after the evening meal – which was much more substantial since Puer had taken charge – Lucius stood up, and asked them all to be quiet. He gave a long speech in which he confessed what he and his brothers had done, and explained that he wished to make amends. And then he formally bestowed the name Marcus on the nameless boy who had changed their family's prospects, and they all toasted him, and drank to his good health.'

In the time that it had taken for Richard to tell his story, Lily had not moved. The sun had risen outside, and light had crept into the room through the gap in the curtains, tiptoeing its way across the sheets to fall across them both. Richard pulled back, now, so that he could see her: and she looked up at him, her face flushed, her eyes sparkling. Her palms, still against his chest, tapped out a familiar sequence.

'I love you, too,' he replied, encasing her tiny shoulders in his hands. They lay like that until they heard the shouts of excited children in the street outside, and then Lily wished her father a merry Christmas, and they got out of bed.

Connie woke up in the bedroom of her childhood, for the first time in over twenty years. She and Nathan were sleeping on a mattress on the floor: there was no furniture in here, nothing to remind her of the years she'd spent in this room. She had wondered yesterday, while they were making the bed, where her old single bed had gone. Had it just been thrown away, along with all the other remnants of her childhood? Or was everything stored, somewhere, waiting to be found?

She could hear the boys stirring in Lily's old room, next door. They were talking quietly, but their voices carried through the thin walls. There was a thump, as if one of them had fallen, and then a shout, and then laughter. She smiled, trying to imagine what they were doing. Loving the fact, even while she was jealous of it, that they had a life that they shared away from her, a world where their parents were largely irrelevant. It reminded her of when she and Lily were young, the secrets they had shared away from their parents' hearing.

Nathan was still fast asleep, his breathing deep and even, his body still. He was the kind of person who fell asleep where he lay and didn't move for eight hours, who slept on his back with his arms at his sides, like a flushed corpse. Connie had always been fascinated by how tidily he slept; sometimes she fell asleep curled up into him, his arm around her shoulders, and if she moved away in the night she would wake to find his arm still outstretched, waiting for her to crawl back into the place she had left.

It was the sign of an untroubled mind, he'd told her once; you could only have truly restful sleep if you could put all your worries aside, leaving your unconscious free to roam through everything else. She wondered, now, if he truly was as calm as he seemed when he was asleep. He had always been stronger than her, less volatile, less reactive; she had found it irritating at times, thinking that he viewed himself as some kind of saint, while she was a mere hysterical woman. She was being unfair, she knew – in many ways she was stronger than he was, and he knew it, and valued that strength in her – but she couldn't help but feel that there was something unnatural about being able to cast your anxieties aside so easily. Did he truly not worry about the future because there was little he could do to change it? Or was he just confident that Connie would never split up their family over one simple mistake? The idea of his self-assurance, his arrogance, made her want to slap him.

She heard Lily and Richard getting up, their door opening, their footsteps making their way down the stairs towards the kitchen. She remembered lying here on Christmas mornings as a child, after Lily had gone away, listening to her parents creeping down the stairs, trying to get the coffee going before she got up and demanded presents and false cheer. Not that she had ever really demanded those things: Christmas had seemed like a pointless holiday, once Lily had gone. Her parents had never been the same as they had been before; their delight in giving presents, in cooking dinner, in celebrating the existence of their family seemed to have dissipated. And Connie realised, with a stab of sadness, that it would be the same in their family, if she were to tell Nathan she couldn't forgive him. Christmases would always be divided, as would everything else. Her children would remember, but never be able to relive, the days when their family had been a unit and there had been something to celebrate.

That evening, after the boys had been dragged to bed, the four of them sat around the kitchen table, two bottles of wine on the go, leftover cheese and biscuits scattered all around them. Despite the lack of Christmas decorations in the kitchen – Lily had run out halfway through decorating the house – the atmosphere was festive, helped considerably by the wine. But Lily found that she couldn't quite settle into it. This room, as always, felt uncomfortable.

It was the windows, she knew: combined with the patio doors, they essentially made for a wall of glass, blackened by the night outside. The result was a feeling of uneasy exposure: the sense that others could see in and you couldn't see out. Lily kept catching glimpses of her reflection in the glass, flashes of movement out of the corner of her eye. Sometimes the flashes weren't reflections at all; but she pushed those to the back of her mind, and said nothing about them.

Richard had been telling them all stories about his bar job, which, Lily realised, in a vague sort of way, he had never told her before. Had she ever asked him about it? She had heard him mention Tim and Rosa, but she had never enquired about the regulars, nor even been into the pub itself. She thought she had been there, once, as a child, but her memory could just as easily be pure imagination. She had vague images of rows of bottles glinting in dim orbs of light, of dark wood tables and deep red patterned carpets.

'Are the carpets red?' she asked, stopping Richard in mid-sentence, startling them all.

'Can't say I've ever looked, actually. Why?'

'Oh, nothing. Just – something I thought of.'

Richard smiled, puzzled, but carried on with his story.

Later, when Nathan was telling them about a work party he'd been to and Connie was preoccupied with listening to him, Richard reached for her hand under the table, searching out reassurance. One long squeeze, and she squeezed his fingers lightly in response, feeling the oddity of his knuckles under the skin. *I'm okay.* He caught her eye, smiled faintly.

Behind him, another, smaller Lily clapped her hands over her mouth, and shook her head exaggeratedly from side to side. *Don't tell.* But don't tell what?

To her right, a larger shape flickered past the glass doors. Lily fixed her eyes on the half-empty wine bottle on the table and said nothing.

'So, anyway, long story short, Bill fell straight through the buffet table, and we were never invited back to the Hilton again.' Nathan laughed, and they all laughed along with him, though Lily had lost the focus of his words and couldn't work out where the humour was.

'He actually fell *through* the table?' Richard sounded mildly impressed.

'Yeah, well, the table was one of those long ones with lots of separate sections that you join together. They're pretty badly designed, actually. So he fell into the middle and the whole thing just sort of collapsed in on itself.' Nathan grinned. 'I like to think he ended up with a trifle on his head, but I'm pretty sure that's just wishful thinking.'

'Well, it makes a better story, and, seeing as none of us was there, we might as well go with it,' Richard said, reaching for the wine bottle and topping up their glasses.

There was definite movement outside now: not just the flickerings of her imagination, nor the reflections of their movements. Connie noticed her squinting at the window.

'What's up with you tonight?' she asked, downing half of her wine in one mouthful. 'You keep looking at the doors as though someone's about to burst through them.'

Lily shrugged. 'I saw something.'

'Something like a person? Or something like a reflection?'

'I don't know.'

'Want me to go and have a look?' Richard was on his feet without waiting for an answer, and Nathan was a second behind him. Connie rolled her eyes at Lily, but didn't try to stop them.

The key hung on a hook next to the fridge. Richard unlocked the door and pulled it open, letting in a blast of cold air as he did so. 'God, that's *freezing*,' Connie muttered, just a bit too quiet for them to hear.

Both men stepped out into the garden and vanished from view. The open door was like a hole of pure darkness in the reflected light of the glass. After a moment of glaring at it, Connie got up and slammed it shut behind them, muttering darkly about men being born in barns.

'Should we go out there?' Lily felt uneasy, the closed door like a barrier.

'Oh, leave them to it. They like nothing better than being manly and protective. And anyway, my coat's by the front door and I can't be bothered to get it.' Connie sat back down and took another long gulp of her wine. 'What did you think you saw, anyway?'

Lily shrugged. 'A person, maybe?'

'Have you seen things out there before? When it's just been you and Richard?'

Lily looked at her, weighing up her answer. 'I don't come in here much,' she admitted after a moment.

'Because of what happened?'

Lily shrugged again. She was toying with the stem of her wine glass, seeing how far she could tilt the glass without it being in danger of tipping over. In her head, it overbalanced, spitting wine across the table in all directions; in reality it stayed upright, resting in a tidy ring of its own dribbled contents.

'How can you stand living here?' Connie asked, softly, which made Lily look up at her.

'You did.'

'I didn't have a choice. I was a child. And I left as soon as I could... You can go anywhere you want.'

Lily thought for a moment. 'We haven't got the money.'

'They're still paying you, aren't they? I'm sure you could survive for a while on your salary.'

'But Richard doesn't want to. And he thinks...' She looked at the door, as if he was going to come bursting through it. 'He doesn't know, okay? About Billy. He thinks being here will be good for me. That I'll get over whatever issues I have with our parents and lay old ghosts to rest, or something.'

It had been a lifetime since Connie had heard her utter so many words in one go. 'Why haven't you told him?'

Lily shrugged.

'Does he know about the institute? About you not talking at all?'

Lily nodded, looking back down at the wine glass. A single drop of red wine worked its way down the outside of the glass, and was almost at the bottom when she caught it with the tip of her finger and lifted it to her lips.

'So why does he think you went there?'

Lily shrugged again. 'I don't know. Stuff to do with Mama, maybe.'

'You told him about Mama?'

Lily nodded.

'I haven't told Nathan much about it,' Connie admitted after a minute. 'He knows about her being ill, obviously, because he knew I went to visit her. But I didn't go into details.'

'Does he know about Billy?'

'No.'

They looked at each other, a new awareness springing up between them. This was it, then. Just the two of them.

The door burst open, bringing in a flurry of cold air and movement. 'Nothing out there,' Nathan announced cheerfully, stamping the cold out of his shoes and pulling his coat off. 'It was probably just our reflections in the glass.'

Lily nodded, and Connie said, 'That's what we were thinking. Thanks for checking, though.'

Richard and Nathan rejoined the table, the cold from outside clinging to their clothes with the ferocity of cigarette smoke. Richard slipped a hand under the table and found Lily's fist, clenched in her lap, and enclosed it with his fingers. 'Feel better?' he asked, softly.

She nodded. 'Thanks.' She looked up, and for a brief moment her eyes met Connie's across the table, and she was surprised by what she saw there: no accusation, no judgement; nothing, really, except compassion. Then they both looked away, and Lily kept her gaze fixed on the table for the rest of the night, the eyes in the glass behind her pricking at the hairs on the back of her neck.

then

Marcus was shaking as he got into the car. All the good cheer he had been carefully cultivating throughout the day slipped out of his grasp and he was left, raging and impotent, wishing for a life that had taken a different course. The things Anna had said boiled in his brain and fizzed beneath his skin, retorts flashing redundantly in his brain now, far too late. Perhaps he would write them down for use in a later argument. It would be a shame to waste them.

He slammed the car door and thought fleetingly of Lily, upstairs, hiding out of their way: would she be okay, left with her mother? Was Anna in such a fragile state that she would hurt Lily? He dismissed the thought immediately. She could be a danger to herself, perhaps, but never to her children.

He felt guilty, though. Leaving on Christmas Day. And when things had been going so well... He would have to make it up to Lily later.

He started the car and pulled out, too quickly, not concentrating on where he was going. He realised that it wasn't just blood fizzing in his veins, and took a moment to steady himself. No point getting arrested just because he was angry. It certainly wouldn't put him in a better mood; in theory they could keep him in the cells overnight if they caught him drink-driving, and he would struggle to hold on to his licence.

He drove carefully through the residential areas, despite the fact that there was no one around. As soon as he got to the outskirts of town he sped up, and registered the release, the sense of exhausted satisfaction as he floored the accelerator and felt the car rumble beneath him. The needle climbed from thirty to sixty, seventy, eighty. He pulled on to a long, straight stretch of country road and got up to ninety-five before forcing himself to ease up and drop back down to the speed limit.

There was a certain amount of satisfaction in acting like an idiot. Doing things that he knew Anna would disapprove of. He had spent so much of his married life being the sensible one, making sure he was together for his children, supporting his basket case of a wife. Putting up with her acting however she wanted, whenever she wanted, without sparing a thought for him. He was sick of it. Connie had known: he was sure that was why she'd gone. She'd finally woken up to the fact that her parents were hopeless, her entire family a sham, and had got out the only way she knew how.

He almost wished she'd taken him with her.

Thinking of Connie, he felt a pull of regret that was so close to being physical pain as to be indistinguishable. If only he'd done something to help. Something to make her realise that she wasn't alone, that she could talk to him, that he would support her and let her be whoever she really was. He had never been frank enough with his daughters, he realised. Never let them know that they could tell him about anything, that he would never judge them the way their mother did.

He'd been too wrapped up in just trying to make sure everyone stayed alive.

He came to a village, and dropped down to twenty. Felt the drop in speed as if it were his own power falling away, rather than the car's. Crawled through empty streets, feeling hemmed in by the slowness, longing to push back up to a speed that felt in tune with his mood.

The wine he'd drunk earlier had exacerbated his rage, and the speed had added to it; now both had faded and he felt drained, dullness seeping in around the edges. He clawed for his anger, wanting it back, but it had been replaced by a numb sense of realisation, a feeling of stuckness. No matter how fast he drove he would not leave behind his reality. He would never be like his daughters, free to escape, to go wherever they chose. He would be forever stuck in a life that he had once viewed as his choice.

A rabbit darted out in front of his car, and he swerved, too violently, almost slamming himself into a tree. He pulled over immediately, his tiredness obliterated by the adrenaline suddenly coursing through his veins. He forced himself to breathe deeply, evenly. Held his hands out in front of his face, and noted the fact that they were shaking uncontrollably. *Close call*, he thought, his breath shuddering in his chest.

He leaned back against the headrest and closed his eyes.

He must have fallen asleep, because when he opened his eyes again it was dark, and he felt disorientated. The road he was on was just outside a village, and there were no street-lights. The dark on the other side of the windows seemed thick, syrupy, and full of movement. The green numbers on the dashboard flashed the time at him: 17:02. He had missed dinner, then.

Stiffly, reluctantly, he switched the engine back on, and tried to get himself into a driving frame of mind.

He flicked the lights on, illuminating the road in front of him and further deepening the darkness of the trees on either side. He was struck by the stupidity of falling asleep in a darkened car at the side of an unlit road: if anyone had come down here without paying close attention they would have careered straight into the side of him, and he would have been crushed. Thankfully there was no traffic on the road, but if it had been any other day he wouldn't have been so lucky.

He pulled out into the road, driving cautiously now, as if to counteract his earlier behaviour. He turned around as soon as he could and began heading back home, driving within the speed limit, trying not to let exhaustion get the better of him. In his post-sleep stiffness he felt bone-weary and emptied; his eyes flickered across the road, taking in nothing, while he strained to keep them open.

It was probably the fact that he was driving slowly that killed him, the coroner said later. At the side of the road, tied to a tree, was what looked like a man in a Father Christmas outfit. It had been hung in such a way that, when the wind blew, it drifted out into the road. Had Marcus been going faster, he would never have noticed it; or at least he wouldn't have seen it clearly enough to think it was a man.

It blew outwards, and for the second time that evening, Marcus swerved to avoid something in his path; only this time he forgot to brake, and the front of his car crunched itself around the trunk of a tree on the other side of the road.

The Father Christmas – a collection of balloons, wrapped in red crêpe paper, and decorated with a Santa hat – floated back towards the other side of the road, undamaged.

now

The air was freezing as they stepped outside the house, breath encasing faces in vaporous clouds. Lily and Connie were dressed virtually identically, in blue jeans, black boots, large black coats. Only their hair was different: Lily had pulled hers back into a ponytail, whereas Connie had hers down, flowing around her face. Richard surveyed them while locking up the house, and realised they could almost be twins: only the tiny creases at the corner of Connie's eyes hinted at the fact that she was older.

The three of them stomped their way down the lane, their voices unnaturally loud in the Boxing Day stillness. Lily stopped often to admire plants at the side of the road, and every time she did so Connie stood impatiently, pointedly not joining in, wanting to be on her way. 'You don't have to look at them all *now*,' she said, when Lily stopped for the fourth time. 'Why can't you look on the way home?'

Lily shrugged, and resumed walking, just a beat behind her sister. They grew silent, and their pace slowed, as they approached the church. It was a small, unimpressive building, on the corner of a lane, surrounded by a low brick wall with a domed top. There was no one around – they were too late for morning service, and the little gate which led to the churchyard was locked. Connie pushed at it a couple of times, frustrated, making Lily laugh.

'What?' Connie asked, indignant. 'I don't want to have to come back tomorrow.'

Lily gave her a mock-scornful look, and leapt over the wall in a single movement, turning to face them from the other side with her arms held out triumphantly. 'Ta-da!'

'All right,' Connie muttered, following suit in a less acrobatic manner. 'Show-off.'

Richard grinned, and followed them both. Frost-coated leaves crunched on the grass on the other side of the wall, and the ground was uneven, strewn with slanted headstones.

'Do you know where it is?' Lily's voice was hushed, as if instinctually not wishing to disturb the slumber of the dead.

'You were at her funeral too,' Connie replied, her voice equally quiet. 'It was round here somewhere, wasn't it?'

They picked their way through the headstones to a less crowded patch of grass, trying not to walk on graves where possible. The headstones here were newer, the marble and limestone gleaming in contrast to the weathered stones nearer the entrance. The lettering was clearly visible, etched deep into the stone: names and dates that meant little to any of them.

'Why didn't we get her buried next to Dad?' Lily asked.

'There was no room,' Connie replied, her voice vague as her eyes skated over the lettering on the headstones.

'But why didn't she buy a double grave? When he died?'

'I don't know.' Connie shrugged. 'I guess she didn't want to spend eternity sleeping next to him. Hardly surprising, is it?'

'But she never remarried.' Lily's voice was puzzled, as if she'd never really thought about it before.

'What's your point?'

'I don't know.'

They carried on searching in silence, splitting off in different directions, and after a minute Richard called out to them both. They gathered around a small headstone in a pale, yellowish stone. The lettering was brief and to the point. *Anna Emmett, 1943–2010. Rest in peace.*

'They only put the stone up a couple of weeks ago,' Connie said. She brushed the top of it with gloved fingers, feeling the cold deadness of the stone through the wool.

'It looks nice,' Richard offered, when Lily said nothing. 'Did you choose it?'

'"Choose" isn't really the right word for it,' Connie said dismissively. 'Mama was pretty specific about what she wanted.'

Lily crouched down in front of the stone, uncomfortably aware that she was standing directly on top of what was left of her mother. She took her glove off and traced the letters of her name with a finger, surprised at the smoothness, the perfection of the carving. 'She was young, really, wasn't she?'

'She got to a good age, considering,' Connie said bluntly. Lily nodded, but didn't reply. She stood up after a moment, her knees cracking in protest. 'Shall we find Dad?'

'Okay, then.' It was only as they began to move away that Lily realised they should have brought flowers, or something to show that they'd been here. She looked around, searching for something suitable. There was a holly bush at the edge of the churchyard, and she pulled off a sprig of holly, adorned with a vibrant red berry, and placed that on the stone. Richard, watching from a distance, nodded his approval. Connie had already vanished into the maze of stones.

Because the graves were in no particular order, it took them a while to find Marcus's. As she searched, Lily caught glimpses of names she recognised, like familiar faces in a crowd: the names of old neighbours, people who had attended her father's funeral, now gone themselves. It made her feel odd: sad, to think that many of the people she remembered from her childhood had not moved on but had simply been laid to rest in her absence; and glad, that they were here, together, all in the same place.

'Hey, Lily.'

She looked up. Connie was invisible for a second, crouched down to look at something, and then she stood up and waved. 'Over here.'

'Have you found him?'

'No.' She beckoned again, and Lily picked her way across the churchyard towards her sister. She looked around for Richard but couldn't see him; he must have gone round the side of the building.

Connie was crouched next to a tiny headstone, about half the size of the others, and she beckoned for Lily to crouch down next to her. The words on the neighbouring headstones had been somewhat obscured by the passing of time, by lichen smothering the stone, but this stone looked brand new. *William Edward Thompson, 1974–1985. Beloved son.*

'It was twenty-five years ago,' Lily whispered, reaching out a hand to touch his name, then pulling it back, almost afraid.

'Makes you feel old, huh?' Connie smiled, but it was a sad smile, and there were tears in the corners of her eyes. They crouched there together, not saying anything, until Richard came upon them a minute later.

'I've found your dad,' he said, peering over the headstone behind them. 'Who have you found?'

'Oh, just an old friend,' Connie said, standing up and brushing non-existent dirt from her jeans. 'Where's Dad?'

Richard led them to the grave, which was near a wall at the back of the churchyard. It was under a covering of trees, so that it felt dark and gloomy, the thin light offered by the grey sky obscured by a cluster of leafless branches. The stones under the trees were more heavily marked than those out in the open, and Marcus's headstone was almost illegible under a coating of dirt and lichen.

'It's so dirty,' Connie murmured, brushing at it with her fingers and knocking off dark clumps of filth. 'Didn't Mama ever think to get it cleaned?'

Lily didn't reply, thinking of the day of his funeral.

'It doesn't look as though she came down here much,' Richard volunteered, his voice quiet and solemn.

The three of them stood in silence for a while. Richard thought of the man he'd never met, who had had such an influence on the woman he loved. He'd never asked Connie about him. Never bothered to find out if they'd been close. But he knew from rare conversations with Lily that the only stability the two of them had had in their childhood had come from him.

After five minutes, Lily turned and walked away, back to the place where they'd jumped over the wall. Richard stayed with Connie, standing silently behind, until she drew herself out of her thoughts and realised that he was there and that Lily was gone.

'I've never bothered,' she said, and her voice was quiet and rough with tears. 'I just thought – well, graves aren't really relevant, are they? This isn't *him*.'

'No,' Richard agreed. 'It's not him. But it's a representation of him.'

'It's a terrible representation.'

'Well, it's dead, and he was alive. So that's hardly surprising. But it's supposed to signify the everlasting spirit, you know? The fact that, even though he's gone, he still made a mark on the world that was permanent and irremovable.'

'It's not much of a mark.' Connie gestured vaguely around them. 'It's the same as everyone else's.'

'It's the only one that has his name on it.'

Connie shrugged. 'What's in a name?' There was a pause, and then they both laughed. 'Sorry. I'll stop it now. I just feel guilty, I guess. Because I've never done anything to show how much he meant to me. I never even went to his funeral.'

Richard was surprised. 'Really? How come?'

'Lily never said?'

'I don't think we've ever spoken about it.'

'Oh.' Connie looked up, to where her sister was perched on the wall, swinging her feet and kicking the concrete lightly with her heels. 'I was away when Dad died. I was in Germany.'

'Oh.' Richard did some quick maths, figured out how old she would have been. 'School trip? They could have waited until you got back, couldn't they?'

'No, it wasn't a school trip. I ran away.' Her eyes were still on Lily, though they seemed to be focused on something else entirely.

'For how long?'

'Maybe eleven months, a year? I meant to ring, but I kept putting it off and putting it off... You assume the world is just carrying on in the same old way, when you're wrapped up in yourself like that. Never occurs to you that things might change. When I finally got round to coming back, he was long dead and Lily had gone back to our grandparents' house and I... Well.'

The sentence hung between them, uncomfortably. 'What did you do?' Richard asked eventually.

'Oh, you know. This and that. My grandparents helped me get somewhere to live. I visited Lily fairly often. And when she went to uni I moved nearby, met Nathan, and, well, the rest is history.'

'Do you regret running away?'

'Yes.' Connie took a last look at her father's headstone, and then started to walk back towards Lily. 'Come on. The kids will be wondering where I've got to.'

Lily had been looking at her feet, but she looked up when she heard them coming, and smiled. The three of them linked arms once they were on the other side of the wall, and walked home in a line, not saying a word, completely unaware that, from the corner of the churchyard, their movements were being watched.

then

Lily awoke on the day of her father's funeral to find the house silent, the sky dark, the world muted and strange. It had been two weeks since the police had delivered the news, and Lily had been numb silence alongside her mother's hysteria, a grieving shadow that blended into the darkness of the surrounding world and left her mother to it.

The police had tried to find Connie, to no avail. The letters had included no addresses. Through the postmark they managed to trace her back to a hostel, which she had left on Boxing Day morning with no forwarding address. They had promised to keep trying, but Lily didn't hold out much hope. Connie would be in touch when she felt like it.

Despite that, Lily spent her time at home waiting for the phone to ring. Making silent bargains with it, as though it were a living being that could locate Connie for her, bring her home and make everything the way it should have been. *Please*, she whispered, as she curled herself up in her blankets and waited for sleep to come. *Please come home. Please don't leave me here like this.*

A week earlier, Lily had gone with her mother to the funeral director's to choose the flowers, the coffin, to set the date. Her mother had pointed at the things she wanted through her tears, and told lies about how happy they had been together. Lily had swallowed her sickness and her grief along with lukewarm tap water, and watched blurred shapes walk past the window. 'He would have liked this one, wouldn't he, Lils?' her mother had said, again and again, and Lily had nodded, not seeing, not believing.

'She doesn't talk much,' her mother had said at one point, confidingly, to the kindly woman who was handling the arrangements. 'Not for years. She's had a difficult childhood.'

The woman had nodded sagely, and treated Lily with extra delicacy after that.

When they got home there was no confiding, no sense that they were in it together, as there had been in the funeral director's. Instead Anna retreated to her room and sobbed herself to sleep, while Lily sat in her room nearby and worried about becoming an orphan.

Her grandparents turned up two days before the funeral. They said little, but they created a cocoon of normality around Lily. They cooked meals, insisted on washing at appropriate times and changing clothes every day. They urged her to do schoolwork and made her mother get out of bed.

The day, when it came, felt as if it had arrived too soon, as if no time at all had passed since her father had been at home making Christmas dinner and confiding that he wasn't happy in his marriage. Lily couldn't quite believe they would go through with it, when a third of their remaining family was hundreds of miles away and didn't even know what was happening, but her mother was determined to get it over with and thought that Lily was being ridiculous.

'You don't just cancel a funeral because someone can't make it, Lily,' she said, her voice stern and impenetrable, like it had been when Lily was very young. 'It's got to go ahead, whatever happens. Your father needs to be laid to rest.'

Lily was fairly certain her father wouldn't mind an extra couple of weeks in the mortuary, if it meant both his daughters attending his funeral, but she said nothing, her grandparents said nothing, and the day went ahead as planned.

It was a quiet affair: only a handful of people, mostly old neighbours and work colleagues. Marcus had spent too much time at home or at work in recent years, and his circle of friends had narrowed accordingly. The service was held in the church in the old village – because, although he had never been particularly religious, he had known the reverend and would have liked to have him presiding over the service – and a cluster of people Lily hadn't seen for years came to pay their respects. She was surprised to recognise Billy's father, in the back row, though he didn't look at her and she didn't try to catch his attention. He had never shown them any warmth, since everything had happened; Lily assumed it was because he blamed them for his son's death. She wondered if he was there because he was sorry about her father, or because he wanted the satisfaction of seeing him in the ground.

The service lasted fifteen minutes, and was accompanied all the way through by the muffled sobbing of her mother. When they picked up the coffin to carry it outside, Anna looked as though she might faint with grief; but she collected herself in time to be the first to walk behind it. Lily followed at a slower pace, delaying seeing the grave.

It was deep, and somehow undignified: a shovel still sat to one side, next to a tree. The coffin was lowered at angles, first one side, then the other, the bearers glaring at each other from each side of the grave as they tried and failed to get their timing right. The gleaming wooden box hit the ground right side first, and Lily imagined Marcus being jostled from side to side, his elbows bouncing off the wood as his arms were clasped over his stomach, and she wanted to howl against the indignity of it, an indignity that her father of all people did not deserve.

She and her mother stood in front of everyone, and she followed her mother's movements as she threw dirt on the coffin, stepped away, made room for the gravediggers to start filling in the grave. It was a cold day, and it began to rain as they stood there. She heard one of the gravediggers mumble something about getting this over with before the rain really hit, and she felt sick with shame. She knew, then, that her mother had truly never loved her father; if she had loved him, she would have given him a better end than this.

All day, Lily watched out of the corner of her eye for Connie to appear, expecting her to show up like a long-lost heroine in a film, breezing in at the last minute and saving the day. But she never came, and when Marcus's parents went home later that evening, leaving Lily and her mother exhausted with each other and with everything else, there was no one to break the silence and make the day feel as though it had been worth something.

now

Richard didn't go back to work until the fifth of January.
The pub was always quiet over Christmas, Rosa had assured
him – even on New Year's Eve they barely had more than
their usual Saturday night crowd – and he had taken the time
gratefully, without argument. It had been less than a month
since Lily had come home from the hospital, and she still
didn't seem quite right, sleeping for long periods of time and
spending days on end sitting up in her old bedroom. She had
briefly seemed to brighten over Christmas, but the second
everyone had left she had retreated back into herself, and
Richard felt as if he was unable to reach her.

He'd considered not going back to work, but Lily had
insisted, in her quiet way: she was fine, and there was no
point him sitting around all day babysitting someone who
was fine. So here he was, propping up the bar, half-heartedly
skimming the newspapers while he watched two of the oldest
regulars playing darts.

'Richard?' Rosa's voice carried down the stairs, along
with the faint thumping of the radio. 'Can you come up here
a sec?'

Richard set aside his newspaper and made his way
upstairs. Rosa sat on the floor in the middle of the kitchen.
The contents of the kitchen cupboards were piled around her,
and she was holding a notepad, apparently checking items off
a list. She glanced up when he appeared in the doorway. 'Is it
busy downstairs?'

'Horrendously.' He grinned. 'John and Jim have got me run ragged.'

'I can imagine.' She rolled her eyes. 'Can you do me a favour?'

'Sure.'

'Ed was supposed to be bringing over some veg out of his garden for me, but he hasn't turned up and he's not picking up the phone – could you nip over and see if he's there?'

Richard shrugged. 'Sure. But, if he's in, wouldn't he pick up the phone?'

Rosa laughed. 'Unlikely. He turns the ringer off most of the time so that he doesn't get disturbed.'

'Sensible man.' Richard grinned. 'Where does he live?'

'It's just a few minutes up the road. Right by your place, actually. Are you sure you don't mind? We can leave the old boys in charge for a few minutes.'

'Of course. That's fine.'

'Oh, you're a lifesaver.' She scribbled something on the notepad, then ripped it off and held it out to him. 'That's the address. He should be in – he's always about at this time of day.'

Richard left, with a nod to 'the old boys', who were left in charge often enough that they knew what to do. It was a relief to step outside. The inside of the pub was always dim, but outside all was bright and clear; there had been rain earlier, but the clouds had dispersed and the winter sun was dazzlingly reflective on the watery ground.

He walked slowly through the village, knowing Rosa wouldn't mind him taking his time. Considered dropping in on Lily, but he didn't want to crowd her. And a part of him was worried that he might find her back in the cellar. Searching for something that had nothing to do with him.

Ed's house was only two streets from theirs, his garden backing on to the same woods, at the end of a narrow, circular close where all the houses looked the same. There was no one around. Richard walked down the front path, eyes on the darkened windows, hoping to see Ed's face appear behind the glass. He could feel eyes on him, twitching curtains, but could see no one.

He rang the doorbell, and heard a shrill, high-pitched ringing on the other side of the door. There was no answering thunder of footsteps down the stairs, or blurry features in the glass panel. He rang again, holding it for longer. Still no answer.

He was about to leave when he noticed that the gate at the side of the house was open: a passageway led round the back. Presumably if Ed was in the garden he'd be out of range of the doorbell. It couldn't hurt to take a look.

He walked down the passage. He realised he was tiptoeing, and forced himself to place his feet normally on the ground, feeling ridiculous. Something about the absence of noise, of people, was making him feel jumpy and strange. But that was no reason to start acting like a burglar.

The garden was much smaller than theirs, the woodland fenced off behind it, but it was still large by Richard's city-bred standards. There were piles of logs to one side, poking out from beneath a tarpaulin. A small stretch of lawn was occupied by a plastic garden chair, spotted with raindrops. The rest of the garden seemed to be one large vegetable patch.

There was a shed at the far end, with its door ajar. If Ed was around, that was presumably where he'd be. Richard picked his way through the vegetable patch on the narrow dirt pathway and knocked lightly on the open door.

'Yep?' Ed didn't sound even slightly surprised that someone would be knocking on the door of his shed. Richard walked in.

It was larger than it looked from the outside, and mostly taken up with tools that hung from every available bit of wall space. But there was an armchair, and that was where Ed sat, sifting through a tub of seeds.

'Ah, Richard. Good to see you. How's it going?'

Richard was glad he didn't need to explain what he was doing wandering round Ed's private property without an invitation. Maybe it was one of those things that was acceptable in villages.

'Yeah, good, thanks. And you?'

'Oh, not so bad, you know. Just getting things ready for spring. Want to take a look?'

'Sure.'

Completely forgetting the reason he was there, Richard followed Ed through the garden, making what he hoped were appropriate noises of interest as Ed pointed out the various features. 'Obviously it doesn't look its best at this time of year. You should come back in a couple of months when things are really getting going.'

'Sounds great,' Richard said, hoping he sounded appropriately enthusiastic. He had never really understood the attraction of gardening.

'You done much with your garden since you moved in?'

Richard shrugged. 'Not really. I don't think either of us are natural gardeners.'

'Yeah, it's a big space, if you're not really interested.'

Richard frowned. 'You've been there, then?'

'I used to do some gardening for Lily's mother. After she went into hospital.'

'You never said.' His voice was guarded. It seemed like an odd thing to have gone unmentioned.

'Didn't I?' Ed shrugged, and carried on walking. 'Was there a reason why you dropped round, by the way, or did you just want to say hello?'

'Oh, sorry, I completely forgot. I'm meant to be at work.' Richard laughed, struggling not to sound uncomfortable. 'It was Rosa who sent me, actually – she said you were supposed to be bringing her round some veg out of the garden?'

'Oh, sure. Come in; I think it's all bagged up in the kitchen.' Ed led the way through the garden back to the house, stopping here and there to snap off a dead shoot. The back door led into a utility room, crowded with wellies and bottles of gardening-related chemicals. A pile of boxes almost obscured the washing machine.

'Don't worry about taking your shoes off,' Ed said cheerfully, leading him through to the kitchen. By comparison this was spotlessly clean – there was nothing on the worktops except for a block of knives and some tins for tea and coffee. A set of red bar stools, garish in comparison to the rest of the decoration, were the only indication of homeliness. Ed opened a cupboard and pulled out a carrier bag of vegetables. 'Here you go.'

Richard smiled and took the bag. 'I take it you grow more than you know what to do with?'

'I don't get through that much on my own. But it's nice to be able to pass it on to friends. Actually, there are some seeds in the shed I was going to give her. Would you mind hanging around a minute while I grab them?'

'Sure, no problem.'

'Great. I won't be long.' Ed clapped him on the shoulder, and went back outside.

The house was silent except for the humming of the fridge. A doorway at the end of the kitchen led through to the living room, and Richard peered round the door, curious. The living room was much more homely – there was art on the walls, framed photos on the mantelpiece. A large, garish rug made the place seem much more colourful.

Richard stepped into the room, intrigued by the photos. The one closest to him was of a little boy – fair-haired, smiling, about six years old. He sat astride a bicycle, both feet on the ground, clearly proud of himself for holding it up. There were gaps in his smile where he'd lost his teeth.

Another photo showed the same boy, but older – maybe ten now. He was on a swing, and a blonde girl of the same age sat next to him. They were both grinning and waving at the camera. There was a note of familiarity, but he wasn't sure what it was.

'Okay?' Ed appeared in the doorway, making Richard jump. He hadn't heard him come in.

'Sorry, I didn't mean – I wasn't snooping.'

'Didn't imagine you were,' Ed said, briskly. There was a moment's silence, while Richard tried to place what was wrong with the situation, and then Ed held out a small bag of seeds. 'Here you go, then.'

'Great. Yes. Thanks.' He took the bag and tried to shake off the awkwardness.

'I'll see you out, if you like.'

'Great.'

Ed showed Richard to the front door, and watched him all the way down the front path. He waited until Richard was halfway up the street before he closed the door behind him.

Lily left the house not long after Richard left for work. The air was cold and damp, rain threatening in the grey of the clouds, and the streets of Drayfield were quiet – just a few pensioners who nodded politely and without recognition as she walked past. She pulled her coat closer and kept her eyes on the ground as she made her way to the bus stop.

It wasn't much of a stop, just a post with a sign and a lone bench with half of its slats missing. A mother, not much older than Lily, perched on the edge of the bench and pushed a buggy back and forth with one hand. She didn't look up when Lily sat down next to her.

It was the first time she'd really ventured out on her own since they'd moved there, and she hadn't been prepared for the strangeness; sitting on the same bench where she'd once sat as a child waiting for the school bus. It was twenty-one years ago and yesterday and somehow another lifetime altogether, all at once. She looked to her right, half-expecting to see the ghost-children standing there, waiting to be whisked off to school. All she saw was empty air.

The bus turned up, with only three other passengers on board. Lily made her way upstairs and sat at the front. She liked looking through the front window in slow traffic: enjoyed the way the perspective made it seem as if the cars below vanished beneath the front wheels of the bus, only to reappear a moment later, unscathed.

The journey was quicker than she remembered; either her sense of time had shifted as she'd got older or there was less traffic at this time of day. Probably a mixture of both. She disembarked in the centre of town, and immediately felt assaulted by people. Farnworth wasn't a particularly busy town, but it had been weeks since she'd been in the company of strangers, and suddenly there were hundreds of them: walking in different directions, walking into her, almost walking through her as though she wasn't there at all. Without paying attention to what she was doing she found herself standing in the corner of the bus station, flattened against the glass, counting her breaths in an attempt to slow her pulse. Her vision blurred, and for a second she thought she was going to faint. Then the crowds cleared, and the moment passed.

It had been raining heavily, and the pavements were slick, dotted here and there with puddles of brown water. There was still a wetness in the air that clung to her skin and made her throat feel damp as she breathed. She set off in the opposite direction to most of the crowds, heading away from the centre of town. Within minutes the streets had expanded, rows of wide, three-storey terraces springing up on either side, their yellowish bricks streaked with sooty residue from centuries of pollution. There were fewer people here, and half of the buildings carried ornate plaques which designated them as non-residential: solicitors' offices, walk-in health centres, dentists. She counted the numbers until she found the one she was looking for: a small bronze plaque announced Mervyn & Partners Health Services, with a list of names and qualifications underneath. His name was at the top. Dr Alastair Mervyn, Consultant in Child Psychiatry.

She'd looked him up before coming here, but, even so, seeing his name printed in bronze triggered an odd mixture of emotions. There was affection, and a sort of longing; she'd often wondered how he was getting on, though she'd never thought to contact him before. But there was also fear: what if he refused to see her? Or, worse, couldn't remember her at all?

She stood outside on the pavement, staring at the plaque. Fat drops of rain started to fall, spotting the pavement around her and landing heavily on her head, but she didn't move. Didn't notice time passing, people shaking their heads as they walked around her on the pavement.

And then the door opened, and some people came out: a father and his son, who couldn't have been older than ten. The father held the son by the hand, helping him down the large stone steps, and a woman stood behind them, holding the door open, watching them go. 'See you next week, then.' She went to close the door, and then noticed Lily standing there. 'Oh, hello, dear. Can I help you?'

Lily hesitated. 'I'm not sure.'

'Why don't you come in?'

The father and son brushed past her, leaving just Lily, standing awkwardly on the pavement. She looked around her, but couldn't think of an excuse not to go in. So she nodded, and stepped over the threshold, letting the woman close the door behind her.

She stepped into a hallway, large and dark and distinctly Victorian in décor. For a moment she was reminded of the institute, but most of that had been much more clinical in appearance; it was only the doctors' offices that had been lined with books and mahogany panelling. This was more homely, with a narrow, burgundy-carpeted staircase leading up to what could have easily been bedrooms. The woman led the way through to the front room – a large, airy reception area, decorated predominantly in green and lined with waiting-room chairs – and made her way behind the desk. There were two other people in the room, a woman in her forties and a girl in her teens, sat a chair apart from each other. The woman was reading, while the girl stared sullenly at the floor.

'So how can I help you?' the receptionist asked, warm yet businesslike, settling herself down in the chair in front of her computer.

'I – wanted to make an appointment.'

'Well, we actually only see children in this clinic. There's an adults' centre just down the road – '

'I want to see Dr Mervyn.'

The woman raised her eyebrows. 'Are you a friend of his?'

'I was – a patient.'

'I see. Well, he's a busy man, and if this is a social call I'd suggest getting in contact with him out of hours.'

'It's not a social call.' Lily looked down at the floor. She could feel the teenager watching her. 'I need to talk to him about – some treatments. That he gave me.' The woman stared at her blankly. 'When I was younger,' she said, trying not to let desperation creep into her voice. 'It will only take ten minutes.'

'I'm afraid he's booked solid for today – '

'Ten minutes? Please?'

The woman looked at her for a moment, as if weighing up her options. 'It might be quite a wait. But, if you sit down, I'll have a word with him when he's free.'

'Thank you.'

She sat down opposite the teenager, whose gaze had moved to the large bay window that faced out on to the street. Lily picked up a magazine and started to flick through it, but the words blurred on the page and made her feel dizzy. She closed her eyes. The room was silent except for the tapping of the receptionist's fingers on the keyboard, and the occasional roar of a car passing by outside.

After fifteen minutes or so she heard a door open upstairs. There was the low murmur of voices; three sets of footsteps on the stairs. The front door opened, and then closed. And then one set of footsteps, coming closer. Pausing at the door. And then the shock of a voice so familiar, speaking an unfamiliar name: 'Jenny?'

Lily opened her eyes. He didn't look at her; his gaze was fixed on the teenager, who looked up, smiled faintly, and stood up. The woman – Lily realised it must be her mother – touched her arm as she stood. 'I'll be right here,' she murmured, but the teenager shook her off and followed Dr Mervyn without looking back.

Lily had no idea how long she sat there. The rain grew heavier outside; the sky darkened and thick raindrops pelted the window. Patients came and went. Sometimes doctors appeared briefly, summoning their patients. Other doctors seemed less willing to come out of their offices, and their patients were escorted by the receptionist, who smiled and took hold of their arms like an elderly nurse.

Lily sat silently, staring at the floor, tracing the patterns of the carpet with her gaze.

Eventually she was the only one left. The receptionist left the room and went upstairs. Lily heard the soft tread of her shoes on the carpet, the creaking of the stairs under her feet. The light rapping of her knuckles on a door upstairs. The low groan of the door's hinges as she eased it open.

Five minutes, in which Lily wondered what on earth she would say to him.

And then she heard two sets of footsteps coming down the stairs.

When he looked at her from the doorway, his gaze was the same as it had been twenty-one years before, and she felt momentarily sure she wouldn't have to explain herself. But there was no recognition in his eyes. 'Do you want to come upstairs?' he asked, his voice kind but puzzled.

She followed him up the stairs and into his office. It was markedly different from the one she had spent so much time in – that had been a school office that he'd borrowed, and the objects within it had been impersonal, meaningless. This was different. The walls were lined with bookshelves, and dotted here and there with framed photographs, diplomas. On his desk sat a family photograph: Dr Mervyn, wife, two daughters. She'd never realised he had children.

Maybe he hadn't, back then.

They sat down opposite each other, separated by his desk, as they always had been. She realised he was in his mid-fifties. The same age as her father would have been, had he lived. The doctor's eyes had stayed the same, but his face had crumpled slightly around them, weathered with age. His hair was mostly grey.

'So, are you going to make me guess who you are?' he asked. His smile was the same.

'Lily Emmett. I was almost twelve, last time you saw me.'

He leaned back in his chair, and gave her a long look; appraising. She couldn't tell whether he remembered her or not. 'And how old are you now?'

'Thirty-three.'

'I'm afraid you're a bit old for me to be able to treat you.' His voice was firm, but his smile was kind. 'Was it treatment you were after?'

The question made her pause. What was it she was after? 'I'm not sure.'

'Well, why don't you tell me what's been happening?'

She said nothing for a moment, clenching and unclenching her hands in her lap. She realised she'd been hoping he would just know, without her having to explain.

'I've been having – similar problems. The same problems as I used to have. And I wondered if you could help.'

Dr Mervyn looked at her kindly. 'I'm a child psychiatrist, Lily. Don't you think you'd be better off with someone who deals with adult problems?'

'But it's the same problem.' Her voice was stubborn.

'It might be related to the same problem. But the nature of it is likely to have changed as you've grown older, and the treatment would be different now.' He leaned back in his chair, fingers clasped in front of him on the desk. 'Do you still have difficulty talking?'

So he did remember her. 'Not really. I don't talk as much as other people, I guess. But I don't avoid it.' She looked him in the eye, to gauge his reaction. 'I'm a lecturer now.'

He laughed. He looked genuinely delighted. 'Really? That's amazing.'

She shrugged. 'I suppose it might seem that way. But it's a different sort of speech.'

'Yes, I can see why you would feel like that. But – ' he leaned forward slightly ' – it's not really, you know. It's all communication.'

She shrugged again. 'It's not that that's the issue.'

'Okay. So what is the issue?'

She looked out of the window. It was dark outside now – the clock behind Dr Mervyn's head said it was past four o'clock – and there was a street-lamp directly outside the window, casting an orangey glow across the corner of the room. It reminded her of the kitchen in her old flat.

'I've been collapsing. Like I used to, only – worse, I suppose. I'm on sabbatical from work. And I...' She wondered if she dared tell him, and then realised that this was the real reason she had come to him. Because she couldn't admit it to anyone else. 'I've been hallucinating.'

'I see. What form do the hallucinations take?'

'They're – me. And my sister. As children.'

'And what are they doing?'

'They want me to go into the garden. To where Billy died.'

They sat in silence for a while, Dr Mervyn tapping the tips of his fingers together as he thought. The ticking of the clock behind him filled the room, marking the rising of the moon. Lily thought that maybe she shouldn't have come.

'Did you ever remember what happened?' he asked, eventually.

'No.'

'Do you want to?'

She looked down at her hands. Didn't reply.

'I don't know if anyone would be able to help you remember. It was a long time ago, and if you've gone this long without any hint of remembering then it's likely that the memory just isn't there. But there are other treatments for dealing with the symptoms you're experiencing.'

'Like what?'

'Talking therapies. Antidepressants. Have you not spoken to any doctors about it in recent years?'

'It's not depression. They said it was, um, conversion disorder.'

'Yes, that would be consistent with my diagnosis of you when you were a child. Did they explain what that was?'

'Sort of.' He looked at her, expectant. 'They said my brain gives me physical symptoms to deal with because I'm not coping with stress properly.'

'Right. The selective mutism you suffered from as a child was of a similar nature. My guess is that, as you've grown older, your symptoms have adapted to ensure that you keep managing them. In cases of conversion disorder, there's often an underlying anxiety problem, and that's why I would suggest antidepressants.'

She nodded. 'Would they help with the other stuff?'

'No. The only way your symptoms are going to get better is if you address the root cause. You need to come to terms with the things that have happened to you, the stresses you have been suppressing since you were a child.'

'It sounds like psychobabble.'

'It's a recognised psychiatric disorder.'

She looked at him, sceptical.

'Here, look.' He walked to his bookcase, pulled out a large grey paperback and laid it on the desk in front of her. *Diagnostic and Statistical Manual of Mental Disorders*. He flipped it open at the index, traced his finger over the right section, entitled *Somatoform Disorders*, and there it was: *Conversion Disorder*. Lily stared at it for a moment, then flipped the book closed. It was enough to see the words, without seeing her symptoms listed in black and white.

'So what would you suggest?'

'Well, I would recommend therapy. With someone who is a qualified adult psychologist. I can recommend a few people.'

'What if I don't want therapy?'

He looked at her over steepled fingertips. 'You remember the exercise we tried? Exposing yourself to various stimuli in order to bring back memories?'

'It didn't work.'

'I beg to differ.' He smiled again. 'If you remember, it had quite an effect on you.'

'But it didn't help me remember.'

'Well, no. But that's not really the object any more.' His voice was gentle, prodding her subtly into agreement. 'It's not important for you to remember, as such. You just need to stop being scared of remembering. You need to confront whatever it is that's causing you distress.'

'So where would I find the stimuli?'

Dr Mervyn raised an eyebrow. 'Have you tried talking to your sister?'

then

Connie stepped out of Gatwick Airport into the wet warmth of late April. She was thinner than she had been when she left, and tanned from working outside, though it hadn't seemed especially sunny when she'd been there. Her hair was lighter, making her eyes appear bluer, and she looked older. She'd been away for nearly a year.

The familiarity was momentarily disarming – the chatter of English voices around her, the signposts and symbols that were instantly recognisable. The line of black cabs, and the patient queue of passengers in front of it, were so British that they made her want to cry. She followed the signs to the train station and emerged on to a busy platform, filled with people of all nationalities standing near piles of luggage, watching the departure screens anxiously.

She got on the first train heading southeast, and secured a cluster of four seats and a table to herself, piling up luggage on the seat next to her and putting her feet on the one opposite. The train crawled lazily through the countryside, past rolling hills, lush trees, picturesque rivers. The sky darkened with gathering clouds, and before long raindrops splattered against the glass, obscuring the view. Connie leaned her head against the glass and closed her eyes.

The train stopped and the doors opened, letting in a blast of excited conversation and cold air. Several people got on, and Connie slid her feet reluctantly off the seat as an elderly man moved towards her. He took the seat diagonally across from her, and nodded at the space next to him, saying, 'You can put them back, if you like.'

She smiled faintly. 'Thanks, but it feels rude, making you sit next to my feet.'

'I've sat next to worse things.'

He leaned back against the headrest and closed his eyes, and after a moment Connie put her feet back where they had been.

The train continued, the sky growing steadily darker, until all Connie could see through the glass was her own face reflected back at her. A ticket collector checked her ticket, and looked pointedly from her feet to the sign above them which expressly forbade her from putting them on the seat. She glared at him and moved them, snatching her ticket back ungraciously. The elderly man laughed at her expression. 'At least you know to pick your battles,' he said, his voice kind, and closed his eyes again.

An hour later, they arrived at the nearest station to the village, and she hauled her bag on to the platform, shivering the second she got outside.

The rain had not abated, and made visibility difficult, but she knew exactly where she was going. The steps into the car park were slippery with rainwater, the car park partially flooded. She grimaced, and hopped across it, trying to avoid the worst of the puddles.

Two cabs waited at the entrance to the station, and she jumped into the first one, giving the driver the address between grunts as she hauled her bag in after her. He nodded and started the engine wordlessly. They drove along the dark roads in silence, as Connie stared out of the window and tried not to think about the reception she would receive. The rain pounded on the windscreen, and the windows were steamy and opaque. Connie traced a 'C' in the condensation, and then rubbed it out, creating a clear patch through which she could see the orange glow of street-lamps outside.

The driver pulled up outside the house, and Connie felt a momentary shock at seeing it still standing there, exactly the same as it had been when she left. There were lights on in the living room; she could see the glow through the gap in the curtains. She paid the driver with a note and told him to keep the change, though she had no idea how much she'd given him.

As she walked to the front door she felt sure she was being watched, the dark windows above her looming like eyes. She wondered whether she should knock, and then shook her head at her own ridiculousness and dug around in the front pocket of her bag until she found her key. It turned easily in the lock, and the door swung open into darkness.

She waited, breathless, but there was no indication that anyone was coming to greet her.

She could hear the murmur of the TV in the living room, and movement in the kitchen: someone making dinner. She closed the door behind her quietly and crept forward, wondering about the best way of announcing herself. She considered shouting hello, but she felt nervous, almost unwelcome. She realised she had been envisaging some kind of hero's welcome all the way home, but now she was here she didn't feel anywhere near so certain of being well received.

Admonishing herself for being ridiculous, she dropped her bag on the floor and stepped forward more confidently. 'Dad?' she called, and she felt rather than heard the movement freeze in the kitchen. No answering call, though. 'Mama?'

Her mother stepped into the doorway, confusion giving way smoothly to relief. 'Connie,' she breathed, rushing forward to hug her, and then hesitating when she was just a step away. 'It's – it's really you?'

'It's really me,' she confirmed, allowing herself to be swept into a hug. She felt her mother's sharp edges digging into her as their collarbones pressed together.

'Oh, darling, I thought you were dead,' her mother whispered into her hair. 'And the last words we ever spoke were an argument – '

'Shh. It's fine. I'm not dead.' Connie stepped away awkwardly, brushing her mother's tears out of her hair. 'Where are the others? It seems quiet.'

Her mother looked anxiously back at the kitchen doorway. 'What made you decide to come back?' she asked, ignoring Connie's question.

'I don't know, really. Just got bored of sleeping in strange beds.' Her mother looked at her sharply, making Connie laugh. 'On my own, Mama. I promise.'

'Good. Good.' She looked behind her again. 'Have you – spoken to anyone? Lily, or anyone?'

'No. You know what Lily's like on the phone.' Connie looked at her mother closely, trying to work out what in her behaviour was so off-putting. She was acting like a trapped rabbit. And she kept looking at the kitchen door as if something horrible was going to burst through it. 'Mama? Is everything okay?'

'Yes. Of course.' Her mother turned to face her, lifted her hands to Connie's cheeks. 'It's so good to see you home.'

'I'm sorry I didn't call. It just seemed – well. I needed some space.' She thought about what she had glimpsed through the kitchen window on the night that she left, and flinched involuntarily.

'It's okay. That doesn't matter now.' Her mother's gaze again, darting back to the kitchen door. What was she afraid of?

'Mama?'

'Yes, darling?'

'Where's Dad? And Lily? Have they gone out?'

Her mother looked down, reaching out for Connie's hands. 'Look at the state of your nails, darling. They're filthy.

Really... really filthy.' She rubbed the pads of her fingers along the edges of Connie's nails. 'You haven't been taking care of yourself, have you?'

'Mama.'

'Don't.' Her mother looked up then, and the expression in her eyes was so desperate, Connie *felt* what she was trying to say, without really understanding it.

'Mama, *please.*'

She opened her mouth, but then shook her head, no sound escaping. From behind her, in the kitchen, a male voice carried easily, though it didn't speak particularly loudly.

'You're going to have to tell her some time, Anna.'

Connie looked up, and found herself looking straight into the eyes of the man she had run away from.

now

Connie opened the door to find Lily standing on the other side of it. She looked lost, and a bit sheepish. 'I went to see Dr Mervyn,' she said, and Connie ushered her inside.

'Are you serious? He's still practising?'

'He's only fifty or so.'

'Yeah, I guess.' Connie walked through to the kitchen. 'Do you want tea? I was just going to make some.'

'Thanks.' Lily stood in the living room, feeling awkward. She was suddenly aware of how quiet the house was, and couldn't remember the last time she'd seen her sister at home without the boys around, drowning out the silence with childish screams. 'Boys at school?' she called.

Connie appeared in the kitchen door, looking puzzled. 'It's gone six,' she said.

'Oh. Yeah.' She remembered now. The darkness setting in while she sat in Dr Mervyn's waiting room. She must have been there for hours. She felt suddenly dizzy. Connie noticed as she reached out a hand to steady herself on the back of a chair.

'Have you eaten?'

Lily tried to remember, but the whole day had condensed into sitting in that chair, waiting. The time she'd been in his office was microseconds, already gone. 'I don't think so.'

'For fuck's sake, Lily, you're thirty-three years old.' But the tone was kinder than the words, and Connie guided her into a seat. 'What do you want to eat?'

'Where are the boys?'

'Karate. Nathan's picking them up. They'll be at least half an hour yet.' Connie disappeared into the kitchen again, shouting behind her. 'Toast? Soup? Pasta? I think I've got some stuff in the freezer if you want.'

'Um.' She felt as though her brain had atrophied, and she couldn't remember how she'd come to be here. 'Soup?'

'Sure.' Banging, of saucepans on counters. And a crackling. Connie rummaging in the freezer. 'Carrot and coriander okay?'

'Yeah. Thanks.'

For a few minutes Connie banged around in the kitchen, and Lily stared into space, wondering why she was here. Dr Mervyn had suggested it, so she had come. But what had he expected her to say, now that she was here?

Connie appeared in the doorway again. 'Does Richard know where you are?'

'No, I don't think so.'

'Do you want me to call him?'

Lily shook her head. 'I will. In a bit.'

Connie ducked back into the kitchen for a moment, and then reappeared carrying a bowl of soup, which she set down on the coffee table in front of Lily. 'Leave it for a minute, it's hot. Are you sure? It would only take a second, to call him. He's probably worrying about you.'

'No. Thanks.'

'Lils.' Connie leaned forward, took her hand. 'Can you tell me why you went to see Dr Mervyn?'

Lily considered the question. 'I think I was scared.'

'Of what?'

'Myself.' Lily leaned back in the chair, so that Connie was forced to drop her hand. 'The collapsing, you know. And, um. Bad dreams, and things.'

'That house?'

'Yeah, partly.' Lily groped for the words, clenching and un-clenching her good fist. 'Dr Mervyn suggested I speak to you.'

'Why? What does he expect me to be able to do about it?' Connie's voice was defensive, and Lily looked down at her hands and didn't answer. 'Does he think I'm the reason you're not well?'

'No.'

'What, then?'

Lily found her eyes crawling the walls, as if searching for what she wanted to say. 'Did you ever read the coroner's report?' she asked eventually.

'Billy's? Or Dad's?'

Lily looked at her, confused. It had never occurred to her that their father's death would also have been investigated: it had been so straightforwardly awful. 'Billy's.'

'Oh. No, I didn't. I don't think I understood what a coroner's report was, at the time. And I doubt Mama would have let me read it even if I'd wanted to.'

'What about when you were older?'

Connie shrugged. 'I was there, wasn't I? So there was no need.'

'You weren't ever curious?'

'What is this? You know what happened, don't you? He fell; he hit his head and he broke his neck. End of story.'

'But – ' Lily's protest sounded feeble, but felt terribly important ' – I don't remember. It feels as though if that's all there was to remember then I wouldn't feel like something was missing.' She looked up at Connie, pleadingly. 'Do you know what I mean?'

Connie's face was blank confusion. She inhaled sharply, as if about to speak; then she shook her head. 'Finish your soup,' she said, her voice tired. 'I'll drive you home.'

They got back to Drayfield after nine. Connie led the way up the front path, pointlessly, because she then had to wait at the door for Lily to find her key. They pushed open the door on to a brightly lit hallway, but no sound.

'Hello?' Connie's voice, louder than usual as she stepped over the threshold. Lily was already kicking off her shoes, walking towards the kitchen, but Connie felt oddly cautious. Something in the silence felt wrong. She was reminded of another time, years before, when she had walked into this house to find things not quite as they should be.

'Richard?' she called, but still no answer. She closed the front door behind her, and followed Lily into the kitchen.

Richard was nowhere to be seen, but the patio door was wide open. Lily stood motionless near the doorway. Her expression was sheer terror, but Connie couldn't understand what she was seeing that would scare her so much.

'Is he outside?' she asked, putting an arm on Lily's elbow, causing her to jump. Lily looked at her briefly, but didn't reply.

'Let's go and look, shall we?' Connie said, her voice halfway between parental and exasperated. She took a step forward, and then heard Richard's voice, carrying in through the open door.

'What the hell are you playing at?'

Both Lily and Connie darted forward at the same moment.

then

Her grandmother looked older than Connie had remembered
her looking, and more tired. Her smile as she opened the door
was genuine, though, and her hug as warm as it had ever
been. 'Look how grown-up you are,' she sighed, and Connie
was shocked to see tears in her eyes. She hadn't registered,
until she was face to face with it, that the loss of her father
had also been the loss of her grandmother's son.

'I'm afraid Grandpa's still finding things a bit of a
struggle,' she said, leading Connie through to the kitchen.
'But Lily will be thrilled to see you. Will you be staying long?'

'Well, it depends,' Connie hedged. A slightly surreal
feeling was setting in: after almost a year of travelling by
herself, of flitting from job to job and town to town without
ever really speaking to anyone, it felt odd and abrupt to be
back on familiar ground. There were school photos of her on
the wall; her and Lily, aged seven and ten, sitting tall in school
uniform. Lily was missing two teeth, and the gaps made her
smile seem wider, somehow.

'How was your mother?'

Connie shrugged. She didn't want to talk about her
mother. She felt very aware that her clothes were dirty, that
she hadn't showered for two days, that she hadn't brushed
her hair or her teeth since the plane had landed that morning.
She'd been lucky that she still remembered her grandparents'
phone number after all these years: she couldn't have stayed
with her mother, and the thought of spending the night in a

random hostel after the shock of her homecoming was more than she could bear.

'Do you know that she's been having some problems? They've been talking about hospitalising her.'

Connie tried to suppress disloyal thoughts: *melodramatic, attention-seeking, weak and pathetic.* Making such a fuss, when she'd never really loved him anyway, while the rest of them carried on as best they could. Her feelings must have showed on her face.

'They were very much in love, once,' her grandmother said gently, and Connie knew it was the nicest thing she could find to say about her.

'Well, she's moved on,' Connie said bluntly. The expression on her grandmother's face made Connie realise she already knew. 'How long?' she asked, not sure she wanted to know.

'As I say, they were in love, once. It was a long time ago. Anna needed comforting, and she found someone who would give her what she needed. Don't judge her too harshly.'

'She cheated on your son. Don't you hate her?'

Her grandma smiled sadly. 'No, dear. I don't hate her.'

'I missed his funeral.' The words, barely a whisper, were uttered in the direction of Connie's feet.

'Oh, Connie. I'm so sorry.' Her grandmother stepped forward to wrap her arms around her. 'We wanted to wait, but your mother just wanted to get it over with. We did try to find you, but – well, you did a good job of keeping yourself hidden.'

'Yeah.' Connie blinked, clearing the tears from her eyes, disengaging herself from the embrace as delicately as she could. 'So where's Grandpa, then?'

'He and Lily have just gone for a walk up the lane. They shouldn't be more than half an hour or so, and then dinner will be ready. Did you want to wash first?'

Connie went up to the room that she and Lily had shared as children, the one that Lily had taken over when she'd moved in properly. Once it had had twin beds, and the only personal items had belonged to her grandparents: a picture of them together in their twenties, framed by a trellis of roses; a dish full of delicately elaborate brooches. It was unmistakably Lily's room now: the second bed had been removed, and there were her books, her school things. A small cluster of make-up on the dresser, half of which had obviously come free with magazines. And a photograph of their father in an ornate silver frame. He was in his late thirties, perched on top of a cluster of rocks, giving a wide smile and a thumbs-up to whoever was holding the camera. She wondered who it was: probably her mother, but had they really ever been that happy?

A camp bed had been set up for Connie, with towels laid out on it, and she dropped her bag on the floor and started to undress. It was a relief to peel off her dirty clothes, to brush out her hair. Most of the places she had stayed had been nice enough, but they hadn't felt homely. The familiarity here might be disarming, but at least it was there.

She had a shower, taking her time, filling the bathroom with steam. The hot water was invigorating, pounding the muscles in her shoulders and soothing the tension that had gathered there. She felt as though she was washing off at least a week's worth of dirt, as opposed to a couple of days' worth; her hair was thick with the scent of other people's unwashed bodies.

Drying off, she rubbed a hole in the steam on the mirror and peered at her reflection. Her skin looked pale and blotchy, her cheeks hollowed out by a year of work and half a day of grief, but her eyes retained some of their brightness. She looked older than her sixteen years, but not so old that people would miss her youth completely.

When she got back to the bedroom, swathed in towels, with damp still clinging to her skin, she found Lily sitting on the bed, staring out of the window. She looked up as Connie entered, and her eyes were dark, a faint accusation hanging in the air between them.

Connie closed the door behind her and sat down on the bed, awkwardly trying to wrap an arm around Lily while still keeping her towel wrapped around her, the cold in the air biting at her bare skin. 'Hey, sis,' she said softly, kissing the top of her head. Lily leaned into her shoulder, closing her eyes.

'You came,' she said, her voice barely a whisper.

'Yeah. I'm sorry it took me so long.'

They sat for a while, arms wrapped around each other, breathing as one.

'I heard – ' Lily stopped, and moved forwards out of Connie's arms, twisting her head round to look her in the eyes. 'I heard you saw Mama.'

'Yeah. She told me about Dad.'

Lily blinked at her, wordless. Her eyes weren't accusing, but Connie found the lack of accusation even more painful, somehow, than the presence of it would have been. 'Lils, I'm so sorry I wasn't there.'

'He died on Christmas Day.'

Connie chewed her lip to stop herself from crying. 'I know.'

Lily stood up and walked to the window. She stood for a while, looking at things that Connie couldn't see. Connie watched the back of her neck, visible beneath the wisps of hair that had escaped from her ponytail. She realised how grown-up Lily looked: almost a teenager now. She'd always looked younger than she was, childish and delicate and fragile. She was still young, but the fragility had morphed, somehow. She'd developed a sort of quiet strength since Connie had last seen her: you might still want to protect her, but she no longer looked as though she needed it so much.

'I really wanted to come home, Lils. You have no idea. How it felt, when she said...' Connie trailed off. Lily hadn't so much as twitched in response.

After a minute, Lily turned around and headed towards the door. 'You'd better get dressed,' she said. 'For dinner.' She closed the door quietly behind her, leaving Connie alone.

Conversation over dinner was stilted. Lily didn't speak at all, and their grandfather sat like a shadow beside her, hollowed out and wordless. Connie answered the questions put to her by her grandmother, but neither of them was really in the mood, and eventually they both gave up. Silence crept in like the darkness, slipping underneath the curtains and lurking in the corners of the room.

After dinner, they all went upstairs to their respective rooms.

There was a tiny TV set up in the corner of Lily's room, and the two girls changed into their pyjamas and watched *Blind Date* without really seeing it. Connie couldn't help thinking of their childhood visits to this house, when they would have stayed up talking into the early hours, listening to the low murmur of conversation and the faint scent of cigarette smoke drifting up from the living room. She could clearly remember the shadows the hallway light had cast upon the room: the way Lily had looked, glowing faintly in the darkness, as they swapped ghost stories and talked about what they would do the next day. Now, they barely looked at each other, and the silence from the rest of the house felt like a gaping wound.

Connie tried to imagine what it had felt like, for Lily, coming to live here full time. To leave their old life behind entirely, but to still be in someone's care: no freedom, and no parents either. In some ways, having spent so much of her childhood here, it must have been more like coming home. But, if Connie had been around, would things have been different? Would they have stayed with their mother, rebuilt some sort of family out of what remained?

At eleven Lily flicked the TV off without asking Connie whether she was still watching it, and rolled over to face the wall. There was a gap at the top of the curtains, and from the glow of the street-lamp outside the window Connie could just about see her sister's back, solid and hard and accusatory.

'I had to go,' she said, her voice feeling unnaturally loud in the darkness. No response. 'I know it must have seemed selfish, but I had a fight with Mama, and I saw some stuff, and I just couldn't stick around any more.'

There was a long pause before Lily spoke. 'But you planned it. You told me.'

'I know I said that. But I didn't mean – I wouldn't have left *then*. Not like that.' Connie sighed, twisting the duvet cover between her thumb and her forefinger, trying to find the words. 'I would have said goodbye, if I'd really planned it like that.'

'You never called.'

'No,' Connie admitted.

'Dad *died*.' Lily's voice was a ferocious whisper.

'And if I'd have thought for ten seconds that something like that might happen then I wouldn't have gone, alright? But I couldn't be in a house with Mama any more. I just couldn't.' A beat. 'I still can't.'

'You went back to see her, though.'

'I thought you'd be there.'

Lily turned over to face Connie. The bed wasn't much higher than the camp bed, and there was a three-foot gap between the two, so they could look into each other's eyes easily enough. 'So what made you leave, then?'

'I – saw something.'

'What? What did you see that was so awful?'

Connie groped for the words to explain it. 'I saw – Mama doing something. And it – it made me think.' A pause. 'I think it made me remember.'

Lily's eyes widened, almost imperceptibly. Connie could feel the tension radiating from her, from both of them, as they waited for Lily to ask the question.

One thousand, two thousand, three –

'Was it our fault?'

– thousand, four thousand, five thousand, six –

'No.'

Exhale. And: hush.

now

When Lily stepped into the garden, she could see Richard straight ahead in front of her, but nothing beyond: all was darkness and shadow, and she couldn't make out what he was shouting at. She wanted to say his name, alert him to her presence, but fear stuck her throat and made it impossible. She reached out a hand instead, finding his shoulder in the dark. He spun around instantly.

'What are you – ?' He stopped when he saw her, and his voice softened. 'Sorry, Lils. You scared me. Where have you been?'

'She was with me,' Connie said, stepping into the garden behind them. 'What's going on? Why are you out here?'

Richard looked momentarily as though he wanted to reprimand her for keeping Lily out without asking permission first, and then he remembered where he was, and spun back around. 'I saw some – *arsehole* running around out here. Trying to scare me, most likely. Or steal something.'

'What would they steal? Weeds?'

'How should I know?' Richard sounded annoyed. 'Maybe they were trying to break in. Don't suppose Nate's with you?'

'What, you need manly back-up?'

Richard shrugged. 'Couldn't hurt.'

They carried on talking, but Lily tuned them out, staring past Richard into the darkness. Her eyes were adjusting now, and she could see movement; a faint flickering in the trees as shadows skittered past. She shuddered involuntarily, took a step back. 'Hey, let's get you back inside,' Richard said, putting a hand on her shoulder, but she shook her head. Could feel the pull of the woods, as if something was demanding her attention.

Ghost-Connie, stepping out of the shadows; beckoning her with a hand.

'Lils.' Connie's voice behind her, tentative: and then more forceful. '*Lily.*'

Lily, already stepping forward, didn't hear her.

– You have to be quiet in the house or Mama will hear us –

Lily's footsteps, sock-slippered, tiptoeing two steps behind Connie's. Skipping the creaking step by instinct. And Connie's hair a blur in front of her face: a torch for her to follow in the darkness.

– But it's dark and I'm scared of the dark and didn't you say Billy was meeting us –

Connie's coldwater scorn, scathing even in the pitch black.

Outside was a slap of cold air. Moonlight trickling through blanket fog and Lily's watch, blue numerals flashing in the dark. Shadows, moving.

And, beyond the shadows, other things.

'What's wrong?'

Connie was at her side, hand on her shoulder, but she felt far away and Lily couldn't tear her eyes away from the woods. The someonethere. In a moment a clear beam of moonlight would illuminate them and then –

And then what?

'Lils, *please*, can you just say something? You're scaring me.'

Lily felt fixed, immovable. Couldn't wrench her eyes from the distance, even though she knew it was important.

Connie's voice filtered as if through layers of pondwater, years-distant and otherwise.

That feeling, so familiar: as if her throat was closing up.

The words, if she had ever had them, were not there now.

Trapped in the shadows, perhaps, with whatever else lurked out there.

'*Lily.*'

And then: Richard at her side, forcibly unclenching her fist. Slipping his fingers between hers. Speaking in a language she could still use. *Okay?*

Yes.

And a face, looming out of the shadows: becoming clearer the longer she looked.

Shadows rippling across the grass. And they had silk-slipped into the woods, plunged into the trees. Branches catching at hair and trailing skeletal fingers across cheekbones and Lily had cringed away, becoming smaller in the darkness.

Connie's whisper-voice, carrying across the years:

– *You need to **keep up** Billy's going to be **waiting for** us at the secret place –*

The woods had seemed to go on forever. Crunch of twigs under toes, glimpses of moonlight through the canopy of trees above. Lily's voice, a hesitant shadow next to Connie's:

– *Do you **know where** we're going? Are you **sure**?*

And still they had plunged ahead, forest bed rustling underfoot.

'Maybe we should get her inside.' Connie's voice was low, troubled. 'This isn't a good place for her, Richard – you don't understand – '

Lily's hand in his, two sharp bursts of pressure.

'She says no,' he said, his voice blunt.

'How do you...?' Connie looked from her sister to Richard, but both of them stared straight ahead, and they didn't reply. Connie followed their gaze.

And the shapes in the trees solidified into something recognisable.

'*You*,' Connie said, and her voice was barely a whisper: a memory stretching out across her entire life. And at the same moment, Richard, bewildered, stepping forward and dropping Lily's hand: 'Ed?'

Darkness had closed in on them. And the silence, blanketing them, shroud-like. So that the snapping of twigs echoed a hundredfold in the night and even the tiniest whisper felt like it echoed through the trees.

– *Where are we* **are we** *there yet where's* **the secret** *place* –

Shhhhh, no words here, just the hiss of whispered footsteps.

Mouth of the den loomed up. Rocks taking the form of teeth in the night, and Connie slipping ahead, to be swallowed by the dark. Lily, unobtrusive ghost-morsel behind her.

There was moaning in the dark.

– *What's that* **noise there's** *something in here* **I don't** *like it shut up stop* **being** *such a baby it's only Billy* **playing** *tricks* –

A step forward, and then: stop.

One shape in the distance, or maybe two: writhing in the dark.

Not Billy.

'What are you doing here?'

Richard's voice sounded half-guarded, half-bewildered. Lily could almost see him grasping for a logical explanation.

Ed stood caged in front of them all, face like a trapped animal. He opened and closed his mouth, but no words came.

'You know him?' Connie's voice, confused, floated out of the darkness from behind Lily.

'*You* know him?' Richard, equally confused.

'Yes, yes, everyone knows me,' Ed said. The swiftness with which he regained his composure made Lily wonder if she'd imagined the anxiety in his expression a moment before.

'How? How do you know him?' Connie stepped forward, into Lily's line of vision.

'He was the one who suggested the bar job to me.' Richard's voice was hard, unreadable. 'How do *you* know him?'

Lily could feel Connie's eyes on her. Felt the suggestion of something in the air: words that she wasn't going to like. An image of past and present, merging together: familiar face from childhood blurring with a spectre glimpsed through adult eyes.

And the hesitation in Connie's breath before she spoke.

'He was having an affair with our mother.'

Shapes unclear, half-seen. Connie stumbled back, too fast, dragging Lily with her before she could see. Only two images, from deep within the den, disconnected and yet not: a flash of blonde hair in the dark, and a low moan nearby.

– *Come on **we've got** to get out of **here** we've got to but where's Billy* –

No time for questions.

Running and not running – feet dragging in the dark and stumbling on buried roots – Lily understanding and not understanding – and behind them, those moans, eerie and animal-like, swelling in the darkness.

Connie's voice a rush of whispered instructions:

– Not far **now we'll** *be home soon Billy* **must** *have already gone home –*

And then she vanished, empty air where her voice had been. A fall, a cry: Connie splayed face-first in the dirt, and Lily standing over her.

Only it wasn't just Connie.

A sudden flash of light as the moon emerged from behind the clouds.

And then a scream, as Connie realised what she'd tripped over.

then

Connie had left her grandparents' house after a few days. It had been nice to see them, and to check up on Lily, but there had been no real reason to stay. She couldn't return to school. She couldn't live there, sharing a room with Lily, pretending she was still a normal teenager. And she couldn't stand the reminder of her father's death which inhabited every moment she spent in that house.

She went to a nearby town and got a job in a café. She told her grandparents where she was going, and she found a room in a shared house, with people not much older than her, mostly university students. Her grandparents helped her with rent until she had built up enough to be able to pay it herself. She was used to living on nothing, and the rent was cheap due to the house being run-down and draughty, so it didn't take long.

On her first free weekend, about six weeks after she'd moved, she took a trip back to Drayfield to see her mother. It was a four-hour train journey, and she spent most of it staring out of the window. She tried to read, but it was a struggle to concentrate. She felt sick with nerves, and she wasn't sure why.

She got a taxi from the train station, as she had done the last time she'd been to visit. It was light this time, and there was no rain, but the sky was overcast and the streets were still deserted.

She knocked on the door this time; she didn't want any surprises.

There was no answer. She waited for five minutes, knocking several times, and then gave up and used her key. The house was silent when she stepped in, and she could feel that no one was home. More than that: there was a different sort of absence. The house felt cold, unheated. Inhabited by stillness.

She went out into the garden. It was overgrown and tangled, a wild haze of lavender springing up between the lawn and the woods. She walked towards the woods, experimentally, but she stopped about two feet away and wouldn't go any closer. They were just woods, but inside there was darkness and she didn't want to see it.

She heard a rustling near the neighbour's fence, and turned; she could see a shape through the gaps in the wood. 'Hello?' she called. A face appeared over the top, a young woman she had never seen before.

'Hi. Are you one of Anna's daughters?'

'Yeah. I'm Connie.' She moved closer, so they wouldn't have to shout. 'Where is she, do you know?'

'She was taken into hospital last night.' The woman leaned her elbows on the fence. She was head and shoulders above Connie; she must have been standing on something that Connie couldn't see. 'I'm Lucy, by the way.'

'Hi.' Connie frowned. 'Hospital?' she repeated.

'Yeah. The place – it's just in the next village. The psychiatric hospital.'

'Oh.' She sifted through the possible responses for one that might seem appropriate. 'What happened?'

'Not sure. I've not lived here long, but her boyfriend popped by, to let us know what was going on.' Connie flinched at the mention of Ed, but didn't comment. 'I think she had some kind of breakdown,' Lucy added, her words measured, as if she was checking their impact as she said them.

'Right. Makes sense.' Connie nodded. 'I should go and check on her, then.' She went inside without another word, though she could feel Lucy's eyes on her all the way up the path.

She remembered the name of the hospital; it had been notorious, back when she was at school, and Eleanor had tormented her with the possibility that she would be sent there. She wanted to get a taxi, but she didn't have enough money for that, so she locked up the house behind her and walked down to the bus stop.

The buses ran in that direction every twelve minutes, so she didn't have long to wait. The journey took about half an hour. She spent the time trying not to think about the state she'd find her mother in. She'd seemed odd, before, but Connie had put that down to having to tell her that Dad was dead. Had she had a breakdown? Or was it just normal grief?

The nurses asked her to wait when she arrived at the hospital. They called a doctor, who introduced herself as Dr Ruskin, and took her into a private office. 'Are your grandparents not with you?' she asked as they sat down. 'We spoke to them this morning.'

'No, it's just me.' Connie didn't offer any further information, and Dr Ruskin looked for a moment as if she was going to ask, then seemed to think better of it. She gave Connie an overview of Anna's situation, then sat back and looked her in the eye.

'I'll be honest with you,' she said, 'she's much better than she was when she arrived, but it's unlikely she's going to be well enough to live on her own again, for a while at least. She's severely depressed, but we also think she may be suffering from schizophrenia. She's certainly not capable of looking after herself right now.'

'Do I need to look after her?'

The doctor looked surprised at the bluntness of the question. 'No. You're a minor, so we're not expecting you to take responsibility for her. But we think she'll probably have to be moved into a long-term care unit.'

'And who would pay for that?'

'A lot of it would be covered under the NHS. But your father also had a life insurance policy, so she has money available. It's unlikely she'd have to sell her house.'

'Unlikely.' Connie said the word aloud, digesting it.

'We'll have your interests in mind as well as hers. It's something that will be discussed with you as time goes on. At the moment we would only be looking to move her into a care unit for an initial period of six months.'

Connie nodded. 'And when are you looking to do this?'

'Actually, the move is already planned for next week. She's agreed to it.'

After that Dr Ruskin took her to see her mother. 'Visitor for you,' she said, opening the door without knocking and gesturing Connie inside. She closed the door behind her, leaving them alone.

The room was bright and sunny, the window looking down on green, rolling lawns. Anna was propped up in bed, eyes on the TV in the corner of the room. She glanced up as Connie entered, but only seemed half-aware of her presence.

'Hi,' Connie said, feeling awkward. She sat on the end of the bed.

'How did you find me?' Anna's voice was drowsy, but she sounded coherent.

'The neighbour told me where you were.'

'Ah. Good.'

'What's going on, Mama?'

Anna shrugged. 'Same old, same old.' Her eyes slid back towards the TV, as if the conversation were now over.

'You've been living with Ed,' Connie persisted.

'I didn't have anyone else.'

There was no apology, no remorse, and Connie felt her fingers tense around the duvet that encased her mother. She wanted to dig her fingernails into her mother's flesh.

'How could you do it, though?' she asked, trying to keep her voice low and reasonable. 'After everything that's happened. Dad's dead, and still you just carry on, having the same affair you always had.'

'Well, there was no point in hiding it any more, was there?' Anna laughed bitterly. 'Your logic seems somewhat skewed, my dear.'

'Didn't you feel guilty?'

Anna closed her eyes. There was a long pause, and for a minute Connie thought she had fallen asleep. But then she opened them again, wearily. 'Of course I felt guilty. But I was also angry with your father.'

'He tried his best.'

'So did I.'

'When? I saw you the night Billy died. And I saw you the night Lily got shut in the cupboard. Did it ever stop? Or were you with him the whole time, all that time Dad was trying to hold our family together?'

'We stopped for a while.'

'I don't believe you.'

Anna sighed. 'No, I didn't think you would. I doubt you'd believe me if I told you your father wasn't a saint, and he didn't always treat me that well, and Ed made me feel a lot of things that he never did. But it's true. And now it makes no difference, because your father's dead and I'm in here and Ed isn't able to look after me, so none of it matters any more.'

'It matters to me.'

'You'll grow out of it.' Anna shifted on the bed until she was lying down. 'I need to sleep now.'

'They're talking about keeping you in hospital for months. Is this it? Are you just going to lie here and let this be your life?'

'It's not a choice that's mine to make.'

'It *is*, Mama. All of this has been your choice. You could have chosen to make it work, chosen to try – '

'And then have it all turn out like this anyway.'

'You don't know that.'

'I know more than you do. Please let me sleep now.'

Connie sat there in silence, until her mother's light snoring filled the room, and then she left. It was a long time before she saw her again.

now

Lily could feel the reverberations of Connie's words as if they were ripples in the air around her. There was a sense of something suddenly falling into place, but that place was obscured, shrouded in darkness.

'An affair?' she repeated, but they didn't hear her.

'I don't understand,' Richard was saying. He was looking back and forth between Ed and Connie, as if not sure which one of them he should be demanding answers from. He turned on Ed. 'You knew who I was when you first approached me?'

'Yes.' Ed looked as if he was going to say more, but stopped.

'And your reason for approaching me was... What, exactly?'

Ed shrugged. His eyes were fixed on Lily. 'You look so like her,' he said wistfully. 'Like your mother.'

Lily looked at him more closely, tuning out the conversation around her. His face was only faintly familiar, a blur of features she remembered from childhood mixed with shadows from the recent past. 'You're Billy's dad,' she said abruptly.

'Yes, of course.' His voice was pained.

'And it was you that I saw in the garden when I collapsed.'

That got Richard's attention. 'What the hell? What are you talking about?'

Ed tensed and took a step back, but Lily ignored them both, turning to Connie.

'An affair?' she said.

Connie looked pale in the moonlight, shadows making odd hollows in her face, so that Lily couldn't read her expression. 'I'm sorry,' she said. 'I shouldn't have said anything.'

'Surely the point is that you *should* have said something?' Lily felt confused, wrong-footed. She couldn't quite understand what was happening. 'When were they having an affair? Why did you know about it when I didn't?'

Connie looked at the ground. 'I didn't want to tell you.'

'But *why*?'

'I was trying to protect you – '

'Protect me from *what*?'

Lily's voice rose to a pitch it hadn't reached for years. She couldn't remember the last time she'd felt that feeling: the tightness in her throat, the straining of her vocal cords, and the release that came with the vibrations of sound.

She felt Richard grasping at her hand, striving to calm her, but she shook him off. Eyes firmly fixed on her sister, who refused to meet her gaze. And Connie's voice, when it came, so small it was almost lost in the darkness.

'I was only trying to help.'

Figures emerging from the dark, clawing at their own clothes, reassembling themselves as they slipped out of the shadows. Two figures splayed out on the floor, two standing in the trees: and Lily crouched between, listening to her sister's quiet sobs.

Billy face-first in the dirt, neck twisted, unnatural. Dark pool underneath his head. Arms spreadeagled: no life in dead hands. And the voices of the tree-shadows reached her, slow in their approach, as if swimming through treacle.

– *What's going on why are you crying that's my son* –

And then Mama's arms around her waist, lifting her off

the ground: legs suspended briefly in mid-air, flying. Same for Connie: both of them standing side by side in the darkness, moon flitting through trees, and Mama hurrying them back to the house, a muttered stream of desperate words receding behind them.

– *He saw us he saw us he saw us* –

Billy left in the dirt with his father: and, later, the distant whine of sirens, heard from the safety of her bed.

'He saw them,' Lily said, her voice slow, as the pieces of the puzzle pushed themselves together. 'Billy saw them together. That's why he fell?'

Connie hesitated, then nodded.

'And you *knew*? You knew what happened and you didn't tell me.'

'I – it's difficult, Lils. They sent you away – and you were only eight, you wouldn't have understood – I didn't understand myself, not then. I saw him running away from something, and I saw him fall, but it wasn't until later that I put it together, realised what he'd seen.' She swallowed. 'What *I'd* seen.'

'But you didn't say anything.' Lily's voice, hard, stubborn. 'You could have told me, when you realised, but you never did.'

'I told you it wasn't our fault, when I got back. I thought that was what mattered. How could it have helped, to know the rest? You weren't even living with Mama any more; you had nothing to do with her...'

Lily waved a hand, brushing her protestations off. '*When* did you put it together?'

'I saw them together. Just before I ran away.'

Lily was dimly aware of Richard and Ed behind her, listening avidly; of the lurking backdrop of the trees, and of the darkness stretching out for miles beyond them. But her attention was focused on Connie, and on trying to piece together the implications of what she was saying. The subtle shift of all the things she'd thought she'd known, merging into the pieces that had always been missing.

'How long did it go on?'

'Forever.' Connie was close to tears now, her voice trembling. 'It never stopped, did it?'

She looked up at Ed for confirmation, but his head was bowed and Lily wasn't interested in his response. 'Did Dad know?'

'I don't know. We never talked about it.'

'But that's why they fought all the time, yes?'

Lily was shaking now. She felt Richard's hands on her shoulders, steadying her. Tried to keep her breathing even, but the realisations were coming too fast, the pieces connecting with a solidity that choked the air in her throat.

'That's it, isn't it?' she said, when Connie didn't reply. 'They fought because Mama was having an affair. Billy *died* because he saw them. And Dad – ' Her voice caught, but she shook her head, forcing the words out. 'Dad died because they fought about it. He was miserable, and then he died, all because of this. And you never told me.'

'Please, Lils, please don't turn this on me. It's him, he's the one in the wrong – ' Connie waved a hand in Ed's direction, but Lily shook her head again.

'No. He was just a stupid man having an affair. You're the one who lied to me.'

'But I was trying to keep you safe. You were never okay, never strong enough...'

'*And why do you think that was?*' Lily's voice rose to a shout, and she felt the stretching in her vocal cords: the feeling of shouting after so many years, of releasing *noise* after years of encasing herself in silence, was like stepping back into the skin of a person she used to be. 'I *knew* there was something missing. Something I needed to remember. You must have known as well, surely? You can't have been that wrapped up in yourself, that you never realised?'

She saw Connie take a step back, cowering from the sound of a voice she barely remembered. 'But you never said what the matter was, Lily, not really. I thought – I thought it was just because of *everything*.' Her voice was raw now, her lips trembling. 'I thought it would be easier for everyone if we just tried to forget about it.'

'But you never asked. You just *assumed*. Made my choices for me, as always.'

'For God's sake, Lils, it wasn't just about you, okay? I was there too. Billy was *my* friend. What makes you think it would have been so easy for me to talk about it?'

For a moment Lily stood glowering, torn, wanting to say more; then, without another word, she turned and walked back to the house. She heard the three of them behind her: Richard questioning Connie, Connie demanding answers from Ed, Ed protesting his innocence. The voices merged together, three separate strands of outrage and confusion blending together as one.

She closed the door on them, and released herself into the silence of the house.

She must have fallen asleep. She awoke on the sofa, with Richard sat at her feet like an oversized guard dog. At some point he'd draped a blanket over her, placed a glass of water on the table next to her head. His hand was absent-mindedly holding on to one of her calves, though he was staring in the opposite direction and his mind was clearly elsewhere.

'Morning,' she whispered, and he whipped his head round. 'Is everyone else gone?'

'Yeah. Connie said she's going to come over later, if you don't mind. She wants to talk to you properly, once the shock's passed a bit.'

Lily nodded. She wasn't sure if she was ready to talk about it yet: didn't want to shelve her feelings, bestow forgiveness, as she knew she would have to do if they were going to move on.

But then, if it was a choice between that and no forgiveness, she would do what needed to be done. A future without Connie was unthinkable, barely a future at all.

'What about Ed?'

'What about him?'

Lily shrugged. 'Did he explain what he was doing here?'

'Sort of. He said he's been coming over for a while, trying to get the garden nice for you. Said he used to do it when your mother lived here and he found it hard to break the habit. He kept talking about your hair and your eyes, how you looked like her – you and Connie, but especially you.'

Lily nodded. 'People have said that before.'

'Well, I think he was hanging around trying to get a glimpse of you. Seems a bit obsessed, if you ask me, but I think he's harmless enough.'

'Let's hope so. He was always a bit weird, after his wife left him. And after Billy died...' She closed her eyes, trying to remember. 'I know there were rumours, about him going crazy, prowling around the woods at night looking for Billy's ghost.'

'When actually he was probably just looking for your mother.'

'Guess so.' Lily stretched and pushed herself upright. 'I think I need a shower.'

'Want me to make some coffee?'

'Sounds great. Thanks.'

She showered slowly, watching the water pool briefly at her feet before swirling away down the plughole. She felt as though the shift in her perspective had stretched outwards from the mere fact of past events, touching everything. She tried to pinpoint the change: it wasn't just the clarity of knowing more than she had done before.

It took almost a minute for her to realise that she was no longer afraid.

When she went back downstairs Richard was sitting at the table sifting through the post, a pot of coffee in front of him. He poured her a cup, wordlessly, and she sat down opposite him and lifted the cup to her face without drinking. Thick tendrils of scent wound their way through the air and into her senses. The doors in front of her, demanding her attention.

'I want to go outside,' she said.

Richard grabbed their coats and they stepped outside into the freezing morning air, their coffee forgotten on the table inside. Lily walked steadily down the garden, feeling the gentle slope of the lawn beneath her. Richard was half a step behind – with her, but letting her lead.

A path of paving stones led through the lavender borders. Last time Lily walked this path the stones had been like slabs, the lavender level with her head: it had been like plunging through a gateway into another world. Now it was just a path, just a few plants; and, ahead, the looming darkness of the trees: just trees.

The woods were smaller than she remembered. Still big enough to get lost in, but Lily could see the edges, feel the borders of the neighbouring fields. When they had been children it had stretched on forever.

She only had a vague memory of where she was going, but it wasn't hard to find. Richard trailed her footsteps; she could hear the crunching of twigs behind her. After a few minutes of walking the mouth of the den opened up in front of them, half-covered by the brambles that had grown around it.

'Was this where your mother and Ed...?' Richard trailed off, as if he was struggling to find a delicate way to word it.

'Yeah. We used to come here too, though, when we were little. It was our hideout.' Lily turned around, pointed through the trees to where a clearing was just visible. 'That's where Billy fell.'

'So you think he was running away and – what? Tripped over a tree root or something?'

'Guess so.' Lily tried not to flinch, the image unnecessarily vivid even in the daylight. Turned back to the secret place, contemplating the entrance.

It was a low cave, not even really a cave; just a hollow in the earth, like an oversized burrow. She stepped forward, feeling it close around her. The ceiling was low enough that she had to duck to enter, and, once you got a few steps in, it dropped to crawling height. It was smaller than she remembered; looking at it now, she was surprised that it could have held three children so comfortably.

Or two adults.

Richard crouched down at the entrance, seemingly unwilling to step over the threshold. 'What's in there?' he asked, squinting to look closer.

Lily got down on her hands and knees and edged forward. Debris was scattered between the tree roots; old newspapers, unidentifiable rags, a few bottles. Nothing familiar. Lily lifted a few things for Richard's inspection, and he grimaced.

'I didn't realise there was a homeless shelter at the bottom of our garden.'

'More likely to be kids than homeless people, round here,' Lily replied, but her voice was distracted. She lifted a few of the newspapers, squinting in the hope of uncovering something significant, a date that resonated. But, despite the fact that they were crisp and yellowing with age, the dates were unsatisfyingly recent.

She became uncomfortably aware that Richard was motionless, watching her. 'Want to come in?' she asked.

He crawled in next to her. The space was just big enough for them to sit side by side, Richard facing outwards, Lily on all fours, still sifting through the rubbish on the ground.

'How often did you come here?' Richard asked.

'I don't know. Connie and Billy played here most days, I suppose. I used to follow them, but I could never find it on my own.' She sat upright, her leg muscles starting to cramp beneath her.

'Is there anything there?' He gestured towards the ground.

'No. Just rubbish.'

He lifted a random newspaper, inspected it briefly, cast it aside. 'This place must hold a lot of stories.'

Lily grimaced. 'Probably not ones I want to hear.'

Richard nodded. They fell silent, and the sounds of the woods settled into the space around them; the whispers of the trees, the conversation of blackbirds overhead. In a distant world, cars rolled past, life moving around the stillness.

'In the beginning was the word,' Richard said, his hand stretching out until it found hers. 'And the word was…?'

She was quiet for a moment. She thought of all that had happened the previous day; all that the afternoon might bring. Her voice, when she spoke, was soft in the gentle stirring of the morning.

'Tomorrow,' she said.

Acknowledgements

There are a huge number of people who have offered their support, guidance, advice and enthusiasm, and, quite apart from not having the space, if I try to list everyone I will inevitably forget someone important and feel hideously guilty. So please just take it as read that, if you have ever offered your support, I have appreciated it. However, there are a few people that deserve particular acknowledgement.

First and foremost, I owe massive thanks to everyone at Myriad Editions for all their support and enthusiasm, and for being so welcoming. Particular thanks to Vicky Blunden for her unfaltering guidance, and to Linda McQueen for exhibiting a pedantry which surpasses my own.

Although this novel didn't require too much in the way of formal research, I would like to thank the Selective Mutism Foundation for providing information about current research and treatment, Sarah Agnew for passing on information about selective mutism, and Leanne McCreery for providing expert advice regarding the treatment of head injuries.

I've been lucky enough to have some truly brilliant teachers over the years, and at the top of that list is Jerry Hope, who will sadly never know how important his guidance proved to be. Thanks are also due to both the tutors and my fellow students at the University of Sussex – particularly those who first suggested, upon reading the prologue, that there might be something more to this story.

My colleagues have all been fantastically supportive, and I am extremely grateful for all the encouragement (especially that which comes in the form of pizza, biscuits, wine and Haribo), but particular thanks are due to Stuart Lewis, both for being so accommodating and for allowing me to work in exchange for printing credits.

Thanks to my early readers and fellow writers: Alex Adams for the years of feedback and creative swearing, Dan Cash for doing everything possible to stop me procrastinating (it didn't work, but thanks for trying), Aleksi Koponen for inspiring and encouraging at every turn, Sarah Calvert for reading not only this book but also every passing thought I have throughout the day, Maria Holburt for simply being the most enthusiastic person in the universe, and Rosie Davis for being so wonderfully supportive.

Particular thanks are also due to the two people who are as close to sisters as I will ever get: Lexi Boyce, for putting up with me the longest and for providing one truly excellent mathematical joke; and Annie Rowling, for all the eggs.

And finally, massive appreciation to Mum, Dad, Paul, Daniel and Lee – for a lifetime of encouragement (or, in the case of my brothers, something that I'm sure resembles encouragement if you dig deep enough), and for always being there. I can't thank you enough.

Sign up to our mailing list at
www.myriadeditions.com
Follow us on Facebook and Twitter

MORE FROM MYRIAD

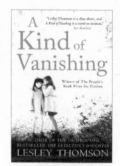

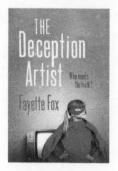

MORE FROM MYRIAD

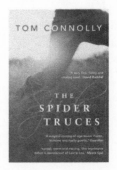

Sara Marshall-Ball has an MA in Creative and Critical Writing from the University of Sussex. An extract from *Hush* was shortlisted for the Writer's Retreat Competition in 2012. She lives in Brighton.